Aiveen McCarthy was born in Dublin and gained a degree [illegible] going on to work for the London Stock Exchange for six years as an analyst programmer. She currently works in software in County Dublin, where she lives with her husband Tom and two children.

WITHDRAWN FOR SALE

By the same author
The Insider
The Courier

AVA McCARTHY

Hide Me

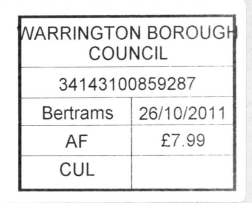

WARRINGTON BOROUGH COUNCIL	
34143100859287	
Bertrams	26/10/2011
AF	£7.99
CUL	

HARPER

This novel is entirely a work of fiction. The names, characters and
incidents portrayed in it are the work of the author's imagination.
Any resemblance to actual persons, living or dead, events or localities
is entirely coincidental.

Harper
An imprint of HarperCollins*Publishers*
77–85 Fulham Palace Road,
Hammersmith, London W6 8JB

www.harpercollins.co.uk

A Paperback Original 2011
1

Copyright © Aiveen McCarthy 2011

Aiveen McCarthy asserts the moral right to
be identified as the author of this work

A catalogue record for this book
is available from the British Library

ISBN: 978 0 00 736388 9

Set in Sabon by Palimpsest Book Production Limited,
Falkirk, Stirlingshire

Printed and bound in Great Britain by
Clays Ltd, St Ives plc

All rights reserved. No part of this publication may be
reproduced, stored in a retrieval system, or transmitted,
in any form or by any means, electronic, mechanical,
photocopying, recording or otherwise, without the prior
permission of the publishers.

This book is sold subject to the condition that it shall not,
by way of trade or otherwise, be lent, re-sold, hired out or
otherwise circulated without the publisher's prior consent
in any form of binding or cover other than that in which it
is published and without a similar condition including this
condition being imposed on the subsequent purchaser.

MIX
Paper from
responsible sources
FSC™ C007454

FSC™ is a non-profit international organisation established to promote
the responsible management of the world's forests. Products carrying the
FSC label are independently certified to assure consumers that they come
from forests that are managed to meet the social, economic and
ecological needs of present and future generations,
and other controlled sources.

Find out more about HarperCollins and the environment at
www.harpercollins.co.uk/green

To my children, Mark and Megan,
who are the reason for everything

Acknowledgements

As always, many thanks to my agent, Laura Longrigg, for her encouragement throughout the writing of this book, and to all the team at HarperCollins for their expert input along the way. Thank you also to Pilar Molina for the Spanish and Basque translations in the text. And a special thanks goes to my husband, Tom, for his patience and support, from Chapter 1 right through to The End.

Prologue

Harry pitched head-first over the cliff.

For an instant, she floated. Gunfire ripped the air behind her. Below her, hulking waves exploded, hungry, ready to swallow. Then the cliff rushed skywards and the ocean slammed into her face.

Don't scream, don't scream!

Water plunged into her sinuses, packed into her ears. She clamped her mouth shut, choking back the scrap of air she had left in her lungs. Then the current sucked her down into a deep, black tornado.

Her brain clamoured. Growling water thrummed in her ears, funnelling her down.

Don't breathe, don't breathe!

The rip tide snatched her. Hurled her in circles. It pitched her upside down and tore at her limbs till her lungs felt ready to burst.

She forced her eyes open. Saw an arrow of white tunnelling past her face. A silent jet-trail.

A bullet?

Jesus! He was going to kill her.

Harry's diaphragm heaved, fighting for the chance to breathe. Panic screeched through her, and she thrashed her legs, bucked her body. Then the ocean whirled her into another violent twister.

Suffocation crushed her chest. She had to open her mouth, had to inhale!

Don't breathe!

Her brain lurched, and she felt her eyes roll. Hunter's face floated before her. Maybe she'd see his body. Was he down here with her somewhere? Had Franco had him killed too?

No more oxygen. Just vapours to fuel her brain.

The undertow grabbed her and whiplashed her into a spiral. She tumbled. Drifted.

Her mother's face. Always so relieved by Harry's absences. What would she think when Harry was dead?

Now you don't have to talk to me, Mom.

Harry glided. Floated in freefall. She felt light. Euphoric, almost. And the reflex to breathe became slowly irresistible.

She couldn't help it. She opened her mouth. Inhaled.

Cold seawater sluiced down deep into her lungs.

1

Twelve days earlier

Cheating the casinos was a dangerous game. A game that could get you killed, if the stakes were high enough.

Harry eyed the roulette wheel, and edged alongside the other punters. Spying on the cheaters out in the open was risky, but she had to get close. She had to know how Franco Chavez was doing it.

'*Coloque sus apuestas.*' Place your bets.

The ivory ball swirled. The fat guy in front of Harry clacked his chips, like a set of castanets, and she stepped around his bulk to get a better view. A tangle of arms reached across the table, and she scanned the faces, wishing she knew what to look for.

She flexed her shoulders and felt them crunch. She'd been in the Gran Casino de San Sebastián for hours, patrolling the high-limit rooms till her feet ached. At this point, she wasn't sure which bothered her more: the nagging sense that she was wasting her client's money, or her growing unease that Chavez knew she was watching.

Harry frowned, and drifted away from the table. It didn't help that no one knew what bloody Chavez looked like.

She slipped into the poker parlour. Roped off from the main floor, it was quieter here. No roulette-rattles, no social chit-chat. Just the tense *snick-snick* of cards against the baize. She wandered between the tables.

'Watch their hands,' her father had said. 'That's where the cheating begins.'

Harry started with the dealers. Given enough practice, a crooked dealer could stack the deck, cull cards, fake a riffle, deal seconds, peek at the top, and all with a deftness that was near-impossible to spot. Harry knew because she could do it herself.

'A good false shuffle is like a monkey tapping away at a typewriter,' her father used to say. 'There's a whole lot of activity, but no end result.'

Harry scoured the dealers' hands for telltale signs, but saw nothing out of place.

She paused to watch the players at one of the busier tables. Four men and a blonde, none of them speaking. The only sound was the chinkle and clatter of chips. Harry sifted through the players' moves, filtering their gestures, looking for patterns, the way her father had taught her. It didn't take long. Her eyes came to rest on the single chip that was placed a shade too carefully on one of the players' cards.

Harry shot him a look. Mid-sixties, thin and morose-looking. She glanced at his hole cards, lying face down on the table, one on top of the other. And at the single red chip that tagged their bottom corner.

The back of Harry's neck tingled. A lot of players protected their hole cards with chips, but to a cheater the exact placement was key. It signalled the value of his hand to an accomplice at the table.

Collusion-cheating. Effective, and tough to prove.

Harry guessed the guy was using the simplest set of signals: top-left corner for a pair of aces; top-middle for kings; top-right corner for queens, and so on. His cohort was probably the blonde seated two places to his left. Between them, they could raise and re-raise the stakes if one of them had a good hand, forcing bigger bets out of the other players.

Harry stared at the man with the gloomy mortician's face and felt her insides droop. Force-out teams could bleed you dry, but this guy wasn't Chavez.

She wheeled away. What the hell was she thinking? Casinos didn't care about poker cheats. Why should they? The money they hustled belonged to the other players, not the casino. This wasn't the scale of cheating her client had in mind, and she knew it.

Harry headed back out towards the main floor, not caring to admit that the poker room had been some kind of refuge. She reminded herself that Chavez couldn't know she was watching, then strode back to the roulette table she'd left a few minutes before. The fat guy was still there, clacking his chips.

'No *pongan más apuestas, por favor.*' No more bets.

The ball curled into the spin. The punters around the table grew quiet, though most gave in to the urge to fiddle with something. The fat guy picked at a scab on his chin. Beside him, a woman twirled a lock of hair so tight it had to hurt.

The ball *tick-ticked* into a slot.

'*Treinta y cinco, negro, impar.*'

The dealer plonked his marker on the winning thirty-five and the table seemed to exhale. People shifted and resumed murmured conversations. The hair-twirler pouted. The fat guy shrugged, rubbed his eyes and went back to playing percussion with his chips.

'Well, *shit*, would you look at that?'

Harry jerked her head up. A heavyset man had approached the table, jabbing a finger at the layout.

'Number thirty-five! *Yessir!*' He punched the air with his fist. 'Five hundred euros straight-up on thirty-five! I believe that makes me a winner!'

His cheeks were flushed and hamster-plump. He whooped and swiped at the air some more, spilling his drink in the process. The crowd fussed over him, mostly speaking Spanish, which he didn't seem to understand. Even the hair-twirler smiled and stroked his sleeve, probably hoping some of his luck would wipe off from it. Rubbing the holy relic, Harry's father used to call it.

Harry's eyes strayed to the dealer. He'd summoned the floorman, who seemed to be giving him a hard time. The lucky winner beamed at them and raised his glass.

'Looks like I hit the jackpot this time!'

The floorman managed a stiff smile, then nodded and stepped away. The dealer turned to make the payout: €17,500.

Harry studied the winner as he stacked his chips. He was probably in his mid-fifties, his hair dusted with grey and thick as an old badger's pelt. The suit looked expensive, and from his accent she'd pegged him as a native of some southern US state.

She stared at his chips. The payout was high, but it happened now and then. Usually, the punter would lose it back to the casino in a matter of days. She watched the American place another €500 bet, this time on number thirty. Half a dozen players followed his lead, the simpering hair-twirler among them. The ball swished around, then rattled into number fifteen.

A groan eddied along the table. The American beamed at his new friends.

'Hey, you win some, you lose some.'

Harry noticed that no one was meeting his eye. He shrugged and gathered up his chips, pushing a generous tip towards the dealer. Then he strolled off in the direction of the other roulette tables.

Harry followed him across the Colosseum-sized room,

and watched him lose another €500 on a table at the back. She shook her head. At this rate, the casino would get its money back inside the hour. She sighed, massaging the nape of her neck. Stupid to think he might have been Chavez. He was just another chip-happy tourist.

Her back suddenly prickled, like an onset of rash; a tip-off from her skin cells that somebody out there was watching her. She did a quick 360-degree scan of the room. The place was busy, the punters working hard to look as rich as their surroundings. Sequinned evening gowns skimmed the marble floors; dinner jackets looked classy against the claret-toned furnishings. But none of them were paying any attention to Harry.

Her gaze drifted upwards, past the crystal chandeliers to the private mezzanine floor. Her client, Riva Mills, was watching her from the balcony.

Harry tensed. The last thing she needed was someone checking up on her. She turned her gaze back to the table, aware that her raised hackles were due to a lack of progress on the job. Maybe tomorrow she'd terminate the arrangement. Riva seemed to think she needed her services, but Harry wasn't so sure.

They'd met by appointment the previous day and talked while Riva patrolled the mezzanine floor.

'Someone's cheating my casinos, Ms Martinez,' the woman had said. 'And I want to know who it is.'

Harry had kept pace with her, studying her profile. She looked to be in her forties, maybe ten or twelve years older than Harry. Her features were fox-like, small and pointed, and her blonde hair was threaded with grey.

'His name is Chavez,' Riva continued. Chips snapped and clattered on the tables below the balcony. 'Franco Chavez.'

'Then you've already identified him?'

The woman threw her a stony glance. 'I know his name. That doesn't mean I know who he is.'

Riva swept ahead and Harry followed in silence, resisting a childish urge to pull a face behind her back. She'd done some digging before the meeting and had to admit, the woman's history was a little intimidating. Raised by her mother in a trailer in Ohio, Riva had left school on her fourteenth birthday and hitch-hiked her way to Wisconsin. She'd lied about her age and got a job as a bunny girl, then lied again to become a casino dealer in Nevada. She'd bought her first casino at the age of twenty-one. Over the next twenty years, she'd built a powerful casino empire, expanding it across the States and into parts of Europe.

Harry eyed the uncompromising set of Riva's back. She guessed you didn't succeed in the corporate gaming world by being all soft and nurturing.

Riva came to a halt at the short side of the mezzanine and leaned her elbows on the railing.

'This Franco Chavez clown is cheating his way across Europe, and my casinos are next.' She glared at the floor below. 'Maybe he's already here.'

Harry moved beside her. Up close, she could see how

age had loosened Riva's skin, blurring a jawline that had probably once been heart-shaped. She tried to picture the underage bunny girl, but her brain shut the image down.

She cleared her throat. 'Can I ask where you got your information?'

'My Chief of Security, Victor Toledo. He's got sources out in the field, and one of them tipped him off. It's my guess this Chavez is using a computer. Some kind of gadget.'

'Is that what your informant said?'

'No, but that's what all the new cheaters try these days. That's why I want you.' She turned a pair of flinty-grey eyes on Harry. 'It's what you do, isn't it? Technology investigations?'

'That's putting it broadly, but yes, in a way.'

'Like I said on the phone, you come highly recommended.' Riva drilled her with an assessing look. 'You've got the technology, plus you're half-Spanish, so I guess you speak the lingo.'

'A quarter Spanish, actually.'

Harry's father had been born here in San Sebastián. She blamed him for her sooty eyes and dark tangle of curls. The rest of her was mostly Irish. Riva went on as though Harry hadn't spoken.

'And if what I've heard is true, you're no stranger to casinos, either.'

Something else Harry could blame her father for. She'd been apprenticed to his gambling career since she was six years old, and there wasn't much she didn't know about casinos. She shrugged in acknowledgement, a sense of misgiving chafing at her insides.

'What about your own surveillance team?' she said. 'Surely the cameras can catch Chavez?'

Riva clicked her tongue and whirled away, heels *snip-snapping* against the floor. If shoes could be bad-tempered, then hers were in quite a snit. Harry trotted to keep up.

Riva spoke over her shoulder. 'Cameras only record the action. Someone on the floor needs to spot the move first before knowing what tape to re-wind. Those bozos in the eye don't turn up much on their own.'

'I thought they were supposed to be experts.'

Riva snorted. 'In the old days, maybe. Vegas used to hire ex-cheaters to do their spying. They knew stuff, those old guys. But nowadays, it's greenhorns fresh out of school with a six-week training course under their belt. They couldn't spot a slick move if the cheater was sitting in their lap.'

'But their equipment's pretty sophisticated, isn't it?'

'Yep. That's half the problem. Shuffle machines, smart card shoes, self-activating cameras. Technology has dulled their edge. I don't need goddamn automated robots, I need proactive surveillance.' Riva wheeled around to face Harry. 'What's the matter, are you afraid?'

Harry stopped in her tracks. 'Afraid of what?'

'The cheaters. You should be. They can be dangerous.'

Harry blinked, and Riva waved a dismissive hand.

'Oh, not the small-time hustlers, they're usually

harmless. I'm talking about organized crews. Colluding professionals. You think you're watching them, but half the time they're watching you.' She must have read the unease in Harry's face, for she went on: 'Just stay in the casino. Nothing can happen in front of the cameras.'

A small shiver scampered down Harry's spine. Riva glanced at her watch and frowned.

'Look, do you want the damn job or don't you?'

Harry hesitated. Good question. She pondered it for a moment, then came to a decision.

'Yes, I want the damn job.'

After that, they'd retired to Riva's office to agree terms, and Harry had started billing hours to her new client the following day.

'No *más apuestas*.' No more bets.

Harry whipped her gaze back to the table. The American had gone, his place taken by a blond guy with an easy smile. She watched him flirt with a redhead beside him, then noticed that the fat punter had joined them from the other game. He was standing next to her, still playing castanets with his chips. Harry glanced up at the balcony. Riva had disappeared.

Harry puffed out a breath. She shouldn't have taken the job, but she'd had her reasons, none of which she cared to examine now. She glanced at the players. Privately, she wasn't convinced Chavez would use an electronic device. Sure, people tried them: laser scanners predicting where the ball would land; radio transmitters designed to control the spins. But that didn't mean any of them worked. And what the hell did Riva expect her to do? Scan the room for electronic equipment? Triangulate in on radio emissions? With everyone carrying mobile phones, there wasn't a lot of point.

'*Treinta y cuatro, rojo, par.*'

The dealer placed his marker on number thirty-four. The fat guy rubbed his eyes, then went back to clacking his chips.

Harry's brain lurched.

The fat guy rubbed his eyes.

Her mind groped with the fuzzy déjà vu, but couldn't slot it into place.

'Well, hey! Looky-here!'

Harry stared. The American was back.

'A lucky five hundred on number thirty-four.' He laughed and toasted the other players with his drink, setting his ice tinkling. 'I just keep on reeling 'em in!'

Harry gaped for a moment, then snapped her gaze back to the fat guy. He'd rubbed his eyes before the last win, too, but so what? Maybe he had an allergy. She studied his pasty profile and suddenly, his hands grew still. He turned his head a fraction towards her. If he'd been a dog, he would've pricked his ears.

He knew she was watching him.

A shiver twitched between her shoulder blades. She slid a glance at the dealer. He'd called in the floorman who supervised his section of the room. They consulted together, but not for long. Harry watched the American

13

collect his winnings. He'd made €35,000 in less than half an hour.

Movement snagged her gaze at the edges. The fat guy was smoothing a hand over his hair, as though a sudden wind had tossed it. Then he pocketed his chips and lumbered away from the table. Almost in the same instant, the American strolled off and headed for the cage to cash out. To anyone else, their behaviour was random. But because she'd been watching, to Harry it was an orchestrated move.

Collusion.

Her heart rate picked up. The American had joined a long queue at the cage. He wasn't going anywhere, not for a while. The fat guy, on the other hand, was heading out of the room.

Harry threaded through the crowd, tailing him into the foyer. She dropped back behind an oversized pillar, watching him blunder through knots of cocktail drinkers as he made his way out the door.

She chewed her lip, debating the wisdom of her next move. Then she eased out from behind the safety of her pillar and followed him into the dark streets of San Sebastián.

2

'You will come with me, *señor*.'

Marty froze. The hand on his shoulder was heavier than a sandbag. He swallowed. Made himself smile. Then he looked up at the plain-clothes security agent.

'Be with you in a sec, pal.' He gestured at the roulette table. 'I've a bet riding here.'

Fingers crushed the tendons in his shoulder. 'You just lost, *señor*.'

Sweat trickled down Marty's back. The ball was still spinning. He tried to shrug, but the hand was cramping his style.

'Hey, what the hell,' he said. 'Wheel's been against me all night, anyway.'

He winked at the redhead beside him and got to his feet, still craning his neck to look the agent in the face. The guy must've been six-seven, six-eight at least. Marty

15

could see his own blond hair and stupid grin reflected in the agent's mirrored shades. What kind of jackass wore those things inside? Maybe he should mention it. *You're a jackass, you know that?* The agent grabbed his arm and Marty kept his mouth shut.

The guy's grip was like a tourniquet. He hustled Marty through a herd of Japanese tourists, then propelled him across the room. Balls *plink-plinked*, playing hopscotch on their wheels. The agent shoved him through an unmarked door and into a deserted hallway, and when he locked the door behind them, the skin on Marty's arms puckered. He'd been back-roomed before, but never in one of Riva's casinos.

He flashed on the image of her leaning against the balcony. The sight of her had jolted him, he didn't mind admitting it. She looked good. The cheekbones were still high, the body still well put together. It was the first time he'd seen her in nearly twenty years.

The agent's fingers dug hard into his biceps, jerking him towards a door near the end of the passageway. Marty read the nameplate:

V. Toledo, Director de Seguridad.

His gut tightened. Jesus, not that prick again.

The agent opened the door and shoved him into the middle of the room. Marty squinted against the harsh fluorescent light. The place was whiter than a dentist's surgery, with the dead-air quality of soundproofed walls.

'Sit down.'

Marty's stomach relaxed a little. The bald guy behind the desk wasn't Victor Toledo.

Marty shoved his hands in his pockets and stayed standing. Keep your mouth shut. That was the rule of survival in situations like these. On the other hand, an innocent person might have said something by now. He cleared his throat.

'Look, what the hell's going on here?'

The bald guy glared. His features were large and blunt, as though thickened by a punch in the mouth. Marty jutted out his chin.

'I'm a paying customer. That goon of yours—'

The agent's boot sideswiped the back of Marty's knees. He felt the crack, the dead legs, then crumpled into the chair behind him. For a moment, he lay sprawled, his chest thumping. Then he eased himself upright, not looking at the agent, and straightened his jacket and tie. The bald guy glanced down at a file on his desk.

'Name?'

'Roselli. Who the hell're you?'

'Age?'

'I'm not talking till I see some identification. How do I know you're not just a coupla hoods?'

The bald guy's head jerked up. Marty's armpits prickled with sweat. Then the guy pushed a casino ID across the desk. *Alberto Delgado, Seguridad de Gran Casino.*

Marty shoved it back. 'That's not what it says on the door.'

'You *will* answer my questions, Señor Roselli.' His Spanish accent was thick, making much of the rolling 'r' in Marty's name. 'Your age?'

'Thirty-eight. What's that got to do with anything?'

'Address?'

'Hotel Plaza.'

That wasn't strictly true. He was renting a room in a cramped house on the other side of the river. It had been recommended to him by the barman in the Hotel Plaza, whose sister-in-law ran the place. The room she'd given him was old and musty, and he shared a bath with six other tenants. It was cheap, but already he was behind on the rent.

'Empty your pockets.'

'What?'

'Everything on the desk. Now.'

Marty sensed the agent's bulk shifting behind him. He took the hint and fumbled in his pockets, tossing items onto the table: a scuffed wallet with forty euros in cash; a fake driver's licence; six red casino chips, worth five euros each; and a stick of gum with pocket-fluff on the wrapper.

Delgado's lip curled. 'This is all you have? No credit cards? No traveller's cheques?' He leaned forward. 'No high-stakes chips?'

Marty shifted in his seat. As his sum of worldly goods, the pile didn't amount to much, but if he was careful it could last out the week. Then again, careful wasn't his style. He shrugged.

'I don't carry all that stuff around. Everything else is back at the Plaza.'

The plain-clothes agent snorted. Marty tugged at his

threadbare cuffs, surprised to find his fingers so steady. Suddenly, a pair of hands thrust his head forward and the desk slammed up into his face.

Pain crunched through Marty's nose. He tried to yell, but his tongue felt thick. The hands pinned him down, crushing his mouth and eyes. Then they wrenched his head back and Delgado's face filled his vision.

'Maybe you should look again,' Delgado said.

Marty coughed, aware of something warm trickling from his nose. He slipped a trembling hand into his pocket, extracting the black chip he'd stolen earlier. It was worth five hundred euros.

Delgado snatched it, nodding towards the agent. 'Luis here saw you lift it from a customer's rack.' He sneered, then stowed the chip in his pocket. 'Don't worry, I'll see the owner gets it back.'

Luis sniggered, then released his grip. Marty's skin felt clammy. He touched his nose and winced. Shit. All this for a lousy five hundred euros. He closed his eyes for a moment. Lousy or not, it would have paid the rent he owed and set him up for another few weeks.

He opened his eyes, backhanding the blood from his lip. Delgado picked up the red chips and rattled them idly through his fingers. Then he slipped them into his pocket. Marty's hand froze halfway to his mouth. He watched Delgado strip the cash from his wallet and pocket that too.

'Hey!' Marty half-stood from the chair. 'Those're mine!'

19

Delgado raised his eyebrows. 'You are a thief. We just proved it. I am confiscating stolen goods.'

He flipped the battered wallet onto the desk. Marty felt his fists curl.

'You can't prove I stole anything. It's just your word against mine.'

'You think so? Maybe we caught you on camera.'

'Bullshit.'

Marty traded glares with Delgado. He guessed they ran quite a sideline, shaking down two-bit grifters. But sometimes it paid to call a bluff. The Gran Casino had hundreds of cameras, but even so, not every angle was covered. Sometimes, surveillance had to spot a move first before knowing to pan after it with the lens.

The reality was, on a floor this crowded, Marty might just have got away with it.

Delgado's lip curled into another sneer. 'You really think you can fool the cameras?'

'Hey, I'm just saying, maybe your pal Luis here made a mistake.'

'You would like to see yourself in action?' Delgado gave a humourless laugh, then clicked his fingers at Luis. '¿Qué mesa?'

'Mesa cinco.' Table five.

Delgado snatched up the phone and barked orders to someone on the other end. Marty's Spanish wasn't up to much, but he was hoping this was the first time they'd bothered to check surveillance.

Delgado ended the call. Then he pointed a remote

control at a TV screen on the wall, and the casino floor snapped into view. He sat back, swivelling in his chair.

'Now we will see how a lowlife operates.'

Marty slid a finger under his collar, his gaze fixed to the screen. Without sound, the roulette floor looked static and dull; just a bunch of well-dressed dummies tossing chips onto the baize. And there he was, hovering near table five.

His blond hair looked tousled, his skin nut-brown from the sun. Marty watched himself flirt with the curvy redhead, re-living the buzz as she responded to his cheesy lines.

Then he saw the mark: short, thickset; mouth as wide as a toad's. Luis pointed at the screen.

'*Esta es.*' That's him.

They watched as the toady guy shoved the redhead aside, thrusting a chip down the front of her dress to keep her quiet. Even seeing it for the second time, Marty felt his temper climb. He knew what had happened next, though you couldn't tell from the screen. He'd opened his mouth to intervene, but the girl had stopped him with a pleading look. Marty had got the message. They were some kind of couple. Step in, and maybe she'd pay for it later. So he'd bitten back his temper and taken revenge the only way he knew how.

Marty peered at himself on the screen. In a minute, he'd move closer to the toady guy, waiting for him to lean across the layout, leaving his rack of chips exposed. Easy pickings for a chip-thief with deft hands. A party

21

of Japanese tourists drifted into view, heading towards the table. Marty spotted Luis, tree-trunk solid, watching from the other side.

Something tapped at Marty's brain. His eyes shot back to the tourists, and he recalled how they'd blocked his exit from the table. He stared as they flocked across the floor. Soon, he'd be completely hemmed in. With that kind of coverage, the camera was going to miss his sleight of hand.

He leaned back and let out a long breath. Then his pulse jolted as he realized something else.

This was Franco's table.

Shit.

Marty's gut clenched. In another thirty seconds, they'd catch Franco's move. Marty scanned the players, spotting Fat-Boy in position. There was Cowboy, placing his €500 bet.

Marty dragged a hand over his mouth. He'd been following that sonofabitch Franco for weeks and had nicknames for all his crew. Then he noticed again the pretty, dark-haired girl standing on the sidelines. He'd seen her clock Fat-Boy's eye-rub and his swift exit signal, but she didn't seem part of their play. Surveillance, maybe? But who'd be dumb enough to tangle with Franco?

He slid a glance at Delgado. The asshole had him cornered, but not in the way that he thought. If Marty let the tape run, he'd probably be in the clear. On the other hand, they'd hit on Franco.

He watched the roulette wheel and his breathing speeded up. Where there was gambling, there was cheating. And where there was cheating, there was money up for grabs. Marty had been down on his luck for ten years, and for a while now he'd figured that coat-tailing on Franco was his only way out.

He held up his hands. 'Okay, forget it, you're right.'

Delgado narrowed his eyes. Marty licked his lips and went on:

'I stole his stupid chip. You can stop the damn tape.'

Delgado's face turned crimson. Slowly, he got to his feet and made his way round the desk, his gaze pinned on Marty.

'You think you can make fools of us? Waste our time?' He snapped his fingers at Luis. 'Maybe you should see what happens to thieves in this casino.'

Luis snatched Marty's arms and wrenched them behind his back. Marty's shoulder muscles screamed. Delgado strode towards him, rolling up his shirtsleeves, and Marty tensed his gut.

Somewhere on the screen, that bastard Franco was making his move and Marty was going to pay for protecting him. Sweat slid down his face.

But hey, what the hell?

After all, once upon a time they'd been friends.

3

Harry nudged through the crowds, following the fat guy along the cobbled streets of the Old Quarter.

Glasses clinked from the tourist-filled bars, and the air was thick with the salty scent of sausage. Harry fixed her gaze on the figure ahead. He must have been a hundred pounds overweight, but it didn't seem to slow him down.

She picked up the pace, trying to fix her bearings. Navigational challenges were never her strong point, and she hadn't been here long enough to tag many landmarks. She scanned the medieval-looking buildings. There were plenty of signs, but most of them in Basque, with its unintelligible x's and k's.

Up ahead, the fat guy moved like a barge, parting the crowds in a backwash behind him. He made a sharp right, and Harry trotted after him into another lantern-lit alleyway.

She recalled how he'd smoothed a hand over his hair at the casino. If her guess was correct, it was some kind of signal, a cue for his accomplices to cut and run. Right now, he was probably headed for an emergency location, or maybe back to wherever he was staying.

Just stay in the casino. Nothing can happen in front of the cameras.

She flicked a quick glance over her shoulder. All she planned to do was pinpoint an address. At least then she'd have something to offer Riva before terminating their arrangement.

Harry winced. Backsliding out of a job made her insides squirm, but the truth was, Riva didn't need her. Harry's expertise was in computer security, investigating forensics and security breaches for criminal and civil litigation. At least, that was the whitewashed version. Actually, she'd been a hacker since the age of nine and that was still what she did best. But whatever her skills, she certainly wasn't equipped to crack open a ring of casino cheaters.

She huffed out a breath, picking her way over the cobbles. The maze of laneways reminded her of Temple Bar, Dublin's alleged Bohemian Quarter, though the cobbles here were easier on her feet. The thought of her native Dublin triggered another squirm. Ever since her return from Cape Town a few months before, she'd had trouble settling back into her hometown. All her ties were there: her parents, her sister, her friends, her business. And Hunter, of course. The detective who'd recently stirred her body chemistry, brewing up something she didn't quite recognize. But still, Dublin left her feeling displaced. Like a jigsaw piece tidied into the wrong box.

The truth had crystallized during a rare phone call with her mother.

'A vagrant, just like your father,' her mother had said. 'You've moved three times in the last twelve months. Different homes, different countries, different jobs. Are you the same with men? Hopping from one bed to the other?'

Harry's cheeks stung at the memory. Jesus, weren't mothers supposed to be on your side? But at least the woman's hostility had made her face facts. Harry's sense of dislocation wasn't new. Nothing like having a frosty mother all your life for making you an outsider in your own home.

Glass shattered on the cobbles behind her. Harry squeezed through a scrum of tourists, still keeping tabs on the fat guy. Her feet ached, and it occurred to her she was wasting her time. Maybe he was just a regular punter who had nothing to do with Franco Chavez.

She squinted through the alleyway. The fat guy shot a glance over his shoulder. Then he dipped his head, switched gears and put more distance between them. Harry frowned. Had he spotted her?

She hung back, her eyes roaming the busy tangle of streets. Tiers of wrought-iron balconies loomed above her, and every alley seemed to converge on a Gothic church spire. Her back tingled. She was worryingly far from her navigational comfort zone.

Something tugged at her gut, willing her to turn back. Was there really any point in following a guy who knew she was there? She slowed her pace, giving in to the notion. Then suddenly the fat guy stopped and spun around.

Harry jerked to a halt. Goosebumps erupted along her arms. He was staring right at her. His gaze drifted over her shoulder, his eyes widening. Then he whirled away and barrelled down the laneway.

Harry whipped her head around. What had he seen? She scoured the narrow backstreet, searching for false notes. She peered at the tourists, at the local Basque vendors, but nothing seemed out of place.

Was someone else following him?

She snapped her eyes back. He'd almost disappeared, and she took off after him at a jog, not sure of her intentions. She followed him to the end of the laneway and found herself on the edge of a large, open square. Sandstone buildings enclosed it on all sides, with rows of balconies rising up like seats in an amphitheatre. At ground level, the square was bordered by a colonnade of shadowy archways.

Harry felt her limbs relax. Finally, a place she recognized: the city's old bullring, Plaza de la Constitución.

She slowed to a walk, scanning the area. It was less crowded in here, and the place scattered echoes like an empty church. You could still see the numbers over the shuttered windows from a time when the balconies were rented out as seats.

27

Harry spotted the fat guy scurrying for cover under the walkway of arched porticos. She hesitated. The porches looked gloomy, in spite of the lanterns dotting the colonnades. Better to stick to the safety of open country. Besides, he had to emerge sooner or later to exit back onto the streets.

She struck out across the plaza in line with the archways, trailing his ample silhouette as he blundered in and out of the shadows. Voices echoed in the hollow acoustics, and for an instant, Harry heard the roar of crowds lusting for blood at the bullfights. An image thrust itself into her head: a quivering animal, slashed and butchered, who could do nothing but stand and bleed. She shuddered, shaking the memory off. Her father had taken her to a bullfight as a child. It was the first time she'd seen violent death.

She blinked and focused back on the porticos, waiting for the fat guy to reappear. She slowed to a halt. Flicked her gaze across the arches.

There was no sign of him.

Shit. Had he doubled back? She whirled around, scouring the square. Nothing.

Dammit.

Harry peered at the gloomy archways. The notion of going in there made her spine hum. She dug her nails into her palms, then edged across the plaza and stepped under the portico, retracing the fat guy's steps. By now, the square was almost empty. Her shoes slapped chapel-like echoes off the walls, and a chill skittered through her. Then something behind her made a bubbling sound, and she turned.

The fat guy was sitting on the ground, leaning against one of the columns. He was staring up at her, his eyes wide. He looked as though he was about to accuse her of something. Then she saw the bloody gash that had ripped his throat open, and she screamed.

4

'You're a long way from home, Miss Martinez.'

Harry eyed the detective perched against the desk in front of her. He was leafing through her passport, his nostrils flared as though he'd found a dead bug between the pages.

'I told you,' she said. 'I'm working for a client.'

She shifted in her chair. Riva was certainly one of the reasons she was here, anyway. The detective regarded her down the length of his nose. It was slightly hooked and, with his close-set eyes, it gave him the look of an eagle.

His name was Vasco. He was an inspector with the Ertzaintza, the police force of the Basque country, and so far he was the fourth guy to interview her about the events of last night.

He turned his attention to a stapled report, probably

her signed statement. Fatigue shuddered through her. The police had grilled her till three in the morning, and had started again soon after breakfast. By now, it was early evening and what little sleep she'd got had been slashed by images of blood-soaked, slaughtered bulls.

'You have been in San Sebastián before.'

Harry frowned. He made it sound like an accusation. And besides, how did he know?

'That was a long time ago,' she said. 'My father brought me on visits as a child. He was born here.'

'You have family in the city?'

She brushed at an imaginary speck of dust on her skirt. 'I'm not sure.'

Her memories of those childhood trips were flimsy as cobwebs. Her older sister, Amaranta, had been there with her, but for reasons Harry had never understood, their mother had refused to come. Harry fiddled with the strap of her bag. Her personal link with San Sebastián was another reason she'd taken the job, but so far, she'd been too busy for cosy family reunions.

Her stomach dipped with an odd emptiness. The alienation she'd felt in Dublin had left a void like a doughnut hole inside her. She'd found herself re-examining her past, as if that would somehow plug the cavity: her nomadic Dublin childhood, where her father's gambling had kept their finances on a pendulum swing; the upheavals from house to house, in line with his cashflow; the upmarket mansions, the low-rent bedsits, the ever-changing schools. She realized she had few treasured memories of 'home', the kind that others called nostalgia and that tied your heart to a place.

Harry swallowed against a pesky fullness in her throat. The job in San Sebastián had come at the right moment. She'd never fully explored the Spanish side of her identity, and it was probably time that she did.

Vasco tossed her passport into her lap, then strutted back around the desk. She took in his tall, elegant frame; the expensive suit and the slicked-back hair. The first *ertzaina* she'd talked to had been a uniformed guard, dishevelled from overwork. This guy looked more like a politician than a cop.

He sat down behind the desk, flipping up his coat-tails like a concert pianist taking position. 'Tell me again why you followed him.'

His English was precise, his accent almost Etonian. The other cops had been relieved to revert to Spanish with Harry, but not Vasco. She pegged it as vanity, but to be fair, his fluency was impressive. Harry sighed.

'I've already explained, I saw him—'

'I know what you saw. Please answer my question. Why did you follow *him*? Why not follow the man you say collected the winnings?'

Harry pictured the American with his thatch of greying hair, queuing up at the cage. 'He'd won a large amount of money. Assuming the casino was following regulations, he'd need to fill out forms with proven ID before cashing in that amount.'

'So?'

Harry shrugged. 'So I figured the casino already had a line on him. The other guy was the unknown quantity.' For an instant, her breeziness deserted her and she was back in the old bullring: *wide, staring eyes; butchered gullet*. She swallowed. 'Do you know who he was?'

Vasco stared at her, hawk-like, and didn't answer. Then he said, 'What is your connection with Riva Mills?'

'I told you, she's my client.'

'And that's all?'

Harry frowned. 'What else would there be?'

'So she contacts you out of the blue. An American businesswoman based in San Sebastián decides to hire a technology expert from Dublin.' He leaned forward. 'Who just happens to be you.'

'It didn't happen *out of the blue*. I was recommended to her by a mutual friend.'

'What friend?'

'Her name's Roslyn Bloomberg.' Harry watched him write it down. 'She's a diamantaire based in New York. My father's known her for years, and it turns out Riva's a client of hers.'

Harry had been surprised when she'd heard that Ros had recommended her. They'd parted on bad terms in Cape Town a few months before. For reasons too complex to sort through at the time, Ros had believed that Harry was a thief. Other people's opinions didn't usually count with Harry, but Ros had come close to being a substitute mother for a while. It hurt to be rejected by two mothers in a row, whatever way you looked at it.

Vasco slapped an eight-by-ten photograph on the desk. 'Take a good look. He was a countryman of yours.'

Harry's skin turned cold. The fat guy's face shone back at her like a moon. His eyes were pale, his skin doughy and bloated. She couldn't see his throat, but guessed that when he posed for the shot, he was already dead. Her insides shrivelled.

Vasco tapped the photo with a pen. 'His name was Stephen McArdle. Does that mean anything to you?'

'No.'

'We've built quite a profile on him. Thirty-four years old, born in Belfast. Started off doing work for IRA splinter groups, then later for Colombian revolutionaries, the PLO, even our own Basque separatists.'

Harry frowned, picturing the clumsy figure who'd barged ahead of her through the backstreets. 'He was a terrorist?'

'He was a hacker, Miss Martinez.' Vasco's gaze drilled into hers. 'Just like you.'

Harry's eyebrows shot up. She was about to reply when the door swung open. A short, stocky man shambled into the room and dropped a folder onto the desk. He stared at Harry. His unshaven face drooped with middle age, and his head looked too large for his body, though maybe that was down to his mess of dark, woolly curls. He took a seat by the wall, his eyes never leaving her face. Vasco went on, ignoring the interruption.

'McArdle hired himself out to anyone who paid him well enough.'

Harry hesitated. The newcomer's stare was unnerving. She cleared her throat.

'Paid him well enough to do what?'

'Help them fund their operations.'

'By hacking?'

Vasco shrugged. 'Terrorists raise funding in all sorts of ways. Drugs, smuggling, kidnapping, prostitution. Now they add cybercrime to the list.'

He picked up the folder and browsed through it. It looked like another set of photographs. He slotted one out for a closer look, and kept talking.

'McArdle had quite the hacker's pedigree. Credit-card company penetration, ATM heists, cyber protection rackets.' He peered at her over the glossy eight-by-ten, his look predatory. 'But then, you know more about this kind of thing than me.'

Harry narrowed her eyes. 'Look, I don't appreciate—'

Vasco smacked the photo onto the desk. 'This man, who is he?'

Harry blinked. She recognized the florid face of the American from the casino.

'He's the one who collected the winnings. I don't know his name.'

'And this one?'

He tossed down another photo, a headshot of a woman. She looked thirty-something, a brunette with good bones, though the layers of make-up masked her features like a veil. Harry shook her head.

'I've never seen her before.'

'And him?'

Another headshot: a man in his late forties, pale crew cut, eyebrows bleached by the sun. His complexion looked mud-stained with freckles.

Harry shook her head again. 'No. Is that Franco Chavez?'

Vasco broke eye contact. Over by the wall, his shaggy-haired colleague stirred in his chair. Eventually, Vasco said,

'We don't have an ID on Franco Chavez.'

'I see.' Harry looked from one to the other, trying to read their discomfort. 'But these others, they're all part of the casino-cheating crew?'

'We believe so.'

'Why do they need a hacker? Are they really using computers to cheat?'

'Maybe.' Vasco tilted his head, as though assessing her. 'Or maybe they need a hacker for something else.'

Harry squinted. What was he getting at? He leaned forward, his eyes probing hers.

'We know a lot about you, Miss Martinez.'

She lifted her chin. 'Such as?'

'We've been in touch with your police force in Dublin. They were very helpful.' Vasco peered at her like a raptor bird, and Harry tried not to squirm. 'You started young. I understand you hacked into the Stock Exchange when you were just thirteen.'

Harry's eyes widened. How the hell did he know about

36

that? No charges were ever filed. A childish misdemeanour, nothing more. Vasco was still talking.

'Then more recently, there was the question of several million euros that went missing in the Bahamas. And later, some diamonds in Cape Town. Also missing.'

Harry's brain raced. She'd sailed close to the winds of larceny more than once, but she'd had her reasons, all of them good ones. Trouble was, she couldn't prove it. Then again, neither could they. She clenched her fists.

'I've never been arrested for anything.'

'Your father has. He served six years in prison for insider trading, didn't he?'

Harry gaped. What was he doing, trying to build some kind of case against her? And for what?

'*Geldi!*'

Harry snapped her gaze to the stranger by the wall. He'd shot to his feet, his expression stony, and was firing out what sounded like orders in rapid Basque. Vasco made a chopping motion with his hand, cutting him off. Then he turned back to Harry.

'Have you talked to Riva Mills since McArdle was killed?'

Harry glared at him. 'No, I haven't had the chance.'

'Well, don't.'

'What?'

He advanced around the desk towards her. Her heartbeat tripped. Behind him, his colleague was shaking his head.

'You have an unusual mixture of skills, Miss Martinez.'

Vasco's eyes bored into hers. 'Think about it. You're a professional hacker who knows her way around a casino. You're part-Irish, part-Spanish. You have a reputation for bluffing and telling lies, not to mention out-manoeuvring the police. You even have a jailbird for a father. This really is a rare opportunity.'

Harry threw him a cagey look and slowly shook her head. Not in denial of his allegations, since most of them were true, but in an effort to ward off what she knew was coming next.

'I have a proposition for you.' Vasco loomed over her like an elegant bird of prey. 'I want you to go undercover, Miss Martinez. I want you to take McArdle's place.'

5

'That's crazy.' Harry stared at Vasco. 'I don't know anything about going undercover.'

But even as she said it, she wondered if it was true. If she was honest, a part of her had always been drawn to the notion of becoming someone else. Her whole childhood, after all, had been a kind of double life.

Vasco's phone rang. He held up a hand, as though halting a line of traffic, then moved behind the desk to take the call. Harry sat back to wait, flicking a glance at his colleague, who'd resumed his seat by the wall. He was scowling across at her, his tangled eyebrows jutting out like twin wire brushes. She shifted her gaze. Vasco was treating the guy as though he was invisible, but there was something about him that Harry found impossible to ignore.

She picked at a fingernail and thought about double

lives, flashing on an image of her childhood self: wild hair, fists clenched as if braced for unexpected combat. Outwardly, she'd been the girl she called Harry the Drudge, whose mother made her sit alone in her room after school so they wouldn't have to talk. The rest of the time, Harry had lived as Pirata, an insomniac who sat at her computer in the dark and prowled the electronic underground. For hours, she'd dialled out over slow modems, sharing ideas and downloading hacker tools. As Pirata, she'd been all-powerful, well respected by her crackerjack comrades. As Harry, she'd led a far more hemmed-in existence.

Vasco wrapped up the call, then looked at his watch, a calculated reminder that he was a busy man. He leaned forward, elbows on the desk.

'This is an important case, Miss Martinez. We've been watching these people for months. I intend to find out what they're up to, and you can help.'

'You've got the wrong person.'

'It's a global investigation.' He straightened his shoulders. If he'd been a bird, his chest would have swelled. 'We're talking about intergovernmental cooperation, very high profile. The United States is involved, Hong Kong, most of Europe, even your own Irish authorities.'

Harry squinted at him. 'For a crew of casino cheaters?'

He waved a dismissive hand. 'Cheating the casinos is just a sideline. These people are involved in something else, something bigger. And I want to know what it is.'

'I'm not trained for this kind of thing. It won't work.'

Vasco ignored her and sorted through the photographs on the desk. 'We know they have links with other criminal organizations. That's how they came to our attention in the first place.' He found McArdle's headshot and tapped it with a manicured forefinger. 'What I want to know is, why did they hire a hacker?'

Harry's gaze slid to the lifeless eyes in the photograph. Her insides flickered, an odd mixture of fear and curiosity. But she bit down on both. This had nothing to do with her.

Vasco was still talking.

'It will be a short, sharp infiltration. Nothing protracted or drawn out. We set things up so that you're taken on as McArdle's replacement. You talk to them, find out who their target is, what they want you to do and why. Then you can disappear. An in-out job. And of course, you'll be well paid.'

Harry lifted her chin. 'I'm sorry, but this is not the kind of thing that I do.'

Vasco paused. 'Perhaps you should reconsider. You seem to forget the awkwardness of your position.'

'Excuse me?'

'You were following McArdle, right up to the moment he died. The casino cameras can place you tailing him out of the building. By your own admission, you pursued him through the streets, all the way to the Plaza. Where he was ambushed and murdered.'

For an instant, Harry's brain shorted out, a synapse

misfiring between hearing words and understanding what they meant. She shook her head.

'You know why I was following him. You can't believe I was involved in his death.'

'Oh, I don't. But naturally, my investigation must be seen to be thorough. My men will need to dig more into your background, check out your family, your father's history, involve the relevant Irish authorities. A long, messy process. And from what I've heard, your relations with the Irish police are already quite fragile.' He raised an eyebrow. 'I could make life very difficult for you, Miss Martinez.'

Harry felt her jaw tighten. 'If you think—'

'On the other hand,' he went on, 'if you cooperate with my request, it might go a long way to redeeming your reputation.'

Harry gaped, her brain still playing catch-up.

Vasco fixed her with unblinking, lidless-looking eyes. 'This case is important to me and, one way or another, I intend to get a result. How cleanly you come out of it is up to you.'

He shot a wrist from his cuff; another showy time-check.

'I have a meeting.' He got to his feet, gesturing at his colleague by the wall. 'This is Detective Zubiri, from our Undercover unit. Talk to him, then give me your answer.'

He snatched a briefcase off the desk and marched out of the room. Harry glared after him, blood seething through her veins. The last thing she needed was to get caught up in a murder case, but Vasco had her in a chokehold. She felt her teeth grind. Suspect or undercover decoy: what kind of half-assed choice was that?

She flopped back in her seat, exhaling a long breath. The silence in Vasco's wake was suspiciously restful, like the calm of a receding rogue wave. She cast a doubtful look at the detective by the wall. His shoulders were stooped, his clothes wrinkled. For the moment, he seemed disinclined to take up where his boss had left off.

Harry glanced around Vasco's office, absently taking in the ordered shelves and the clutter-free desk. She recalled the Dublin base where Hunter worked: the unwashed mugs, the overloaded in-trays, the Post-its curling up like tongues from the files. She pictured his face, lean and tired, his sandy hair short as a school-boy's, and waited for the pang of homesickness to hit her.

It didn't.

'You can go.'

Harry's eyebrows shot up. Zubiri was ambling towards the desk, his untidy hair coiling out of his head like springs. He gathered up the photos.

'This is no job for someone like you.' His voice was low, his Spanish accent distorted by transatlantic tones that probably came from watching American TV.

Harry glanced at the door. Zubiri followed her gaze and shrugged.

'Why should you get involved? Just so he can look

43

good to the Chief?' He blew out air with a *pff* through his lips.

Harry picked at her nail, but made no move to go. She watched him slot the photos back into the folder, McArdle's bloated face now hidden from view. She leaned forward in her chair.

'Who are these people? Why are you so interested in them?'

Zubiri shook his woolly head. 'It's none of your concern.'

'Inspector Vasco mentioned criminal organizations. What kind of crimes are we talking about here?'

'Every kind. The worst kind. Drugs, human trafficking, extortion, armed robberies, fraud . . .' He slapped the folder onto the desk. 'These people crop up in a lot of unconnected cases.'

'And they operate out of San Sebastián?'

Zubiri shrugged. 'Spain has always been important to criminals.'

'For drug trafficking?'

'For everything. Spain is a gateway to Europe, especially for the Moroccans and the Colombians. And Latin Americans can exploit the shared language and culture. Even the Italian clans look on it as a home from home.'

'I thought all the crime bosses holed up in the south. In the Costa del Sol. Not here in the north.'

Zubiri fixed a pair of black eyes on hers, and Harry shifted in her seat. She was stalling and she knew it, caught between a survival instinct to back away and a more ignoble curiosity. Eventually, he answered her.

'The northwest has a long history of trafficking with the Colombians. But security on the Galician coast has tightened up. Now the criminals turn to the ports of *Euskadi*. The Basque country. My country.'

Harry blinked. The intensity of his stare was unnerving. She gestured at the folder on the desk.

'So where do the cheaters fit in?'

'Who knows? Dealers, mules, middlemen, hitmen . . .'

Hitmen. Jesus. An image of McArdle's white face floated before her, the life gushing out of it in bloody bursts. Her insides slithered.

'Who do you think killed him?' she said.

Zubiri didn't need to ask who she meant. 'We don't know. But why should you care?' He leaned forward, supporting his weight on the desk with his knuckles. The backs of his hands were dark and hairy. 'McArdle was nothing to you. Just a fat Irish hacker working for criminals.'

Harry flinched. A shard of guilt twisted in her chest. She knew she'd blanked McArdle out. Hadn't thought of him as a person. Hadn't liked him much, if it came right down to it, though they'd never even spoken. She'd dubbed him 'the fat guy', and then found him dead.

She looked up at Zubiri. 'What else do you know about him?'

He shrugged, straightened up. 'Quite a lot.'

'Was he good at what he did?'

Another shrug. 'So they tell me. Started hacking as a kid. Broke into school networks, messed with phone systems, that kind of thing.'

Harry looked at the floor, as if he might catch a glimpse of her own shady past in her eyes. Zubiri went on:

'It might have ended there if it hadn't been for his sister. She got into debt with a heroin habit. McArdle cut a deal with her suppliers in Belfast: he'd repay what she owed by working for them.'

'As a hacker?'

Zubiri nodded. 'He needn't have bothered. He found his sister's body in an old warehouse a few weeks later. Overdose. The needle was still stuck in her arm.'

'Jesus.' Harry closed her eyes briefly, trying to blot the image out. 'But he kept working for them?'

'Once you're in, it's hard to get out. Just knowing these people, knowing what they do, is enough to put you at risk. They own you. Try to leave and you end up dead in a ditch.'

'How long was he with them?'

Zubiri paused. 'Eighteen years.'

Harry's eyes widened as she worked it out. McArdle was thirty-four. Which meant he'd signed over his soul when he was just sixteen. She shook her head, recalling herself at that age: masquerading as Pirata, flexing her hacking muscles. Just like McArdle.

Pirata: Spanish for pirate. Just a curious explorer on the electronic high seas, testing the limits of technology. But it wasn't all innocent. She'd breached securities, trespassed where others wouldn't. She'd felt the searing heat of true piracy in her soul, and had struggled not to abuse her power. One wrong choice and things might have turned out differently.

They almost had.

At the age of thirteen, she'd given into temptation and hacked into the Dublin Stock Exchange. Fuelled by an illicit rush of adrenalin, she'd tampered with financial data. The authorities had tracked her down, but she'd been rescued by a mentor who'd schooled her in the ethics of hacking. She'd stuck to the code of honour ever since.

Well, more or less.

Harry slid a glance at the folder of photographs. If things had been different, could she have ended up like McArdle? A hacker for hire to the wrong kind of client?

Zubiri followed her gaze, then picked up the folder and tucked it under his arm. 'You should leave. Go home. Forget about this.'

'And let Vasco loose on me?'

Zubiri looked away. Harry didn't move.

Go home. To what? To Hunter? Her mother? Her rocky relations with the police? She pictured Vasco raking over her past, maybe even grilling her father. Her muscles tensed. She thought about McArdle, about her San Sebastián roots; about a whole mess of things that together stirred up an urge to hide away and become someone else for a while.

Suspect or decoy?

Zubiri leaned his knuckles back against the desk, dipping his large head so that he looked up at her from under his brows.

'Go home. Pretending to be someone else is tougher than you think.'

Harry shot him a surprised look. He leaned in closer. His five o'clock shadow looked coarse enough to strip paint. He continued in his low, oddly accented voice:

'Not everyone is cut out to work undercover. You need discipline, control.' His knuckles tightened into fists against the desk. 'You can't forget your cover, not for a day, not for a minute. You must become one of the bad guys, laugh at their jokes, do what they do. And keep your fears to yourself.' Sequins of sweat broke through the stubble. 'These people are not like you and me.'

'Vasco said it would be quick. In and out.'

'Vasco doesn't know shit. He has never worked under-cover. Things get ugly, plans go wrong. You need to think on your feet.'

When Harry didn't respond, he shook his head and went on:

'You will be alone. Really alone. More alone than you've ever been in your life.' A small muscle pulsed in his eyelid. 'You can't leave at the end of the day to relax with family and friends. You're cut off. Isolated. You have no one to talk to about what you're going through, except your contact agent.'

Harry gave him a steady look. 'Would you be my contact agent?'

He held her gaze. 'Yes. But I will not be your guardian angel.'

She stared at him for a moment. His disapproval was a little hard to take, though she wondered why she cared. Then she pictured McArdle's pale, dead face, and slowly got to her feet.

'You're right,' she said. 'This is none of my concern.'

6

Marty patted the three decks of cards in his pocket, then turned up his collar against the wind. One thing was for damn sure, there was nothing continental about northern Spain in March.

He traipsed past the shuttered apartments and shops, heading for the boardwalk by the river. The salty funk of seaweed hung in the air. He squinted across the water towards Alameda del Boulevard, the big-city street that butted up against the old part of town. He fingered the cards in his pocket. Time to scare up some cash, or he'd end up sleeping in a doorway.

His landlady had ambushed him the night before. A fierce-looking Basque with hennaed hair, she'd chewed him out about the rent. He'd tried to flirt, sweet-talk her round, but the beating he'd taken in the casino hadn't helped. The blood had made him look like a street brawler. In the end, she'd given him a day to come up with the money.

Marty fingered the plump wallet in his inside pocket, the one he'd stuffed with newspaper and a few counterfeit notes before he'd left his room. The counterfeits were cheap, a shoddy job that in a good light wouldn't fool anyone. But Marty didn't plan on handing them around for inspection.

He cut left across the Zurriola Bridge where the river surged out into the bay. The tide was high, whipping the estuary into violent swells that boomed off the embankment walls. Marty hunched his shoulders against the driving wind. Water was loud everywhere in this damn city.

He eased along the Boulevard, wincing at the tenderness in his ribs. Last night had been dumb, his own stupid fault. He'd broken the golden rule: never let yourself get back-roomed. He should have kicked, screamed, run, anything. Marty sighed and shook his head. Truth was, he hadn't wanted to look like a bum in front of the redhead. He rolled his eyes skyward and fingered the crusty gash around his nose. He'd sure paid for that piece of vanity.

Halfway down the Boulevard he turned right, ducking into the alleys of the Old Quarter. It was darker in here. The narrow streets stood huddled together, dodging the evening light. He peered into the open bars, searching for a likely mark.

It was Riva who'd first taught him that the world was divided into two.

51

'Suckers and scammers,' she'd said, her slate-grey eyes fixed on his. 'That's all there is in this life. One's smarter than the other, that's the only difference between 'em.'

She'd been just fourteen, only three years older than him, though with fancy clothes and make-up, she could look a whole lot more. He'd bitten his lip, a little nervous about contradicting her.

'But isn't one more dishonest than the other, too?' he'd said.

Riva snorted. 'Honesty don't come into it. Would a sucker jump at the chance to hold the upper hand, assuming he suddenly got smart enough? You bet he would. He'd turn those tables quicker'n spit.' She shook the fine blonde hair from her face. 'It's a simple choice, Marty. Sucker or scammer. Top dog or victim.' Suddenly she'd wheeled away, her bony fists clenched. 'I know which I'd rather be.'

Cutlery clinked from inside the bars. The sweet scent of onions pepped up Marty's nostrils. He watched the customers help themselves to *pintxos*, the Basque equivalent of fast finger-food. He dragged his gaze away. Food was for later, when he could pay.

Marty spotted the mark in the next bar: tall, thin; designer croc on the shirt, sharp crease in the jeans. He was mouthing off to a pale young woman hanging on his every word. Marty eased closer to the open door.

The guy spoke with an educated, English voice. A completed *Times* crossword lay ostentatiously on the bar beside him. He was swirling the wine in his glass, poking his nose over the rim for a sniff every now and then. Marty smiled.

'Almost everyone is a potential mark,' Riva had said to him once.

'Everyone?' He'd still only been eleven and hadn't gotten used to the fact that Riva was always right. 'Aren't a lot of people too smart to be taken in?'

'They sure think they are.' Her thin, heart-shaped face had split into a smile. 'That makes them the best marks of all.'

Church bells chimed somewhere behind him, and Marty came to a decision. He rumpled his hair, loosened his tie, then lurched full tilt through the door. The babble of Spanish hammered his ears. He bulldozed his way to the counter, collecting gripes along the way, and collided with the English guy.

'Hey, sorry, buddy.' Marty belched into the man's face. 'Didn't see ya there.'

The English guy stiffened. Marty made as if to flag the barman down, but managed to knock the guy's glass over instead.

'Jeez, look at that.'

A Rioja-tinted stain was seeping over the crossword. The guy's face grew tight, and Marty winked at the mousy-looking woman beside him.

'Least it missed his clothes. Them fake designer brands don't wash too well, do they?'

The woman's eyes widened. Marty waited a beat. Then

53

he burst into a wheezy laugh and punched the English guy on the arm.

'Just kiddin', pal. Whooo!' Marty patted himself on the chest. 'Here, lemme buy you another.'

The English guy closed his eyes briefly. 'No, thank you, we're just leaving.'

'Aw, come on.' Marty spread out his arms. 'Hey, I know I've had a few, but I'm celebrating. Look—' He glanced over his shoulder, then dug the fat wallet out of his pocket and slapped it onto the counter. A wad of fifty-euro notes curled out over the sides. 'See that? Casino money. Poker action was sizzling and I cleaned 'em out! Know what else?' He fumbled in his pocket for a pack of cards. 'I stole one of their decks as a keepsake!'

Marty wheezed out another laugh, and thumped the English guy on the shoulder. At the same time, he moved in front of him so as to block his exit, and slipped the cards out of the pack.

'Hey, I'll play you for that drink, buddy, just one poker hand for fun.' Marty bungled a shuffle, dropping some cards on the floor. Then he straightened up and dealt two sloppy hands of five. 'I just can't lose today.'

The English guy edged away, sending his friend a snippety, drink-up signal. 'Another time.'

Marty poked him hard in the chest with the cards he'd just dealt him. 'Whassamatter? You afraid to lose in front of your lady friend?'

The guy narrowed his eyes and glanced down at his chest. Something flickered across his face, and he hesitated. Marty knew what had snagged his attention. The cards were spread in a clumsy fan that allowed the guy a peek at what he'd got.

It was hard to ignore four kings.

Slowly, the English guy took the cards from Marty and set them face down on the counter. His fingers hovered over them. Marty twisted away, as if in search of a drink, and treated the guy to a seemingly accidental flash of the other hand. He knew what he'd see there: three jacks and two odd cards. Marty swivelled back, and the guy flicked a furtive glance at the floor.

'You still chicken?' Marty picked up his wallet and peeled a crackling note from his wad. 'Or maybe you'd like to make it more interesting.' He leered at the colour-less woman beside them. 'Whaddaya reckon, fifty bucks too rich for your pal here?'

Marty smacked the fifty-euro note on the counter, covering it with his palm. The English guy's lips disappeared into a thin line, and Marty could almost see the wheels turn. Fact was, the guy's four kings beat Marty's three jacks hands down. Even if Marty changed the two odd cards and drew the fourth jack, it still wouldn't beat four kings.

The guy's jaw pulsed a little. Maybe he suspected he was being hustled, but at this point, chances were he thought Marty had botched the deal.

The guy reached for his wallet. 'One hand.'

The disdain had left his face, replaced now by something craftier. He flicked a fifty-euro note next to Marty's.

Immediately Marty picked it up and used it to cover his own. Another of Riva's rules: bury the funny money. In case anyone got too curious.

Marty examined his cards and chuckled. 'So how many d'you want, pal?'

'I'll stay pat.'

Marty frowned. 'No cards?' He double-checked his own. 'Alrighty. Well, I'll take two.'

He discarded two of his cards onto the counter and dealt another couple from the pack. He palmed his five cards and squeezed them into a tight fan. He let out another belly laugh.

'Woo-hoo! What'd I tell ya? I just can't lose today.' He rummaged in his wallet, lurching up against the bar. 'It's gonna cost you another hundred to see these babies.'

He smacked two more fifties on top of the others, again covering the duds with his palm. The Englishman glanced at his cards, ground his teeth a little. Then he produced two fifties of his own and tossed them onto the counter.

'I call your hundred.' A smile slid over the Englishman's face. 'But you won't top these.'

He spread his cards on the counter with a snap. Four big kings, fat and important-looking. Just the way Marty had dealt them. The English guy reached for the cash, but Marty smacked his hand away.

'Hold on, not so fast.' He fanned his cards out on the counter. 'Where I come from, a straight flush whups four kings every time.'

The English guy's mouth opened and the woman beside him gasped. For a second, they stared at Marty's hand: seven, eight, nine, ten and Jack, all in a tidy row. And all of them suited hearts.

Marty gave them another second to take it in, then snatched up the cash, whirled around and shouldered his way to the door.

His heartbeat drummed against his ribs. He raced outside, wheeled left then right, criss-crossing the rabbit warren of streets. Adrenalin blasted through him, dulling the pain in his torso and setting his fingertips tingling.

He ran till he'd put a safe distance behind him, then slowed to a walk to cool down. He glanced over his shoulder, panting hard. Jesus, he was too old for this.

He stepped into a doorway to count his haul of notes, separating out the phonies. The English guy would work it out soon enough. He'd realize Marty hadn't changed his two odd cards, but had thrown two of his jacks down instead. For a second, he'd probably wonder who the hell would do such a thing. But only for a second. The answer, of course, was a conman who'd stacked the deck.

Marty stowed the genuine notes into his pocket and slipped the duds back into his wallet. Truth was, the guy had been suckered because he thought he'd sneaked a preview of the cards. He'd been happy to fleece an obnoxious drunk, once he thought he had leverage. Marty was with W.C. Fields on this one: you can't cheat an honest man.

Marty did a few neck rolls to loosen his muscles and felt his spine crunch. Pain lanced across his ribs. Jesus. He'd taken quite a beating to cover up for that bastard Franco. The question was, would it be worth it?

He slumped against a wall, waiting for the spasm to pass. One way or another, he planned on using Franco to generate some cash. He'd work with him or against him, he didn't care which. Marty sighed. Well, not really.

He patted the remaining decks of cards in his pocket, letting his gaze roll over the drinkers across the alleyway.

Another bar, another sucker.

His limbs felt heavy. He stayed where he was and closed his eyes. An image of Franco's crew drifted into his head, and for an instant he felt the rush of the glory days when he'd been a part of it all. His pulse thudded. He remembered the exhilaration of pulling a con; the electric highs, the close calls, the camaraderie on the road.

He wondered about the crew Franco worked with now, and whether they were as good as him and Riva. He smiled and shook his head, his eyes still closed. Franco, him and Riva: together, they'd been on fire. No one could touch them without burning.

Marty opened his eyes, readjusted to his surroundings, and felt his shoulders slump. Now he was back where he started: a chip thief and a hustler.

He shrugged himself away from the wall, then trudged across to the bar. A dark-haired girl eyed him from inside the doorway. She was petite and striking, like a lot of these Spanish types, and reminded him of the girl who'd been watching the crew at the casino.

Marty hesitated. Something about that girl had bothered him. She'd seen Fat-boy's eye-rub, but she'd stood apart, hadn't blended in like one of the crew. Hadn't looked much like a real punter, either. The other women had been all gussied up, but she'd been wearing a suit.

Was she working for the casino?

Marty's skin prickled, and he fingered the paltry fifty-euro notes in his pocket. Maybe Franco would like to hear about her.

Maybe someone should tell him.

7

'Are you out of your mind?' Hunter said.

Harry bristled at his tone. She switched the phone to her other ear and yanked the satchel higher on her shoulder.

'Haven't you been listening?' She crossed the street and turned left along the beach promenade. 'I told them I wouldn't do it.'

'Then why are you still talking with them?'

'They want to give me more details, no strings attached. Look, I'm curious, I admit it. But it doesn't mean I'll go along with it.'

'Doesn't it?'

'Would it really be so bad if I did? It's just an in-and-out job. I find out why they want a hacker, then I leave.'

Harry knew she was being contrary; an instinctive

buck against his assumption that he had some kind of say.

'Who's in charge over there?' he said.

'I'm mostly dealing with a Detective Zubiri, but his boss is a guy called Vasco.'

'That prick. What the hell does he know about under-cover operations?'

Harry blinked. 'Vasco? You know him?'

'He phoned a couple of days ago, asked a lot of questions. Sounded like a puffed-up desk-jockey to me.'

Harry recalled Vasco's slick self-importance, and privately she had to agree. She peeked at her watch, then quickened her pace, her shoes scratching against the grit of sand on the pavement. To her left, the grand façades of apartments and hotels lined the shell-shaped coast. To her right, the waves thwacked in a fizz of foam against the sand.

'Look, it's a paying job.' Harry clutched the lapels of her jacket to stop them flapping in the wind. 'A consultancy gig with the police. You're always saying I should work more on the side of the angels.'

She heard him exhale a controlled breath, and pictured him massaging tired, hazel eyes. She chewed her bottom lip, regretting her contrariness. Just once, it'd be nice to have a conversation where they didn't butt heads.

They'd met a few months earlier when one of Harry's clients had framed her as a suspect in a murder. Hunter had been the lead detective on the case, and right from

61

the get-go, he'd pegged her as a liar, though eventually she'd cleared her name. Well, more or less.

Afterwards, Hunter had seemed to reassess her. He'd vouched for her with the Garda Tech Bureau in Dublin, who'd since hired her twice as a computer forensics consultant. She'd worked alongside Hunter on one occasion, but in spite of the plug he'd given her, she could tell some of his wariness lingered. They'd met for lunch a couple of times, had even gone to dinner when they'd both been working late. But so far, one thing hadn't led to another, and Harry had to admit she was probably to blame. Then again, he had complications of his own to sort through.

'So who are these casino cheaters?' Hunter's voice was taut, spiked with the kind of crankiness that comes from lack of sleep.

Harry shrugged. 'I only know a couple of names. Franco Chavez, he seems to be the ringleader. The hacker was from Belfast with paramilitary connections, a guy called Stephen McArdle.'

'I'll check them out, see what I can dig up.'

Harry paused, her pace slackening. 'There's no need. Really, I can handle it.'

Silence thickened the airspace between them. She closed her eyes briefly.

Dammit.

The line between interference and support was a fine one, and she'd be the first to admit she had trouble telling the difference. In her defence, she'd learned the hard way to rely on no one but herself. That was the natural fallout when your father was absent and your mother was indifferent all your life. On the upside, it saved on disappointments, but she'd noticed other people found her independence hard to take. She'd yet to decide if that was their problem or hers.

She cleared her throat. 'Look—'

'I get it. You don't need anything. Just let me know how it works out.'

The line went dead. Harry glared at the phone and, for a moment, considered calling him back. Then she sighed and slipped the handset into her pocket. The conversation had already stalled and crashed. Salvaging the wreckage didn't seem too appealing right now.

She tugged her jacket tighter across her chest. The air was damp and salty, the water a leaden-grey. She'd heard that the Basque country got as much rain as the west of Ireland. Next time, she'd take her cue from the locals and carry an umbrella.

Her phone buzzed against her hip. She whipped it out to check the caller ID: her sister, Amaranta. Mentally, Harry poked a tongue out at herself for hoping it might be Hunter, then debated whether to take the call. Amaranta specialized in big-sister guilt trips, and Harry wasn't in the mood for one right now. She cursed and put the phone to her ear.

'Amaranta?'

'At last. I was about to hang up.'

Harry rolled her eyes and didn't answer. She pictured

her sister: ash-blonde and elegant, just like their mother. Harry was the one who'd inherited the dark Martinez looks, but it was Amaranta who'd got the exotic Spanish name. By the time Harry was born, her mother had tired of all things Spanish and had christened her Henrietta, after her own mother. It was her father who'd rescued her and shortened the name to Harry.

Amaranta huffed into the silence, then quickly got to the point. 'You know that Mum's in a complete state because you're in San Sebastián?'

Harry squinted into the phone. 'Why would she care where I am? And how does she even know? We haven't spoken in over a month.'

'Exactly. Don't you think you should call her?'

'No.'

Harry let that one sit. She knew it sounded truculent, but had no intention of being drawn into explanations. Her relationship with her mother was like a wound that wouldn't heal. Their exchanges usually ended on a sour note, and Harry often broke contact for weeks at a time to give them both a chance to recover. Eventually Harry would go back, peeling off whatever scab had managed to form and exposing herself to another injury. Never once had her mother initiated a reconciliation. Harry suspected she was secretly relieved by her daughter's occasional absences.

'You're being childish,' Amaranta said eventually.

'Not really. We both know she doesn't like me, so why pretend?'

'That's putting it way too strongly, and you know it.'

'Just because she's different with you doesn't mean it isn't true.'

'You were Dad's favourite and I never objected.'

'Well, maybe you should have.'

Harry bit her lip, and for a moment, neither of them spoke. Waves crashed like thunder-claps into the silence, and even Amaranta didn't rush to fill it this time.

Their family had always been split into two teams: Amaranta and their mother versus Harry and their father. It was something she and Amaranta had accepted many years before, and it had brokered a sort of truce between them. Sure, they still bickered, but sibling rivalry was never the cause. The truth was, the family pairings had suited them. For Harry's part, she'd stopped craving her mother's affection so badly. Her father had become her safe haven and proved that her mother might be wrong; that Harry might be lovable after all. She guessed it must have been the same for Amaranta.

Harry kicked a pebble along the promenade. At the time, the arrangement had seemed well balanced, but as an adult the after-effects were starting to feel a little unstable.

Amaranta sighed into the phone, and when she spoke again, her voice was softer. 'It's a little late for all that now, isn't it?'

'Maybe. Maybe not.'

'Look, why not just call Mum?'

Harry's brain jangled at the thought. 'I don't get why

she's so uptight. What's wrong with me being in San Sebastián?'

'You tell me. It's just another job, isn't it?'

Harry closed her eyes briefly. 'More or less.'

They kicked the topic around for a while, but could shake nothing else from it and so wound things up and said goodbye. Harry stowed the phone away and tried to put the exchange out of her head. Thinking about her mother had never brought her much comfort.

She continued along the promenade for another hundred yards, then turned left on to Calle de la Infanta Cristina. Her stomach muscles tightened. In front of her stood the grey, triangular block that housed the Ertzaintza station. She straightened her shoulders, smoothed down her hair, then marched through the door and asked for Detective Zubiri.

An officer escorted her down a narrow corridor, and she trotted behind him, her shoulder aching from the weight of her satchel, which held her laptop and computer forensics toolkit. She probably wouldn't need them, but if she was supposed to be a hacker then she may as well look the part.

The officer showed her into a room and clicked the door shut behind her. Harry did a quick survey of her surroundings.

She was alone in the room. The lights were dimmed, the blinds drawn. The only illumination was the glow of a projector and laptop on the conference table. The projector whirred. Dust motes swirled in the slanting cones of light, and Harry moved closer, peering at the image cast up against the wall. It was a headshot of Riva Mills.

Harry stared at the pointed features and taut lips. The blonde hair was fine and silky. It was the only thing soft-looking about her.

'You're late.'

Harry turned to find Zubiri watching her by the door. His shaggy hair hung low over his brows, obscuring his eyes a little. She glanced at her watch.

'Not really.'

He stomped across the room, his large head dipped low like a charging bull. He took a seat in front of the laptop, gesturing for Harry to sit to one side, presumably so she could view the slideshow on the wall.

She pulled up a chair, nodding towards the photo of Riva. 'We're starting with her?'

'We start where I say. Tell me what you know about her.'

Harry settled her satchel by her feet, playing for time while she coached herself to let his rudeness slide. She counted to three, then straightened up.

'I only know what I could find out from public sources. She's from Ohio. Ran away from home at the age of fourteen, bought her first casino when she was twenty-one.' Harry turned to study the striking face projected on the wall. 'I guess a lot must have happened to her in those intervening years.'

Zubiri grunted. 'What else?'

'She owns eleven casinos, three of them here in Spain. She's lived in San Sebastián for the last ten years, though I'm not exactly sure what her link with the place is.'

She threw Zubiri a questioning look, but he didn't fill her in. Instead, he jabbed at his keyboard. Riva's headshot disappeared and another photo flashed into view: Riva shaking hands with some guy on a podium. The man wore a broad smile and a ceremonial chain, but Riva's expression was sombre.

'She's well respected in the community here,' Zubiri said. His American-flavoured accent seemed more pronounced, as though he'd been practising overnight with CNN. 'She's on the board of trustees for two children's homes. Contributes to local causes. Fundraises for local schools and hospitals. A real philanthropist.'

Harry caught his tone and shot him a sideways look. 'Are you saying it's a front?'

'I'm saying there's a lotta stuff people don't know about Riva Mills.'

'Such as?'

Zubiri flipped ahead to the next slide. A mugshot: the profile and front-view of a young girl. A waif, really. Maybe thirteen or fourteen, with bony shoulders and a pinched, heart-shaped face.

Harry blinked. 'She has a criminal record?'

'Juvenile. Back in the United States. Fraud, cheque forgery, theft.'

'Did she go to prison?'

Zubiri shook his head. 'They gave her a break on

account of her background. They say her mother was abusive. Unstable. Plus there was a younger brother, some problem kid, that Riva mostly took care of.'

Harry stared at the photo, at the razor-sharp cheekbones sloping into dainty features. She had trouble reconciling this undernourished girl with the businesswoman who ran a casino empire. She glanced back at Zubiri.

'Okay, so my client isn't all that she seems. God knows, it wouldn't be the first time. But what's that got to do with the casino cheaters?'

Zubiri leaned back in his chair and took his time about answering, almost as though he begrudged her the information. Eventually, he said,

'She may be involved.'

'In what? Ripping off her own casinos?'

Zubiri laced his hands across his wrinkled shirt. 'Who told her about the cheaters?'

'Her Chief of Security, Victor Toledo. He got a tip-off from a source.'

'What source?'

Harry shrugged. 'I don't know. Does it matter?'

'What about the scam the crew pulled in the casino? Do you know how they did it?'

'No. But now we know who to watch, we could pull the surveillance tapes. They might tell us something.'

Zubiri shook his head. 'Pulling the tapes would alert Riva to their identity. I don't want the cheaters stopped. Not yet. Not if we want them to recruit you.'

Harry stirred in her seat, aware of a shifting in her

gut. Now they were getting to the real reason she was here.

'I haven't agreed to do it yet.' She clasped her hands in her lap. 'But assuming I did, how exactly would they end up recruiting me?'

'Same way they ended up recruiting McArdle. Through recommendations from Irish paramilitaries.'

Harry's heart did a quick flip. 'You're kidding.'

Zubiri was watching her closely. 'That's how McArdle got most of his clients. Word of mouth, vouched for by his oldest employers. And we know Chavez's crew has links with terrorists. It's one of the reasons we're watching them.'

Harry's palms felt clammy. 'So Chavez put the word out that he needed a hacker and his contacts in Belfast put him in touch with McArdle?'

'Exactly.'

Harry shivered, the hairs spiking up along her arms. Terrorists and paramilitaries. The words conjured up an underworld of hatred and fanaticism, generations of rage that had nothing to do with her. She swallowed.

'And now you think Chavez will put out feelers for a replacement?'

'Yes.'

'But how will you know?'

Zubiri sighed and rubbed his eyes, suddenly looking jaded. 'The Irish and the Basques are closer than you think. Your paramilitaries have been buddies with our ETA separatists for almost forty years. Explosives in exchange for training. Handguns for solidarity. Our police force has had undercover agents in your country for decades.' He leaned forward, every line in his face etched deep. 'There are no guarantees Chavez will approach Belfast again. But if he does, our operatives will know about it.'

'And do what?'

'Intercept the enquiry. Redirect it to us and let Chavez know a replacement is on the way.'

Harry's mouth felt dry. Zubiri fixed his eyes on hers and nodded.

'And then you go in.'

8

'Would I wear a wire?'

Harry was surprised at how normal her voice sounded. Zubiri shook his head.

'Waste of time.'

'But don't you need evidence?'

'All we need is information. Wear some piece-of-shit recorder, and you just spend time changing the batteries.'

Harry peered at him through the artificial twilight of the room. The projector beam had excavated lines like dugouts in his face.

'I thought devices were more hi-tech these days,' she said.

Zubiri snorted. 'The Ertzaintza budget doesn't stretch to hi-tech equipment. They keep that stuff for National Intelligence. Even if we could afford it, they wouldn't let us use it.'

'Why not?'

'Because we gotta explain our technology in court. Show how we acquire our evidence. If we use the smart stuff, the gadgets get exposed and so does National Intelligence. They prefer to keep their box of tricks a secret.'

'I see.' Harry's mouth felt dry. 'So no wire?'

Zubiri leaned forward in his chair and started itemizing things on his fingers. 'Look, this crew is professional. They're going to frisk you, they're going to confiscate your phone, your laptop, your jewellery, anything that looks like it could be a recorder, a transmitter or a GPS device.' His sombre eyes locked onto hers. 'These guys catch you wired and you're dead.'

Harry swallowed, and a bead of sweat began a lazy trickle down her back. Zubiri's eyes raked her face, as though hunting for signs of weakness. She lifted her chin.

'Okay, so no recorders or transmitters. How would you know where I was?'

'You'd have backup.'

'Where?'

He shook his head. 'Basic rule of undercover: you never get told where the backup's gonna be.' He tipped his chair back, linking his hands behind his head. 'Think about it. You rendezvous with a target and you know we got a sniper on the roof? You can't help yourself, you'll look up to check he's there.' He shook his head again. 'You won't ever know where we are. It's for your own protection.'

Harry suppressed an involuntary shudder. She'd have to be crazy to get involved in a stunt like this. Then she caught the challenge in Zubiri's gaze, and could tell he didn't expect her to take the job either.

She shifted in her chair. The projector light flickered as Zubiri's laptop dozed into standby mode, obliterating Riva's image from the wall. The room sank into shadow. Zubiri rocked on his tilted-back chair, and Harry glanced at his large, craggy face and thought about his boss, Vasco.

He'd threatened to embroil her in a murder case, to blacken her already tarnished name. She clamped her teeth shut. Her credentials with the Irish police had taken a beating the previous year and, in truth, she was tired of being the bad guy. She'd worked hard the last few months to redeem her reputation, and bit by bit, she'd sensed a growing respect, at least from the Tech Bureau guys. The last thing she wanted was to jeopardize all that now.

The hairs along her arms twitched. It was an in-and-out job. All she had to do was pretend to be a hacker. How hard could it be?

She eyed Zubiri's face, kept her gaze steady. 'Let's assume, for the sake of argument, that I'm going to do this. I presume I'd need an alias?'

He missed a beat, as though adjusting for an unexpected turn of events. Then he let his chair drop with a snap back to the floor.

'We'd prepare some background paperwork. False

74

name, credit card, driver's licence.' He cocked a tangled eyebrow in her direction. 'Unless you have those already?'

Harry felt the colour rise in her cheeks and wondered how much he knew about her occasional identity switches. If he knew about her trespassing caper on the Stock Exchange, then he probably knew about Pirata. Chances were, though, he didn't know about Catalina.

Catalina Diego had started out as an imaginary friend when Harry was five years old. She took most of the blame for Harry's misdeeds; she was blonde and beautiful, and her mother loved her. As Harry got older she'd abandoned Catalina in favour of Pirata, but later reinvented her when she began her hacking scams. By the time Harry was fourteen, Catalina had her own email account, driving licence and even a credit card. Harry still used her whenever the need arose.

She shrugged. 'We could use Catalina Diego. It's a persona I've built up in my professional capacity.'

'Oh?'

Harry returned his unblinking gaze. 'I use it occasionally on authorized security tests. She's got established credentials, a credible paper trail. Plus, I'm used to the name. I won't blank if someone calls me that.'

Zubiri's eyes probed hers, then he nodded. 'Okay. We'd set up a couple of hello phones, get some people to backstop you in Belfast.' He must have seen her expression, for he went on to explain. 'Just numbers and contacts who'll confirm Catalina's background if anyone

75

asks. We'd use McArdle, too. You could say you knew him, you were in the same line of business.'

'Why?'

'He's a dead guy, that's why. Dead guys can't deny knowing you.'

Harry blinked. Zubiri went on.

'You said you had family in San Sebastián.'

'I said I might have.'

'You'd need to stay away from places they might be. In case they blow your cover.'

Harry shook her head. 'No one knows me. I haven't been here since I was a child.'

Zubiri nodded, satisfied. 'Stick to the truth as much as possible. The fewer lies you tell, the fewer you need to remember.'

'What happens if they just don't believe me?'

For the first time, Zubiri's gaze faltered. 'They will.'

'But if they don't?'

He jabbed at the keyboard, kick-starting his laptop. Then he trained his eyes on hers. 'No matter what happens, never, ever break cover.'

Harry experienced a sudden, dizzy rush, like the falling sensation that jerks you out of sleep. Her heart pounded. She eased back in her chair, covering her jitters with slow movements. Zubiri turned to his keyboard, pecking out the password to unlock his snoozing laptop.

Harry's gaze slid to his fingers. Instinctively, she found herself trying to shoulder-surf his code, and had to refrain from craning her neck. But she couldn't make it out. He was hunched over, shielding his hands, as though trying to stop her cheating on a test. All she could tell was that the password was long and, from the way his hands moved, contained numbers and symbols as well as letters.

She awarded him a mental thumbs-up. A hacker would work up quite a sweat trying to power-drill his way through that one.

Light bounced against the wall. Riva's mugshot flickered back into focus, and Harry noted from the information bar that they'd reached slide four in a total of fourteen. She snuck a glance at her watch. Zubiri hadn't struck her as the show-'n'-tell type. Just how many mugshots did he have?

He hit a key and Riva vanished, replaced by McArdle's post-mortem shot.

'We've managed to identify four members of Chavez's crew. McArdle you already know.' Zubiri flipped ahead to the next photo. 'And this guy too, though maybe not his name. Washed-up actor called Clayton James. Also known as James Clay and Jimmy Clayton.'

Harry stared up at the sweaty, florid face and the greying thatch of hair. It was the American who'd collected the crew's winnings at the casino.

'We've run him through our databases, the FBI did the same.' Zubiri switched in another shot, this one showing Clayton drinking in a bar. 'Compulsive gambler, dumped by his wife and kids, left the movie business thirty years ago and turned to forgery, theft, embezzlement and serious fraud.'

Harry took in the man's breezy smile, and the eyes that didn't quite share in the joke. Zubiri moved on to the next shot, one that Vasco had already shown her: the thirty-something brunette with the stage-make-up look.

'Virginia Vaughan, known as Ginny.' Zubiri cued up another slide, showing the brunette standing on the steps of the Gran Casino. 'She travels on an Irish passport and doesn't have a record. We think she's close to Chavez, but we don't know for sure.'

Harry studied the woman's striking face. Despite the showgirl pancake, there was something chic about the exotic planes and angles of her face.

Zubiri moved on. Another photo. Vasco had shown her this one, too: a man in his late forties, red-gold hair cut like a Marine's; straight, bleached brows.

'Name's Gideon Ray.' Zubiri switched to a shot of the man crossing a sunlit plaza. He looked tall and lean, his freckled face creased in laugh lines at some kids kicking footballs through the archways. Belatedly, Harry realized he was in the Plaza de la Constitución. She glanced at Zubiri.

'Is he another conman?'

Zubiri gave her a level look. 'All we know about Gideon Ray is that he kills people.'

Harry's breath caught in her throat. Slowly, her eyes crept back to the smiling man in the photo. 'Who does he kill?'

'Drug traffickers, terrorists, an occasional arms dealer.'

'Why?'

'We don't know.'

Harry hesitated. 'Did he kill McArdle?'

'They work on the same side, so we don't think so.' Zubiri shoved his chair back, stretching out his stocky legs. 'There might be others in the crew, but if so, you'd meet them when you went inside. Along with Chavez.'

Harry's brain suddenly felt swamped, the reality of the situation hitting her like a landslide. If she took this job on, she'd have to mix with these people. Talk with them, work with them, do what they do. She'd have to blend in and fool them into thinking she belonged. Harry's pulse accelerated. She looked up at Gideon Ray's smiling face; recalled Ginny Vaughan's glamour-girl mask, and Clayton's phoney warmth. A part of her wondered what was behind all the camouflage, but mostly she intended never to find out.

Zubiri fixed her with a stern look. 'Don't forget, just because you're undercover doesn't mean you try to be something that you're not. If you don't drink, then don't drink. If you don't take drugs, don't start now. And never say you've been to prison if you haven't.'

Harry nodded, her head still reeling. Zubiri went on.

'These people are lifelong criminals, and you'd be part of their world. But remember: you can't commit a crime when you're undercover. It's a strict rule. If you do, the department will not support you. Under any circumstances.'

Harry studied his intense, deep-set eyes, the unruly

curls, the rumpled shirt, and couldn't help comparing his bohemian image with Vasco's slick efficiency. She cocked her head to one side.

'Did *you* follow that rule when you worked undercover?'

He blinked once, but didn't look away. Eventually, he said, 'Attack is the best form of defence. Always answer a question with a question, and if you have to lie, look up at the ceiling.'

Harry felt her eyebrows knit together, and for the first time, Zubiri smiled.

'I learned that one from the RUC in Northern Ireland. If you're asked a question, you usually picture the answer in your mind's eye, so you look up for it. When you lie, there's no picture, so you look down. They used it when interrogating terrorists.'

'You worked undercover in Northern Ireland?'

'I worked undercover in a lot of places.'

'Inside ETA?'

The smile faded. 'For many years. Some of my superiors worried I was really with ETA, working undercover as a cop.'

'Was Vasco one of them?'

Zubiri blew a characteristic *pfft* through his lips. 'Vasco, he's just a handshaker. Doesn't know shit about undercover work. Doesn't even speak Euskara very well. Me, I've spent a lifetime hunting criminals, and I've found them, too. Some were even wearing the same uniform as me.'

Harry contemplated his large, slab-like face. He returned her look, as if trying to reassess her. That happened to her a lot these days.

Suddenly, he seemed to make up his mind about something. He snapped the laptop shut, then got to his feet, slipping a phone from his pocket.

'I have a call to make.'

Harry sat upright in her chair. 'What, no more slides?' By her calculations, they still had three more to go.

'None that concern you.' He shot her a challenging look. 'Or so my superiors tell me.'

He held her gaze a shade longer than necessary, then turned and headed for the door. She stared after his blocky, shambling frame as he disappeared into the corridor, leaving the door slightly ajar. Harry's eyes slid back to the laptop.

Three slides left.

None that concern you.

A charge whispered down the back of her neck.

Slowly, she reached across the table and clicked the laptop open.

9

Breaking into a laptop was like picking a lock: all you needed was time. Harry shot a glance at the half-open door. Right now, time wasn't on her side.

She edged around the desk to get a better view. The laptop was locked, password-protected. Her skin prickled as she tuned into Zubiri's voice outside in the corridor. He was drilling quick-fire Basque at someone on the phone. She eyed the projector, then reached out to switch it off. No sense in magnifying her snooping to wall-sized proportions.

The projector hum died away. The room darkened to a charcoal dusk, somehow intensifying the silence. Her fingers hovered over the keyboard.

Infiltrating a cop's laptop had to be a crime, whatever way you looked at it. Computer intrusion, property violation, data theft. On the other hand, the police wanted to set her up as a decoy. Surely that gave her dibs on all the facts? Harry shook her head, shelving the debate. Rationalizing her morals was a luxury for later. Right now, she needed information.

She pulled up a chair and thought about Zubiri's password. She could acquire it any number of ways, but the important thing here was speed. Mentally, she raced through her options.

If she knew more about him, she'd probably hazard a guess. Most people chose easily remembered words, no matter how often you warned them. The dog's name; maybe the wife's. Perhaps with a couple of digits appended, as if that would be enough to confound the bad guys. Harry made a face. Zubiri didn't strike her as the type to care for dogs or wives.

She drummed her fingers on the table. Simple brute force often worked best. Take a crowbar to something and eventually it had to cave in. Her sledgehammer of choice was usually a dictionary attack, a program that stepped through thousands of words hoping to jimmy the lock open with one of them. Trouble was, Zubiri's password had looked long and complicated. Hitting the right word and number combination could take her several hours. Besides, if there was one thing she'd sensed, it was the man's fierce national pride. She was willing to bet his password was in Basque, and while her attack program incorporated most foreign dictionaries, his ancient ancestral language wasn't among them.

Harry stirred in her chair. Zubiri's voice ramped up

outside, his consonants growing harsher. As far as she could tell, he was only a few feet from the door. Her heart cantered for a beat or two. She had one option left, but it was far from ideal. It would leave telltale tracks, unmistakable footprints that would lead directly to her. She darted another glance at the door, then hauled her laptop bag onto the table.

She ripped open the front Velcro pouch, rummaging inside for a USB memory stick, which she jammed into the side of Zubiri's laptop. Then she stabbed at the power switch and rebooted the machine.

The laptop hummed. She fixed her eyes on the screen, tracking the startup messages. Outside in the corridor, a copier stuttered to life, its mechanical clacking drowning out Zubiri's voice. Harry kept her gaze on the laptop. Then she hit a key, interrupting its routine, redirecting it to follow orders from her programmed USB stick. The laptop whirred. Sniffed at the stick. Then it swallowed her program like a dog with a biscuit, blithely passing control of its own innards over to Harry.

Her fingers rattled across the keys. She bypassed the rest of the startup grind and instead hooked into the bowels of the hard drive, probing its recesses till she found the list of users permitted to access the machine. There were two: Zubiri and the familiar Admin account, the built-in user that administered the computer. Both had passwords. Both were encrypted. No time to unscramble either one of them now.

But then again, she didn't need to. Why go to the

trouble of decrypting cyphertext when she could erase the password altogether? Remove the lock, and you were left with an open door.

With a few deft strokes, Harry blanked the Admin password, leaving Zubiri's intact. Then she whipped out the USB stick and rebooted the laptop one more time.

Her spine buzzed. Leave no trace. That was the cardinal rule for delinquent snooping, but in this case she'd had no choice. The next time an Admin user tried to access the laptop, they'd know its security had been breached. And it wouldn't take them long to trace things back to Harry.

She closed her eyes briefly, then refocused on the screen. This time, she let the bootup drill run its course, until finally the logon prompt appeared. Username: Admin. Password: Who needed it? The laptop sprang to life and she was in.

Immediately, she keyed in a search for slideshow files. Then she leaned back to wait, straining for sounds of Zubiri over the clatter of the copier outside. For all she knew, he could have finished his call and was on his way back to the room. Her armpits felt damp. Maybe she was wasting her time. After all, what did she expect to find?

The search threw up a single slideshow file. She flipped it open and stared at the words on the opening slide:

TCO NETWORK

TCO. What the hell was that? The slide was dated 5th March, and was accredited to one Chief Inspector

Eli Vasco. Harry had been right. Zubiri had borrowed the slides from his boss. She noted the English words and wondered about the intended audience.

She jumped to the next slide, the first photo of Riva Mills, then flashed through the procession of now-familiar faces: the adolescent Riva; Stephen McArdle; Clayton James; Ginny Vaughan; the smiling Gideon Ray. Finally, she reached the last three unseen slides.

The first was a list entitled 'Criminal Sectors'. Harry's eyes widened as she scanned down through it: drug trafficking, armed robbery, sex trade, extortion, corruption, human trafficking, smuggling, tax fraud, arts fraud, cybercrime, forgery, gunrunning, commodities fraud.

Harry's brain reeled. She raced ahead to the next slide. Two lists, the first headed 'Transnational Criminal Organizations'.

Harry blinked. *TCO.*

She flashed down the first column, her skin turning clammy: Colombian cartels, Chinese Triads, Japanese Yakuza, Russian Organizatsiya, Italian Mafia. Her vision blurred. The list went on. Jamaican Yardies, Bulgarian Mafiya, Albanian Fares, Mexican Federation, Nigerian organizations.

Jesus. Her eyes darted to the second column: 'Terrorist Organizations'. Another long list. Japan's Red Army, Peru's Shining Path, Colombia's FARC, IRA splinter groups, Islamic Jihad movements.

Something cold slid into Harry's stomach. The list read like a roll call for murder and mayhem.

The copier outside juddered to a halt. She jerked her head up. Zubiri had gone quiet. Her gaze shot to the door, but she couldn't get a fix on him. A torrent of adrenalin drenched through her veins. She flew ahead to the last slide, caught her breath as she took in the single line of text. Then she powered the laptop off, snapped the lid shut and two-stepped back to her seat.

Blood pounded in her ears. Behind her, she sensed Zubiri entering the room. She wiped her palms along her thighs, the last slide still scorched on her retinas like afterimage burn-in:

Criminal Proceeds for last six months: $900 million.

10

'So you still told them no?'

'Of course I told them no.' Harry's initial flash of pleasure at receiving Hunter's call was definitely starting to wane. 'Why would I do otherwise?'

'Exactly. One dead hacker's enough. No sense in offering up two, right?'

Harry swung her legs off the bed, biting back an unreasonable urge to bait him by saying she might still change her mind. She pictured him at his desk, the phone wedged into his shoulder, his sandy hair spiked up from shoving his hands through it. She flung aside the map she'd been studying when he'd called, then closed her eyes, relenting slightly. Hunter was only concerned for her safety, after all, and if she was honest, her frustrations had nothing to do with him.

It had been a couple of days since she'd talked to

Zubiri. She'd left his office, thanking him for his time and firmly declining his proposition. Then she'd walked away, expecting to feel relieved, but instead she'd felt oddly empty.

Her gaze roamed her bland hotel room, sliding over its neutral tones of greys and creams. She felt aimless. Directionless. Soon she'd terminate her arrangement with Riva, and after that, she'd have nothing. No client, no assignment. No reason to stay on in San Sebastián. She fingered the map on the bed beside her, tracing the route she'd marked out in thick red pen. No professional reason, anyway.

'Harry?'

'Sorry, you're right. It's too risky, I'd be a fool to do it. But I can't help feeling involved.'

'Because you found McArdle's body?'

Harry shrugged. 'I'd just like to know what happened to him, that's all.'

'Your pal Zubiri doesn't know?'

'If he does, he hasn't told me.'

She flashed on Zubiri's slides: drug trafficking, armed robbery, Colombians, terrorists. Proceeds of $900 million. The scale of it was staggering, but in her humdrum hotel room, the whole thing seemed frankly unreal. She was tempted to relay everything she'd learned to Hunter, but she'd given Zubiri her word that their discussions would remain confidential. Though right now, she wasn't sure she owed him anything.

Hunter cleared his throat. 'Look, I know you told me

not to go digging, but to hell with that. I went out on a limb and did it anyway. Hold on a second . . .'

She heard the quick snap of pages being turned, and imagined him frowning, his tie probably loosened and his collar undone in the manner of a man who couldn't abide restrictions.

'Got it,' he said. 'Okay, Stephen McArdle. You know his background: hacker from Belfast, paramilitary connections. Did you know he wanted out?'

'After eighteen years?'

'Word is, he was spooked. Turning paranoid. He knew too much about the organizations he worked for. Maybe someone back in Belfast thought so, too.'

Harry recalled what Zubiri had said: *Try to leave and you end up dead in a ditch.*

'So you're saying he was killed by paramilitaries? Which ones?'

'Take your pick. He seemed to work for them all at one time or another.'

'Where'd you hear this?'

'I poked around. Stepped on a few toes, exceeded my jurisdiction.'

'I thought you were meant to be keeping your nose clean.'

'I am. But somehow, you keep getting in my way.'

Harry bit her lip. Hunter's career had almost imploded the previous year after he'd had an affair with a suspect in a fraud case. He'd worked hard to toe the line ever since, but playing by the rules didn't suit him any more than it did Harry. They'd knocked heads on the case that had taken Harry to Capetown, but he'd seemed inclined to trust her in spite of the lies she'd spun. That hadn't played out well with his superiors.

He never spoke about the fraud case or the woman he'd slept with, and Harry often found herself wondering what she was like. Someone once said Hunter had a weakness for women who told lies. When she'd put it to him, the look he'd turned on her had been speculative and intense.

Pages crackled on the other end of the phone. He was probably rummaging through a jumble of files, his shirt-sleeves rolled up on lightly tanned forearms. She'd told him more than once he should never have been a cop. A demolition expert, maybe, or a war correspondent. Something that required helmets and nerve and a healthy dose of rage. He hadn't disagreed.

She smiled into the phone. 'Thanks for digging, Hunter. I mean that. But don't get your ass in a sling on my account.'

Hunter grunted, barely listening. His first name was Jack, but for some reason Harry never used it. That alone should have told her something about their arms-length relationship. If a relationship was even what they had. Sometimes she wondered if the electricity between them was mostly being generated by her.

'I lucked out on Chavez,' he said at last. 'Couldn't find anything on him. But I did get hold of some background on your client, Riva Mills. Seems she has a juvie record.'

'So I'm told.'

Hunter clicked his tongue. 'You have a real talent for picking crooked clients, you know that, Harry?'

'Hey, don't get too sanctimonious. Your track record for sound judgement's no better than mine, remember?'

He let that one slide. 'Her home life was no picnic. Mother moved around a lot, ended up in a place known as The Bottoms, some hard-knock neighbourhood along the Ohio River. Riva slept rough half the time, whenever the mother was on the rampage. Got picked up on a couple of minor charges.' He paused to digest a little more. 'Jesus. Mother sounds like one crazy bitch. Arrested for assaulting Riva with a meat mallet. Christ.'

Harry's eyes widened. Could a mother really hate her daughter that much? At least with Miriam, it wasn't hate. Indifference was more her style.

She recalled suddenly how she used to sit next to her mother as a child, watching her sister claim Miriam's lap. Somehow, it was never Harry's turn to be cuddled. But Amaranta was different. Mothered and motherly. She used to complain that Harry was no good at playing dolls, but the fact was, Harry didn't know how. How could she mother a doll when she'd had no role model to copy?

She listened to Hunter whipping through his report, and wondered why she always pulled away from him. Her lessons about love had come from her mother, and she'd grown up confused about how it was meant to feel. As a child, love had seemed like something angry and cold. Something painful. The psychobabble would have you believe she preferred men who echoed her mother's low opinion of her. Harry rolled her eyes. Not everything could be her bloody mother's fault.

Hunter's voice cut back in. 'That's as far as I'd got on Riva. But you don't need this now anyway, do you?'

Harry picked at a fraying thread on her duvet. 'I suppose not. But I've got a few more names. If you had the time, it might be interesting to find out about them.'

'What for? You said you weren't going to do it.'

'And I'm not. You were right, one dead hacker's enough. But it doesn't stop me being curious.'

Hunter was silent. The line crackled with unspoken suspicion, and Harry rushed on, giving him the names of Chavez's crew.

'Zubiri doesn't seem to know too much about them. I shouldn't really tell you any more, but if you can find anything out, I'd be interested.'

The silence stretched on, like a taut rubber band straining to snap. Eventually, Hunter said,

'How long will you be out there?'

Harry wound the fraying thread tightly around her thumb, choking off the circulation till her fingertip turned white.

'Only a few more days.' She glanced at the map on the bed beside her, eyeing the red-inked route. 'There's just something I need to do before I leave.'

11

'I just cannot understand what you're doing over there. It's totally bizarre.'

Harry, resisted the urge to make faces into the phone. Her mother had uncharacteristically initiated the call, and so far had used the word 'bizarre' three times.

'I mean, San Sebastián, Harry. Why on earth?'

'I've already explained.' Harry rounded a bend in the path, her calf muscles knotting against the steep climb. 'I've taken a job here.'

'In your father's hometown?'

'Is there a problem with that?'

'Don't be ridiculous.'

Harry heard the testy *snick-snick* of a lighter as her mother fired up a cigarette. She pictured her mouth puckered like a drawstring purse around it, the sunken cheeks accentuating her dramatic bone structure. Her mother was one of the few people who could still smoke with an air of vintage Hollywood.

Harry tugged her map out of her jeans. She'd been walking uphill for the past half-hour, and by her calculations she had to be almost there. She glanced over her shoulder. The road wound away from her in serpentine loops, the traffic now a distant sigh. She continued along the climbing path, the morning sun toasting her bare arms.

Her mother exhaled a hard, impatient puff. 'It's quite a coincidence, though, wouldn't you say? Ending up there, of all places?'

'Maybe.'

'What kind of answer is that? Is it a coincidence or isn't it?'

Harry winced, and considered dodging the question, but what would be the point? Like a bullet from a machine gun, there'd be plenty more where that one came from.

'The job's just one of the reasons I came here,' she said.

'Oh?'

Harry closed her eyes briefly. The urge to duck the conversation was overwhelming. She tightened her grip on the phone.

'It's really not a big deal, Miriam.'

She'd been calling her mother by her Christian name since the day she'd turned eighteen. Her mother had never objected. In fact, she'd seemed relieved, as if she'd never really liked being called Mum. Not by Harry, anyway.

'If it's not a big deal,' Miriam said, 'then why all the secrecy?'

'There's no secrecy. Look, I just thought I'd take the opportunity to do a little digging, that's all.'

Miriam sucked hard on her cigarette, the line almost crackling with the hiss of flaring embers.

The Martinez lineage never had much airtime when Harry was growing up. Her mother had always managed to sideline the topic, and oozed disapproval whenever Harry and her father spoke Spanish around the house. Not that it happened often. Her father's long absences and his stint in prison had turned Harry against him for a while, and until recently she'd been more focused on shutting him out than on embracing his family tree. But now all that had changed.

Miriam exhaled.

'If, by digging, you mean looking up your father's family, then I think you're a little late.' She expelled the last of the smoke with a short laugh. 'They're all dead, as far as I know.'

'Not all of them.' Harry leaned into the climb, head down. 'What about Olive?'

Her mother paused. Harry rounded another bend, then stopped. The shadow of a crucifix pooled across the road in front of her like an inkspill. She looked up to see a yellow sandstone church, its gothic spires piercing the sunlight. Crazy-paving brickwork jigsawed across its façade. Next to it was an archway and a sign that read *Cementerio de Polloe*.

'That woman's not family,' Miriam said eventually.

'She had a child with Dad's brother, didn't she?'

'And that's all she did. She never married Cristos, had very little to do with any of us after he and Tobias were killed.'

Harry crossed the small courtyard and tried to recall Olive's face. She hadn't seen her since she was four or five, and the memory was hazy: black hair, white skin; sullen mouth too large for her plain face. To a child, she'd looked ugly.

Harry stepped under the archway and into the cemetery. A ribbon of tarmac unravelled into the distance, lined by gloomy, monolithic tombs. The birds seemed noisier this side of the archway, but maybe it was just that all the other sounds had died away.

'Harry? Are you still there?'

'I'm here.'

'You can't want to talk to that woman.'

'Why not?'

'She was nothing to do with us. That's probably why she left. She didn't belong, and she knew it.'

Harry experienced an odd pang on Olive's behalf. Someone else who didn't belong in her mother's world.

She shook the feeling off and strolled along the tarmac, eyeing the ornate crypts on either side. Some were bigger than garden sheds, and designed like mini-churches with their own spires and stained-glass windows. Harry noted the elaborate coats of arms on the doors and raised her eyebrows. This was how the wealthy got interred.

Miriam's throaty voice cut back in. 'Anyway, who knows where Olive is by now? She could be anywhere.'

'She's still here in San Sebastián.'

'How do you know?'

'Dad told me a couple of weeks ago.'

'And how on earth would he know, after all this time? Keeping in touch is hardly one of Salvador's specialities.'

Harry recalled her father's chronic domestic truancy and had to admit, her mother had a point.

Harry made her way further along the avenue. The cemetery was laid out in a vast grid that must have stretched for almost half a mile. Daubs of colour stippled the view: reds and yellows; lilacs and pinks. The sea of flowers spoke of a recent church ceremony, and their sweet scent drenched the air.

'You know how they died, I presume?' Miriam's voice sounded thick with smoke. It had deepened over the years to a near-masculine pitch from all the tar. 'Cristos and Tobias, I mean?'

'Dad always said it was a car accident.'

'Well, that's one way of putting it. Sal never did like to face unpleasant facts.' She paused to inhale on her cigarette, then said, 'They were killed twenty-odd years ago in an ETA car-bomb attack.'

Harry stopped in her tracks. 'Jesus. I didn't know that. Poor Olive.'

Miriam made a vexed sound, as though sorry she'd inadvertently evoked sympathy for an old enemy. Harry pictured her peeved expression, probably heightened by the knot of silver-blonde hair that yanked her brows into a haughty arch. She looked a good decade younger than her sixty years, though Harry often wondered what would happen if she loosened her hair. Would her face collapse like a punctured sack of flour? She couldn't remember ever seeing her mother without her merciless topknot. Maybe it was just another way she had of staying in control.

Harry continued along the wide path, inhaling the dense perfume of flowers. By now, the grandiose crypts had given way to traditional headstones, though these were still large and imposing. Most were engraved in Spanish, but some bore inscriptions in Euskara, the impenetrable language of the Basques. Language seemed to define this unique people. Ancient, complex and once-forbidden, it seemed to be the crux of who they were, along with their fervent independence. Everyone knew the Basques were fiercely proud of their identity. Harry envied them that.

'Look, for heaven's sake, Harry, just what is all this about?'

Harry took her time about answering, the only way she had of imposing any control. She strolled past the headstones, browsing through the names: *Familia Alvarez*; *Familia Hernando*. Eventually, she said,

'Everybody needs to know where they come from, don't they?'

Familia Constancio; *Familia Corrales*.

Miriam snorted. 'Is that what this is about? Discovering your roots? Believe me, you can know too much about

99

those.' She took a quick pull on her cigarette. 'And once you know a thing, you can't shake it off again, either.'

Harry turned off the main path into a narrower walkway. The graves were smaller here. Many bore photographs that had been glazed on to black ceramic plaques. Harry stopped in front of one, a portrait of a silver-haired lady with a shy smile. She read the inscription:

Tu hija no te olvida. Your daughter will never forget you.

Harry blinked, aware of her throat constricting. She swallowed and moved on.

'All I want is a sense of where Dad grew up. Where his home was, what his family was like.' She managed a smile. 'Who knows, I might even settle down here.'

Her mother gave a shriek of laughter. 'Oh, God, don't be naive, Harry. You never settle anywhere, do you?'

Harry's cheeks burned. Miriam went on.

'Let's face it, fitting in just isn't your thing, is it? You don't have the knack. Even at home, you were always the odd one out.' Her mother paused, and when she spoke again her tone was faintly mocking. 'You don't really belong anywhere, do you?'

Something shifted in Harry's chest, something hard that ached. Suddenly she was seven years old again, lying on the floor for hours outside her mother's room, her face pressed to the crack under the door, wondering when her mother would come outside again and talk to her.

Harry clamped her mouth shut. Jesus, she'd thought she was over all that crap. She picked up her pace, her eyes still flicking across the headstones, and aimed for an offhand tone.

'Well, it doesn't much matter.' *Familia Cortez; Familia Barillas.* 'For all I know, this job won't even come off.'

'I see. And if it doesn't, you'll leave San Sebastián?'

'Maybe.'

Miriam paused, then abruptly wound up the call, as though suddenly she'd lost all interest. Harry sighed and shoved the phone back in her pocket. Stupid to have shared anything personal with her. The woman pounced on vulnerability like a hawk on a fieldmouse, and it wasn't like Harry to let her guard down. The damn graveyard must have made her sentimental.

She continued browsing through the headstones. *Familia Soliz; Familia Verano.* Then her step faltered, and she felt her extremities tingle.

Familia Martinez.

Harry held her breath and moved in closer, a light buzz travelling along her arms. She scanned the most recent inscriptions, just to make sure:

Cristos Martinez, 1 Martxoa 1947 – 3 Apirila 1987

Tobias Martinez, 8 Maiatza 1971 – 3 Apirila 1987

Harry stared at the dates. Her cousin, Tobias, had died a month before his sixteenth birthday. She'd been barely seven at the time. She shook her head, fingers pressed to her lips, and scanned the older generations of her family that lay here; all long gone, and none of whom she'd ever met. The notion triggered a squeezing sensation in her chest.

101

Her father's knowledge of his own ancestors was infuriatingly sketchy. He'd only lived in San Sebastián until he was ten, at which point his mother, Clara, a robust and cheerful Dubliner, had insisted on moving home in order to give her sons an Irish education.

'At least, that's the excuse she gave,' Harry's father had said, when they'd talked in Dublin a few weeks earlier. 'If you ask me, she just wanted to escape her Basque mother-in-law.' He'd winked at her, smiling. 'My grandmother was a formidable woman. Aginaga, her name was. Cristos and I used to call her Dragonaga. She tried to prevent us from leaving San Sebastián, but my mother got her way in the end.'

Harry found their names on the headstone: Clara Martinez and her husband, Ramiro. Both had died before Harry was born. Far below them, she found Aginaga, who'd died at the age of ninety-four. Harry blinked. If she was reading the names and dates right, the old lady had outlived all five of her offspring. Harry felt an ache of compassion for her formidable great-grandmother. What use was longevity if it meant you saw your children die?

The only other ancestor her father remembered was his own great-grandmother, Irune. 'She was Dragonaga's mother-in-law. I was six when she died, and all I remember is feeling very relieved. She was terrifying. Even Dragonaga was afraid of her.'

He couldn't remember much about his uncles or aunts, except that they were all dead, along with the few cousins he'd ever had.

'I never think of you as Basque,' Harry had said, contemplating her father's dark, even features. 'You don't even speak the language.'

'Ah, but the first Martinez in the San Sebastián blood-line wasn't a Basque.' Her father had smoothed a hand over the trim, snow-white beard that emphasized his olive skintone. 'He was a fisherman from Cadiz. Bit of a scoundrel, or so they say. He fled north to the Basque country after some fuss about money, and married a whaler's daughter.' Her father's dark eyes had twinkled at her. 'You come from a long line of fishermen, whalers and shipbuilders, Harry.'

And scoundrels, she'd thought, smiling back at the mischief in the face that looked so much like hers. She'd been told all her life how similar they were. The same dark eyes and brows, the same straight nose. The same loose attitude to rules and regulations. It was one of the reasons her mother didn't like her.

The other reasons were more complicated and, in truth, Harry wasn't even sure what they were. But one thing she'd learned the previous year was that Miriam had had an affair before she was born. She'd met her mother's lover and heard the story for herself. Miriam had been ready to leave her bankrupt husband, but then became pregnant with Harry. Sal was Harry's father, there was no doubt of that, and Miriam's lover had back-pedalled out of his promises fast. She'd lost her bid for a better life, and whose fault was that, if not Harry's?

Harry closed her eyes, her chest heavy with some

103

nameless ache. Did that really explain things? Did it really answer that burning question from her childhood: why didn't her mother love her?

Her eyes flared open. To hell with this crap. She wasn't a kid any more. None of it bloody mattered. She shook her head and refocused on the headstone in front of her.

Near the top, she picked out another familiar name: Irune Martinez. The engraved letters were shallow from decades of erosion. She took in the dates, and raised her eyebrows. The Martinez women seemed to live well into their nineties, while the men rarely made it past middle age. Harry thought about the strong matriarchs in her father's lineage. According to him, it was the women who'd ruled the harbours and worked the farms, while the men went to sea for half the year; it was the women who, at one time, inherited all property and titles, since they were the ones doing all the work. She stared at the headstone and felt a tug in her chest, a mix of awe and gratitude for the chain of strong women that had led to her own existence.

Her eyes dropped to the single urn of lilies on the grave. The petals were fresh, their incense rich and heady. She glanced again at Tobias's name. He was her only cousin, and he was dead. Maybe her mother was right. Maybe it was too late to reconnect with her father's family.

She hunkered down and touched the lilies, fingering their crisp petals. Then a hand touched her shoulder and a woman's voice said,

'Harry?'

12

Harry scrambled to her feet. The woman who'd spoken was small and dark, with a heavy black coat buttoned up to the neck. Her pale, slack skin put her somewhere in her sixties.

Harry flashed on her childhood memory: a woman's sullen, ugly face. Then she smiled and extended a hand.

'You must be Olive.'

The woman stepped closer, ignoring the gesture, and peered into Harry's face.

'So you're Miriam's daughter.' Her voice was low, with faint Irish traces.

Harry let her hand drop. If she'd been wary of an emotional reunion, she needn't have worried. Her smile slipped a little.

'Thank you for agreeing to meet me.'

'I almost didn't.'

Harry recalled Olive's unwelcoming manner on the phone. At the time, she'd put it down to shock at the sudden call, but now she wasn't so sure. Maybe uncompromising rudeness was a permanent state with Olive.

The woman was still staring at her face.

'You look like my son. Like my Tobias.' Her eyes turned flat and cold. 'Or how he might have looked if he'd lived long enough.'

Harry flicked her gaze to the headstone; to the grey, chiselled dates that bookended her cousin's short life. It was Olive who'd suggested meeting at the family grave. A morbid choice, Harry had thought. Or sentimental, maybe.

But there was nothing sentimental about Olive.

The woman tilted her head. Her dark hair lay flat against her skull, the cut unflatteringly short. 'Well, well. Miriam's little Henrietta. Sal tells me they call you Harry.'

'He keeps in touch?'

'From time to time. He's helped me financially now and then over the years.' Olive slid a scornful look at the grave. 'More than the rest of them ever did.'

Harry shifted her feet. The conversation kept slipping into hostile waters, like a shifting riverbank collapsing beneath her. Harry groped for a topic that would haul her back to dry land.

Olive took a step closer. 'Why did you call me? What is it you want?'

Harry blinked. 'I don't want anything. I'm in San Sebastián on business, so I thought I'd take the opportunity to meet you. To connect with someone in the Martinez family.'

'I'm not part of the Martinez family. Never was, never wanted to be.'

Harry stared at the woman: at the pallid skin, the too-dark hair; the mouth that was too large for her face. Something baleful seethed behind the eyes, and Harry already found herself wondering how to cut the meeting short.

Olive folded her arms. 'Does Miriam know?'

'That I'm here? Of course.'

The woman shook her head. 'That you planned on talking to me. I can't imagine she approved.'

Harry hesitated, and something sly flickered over Olive's face.

'I didn't think so,' Olive said. 'So tell me, is she still beautiful?'

Harry pictured her mother's face: the haughty bone structure with its near-Slavic angles and planes. 'Yes, she is.'

Olive's broad lips curled. She gestured at the headstone. 'They were all beautiful. Even bloody Aginaga. The Martinez men never chose any other kind.' Her smirk widened. 'Except for Cristos. He defied them all and picked me.'

Harry looked away, unsure how to respond. The woman had a knack for steering the conversation along uncomfortable lines. Olive continued in a rush.

'Miriam and Sal are separated, aren't they?' Her

eyes probed Harry's. 'Has she found herself another man?'

Harry almost flinched. Not at the words, but at the voracious light in Olive's eyes. Harry shook her head.

'I don't know. Look, if you don't mind—'

'What's the matter? You don't like me prying into Miriam's affairs?'

Olive's eyes looked feverish. Maybe the chance to hear news of an old enemy was too good to miss. Harry backed up a step.

'I'm sorry, but maybe this was a mistake. You don't seem to—'

'What made *you* so bloody loyal? After all, she never even liked you.'

Harry froze. It was the first time anyone else had ever said that out loud. She stared at Olive, and the woman pressed home her advantage.

'Don't tell me she's any different now. Things like that never change.'

Harry found her voice. 'We don't get on, that's all. Just normal mother–daughter stuff.'

'Normal? You think so?' Olive smiled, her face creased with spite. 'I know things about your mother. She's not so perfect, no matter what that bloody Martinez family thought.'

'Look—'

'I was the only one who knew the truth. Why do you think Miriam doesn't want you to talk to me?'

Harry felt a clutch of apprehension. 'I don't understand.'

'I saw how she was with you right from the start. It wasn't natural. Other people didn't always notice it.' Olive's eyes burned with malice. 'But then, they didn't know what I knew.'

A cold weight settled in Harry's chest. She shook her head, fighting the urge to ask Olive what she meant. Better to close her eyes, stick her fingers in her ears. This woman could have nothing good to tell her.

Olive was eyeing her closely.

'I used to watch you with Miriam. You'd sit down next to her, put your arm around her waist and wait for her to cuddle you back. She never did. What kind of mother doesn't hug her own child?'

Harry stiffened, as though bracing herself for pain. But what the hell for? She knew how her mother was. It didn't matter any more.

Olive continued. 'She never talked to you much. She'd lock herself in her room for hours to read, and you weren't allowed in. Amaranta was sometimes, but not you. You were like a little outsider looking in, half the time.'

Harry squeezed her eyes shut. 'Please. I don't need to hear all this.'

'Oh, I'm not saying she was all bad. She looked after you in practical terms. If you fell over and hurt yourself, she'd pick you up. But she'd put you down again just as quick.'

Harry clenched her teeth. 'This was all a long time ago—'

'It was obvious from the start that something wasn't right. When you were born, she didn't want to touch you. Asked the nurse to take you away. The midwife warned us to look out for postnatal depression.'

Harry's jaw relaxed slightly. 'Is that what it was? That's what made her so distant?'

Olive smirked and shook her head. 'It would have been a good excuse, wouldn't it? But Miriam wasn't depressed, believe me. This all started before you were born.'

Harry recalled the man her mother had had an affair with long ago. She shook her head.

'Look, I already know about this. She was going to leave my father for somebody else, only I came along and spoiled her plans. She's blamed me ever since. Big deal.'

'Well, well.' Olive's smile was crafty. 'Thank you, dear, I always suspected there was someone else, but I was never sure. But no, this had nothing to do with him. Miriam was far on with you and happy to be back with Sal. He had plenty of money again, you see, and that's all that mattered to her.'

Harry frowned. Miriam and Sal, the happy couple? The notion didn't fit the neat rationale she'd constructed to explain her mother's attitude.

'Henrietta,' Olive said, as though sampling the name. 'Bloody awful name for a child. Miriam's choice, of course.'

'She named me after her own mother.'

'Trying to please the woman, I suppose. Did you ever meet her?'

'Once or twice.' Harry's memory of her namesake was vague: a tall, elegant dowager; critical and bossy. Like Amaranta in dress-up clothes.

'Cold bitch of a woman,' Olive said. 'I met her at Sal and Miriam's wedding. Aginaga was bleating on about how beautiful Miriam was, thinking it'd please the old bat. You know what Miriam's mother did? She rummaged in her bag and produced a photo of herself as a young girl. "You see?" she said. "I was far better looking than Miriam."' Olive shook her head. 'It was the only time I ever felt sorry for your mother.'

Harry's brows shot up. So Miriam had had mother-issues of her own. Jesus. Did a negative maternal bond just get handed down across generations? Like some kind of poisoned baton?

Olive's eyes never left Harry's face. 'Reminds me of Snow White and the evil stepmother who tried to have her killed. Mirror, mirror, on the wall. Remember that?'

'It's just a story.'

'But in the original fairytale, there was no evil step-mother, did you know that?' Olive moved in closer. 'It was the girl's natural mother who tried to kill her. They had to change it, of course. People couldn't accept that a mother could be so cruel.'

Harry shifted uncomfortably. Olive stepped up beside her and turned to the grave for a moment. When she turned back, Harry was shocked at how haggard and desolate she looked. Olive clutched Harry's arm.

'My son was my life. My *life*.' She squeezed Harry's flesh, her eyes bleak with pain. 'But I lost him. I loved him, but he was taken away from me. So tell me. How is it fair that Miriam still has you, even though she never loved you?'

The words stabbed at Harry's insides, re-opening old wounds. She looked away, shook her head, fought with a dull ache in her throat. How could she answer a question like that?

Olive's eyes sought hers, raking her face, as though memorizing every detail, greedy for the features that looked so like her son's. She dug her fingers into Harry's arm and shook it.

'Do you see?' Olive's voice cracked, and her large, ugly mouth trembled. 'Your mother tried to kill you, but still she got to keep you. Tell me what's bloody fair about that? Tell me!'

Harry's brain jolted. For a second, she couldn't speak. Then she whispered, 'What did you say?'

Olive blinked, then looked away. She seemed to hesitate, as though realizing she'd gone too far. Her eyes flicked to the grave. Back to Harry. Then she lifted her chin, her gaze hard and unrepentant.

'She tried to have you aborted.'

Harry gaped. A lurch of nausea swivelled in her gut. Slowly, she shook her head. Backed away. Olive released her arm and went on.

'She tried several clinics, but she'd left it too late. They wouldn't do it. I found out by accident.'

Harry hugged her arms across her chest, suddenly cold. 'I don't believe you. Why would she do that if she was back with my father?'

Olive shrugged. All the fervour had drained away from her face, leaving her flat and lifeless.

'She was warped. Damaged. A failed mother, and she knew it.'

'Not with Amaranta.'

'Only up to a point. They're alike enough, that helps. She could pretend better with Amaranta. But she didn't even want to try with you.'

Harry's stomach slithered, and she pressed her fingers to her lips. She suddenly felt dizzy. Out of whack with her surroundings. She'd constructed so many plausible explanations over the years: she was too much like her father, the husband Miriam despised; she'd ruined Miriam's chance of a new life with her lover.

But now it seemed the reason her mother didn't like her was simply because Harry was alive.

She closed her eyes briefly and felt herself sway.

'I didn't expect – I'm sorry, but I can't deal with this now. I should go. Sorry.'

The ground seemed to spin away from her. She stumbled past Olive, blundered past the endless rows of headstones, away from the grave, away from her ancestors.

She felt short of air. Jesus. Had her mother really tried

to abort her? What was she supposed to do with that? Try to justify her existence to Miriam?

Look, Mom, see how well I turned out? Aren't you glad now you didn't get rid of me?

Harry's brain went into lockdown. Felt numb. Too paralysed to examine her mother, or even herself. She broke into an unsteady run, desperate to reach the exit. The need to bury what she'd learned was like a physical surge.

Harry fled past the tombs and the ornate vaults; the gaudy celebrations of death and family. Suddenly, they repelled her. Family repelled her.

She raced through the cemetery gates, then slowed to a jog as she emerged back onto the road. She didn't look back. Couldn't look ahead. Couldn't think what to do next. Her head reeled, and she stopped in the middle of the path, covering her face with her hands, overwhelmed with the need to block things out. To hide away.

She stood still for a moment.

Hide away and become someone else for a while.

Slowly, Harry uncovered her face. She fished out her phone. Stared at it. Then she dialled Zubiri's number. When he answered, she said in a level voice,

'Tell Vasco I'll do it.'

13

Marty crossed the street and headed for the riverbank, back towards the Zurriola Bridge. The salty sea breeze packed a punch up his sinuses, a welcome pick-me-up after the foody smells of the Old Quarter. He'd emerged from those dark, narrow backstreets feeling like a damned mole.

He picked at the little fingernail of his right hand, scraping off the thready remains of glue. He'd spent the last few nights at the blackjack tables, improving on his odds with the help of some artful accessories. In the trade, they were called glims; otherwise known as concealed mirrors. Or in his case, a shard of silver Christmas ornament glued to his little fingernail.

An old timer called Twinkles had taught Riva the technique. Twinkles had specialized in glims all his life, spent fifty-five years perfecting disguises for his tiny, covert mirrors. A polished thumbtack pushed into the end of a cigar; a gleaming pinkie ring; a sliver of sweet wrapper. Even a cup of black coffee, correctly positioned, had a reflective surface Twinkles could use. But eventually his frail old hands had betrayed him. Riva, a rookie dealer at the time, had spotted the quivering, reflected light that had played along the casino ceiling. But she hadn't reported him, and in exchange, he'd told her how it was done. As always, she'd passed the ruse on to Marty.

'Sit on the dealer's left and keep your eye on the glim.' Her thin fingers had held his as she'd glued a mirrored fragment to his nail. He could still remember his surprise at how warm her fingers had felt. 'When the blackjack dealer takes his own hole card, he'll tuck it under his face-up card. The corner should be picked up by the glim.'

The sea breeze stung Marty's face as he trudged along the riverbank. Glims worked best with greenhorn dealers, but the last few days he'd had a run of sharp-eyed pros. He'd been working the smaller establishments, avoiding Riva's casino. He'd taken a risk going there in the first place, but had been driven by an urge to spy on Franco's crew and, if he was honest, to catch a glimpse of Riva.

He stepped onto the bridge. The riverbank was deserted at this late hour. Enormous black waves pounded against the walls. He'd never seen such crazy river water. It was like some kind of caged humpbacked whale, thrashing around against captivity. Ahead of him, the cubed Kursaal Auditorium blazed its lights onto the

116

water. The geometric façade seemed out of place among the fussy, ornate sandstones on the other side of the river.

Marty yawned. Fatigue rolled over him, weighing him down, which was more than he could say for his damn wallet. He shoved his hands deep into his empty pockets.

Maybe he'd been wrong to protect Franco. Maybe he should cash in on what he knew now, instead of holding out for a bigger play. His gut squirmed at the notion. Then he lashed out at a pebble with his foot, sending it clattering along the bridge. What the fuck did it matter if he ratted Franco out? Those old loyalties were blown to hell and back, and it wasn't Marty's fault. He wasn't the one who'd lied.

'Roselli!'

Marty's head jerked up. Three men stood facing him at the end of the bridge. Their faces were hidden, their figures mostly in silhouette. But Marty still recognized the slightly built guy in the middle. Elderly, white-haired, deceptively frail; the walking stick standing to attention beside him like some kind of third leg.

Victor Toledo, Riva's Chief of Security.

Marty ran his tongue over dry lips. Flanking Toledo were two bull-chested types whose suits looked a size too small. Marty flicked a glance back the way he'd come. Two more goons stood shoulder to shoulder, blocking the sidewalk at the other end of the bridge.

'Roselli!'

The old man's voice was hard and gravelly. Marty stayed where he was, unpleasantly aware of his own

117

heartbeat. Then he figured he should probably obey the summons. With those gorillas around, what choice did he have?

He dawdled along the bridge, hands still in his pockets. Beneath him the river thundered as the tide funnelled in from the bay. Marty stopped a few yards from the old man. The guy had to be over seventy with that withered, crêpey skin, though his back was still ramrod straight.

'You've been avoiding me,' Toledo said.

Marty shrugged. 'Not really. As a matter of fact, I was in your office last week. Courtesy of one of your employees, some guy called Delgado.'

'So I heard. I hope he treated you well?'

'Can't say he did.'

Toledo nodded. His lipless old mouth had a discontented look, as though somewhere along the way, life had sold him short. Welcome to the club, Marty thought.

Toledo's gnarled fingers tightened over the top of his cane. 'You said you'd bring me more information.'

'Hey, I also said it'd take time.'

'It's been two weeks.'

Marty shifted on his feet, not caring to re-examine his last meeting with Toledo too closely. He'd been drunk at the time, had sought the old man out, offering to sell him information. His stomach flinched at the memory. In exchange for a lousy one hundred euros, he'd told him how Franco was targeting Riva's casinos.

'This man Chavez,' Toledo said. 'Or whatever his real name is. I want to find him.'

Marty shot him a look. The old coot was sharp, no doubt about that. Naturally, Chavez wasn't Franco's real name. Any more than Roselli was his. Marty took his hands from his pockets and spread them out, palms upwards.

'Like I said, I can find him for you. I just need a little more time.'

Toledo rested both hands on top of his cane, his fingers as crooked as a bird's claw.

'Tell me what he looks like.'

Marty pictured Franco's tall frame; the strong nose, the dark hair worn long, Apache-style. 'I don't know. I've never seen him.'

'Then how can you find him?'

'I hear things.'

'From whom?'

Whom? Jesus, the guy's English was better than his. Marty tried a weak smile. 'If I tell you my sources, then I'm cutting myself out of the deal.'

One of the gorillas jerked forward, and Marty's muscles tensed. But Toledo stayed the guy with his hand. The old man glared at Marty, his hand still outstretched. His upper eyelids drooped in folds so heavy they had to obscure his vision. Even so, Marty was the first to break eye contact.

Toledo rested his hand back on his cane. 'Do you know Riva Mills? Have you any idea who you're dealing with?'

Marty kept his gaze lowered.

Do you know Riva Mills?

He flashed on a memory of the first time he'd seen her. He'd been eleven years old, hanging out at the International Dealers' School in Vegas. His mother used to work there after her graveyard shift at the casino, and sometimes he'd drop by to check up on her. She'd been a dealer since before he was born, and not just in cards. Drugs, alcohol, abusive men. Ultimately, she'd dealt in death. She'd died of AIDS before Marty had turned twelve.

But that morning she'd been helping the instructor with dozens of students, and Marty had settled in to watch. Blackjack, craps and roulette tables had stretched the length of the room, the bright chips littering the green baize like petals. Students had clustered around, taking turns to deal, and the tinkle of chips along with the heat of the day had been making Marty drowsy. He'd thought about taking off, maybe bunking into one of the hotel pools along the Strip. Then Riva had slipped in through a window at the back of the room.

No one else seemed to notice her. She slid into a chair at the nearest blackjack table and quietly watched the play. She was rail-thin, and moved with a purposeful air. But Marty could tell from her darting eyes that she'd no idea what to do. He strolled towards her table. One of the students tapped the dealer on the shoulder, preparing to switch roles. The dealer clapped his hands, held them palms upwards, then handed over his spot. Marty saw Riva's frown, and sidled up closer.

'You gotta show your hands to the cameras,' he whispered. 'So they can see you haven't palmed any chips.'

Riva flicked him a look, then turned back to the cards as though he hadn't spoken. But later at breaktime she'd shared her can of Coke with him outside.

She came to the school every day after that. She learned faster than the others, was soon an expert at handling cards and cutting chips. Maybe that was why the instructor had turned a blind eye and let her stay. Riva spent all her breaks with Marty, and seemed disinterested in anyone else. Something told him she was more ambitious, had more at stake in all of this than they did.

One morning, as the Coke can had turned warm in the sun, Riva told him how she'd left home six months before, taking her younger brother, Andy, with her. She gestured to a boy of about Marty's age, who was swinging his legs on a nearby wall and flicking pebbles at passersby. The boy looked up and waved. He seemed a friendly little guy, though Marty could tell there was something off-centre about him. Later, as he got to know him, he'd wonder if Andy was the normal one, and it was the rest of the world that was off-course.

Riva had swirled the last of the Coke around in the can, and told him about her job as a bunny girl in Wisconsin, where she'd spend too many nights fending off drunken clients who'd been fooled about her age. She'd left and hitched a ride to Vegas, planning to become a dealer, only she couldn't afford the school fees. So

121

instead she'd just snuck in. She'd only been fourteen, but no one had challenged her yet.

Water thrashed against the embankment walls, and Marty shivered in the breeze. *Do you know Riva Mills?* He raised his eyes to Toledo's face and shook his head.

'No, I don't know her.'

Toledo shuffled forward a step. His sidekicks moved with him, like chess pieces protecting the king.

'What about Chavez? Does he know her? Is that why he's targeting her casinos?'

'Not that I've heard. But I can find out for you.'

Marty kept his face passive. He was a good actor. Even Franco had said so. Toledo would never guess from him that Franco had known Riva since she was eighteen.

She and Marty had been on the road for three years by then, ever since his mother had died. Together they'd worked scams and looked after Andy. The little guy was fifteen, just like Marty, but still couldn't lace up his own shoes. Riva paid the rent by dealing cards at the casinos, which was where she'd caught Franco cheating. He'd been about thirty at the time; well dressed; throwing cash around; colluding at a poker game with a player whose moves weren't quite as slick as his. Some guy with freckles whose name Marty later learned was Gideon. But as with Twinkles, Riva hadn't called Franco out. Instead, she'd demanded he cut her in, and from then on, they'd been a team.

Pinpricks of river spray needled Marty's skin. Toledo was staring at him with his hooded, crocodile eyes.

'You promise to find out many things, Roselli. It makes me wonder how much you already know.'

Marty coached himself not to react. Toledo went on:

'When you came to me first, I thought you were lying. This Chavez person probably didn't even exist. But I've done some investigating since we last spoke . . .' Toledo's deformed knuckles tensed on his cane. 'Our casinos have been badly hit in recent weeks. Losses are up. Significantly.' Veins stood out like blue cables on the backs of his hands. 'Without doubt, someone is cheating. And if it's your friend Chavez, then he's taking us for a lot of money.'

'It's him, all right.'

The old man nodded and sighed. 'Perhaps you are telling me the truth.' He stared down at the turbulent water, his hands relaxing on his cane. Then he shot Marty a look. 'But I still think you know more than you are saying.'

Toledo signalled with his finger, and the two men either side of him grabbed Marty by the arms. Marty's muscles turned rigid.

'Hey!'

Between them, they hustled him across to the railings, then hoisted him up in the air. It was like being lifted by a winch. The old man's voice rasped over the crashing waves.

'Do you swim, Roselli?'

Marty's gut did a somersault. The two men rammed him up against the railings. Then they jacked him higher, grabbed his ankles and pitched him over the top. Marty yelled. For an instant he was weightless. But his ankles were still manacled, and he swung down like a pendulum and slammed face-first into the bridge. Pain shattered through his nose and skull. His brain ricocheted as he hung there, stunned, suspended by his ankles over the water. The drop had to be thirty feet.

'You were easy to find, Roselli! A friendly talk with the Plaza barman was all it took. I can find you again any time I need to.'

Marty moaned. Black river water crashed below him. Blood packed down into his head, and his eyeballs felt close to bursting. He bucked against the concrete girder, powerless as a trussed chicken.

'Nobody cheats my casinos, Roselli! If you know something, then now is the time.'

Marty's arms dangled, already numb, and his heart screamed with the strain of pumping uphill. A monstrous wave swelled towards him.

'I'm not a patient man, Roselli!'

Icy water whacked Marty's face. It flooded his mouth, surged into his nostrils, drenching his head and shoulders. He swallowed it, gagged, waited for it to pass. Then he dragged in a breath and yelled.

'Let me up! I can find him!'

His voice sounded small, snatched away by the waves. He scrabbled at the concrete, his breathing ragged. There had to be something to hold on to, something he could use to heave himself up. But the surface was flat and cold.

The grip on his ankles loosened, and Marty's heart slammed into his chest.

'No! Wait!'

He twisted into a backbreaking sit-up, but the weight of his own torso beat him down. Pain ripped through his legs. He felt his eyes bulge, engorged with blood. Then a gigantic wall of water loomed towards him.

'Toledo! Get me up!'

The hulking wave surged. Marty gulped in a breath, squeezed his eyes shut. A deluge of water thrashed into his face, snapping his head back. The water engulfed him, filling his ears with a hollow, blocked-up sound. It shouldered into him, flung him around. His brain felt congested, his lungs bursting. When would it stop?

His chest pumped for oxygen. He had to breathe, had to open his mouth. Dear Jesus, he was drowning.

Then suddenly, it stopped. The wave receded. Marty gasped in a lungful of air, his chest heaving, the crash of water loud in his ears.

'Toledo! You hear me?' His voice was cracked and his throat burned. 'I can hand him over! I know how he operates.'

He'd tell him everything: where Franco and his crew were holed up; the moves he'd pulled; the cons he had in play. Why the fuck not?

He licked his lips, tasted the salt. Despite all the water, they felt dry. Franco's face flashed in front of him: the wide cheekbones, the dangerous smile. Then another snapshot: Franco playing baseball with him and Andy, letting the little guy win. Marty screwed up his face in pain. Then he yelled till he could feel the tendons standing out like cords on his neck.

'You listening, Toledo? He's working up to a big play, he's going for more. Get me up and I can find out where!'

His ears strained over the roar of waves. Up ahead, the river swelled towards him again, and his head reeled. Suddenly, the grip on his ankles tightened. Hands grabbed at his calves, hauled him up. Concrete grazed his skin. Metal bit into his shins, his thighs, then his belly, until finally, the hands dragged him back over the railings and dumped him on the ground.

Marty lay there, slumped and shivering, his face on a level with Toledo's knees as the old man waited for him to speak. Marty couldn't meet his eyes.

Regret tore at him like jagged glass, a piercing longing for the way things used to be. For a time when he and Riva and Franco had been bulletproof. An invincible trinity. But things would never be the same again, and he knew it.

Nothing had ever been the same after Andy had gotten killed.

14

Pretending to be someone else is tougher than you think.

Zubiri's words rattled around in Harry's head, as she nosed her rented Fiat through a dark, narrow laneway in search of the Kanala Bar. Cold sweat lathered her skin.

She'd spent the last few days in a state of raw anxiety, pacing her hotel room and wondering what the hell she'd just done. She'd found herself hoping that nothing would happen; that Zubiri would never hear from his Belfast informant; that maybe Chavez, whoever he was, wouldn't need a replacement for McArdle. She'd found herself wondering if maybe she should just go home.

Then Olive's words had axed through her, and her brain had shut down, grinding away at the memory of what she'd said with an almost audible hum. That was when Zubiri had called to tell her it was time.

Harry's fingers clenched around the wheel. She'd been

driving now for over an hour. Zubiri's directions had led her west out of San Sebastián, first along the coastline, then further inland through miles of swooping valleys and hills. In daylight, she knew the grasslands would blaze a lush green that would remind her of Connemara. But in the dark, her headlights had washed the hills a watery, ghostly grey. She'd climbed and dipped with the eerie farmland until finally she'd arrived at an isolated hamlet on the bank of the River Deba.

She edged the Fiat into another dark side street, bordered on either side by ramshackle buildings that seemed to sag and shore each other up. Graffiti defaced the grimy whitewash, and the shutters looked cracked and peeling. Up ahead, a sign glowed: *Kanala Taberna*.

Something cold fingered Harry's spine. She cruised to a halt on a crop of scutch grass that seemed to pass for a lay-by in these parts. Then she doused her headlights, and immediately wished she hadn't. The darkness buried her, tumbling like a black landslide. Her heartbeat pounded in her ears.

Why the hell had Chavez arranged to meet in such a godforsaken place?

Car metal ticked into the silence. She climbed out, laptop satchel in hand, and a fine, misty rain settled on her skin like gauze. She glanced over her shoulder. Moonlight dappled the wet cobbles, picking out a path that seemed to invite her back the way she'd just come.

'You can come out any time,' Zubiri had said, when she'd met him for a final briefing. His eyes had probed hers from beneath his shaggy brows. 'We'll need an emergency word.'

'A what?'

'A pre-arranged word. If you use it over the phone I will know to take you out.'

Harry blinked. 'What kind of word?'

'Anything. BMW, paperclip. Something you can slip easily into a conversation when other people are listening.'

'But you said they'd take my phone.'

'Find a reason to use one of theirs. And memorize this contact number.'

He'd torn a sheet of paper from a pad on his desk, then scrabbled around in search of a pen. Harry's palms had turned clammy. An emergency word. Jesus. Her brain went numb as she'd tried not to conjure up a scenario where she might need one. The urge to flee had twitched through her, and she'd started to pace the room.

'Isn't this a good reason for me to wear some kind of wire? So you can hear what I say all the time?'

'Doesn't work that way. We'd need to be in constant range to keep picking up the transmission. That won't always be possible.' Zubiri flung a mess of paperwork to the floor. 'I told you, they catch you with a wire and you're dead.'

He yanked open a desk drawer so hard it crashed to the ground. He roared at it in Basque, then lashed out with his foot, and it occurred to Harry that Zubiri was as wound up as she was.

She'd studied his dark, morose-looking features. Had

129

he deliberately let her see those slides? Vasco had probably censored them, ordering him to withhold the full scale of things in case it scared her off. But maybe Zubiri thought she had a right to know, though telling her straight might have compromised him. Maybe he'd found his own mule-headed way around the rules, a tactic Harry suspected he used a lot in his line of work. Truth to tell, so did she.

A shutter banged somewhere in the wind. Harry hunched against the melancholy drizzle and headed towards the Kanala bar. A stray dog tracked her progress, his nails *tick-ticking* along the cobbles. If it wasn't for the regular pulse of crickets, she could've been in some dismal Irish town.

She drew closer to the bar, taking in the wall graffiti along the way: *Gora ETA, Gora Euskadi*. The paint had dried into long, chilling drips, like a parody of some horror-movie title. A shiver frisked around Harry's shoulders.

She tried to focus. Catalina Diego, that was her name now; the name she'd drawn up around her like a comforter since she was a child, slipping into new personas because it had seemed so much easier than being herself. She suppressed another shudder. Right now, escapist role-play wasn't having its usual therapeutic effect.

Harry reached the bar and hesitated. A life-sized mural dominated the dingy façade: a soldier in army fatigues and a black beret, a scarf obscuring half his face. His automatic weapon was aimed directly at her.

Other murals snapped into her head: the Belfast graffiti she used to see on the news, alongside a cache of detonators and orange Semtex; walls daubed with militants in ski masks brandishing submachine guns, locked in their own time warp of executions and bloody reprisals.

The resemblance was eerie.

She glanced at the slogan scrawled over the door: *Bietan jarrai*. She didn't know what it meant, but sensed intrinsic echoes with the IRA motto: *Tiocfaidh ár lá*. Our day will come.

She flexed her fingers on the strap of her satchel. Her doggy companion was still watching her, his head tilted to one side. Then suddenly he turned and disappeared into the night.

You will be alone. More alone than you've ever been in your life.

Hairs quivered on the back of Harry's neck. She took a deep breath. Then she lifted her chin and pushed through the heavy timber door.

15

Harry stepped inside the bar. Warm air mugged her face, an underlay of smoke catching in her throat. Wooden chairs creaked as people turned to stare.

She scanned the room. The patrons were mostly gnarly old men playing cards, though a few younger types stood drinking by the bar. All of them watched her with open curiosity. Her stomach flipped. Was one of them Chavez?

Harry moved towards the bar. The place looked as if it had once been somebody's house, the main section no bigger than the average living room, with cosy snugs tucked away to one side. Everything was panelled in crude timber, from the scarred walls and grimy ceiling to the dusty, pockmarked floors. A row of photographs hung over the bar: headshots of unsmiling men. The Basque flag was stapled to a knotty beam above them.

'Catalina Diego?'

Harry spun around. A slender brunette was eyeing her through ringlets of cigarette smoke. She wore form-fitting trousers and what looked like a man's dress shirt cinched with a belt at the waist. Dull pancake make-up deadened her skin, but the bone structure was strong and arresting. It was Ginny Vaughan, the woman on Zubiri's slides.

Harry's fingers tightened around her satchel and she managed a curt nod. The woman didn't move. She was hugging her waist with one arm, propping the other elbow on it so that her cigarette stayed close to her lips. She narrowed her eyes and took a long pull.

Maybe it was the long, tense drive, but suddenly Harry didn't feel like playing games. Was the woman here to communicate, or had she just come to stare her down? Maybe there was a protocol for this kind of rendezvous, but right now crankiness seemed as good an approach as any.

'I need a drink.' Harry wheeled away towards the bar. 'That drive was hell. Half the damn signs had the Spanish names blacked out, and who reads Basque?'

'Wait!'

Harry stopped and threw the woman a testy, *what-now* look. Ginny watched her for a moment through half-closed eyes, then flicked her cigarette to the floor.

'Follow me.'

She sashayed off across the room, not bothering to wait for a response. Harry hesitated, then trailed after her with a weary air that was only half pretence. Her knees buckled slightly.

Ginny led her into the ladies' room. It was small and bright, and surprisingly clean. Judging from the gender of the clientele outside, Harry guessed it was rarely used. Ginny indicated the countertop running beneath the mirror.

'Put your bags there.'

Harry did as she was told, picking up on the Irish tones in the woman's voice, the way you did when you were abroad and your radar for fellow natives was heightened. Ginny dumped the contents of Harry's handbag onto the counter.

'Hey!'

The woman ignored her, fishing through her haul: keys, coins, wallet, phone. She turned to the satchel and stopped up short. Her fingers touched the silver logo engraved across the front flap. She flicked Harry a cagey glance, then fumbled with the clasps, removed the laptop and emptied out all the side pockets. In moments, the counter was a viper's nest of knotted cables and hardware.

'Take off your clothes.'

Harry gaped. 'What?'

'Take them off. Everything.'

Ginny leaned back against the wall, slipping a pack of cigarettes and a lighter from her shirt pocket. She lit up with unhurried movements, thumbing the lighter wheel a couple of times before touching the cigarette to the flame. Her eyes stayed locked on Harry's.

Harry folded her arms across her chest. 'Look, why the hell—'

'If you want to work for us, you strip. Otherwise you leave.' Ginny shrugged, blowing smoke at the ceiling. 'Up to you.'

They traded looks for a moment. The woman's lazy drawl matched her indolent posture, and spoke of privileged Dublin: expensive schools, ponies for birthdays, maybe a Porsche when she'd turned eighteen. Harry noted the soft glaze across her eyes, and figured some of the languid air was probably down to alcohol.

Ginny gestured at Harry with her cigarette, her eyebrows forming a question. Harry tensed. Then she kicked off her trainers and began to unbutton her jeans.

She peeled them off, folding them neatly on the wash-stand, then pulled her T-shirt up over her head. She stood there in her socks and underwear, clenching her fists so that her hands wouldn't start to shake. Jesus. Zubiri had been right. What the hell would have happened now if she'd been wearing a wire?

Ginny fixed her with a level look. 'I said, everything.'

Harry closed her eyes briefly, then slipped her socks and underwear off. The tiles were cold on her bare feet, and goosebumps rippled over her flesh. She felt Ginny's gaze lingering on her body, coming to rest on the bullet scar that puckered her right arm.

Harry's cheeks grew warm. She glimpsed her own reflection: sallow bare skin, a tumbling shock of curls too heavy for her slight frame. Her posture looked vexingly submissive. She forced her shoulders back and

135

clamped her fists by her side, resisting the urge to cross her arms over her nakedness. What was it about stripping that made you feel so damn vulnerable?

Ginny clicked her fingers, her hand outstretched. 'Earrings. Watch.'

Harry complied, handing them over. Ginny tossed them on the counter, then eased herself away from the wall. She sauntered over to Harry, brushing too close, before bending to retrieve a bag from behind the single cubicle door. She dumped it at Harry's feet.

'You can put these on.'

Harry inspected the contents: white cotton sundress, navy sweater, underwear, a pair of flip-flops. Everything looked a couple of sizes too big. She ignored the bra, and stepped into the loose panties, then slipped the sundress over her head, tying the sash twice around her waist. The sweater reached almost to her knees. She rolled up the cuffs, and slotted her feet into the flip-flops. If she bunched up her toes, the things just might stay on.

Harry glanced at her possessions on the counter. 'What happens to all my stuff?'

'It'll be looked after.'

And examined, Harry guessed. The notion made her fidgety, though she knew there was nothing to find. The laptop had been wiped, purged of everything except her hacker toolkit. The phone was a new one from Zubiri. He'd recorded a few carefully selected numbers, Belfast contacts who'd backstop her if anyone asked. The keys were for the rented Fiat outside, which bore no trace of her identity, forged or otherwise. Zubiri had instructed her not to carry any ID.

'In the real world, criminals travel light,' he'd said. 'They have cash, cigarettes and keys. Carry ID and you look like you have a lie to prove.'

Harry hugged her arms across her chest, seized by a shuddery chill in spite of the oversized sweater. Ginny lounged back against the wall, and seemed in no hurry to move. She pulled hard on her cigarette and shot a stream of smoke at the ceiling, nudging ash onto the floor with a lazy finger-flick. The studied cigarette rituals were beginning to get on Harry's nerves.

Ginny reached for the empty satchel. 'What's this?'

'My laptop case.'

'I meant the logo.'

'Oh.'

She watched as Ginny stroked the faded emblem. The word *DefCon* was engraved in silver across the leather, the letter 'O' framing a grisly skull and crossbones.

Stick to the truth as much as possible.

'DefCon,' Harry said. 'It's a hackers' convention held every year in Las Vegas. I won the satchel in a contest there when I was thirteen.'

Ginny paused. 'Stevie had a leather jacket with the same thing printed on the back.'

Stevie? Stephen McArdle. Harry's pulse jumped a little faster.

Ginny was still caressing the logo, and when she spoke again, her voice was low.

'He loved that dorky jacket. Said he won it in Vegas too. Years ago, he said. I thought he meant in a poker game.'

Harry pictured McArdle's plump form; imagined him younger, pink with pride, as he lumbered up to a podium to the cheers of black-hat hackers. Another image crowded in: McArdle slumped in the old bullring, eyes and throat gaping.

Harry squeezed her arms tighter around her chest, choking the memory down. Eventually, she said,

'The DefCon jacket's quite a badge of honour.'

Ginny looked at her with interest, and for the first time seemed to forget about her cigarette.

'How would he have won it? What kind of contest?'

Harry shrugged. 'Could've been anything. A capture-the-flag contest to crack open a live system. Or some kind of social-engineering challenge.'

Ginny threw her an enquiring look. Harry went on.

'It's when hackers scam people into giving confidential stuff away. Takes a bit of role-playing, and a knack for telling lies. Like being a conman, really.'

Ginny glanced at the satchel. 'Is that how you won yours?'

Harry nodded. 'I had to call up some random stranger and trick him into giving his bank account details and PIN over the phone.'

'Just like that? A cold call?'

Harry gave another shrug. 'It was easy.'

Ginny stared at her for a moment. Then she lowered her gaze, worrying at the DefCon emblem with a nail.

'Did you know Stevie?'

Her voice was hesitant, the lazy air dispelled. Harry wondered what was behind the softened demeanour, and tried picturing her and McArdle together. The princess and the frog. The pieces wouldn't go.

'I met him once or twice,' Harry said, sticking to the script she'd worked out with Zubiri. 'We worked together on a job, hijacking some government databases. Charged them a shedload of money to get them back, too.'

Ginny frowned. 'He told me he preferred to work alone.'

'Hackers usually do. It's a hubris thing. But occasionally we admit that we need each other's help.'

Ginny continued stroking the DefCon emblem. By now, her cigarette ash was precarious. 'He was clever, wasn't he?'

Harry recalled McArdle's exploits, detailed to her by Zubiri: online extortion, cyber-terrorism, zombie armies, cyber-hijacking with ransom demands.

'Yeah, he was clever enough,' she said.

Ginny snapped her head up. 'But you think you're cleverer, is that it?'

Harry blinked. She hadn't intended to come across that way, but it wouldn't be the first time she'd drowned out fear by overcompensating with arrogance. Better to appear cocky than afraid.

She lifted her shoulder in a casual shrug. 'Probably.'

'Save it.' Ginny flicked her cigarette into the sink, where it hissed into a soggy finger of ash. 'I'm not the one you need to impress.' She turned and drifted towards the door. 'Time to go. Franco's waiting for you outside.'

16

Harry followed Ginny out of the restroom and back to the main bar. A tremor quivered through her legs, as though she were stepping out onto a tightrope.

She slid a glance at the old men playing cards, catching their curious stares. The slap of her flip-flops sounded faintly indecent, like some tacky day-tripper intruding on the locals in her beachwear. She eyed the huddle of men by the bar, and wondered if Zubiri's backup was among them. It didn't seem likely. The place looked like a tight nest of natives, a band of Basques who'd probably known each other's families for generations. Even Zubiri couldn't hide a stranger in here.

'This way.'

Ginny had turned towards the exit. Harry frowned, casting an uncertain look around her.

'But I thought—'

Ginny ignored her, pushing out through the door, and Harry followed, a whispering dread brushing along her spine.

The night air was fresh after the smoky fug of the bar. Headlights floodlit the narrow street, courtesy of a dark, brooding Volvo idling by the kerb. Ginny opened the rear door.

'Get in.'

Harry bent to peer in at the driver. Leather jacket, rangy torso. She couldn't make out his face. She flicked a glance over her shoulder, at the clannish den where she knew she had no allies. Even so, it seemed like a better prospect than getting into a stranger's car.

'I thought Franco was in the bar.'

Ginny lifted a shoulder in a lazy shrug. 'Get in or leave, I don't care.'

Harry chased the alternatives around in her head, a pulse beating high in her throat. Then she made a decision and ducked into the back seat. The interior reeked of cigarettes and old leather. She fixed her eyes on the back of the driver's head, noting the clipped, light-coloured hair that bristled across his neck. Ginny closed the door with a *thunk* and slid into the passenger seat, and when the driver turned towards her, Harry felt a lurch of recognition.

Furrowed laugh lines, sun-bleached brows.

All we know about Gideon Ray is that he kills people.

An electric current buzzed through Harry's frame.

Ginny gave another careless shrug. 'She's clean.'

142

The man called Gideon nodded. Then he gunned the engine and the car torpedoed forward. The force of it pitched Harry backwards against the seat, sucking her in. Gideon sped along the narrow street, pale insects whirling in the headlights, like a flurry of snow against the windscreen.

Where the hell were they going?

Gideon slalomed around black bends in the road, and even Ginny had to brace her hands against the dashboard.

'Jesus, Gideon, take it easy!'

Gideon laughed and slammed the gears up a notch. They hurtled along the road for another few minutes, then he took a hard left and careened onto a rough track. They juddered for a while over bumpy terrain until Gideon yanked the wheel again and spun them in a one-eighty turn. Harry's insides lurched. Slowly, the car rumbled back along the track, then Gideon killed the engine, snuffed out the lights and sat back to watch the road.

The silence was unnerving. Eventually, Harry found her voice.

'Look, what the hell is going on here?'

No one answered. Another car engine whined in the distance, and she peered out at the road. Cones of light pronged the darkness, magnifying slowly, emerging from the same direction they had. The car roared past, its taillights shooting like red stars into the night.

Harry stared after it. Was that Zubiri's backup? Had

someone been detailed to wait outside the bar, ready to follow if she left? A charge travelled down her spine. Maybe she'd had a guardian angel all along. The notion would have been comforting if she hadn't just gone and lost him.

Gideon fired up the engine and headed for the road, turning back the way they'd just come, and five minutes later they pulled up at the Kanala Bar. Harry clambered out after Ginny and followed her inside, her heart still thumping from the ride.

Low voices rumbled through the room. She was aware of Gideon lurking somewhere at the rear as together they filed past the card-playing patrons and in through a door to a small snug beside the bar. It was maybe six foot square, boxed in on three sides by frosted-glass panels that screened it from the other drinkers. The claustrophobic dimensions reminded Harry of a confessional. But the man sitting at the table looked nothing like a priest.

'Sit down.'

His face was strong and big-boned, with the kind of proud, prominent profile you'd see carved on a totem pole. He looked to be in his early fifties, with dark hair scraped into a thick ponytail running halfway down his back. It should have been effeminate, but somehow with his high, wide cheekbones it made him look like a Comanche warrior.

Harry remained standing and tried to work some indignation into her voice. 'What the hell was all that about back there?'

He contemplated her with black eyes that were set too close together, crowding in around the bridge of his nose. 'Dry cleaning.'

'What?'

'Anti-surveillance technique.'

'You think you're under surveillance?'

'No, but you might be.' His accent was American, with no hint of Spanish. 'I said, sit down.'

Harry did as she was told. Those close-set eyes had an intensity she didn't like, and she suspected the guy wouldn't tolerate too much backchat. Ginny slid into a seat opposite her and sloshed some wine into a glass from a bottle on the table.

'There *was* a car,' Ginny said.

Harry tensed. Her eyes flicked to the guy's face, but his expression was unreadable. Ginny sucked in a deep draught of wine, then went on:

'But we shook it off too easily for it to be a professional tail. She seems clean, Franco.'

'*I'll* decide who's clean.'

Harry swallowed, the cigarette smoke scratching at her airways. Franco narrowed his eyes. Like Gideon, he wore a black leather jacket, loose and supple-looking, over a black crew-necked sweater.

'Catalina Diego.' He savoured the name, as though weighing it up, checking it out for flaws. 'You don't look like a Catalina to me.'

Harry's muscles went rigid. He stared at her for a long moment.

145

'I'll call you Diego instead.'

Relief trickled through her like a warm shower, but she worked hard not to let it show. Franco was still watching her closely.

'You Spanish?' he said. 'Or just Black Irish?'

'Bit of both.'

'Cross-breed, then.'

'Like you, you mean?'

His face grew dark, the close-set eyes almost crossing. Ginny froze, her glass halfway to her lips, and Harry sensed Gideon shifting behind her. She made a mental note to watch her mouth.

Then Franco threw his head back and laughed. 'She's right. Diego's right.'

Ginny looked relieved, and set about draining her glass. Franco went on, directing his comments at Harry.

'My old man was some bastard mix of Spanish and Iroquois. Didn't make life easy for either one of us.' He jabbed a finger in the air. 'But my old lady, she was pure Basque. Came from these parts.'

He spread his arms wide, inviting Harry to look around. She played along, disinclined to disturb his expansive mood. Ginny carefully poured herself another glass of wine. Over by the door, Gideon had grown still. Maybe they didn't want to break the mood either.

Franco was still talking.

'Place was a whaling village back in the day, then went to sleep for three hundred years and woke up as an ETA stronghold.' He gestured through the open wall of the snug towards the bar, pointing out the photographs Harry had noticed earlier. 'ETA prisoners. All locals, doing time for political crimes.'

Harry scanned the stoic-looking faces in the photos. She noticed the bell jar of money on the counter. A collection for their families? The Basque flag was draped around its base, the national colours of red, white and green echoing the hues of the Basqueland: red-trimmed houses; whitewashed walls; dark green hills.

She glanced back at the photos. A line-up of freedom fighters or murderous terrorists, depending on your point of view. A coldness slid over her as she wondered if any of them had blown up her fifteen-year-old cousin.

She stared at Franco. 'So you're a terrorist?'

'Is that what they told you in Belfast?'

'They didn't tell me anything in Belfast.' Another angle she'd worked out with Zubiri. 'They never do.'

Franco nodded, and Harry tried again.

'So what are you? Terrorist? Drug dealer?'

His smile looked dangerous. 'Who says I'm either?'

Harry studied his near-ugly features, not liking the fanatical light in his eyes. She pictured him in fatigues, in a Che Guevara beret, then shook the image off.

An in-out job. Find out who their target is . . . Then you can disappear.

She leaned forward in her best businesslike manner. 'Look, I really don't give a shit one way or the other. I'm here to do a job, so let's cut right to it. They tell me you need a hacker. Just what is it you want me to do?'

147

Franco's smile vanished, like a light snuffed out. He reached behind him, whipped out a knife and slammed it flat on the table. Harry flinched. Franco kept his palm over the handle. The blade had to be ten inches long and was wide and smooth, like something out of a butcher's block.

Harry's heart rate kicked into overdrive. Ginny averted her eyes and slugged some more wine. Franco glared at Harry.

'*I* decide when you're ready to be told. You got that? You're not in charge of anything around here.'

Harry's heart was still galloping. Franco leaned across the table towards her.

'People don't do business that way, you should know that. What's the matter with you? You think if I was a drug dealer I'd give a wad of cash to a supplier I'd never worked with before? That I'd buy a kilo of coke from a guy I've only just met?' He whacked the table with the flat of his hand. 'No. I'd start small. Do a test run. Buy like maybe half an ounce, or even better, get a gram for free. Then I'd check out the merchandise, test it for impurities. You gotta build up a relationship, bit by bit. That way everyone knows they can trust each other.'

Sweat slipped down Harry's back. Shit. How was she to know he'd want to pussyfoot around? But maybe that was the point. Maybe Catalina Diego should have known.

Franco picked up the knife and twirled it in his hands, watching the light splicing off the blade.

'Establishing trust is a real subtle business. Like

148

seducing a woman.' His eyes raked the length of Harry's body. 'Everything counts. Small impressions, little tests, quiet understandings. It'll be the same with you and me.'

Harry swallowed. She needed to redeem herself, but something told her it would be a mistake to backpedal now. She got to her feet.

'You want to check out the *merchandise*? You have my credentials, check out those. My expertise speaks for itself. And just so you know, your friend here took my laptop, so I won't be doing any hacking, test runs or otherwise, until I get it back.'

She returned Franco's glare, glad he couldn't see the basting of sweat on her torso. He stood up slowly, his fingers tightening around the knife.

'You'll use McArdle's laptop. That way, I know your equipment is clean.'

Ginny jerked her head up, eyes darting between them both. Harry looked at the blade. Flashed on McArdle's crimson throat. Franco gripped the knife with both hands.

'But first, a little test.' The dangerous smile was back. 'And you won't need a computer for this.'

He raised his arms and plunged the blade into the table. Harry jumped. So did Ginny. Franco released his grip, letting the blade stand upright, the tip submerged half an inch into the wood. Franco laughed, his Indian-brave features turning dark and ruddy. Then he leaned forward, his knuckles on the table.

'I want you to stab someone.'

17

Harry stared at the knife. At the manic look on Franco's face. The blade was like a lethal stake in the ground between them.

She shook her head, dazed. 'What are you talking about?'

'You heard me. I want you to stab someone. Someone in the bar.'

'I'm a hacker, for God's sake, not some kind of hired gun.'

'You want to work for me, you're whatever I tell you to be.' Franco's wide face darkened. 'And right now I'm telling you to stab someone in the bar.'

Oh Jesus. Was the guy nuts?

Harry cast a desperate look across the counter. The barman had disappeared, and any patrons within range had long since turned their backs, preserving a discreet distance. Her brain staggered, groping for reality.

'Look, you've got the wrong person. If you want someone stabbed, then get your friend Gideon to do it.'

'Gideon's loyalties are not in question here. Yours are.' Franco fixed his close-set eyes on hers. 'Call it a test of allegiance.'

Shit. Was he trying to flush her out, maybe betting a covert cop wouldn't do anything criminal? That was bullshit, of course; they probably broke the rules all the time. But maybe most of them would draw the line at stabbing someone.

Harry shot a glance at the door. Gideon was blocking it, a smirk nudging at the laugh lines on his face. Franco was still leaning with his knuckles on the table and beside him, Ginny nursed her wine, her face ashen under the make-up.

Harry stuck out her chin. 'And what if I refuse?'

'Then you go for another ride with Gideon. Only this time, maybe you don't come back.'

Her heart skipped a beat. Ginny flicked her a glance, then looked away. A microwave pinged somewhere over the counter but the barman was still nowhere to be seen.

'This is insane. How can I stab someone in a room full of people? I'd never get away with it.'

Franco shook his head. 'We'll take care of it. Take it from me, there won't be any trouble.'

Harry's eyes skimmed the room. The whole bar was behaving as though they were invisible, and she had the feeling things would stay that way no matter what.

'What about McArdle?' she said. Ginny's head snapped

151

up at the name, and Harry read the alarm in her eyes. 'Did you test his allegiance too?'

'No need. His credentials were a lot better than yours, Diego.'

Harry shifted her feet. Ginny dropped her gaze and fiddled with her glass, and Harry wondered again at her relationship with Stephen McArdle. Franco straightened up, gesturing at the knife.

'Take it.'

A tight coil of panic twisted in Harry's chest. She pictured the old men playing cards outside, and the younger ones built like well-fed farmhands near the bar.

'Who exactly am I supposed to stab?'

'I don't care.'

'What?'

'Pick any one of the dumb fucks out there. You think I give a shit who you choose?'

Harry gaped. Was he insane? Reality seemed to splinter, the pieces spinning out of control. She groped for the back of a chair, as if that might help steady things.

'Do it, Diego.'

'This is madness.'

'Are you calling me crazy?'

Harry shook her head. Her brain felt waterlogged, the buzz of distant bar-talk too loud in her ears.

These people are not like you and me.

Zubiri's words cut through the logjam. She held Franco's gaze, her insides recoiling at the fanatical light in his eyes. *FARC, Red Army, Islamic Jihad movements* . . .

'Take the knife, Diego.' His voice was low, urgent. 'You hear me? Take it, or it's over right now.'

She tried not to flinch. This guy understood strength. That was his language. Any show of weakness would be a mistake.

'Do it, Diego.'

Slowly, Harry reached for the knife. She grasped it in both hands and yanked it out of the table. Her mouth felt dust-bowl dry. Did anyone ever say 'no' to Franco?

She tightened her knuckles around the handle. Then she raised the blade and plunged it into Franco's arm.

For an instant, everyone was paralysed. Then Ginny gasped, and Harry released the knife, her fingers still vibrating from where it had struck something solid. Muscle? Bone? Her stomach slithered. Franco was gaping at her, wild-eyed, the blade still stuck in his arm. He grunted, stepped back. Harry stared, transfixed, at the blood seeping out through his jacket.

Gideon grabbed her wrists and yanked them behind her, shoving them high up her back till her shoulder muscles screamed. Then he slammed her forwards across the table. The wine bottle crashed to the floor. Gideon's weight crushed her lungs, blasting the air from them as she gave a muffled cry.

'Are you out of your mind?' Franco's voice sounded hair-trigger controlled. 'Are you out of your fucking *mind*?'

The blood pounded in Harry's jugular. She squeezed her eyes shut against the pain in her arms, and an image of Hunter's face rushed inexplicably into her head.

She twisted, peering up at Franco. His strong features seemed enlarged, suffused with bewildered outrage.

'I stabbed someone, Franco.' Harry's heart banged so hard against the table it was difficult to breathe. 'I reckon I passed your stupid test.'

Franco narrowed his eyes. Being mouthy was unlikely to save her now, but in truth she didn't know how else to be.

'Get her out of here,' he said.

Gideon hauled Harry upright and wheeled her towards the snug door. She sensed Ginny leaping to her feet, probably to tend to Franco's arm. Harry struggled against Gideon's grip, her body drenched in sweat as he clamped her wrists in one hand and reached for the door with the other. She flashed on the emergency word she'd agreed with Zubiri. *Mother*. Stupid. Did she think saying her mother's name might save her? Like some kind of talisman that was actually on her side?

Gideon wrenched open the door and Harry got ready to scream. Then Ginny's voice drawled across the tiny space.

'Seems to me she passed your test fair and square, Franco. Maybe not in the way you expected, but all the same . . . Besides, I thought you needed her?'

Gideon paused, his fingers a vice-grip on Harry's

154

wrists. The slap of a cash register rattled across the bar. Harry held her breath.

Suddenly, Gideon dropped her arms, like a dog responding to a signal. Harry turned, rubbing her wrists.

Franco was still standing, the knife now on the table, and Ginny was examining his wound. He regarded Harry with a mixture of rage and doubt. Then he nodded slowly.

'Okay, Diego.' He kept on nodding. His voice still betrayed a simmering fury, but his eyes had registered a sudden, sharp interest. 'Okay.'

18

Marty was sixteen when Franco first taught him the art of the long con. Up till then, short cons had been their racket, his and Riva's: the deft moves, the quick getaways. And yeah, maybe the low returns. But once they met Franco, he'd started grooming them for the next level.

The day Marty made the grade, he was holed up in a Vegas motel room with Riva and her brother, Andy.

'Open a window, Marty, there's a good kid.' Riva reached across the table for another bottle of nail-polish remover. 'This stuff's giving me a headache.'

Her blonde hair slipped over one shoulder, like some kind of silk scarf. Marty noticed she was letting it grow, maybe trying to look more sophisticated now that she'd turned nineteen. Her curves, always evident, were filling out more, too. He would've liked it if the long hair was for his benefit, but he was smart enough to know that it wasn't.

Riva poured the nail-polish remover into a shallow pan on the table. The pungent fumes kicked up Marty's nostrils. Between them, they'd already used five bottles of the stinking stuff.

'Window, Marty.'

Andy flashed them a smile. 'I'll do it.'

He hopped to his feet, as Marty had known he would if he managed to stall for long enough. He watched Andy skip towards the window. He was smaller than Marty, though older by three months. The boy's hair was the same pale shade as Riva's, his features just as pointed, like an underfed fox. But his eyes were different. Smaller, set too far apart, with thick eyelids that drooped like half-closed blinds.

There wasn't a name for what Andy had. Or if there was, then Marty didn't know it. 'Retard', people called him most of the time, at least when Marty wasn't there to smack them around. But whatever its name was, Riva said her mother was to blame. The woman was a drunk who'd lurched through her second pregnancy on a permanent vodka bender. For nine months, the little guy's brain had been soaked in 100 per cent proof liquor.

Over by the window, Andy grunted with frustration as he tried to force open the latch. Marty sighed and got up to help. No matter how often you showed the guy, he never remembered how to do it. Any minute now, his small face would shut down, tears of bewilderment starting up.

Marty eased him aside and cranked the window open. Baked air breathed into the room, the dry, stifling heat of the Mojave Desert. It did nothing to alleviate the choking chemical smell. Marty sat back down and ripped open another envelope from the pile on the table. He smiled as he pulled out another cheque.

Franco wouldn't approve, but Marty and Riva had been washing cheques for years. Riva liked the steady trickle of extra money, and relied on it to pay rent and to buy Andy's medication. Marty just liked how easy it was to make a quick buck.

He examined the cheque in his hand. It was for two hundred dollars, made out to someone called Vegas Catering and signed by the controller of a large engineering company.

It was the sixth cheque they'd netted from their haul earlier that day, when they'd cruised the business parks, waylaying mail from some of the larger corporations. The end of the month was always a good time to score cheques being sent out to settle bills.

Marty tore off a strip of Scotch tape, stuck it across the signature, and matched it with a second strip on the back. Then he dunked the cheque in a pan of nail-polish remover, submerging it with the tip of a pencil.

The sweetish vapour scorched up his nose, and he pulled back out of range. In twenty minutes, the acetone would strip the cheque. Ballpoint pen;

typewriter print; dot matrix printer output. Anything that wasn't a base ink would get eroded. Only the bank name and cheque number would stay intact, along with the signature protected by the tape.

Marty watched the dark, inky threads curling up through the solvent. Soon he'd be left with a blank, signed cheque, which he'd fill out for three or four hundred dollars and cash in at a local bank. Any more might attract attention. He'd found that out the hard way, back when Riva had first taught him the scam. He'd ignored her warnings and tried to cash in two thousand dollars. But the teller had rumbled him and he'd almost got caught. Riva hadn't trusted him for months after that.

He glanced at her sharp profile. She was watching Andy soak an old envelope in water, his brows drawn together in a vexed line as he tried to work out why the ink wasn't vanishing. Something snug and warm spread across Marty's chest, like a comforter. It was just like old times; just the three of them. The way things used to be before Franco had come on the scene.

Franco spent all his time with them now. Even his pal with the freckles had disappeared, as though he'd taken a dim view of Franco getting so tight with Riva. Marty wasn't wild about it either, but sometimes you had to step aside for the better man, right?

A key snicked in the lock, and Franco breezed into the room as if on cue. Riva stirred, as if she'd just been plugged in. Andy leaped up and flung himself at Franco like an overjoyed dog. Franco laughed, ruffled his hair. Then he threw his shades on the table and gave Marty a high five. Marty grinned, got to his feet and felt himself trying to match Franco's swagger. The sudden energy in the room buzzed like a power line.

Franco took Riva's hand in his and kissed her upturned palm. She closed her eyes, suppressed a shudder. Marty looked away.

'You ready?' Franco's voice was soft.

'Sure I'm ready.'

Riva stood up, and for the first time Marty noticed she was wearing a plain skirt instead of her usual faded jeans. He took note of Franco's get-up, admiring the grey lightweight suit, the crisp shirt and tie. No one could carry off a sharp suit like Franco. His dark hair was slicked back, the ponytail tucked discreetly out of sight.

'Where are you going?'

'Get changed, kiddo.' Franco crossed the room to the dingy wardrobe, bending down to open the safe that was bolted to the inside. 'You need to be in on this.'

'In on what?' Marty eyed the tiny strongbox, his heart rate speeding up to a panicky *uh-oh* kind of beat.

'The pay-off, what else? You were there at the set-up, you get to play at the endgame too.'

Franco retrieved a large, bulky envelope from the safe. Marty stared at it, his mouth turning dry. His mind raced over the recent scams they'd pulled, but he knew which one Franco meant.

'You mean the Forecaster?' He hovered close to Franco

as the older man strolled back to the table. 'But that's done with, right? We got the guy's money, more than once.'

'Three times.'

'Yeah, exactly.' Marty laughed, hoping it sounded casual. 'So we're good, we're done. Why risk another squeeze?'

Franco gave him a long look, and Marty felt himself fidget. Those close-set eyes always seemed so damned intense. Franco ripped open the envelope.

'That's the problem with you, kiddo. You only got eyes for the short con. You need to think big, think long term. Sure, we got him three times, but that was just the convincer.' He dumped the contents of the envelope onto the table: five thick wads of fifty-dollar bills. 'Now we go for the jugular.'

Franco took a seat and started thumbing through the stacks, counting out the bills. Marty sank into a chair, keeping his limbs loose so he didn't look braced for disaster.

Franco reached the end of the last stack, and his face grew tight. 'Some of it's missing.'

Riva flicked Marty a look, sharp as a paper cut. Then she reached out for one of the wads.

'Here, let me count it.'

Marty didn't move. *Shit, shit, shit.* He'd intended to pay the money back before Franco found out. How was he to know he'd come looking for another stake so soon?

'I'm telling you, it's short.' Franco smacked the table

with his hand and Marty's gut tensed. His eyes raked the room, as if it could offer some way out. His gaze settled on Andy.

'There should be fifteen grand there.' Franco picked up one of the bundles and slapped it back down. 'We're missing five hundred bucks.'

Riva ignored him, tuning him out while she counted. Andy was watching her open-mouthed, fascinated by how quickly she could riffle through the bills. Marty stared at his face, at the heavy-lidded eyes. His palms started to sweat.

Supposing he said Andy took the money? No one would blame the guy; he was just like a little kid. Everybody loved him; strangers felt sorry for him. 'Poor guy,' they'd say, and shake their heads. But look how damned happy he was. Heck, he was the happiest person Marty knew. Marty was the one they should feel sorry for. Andy never had to hustle cons on the streets; he didn't have to grow up and take responsibility, or pay for his mistakes the way Marty seemed to do more and more these days.

Riva stopped counting. 'You're right, we're five hundred short.'

The room fell silent. Franco and Riva turned accusing looks on Marty. He mustered up an indignant expression, then slid his eyes towards Andy. The kid was gazing up at him like some kind of puppy dog, the only one in the damn room who trusted him. Including himself. Marty's stomach turned sour. Jesus Christ. What the hell was he thinking?

He held up his hands. 'All *right*. God. You don't have to make such a big *deal* out of it. So I borrowed the money. Here.' He got to his feet, then reached into his back pocket and tossed a crumpled fold of bills on the table. 'Take it. I was gonna put it back in the morning anyway.'

Riva rolled her eyes. 'Jesus, Marty.'

Franco jerked to his feet, knocking his chair to the floor. 'What's the matter with you? What the *fuck* is the matter with you? You want to ruin everything? You know how long I been setting up this play? Six weeks, that's how long.'

'But we've already got his money, why not just take it and run?'

'Always the fast buck with you, isn't it? You want to waste your life on short cons? Washing cheques, bar bets, street hustles? Is that what you want?' Franco thrust his face close to Marty's. 'When are you going to fucking learn?'

'Okay, okay. So I jumped the gun.'

'Damn right you jumped the gun. Don't you under-stand?' Franco whacked the table for emphasis. 'The long con takes patience. Planning. You gotta reel the mark in a little at a time. Think big, but start small. Build up trust. Play the convincer. Then you move in for the kill.' He glared at Marty, then shook his head, exhaling long and hard. The lines of anger gradually dissolved from his face like the ink from one of Marty's cheques. 'You can't keep letting us down like this, kiddo.'

Marty's face felt hot. He dodged Franco's gaze. The explosive temper he could handle, along with the quicksilver moods. But the disappointment in Franco's eyes was hard to take.

'You're right, I'm sorry,' Marty said. 'The Forecaster's a good scam, I should've waited to play it out.'

'I'm not just talking about the Forecaster, Marty. I'm talking bigger than that. Much bigger. Me and Riva, we've been busy. Things are in motion. We got contacts in Vegas now, done favours that'll step us up a level. Question is, can we afford to take you with us?'

Marty shot Riva a look, and she returned it with a challenging one of her own. Contacts in Vegas. He knew what that meant; he'd heard them talk about it before. The Cosa Nostra still had a hold on parts of the city, but he'd already warned Riva against it. Once you got involved with those guys, you never got out from under. Shit, he should know. His father had worked for them a couple of times, back when Marty was nine years old. Then his old man had tried to leave. It was Marty who'd found his body in the dumpster.

But Riva was stubborn, said she wanted something more than hustling for her and Andy. Hey, he could understand that. But the mob, Jesus. The mob had cost him a father.

He watched Franco slot the wads of notes back into the envelope, and a hard knot lodged in his chest. Why the fuck had he taken the money? He could have waited, even asked. Stupid, stupid. How could he expect Franco to respect him now, to talk to him like an equal?

Franco glanced at him and must have read the thought in his face. 'I can't treat you like a grown-up till you start acting like one, kiddo.'

Then he walked away, opening the door for Riva. She marched out of the room without looking at Marty, pausing only to give Andy instructions.

'Usual rules, Andy. Put the chain on, don't open the door, and don't tell anyone where we are.'

Andy nodded, jumping to his feet. Marty stood there beside him, feeling abandoned. Riva disappeared down the hall, then Franco turned back and pointed a finger at Marty.

'You got two minutes to get changed and meet us out front.' He slipped on his sunglasses. 'Watch and learn, kiddo. Watch and learn.'

They took a cab to Eastern Avenue. Marty sat in the back, listening to Riva argue with Franco about scaling up their pitch.

'We got to push for more than thirty-five.' Riva's pert chin looked set. 'We need it now, Franco, you know that as well as I do. I won't lose this chance.'

'Sell it too high and you'll just scare the sucker off. It's a question of balance.' Franco took her hand in his. 'Look, that other deal's going to stay on the table, those guys are in. We've got time. Trust me, we're not going to lose anything.'

'You think we're the only ones they're talking business with?' She pulled her hand away, her dove-grey eyes stony. 'I mean it, Franco. I won't miss this chance.'

Franco raised his hands in a helpless gesture. The guy had a knack for inspiring loyalty in people around him, but Riva was the only one Marty knew who ever stood up to him.

Marty slid his gaze to the window, not wanting to get involved. As far as he was concerned, that whole mob deal could get flushed right down the pan.

The sun simmered hot and yellow in the sky, as though the earth was frying itself up a big old egg for lunch. Marty's eyes drifted over the plush hotels; the waterfalls, the whirlpools, the rich green foliage; a haven designed to make the suckers forget that the city was built on sand. But the desert was always close, with its coyotes and rattlesnakes and the kind of arid heat that could kill a man in a day.

Riva always complained about the heat, and Franco would tell her about Spain, where his old lady had come from. Not the parched plains of the south, which he said were as much a desert as the Mojave. But northern Spain, with its green hills and forests, and the rain that could fall any time. He made it sound like an oasis.

The cab finally pulled up outside Executive Suites, the luxury tower block where Franco had rented an office for the last six weeks. Marty followed him through the entrance, Riva bringing up the rear. With all the fountains and yucca plants, it was more like a hotel than a workplace, and Marty had flinched when he'd heard how much it cost. But Franco's response had been predictable: 'Without the set-up, there's no pay-off. How long before you get that, kiddo?'

Franco led the way across the lobby, his footsteps snapping against the marble tiles. With his black hair and fierce profile, the guy looked like a proud Indian brave, ready to conquer the corporate world. Marty tried to mirror his posture, squaring his shoulders as if it were some tribal code that would win him acceptance from the chief.

The office suite was located on the fourth floor, with a brass plate that read *Morehampton Investment Management*. Franco unlocked the door to the outer reception and Marty followed him inside. A second door led to a spacious inner sanctum, the whole of it jazzed up in gilt and dark wood.

Riva took a seat behind the reception desk, while Franco stood by the window to stake out the tower-block entrance. Marty pulled at his shirt collar, not used to its chokehold. His heart pumped. He guessed this was how actors felt before they went on stage.

The mark's name was Jed Sanders. They'd snagged him six weeks earlier when Franco had cosied up to a party of high rollers at the MGM Grand. Jed was an overweight, middle-aged businessman, probably in over his head at the poker table, but not about to lose face by admitting it. Over drinks and extravagant macho losses, Franco had let it slip he was a stock-market dealer with his own investment firm. At the end of the night, he'd taken Jed aside.

'Jed, buddy, you're a good guy, and I'm going to do you a favour. Take a tip from a man who knows: buy PariBank shares, they're on their way up.' He raised his hands, warding off Jed's scepticism. 'Don't give me your money, I don't want it. Just thought I'd do you a good turn. You keep an eye on PariBank, see if I'm not right.'

Over the next few days, PariBank's share price rose, just as Franco had said it would. When he met Jed again later that week, it was Jed who first mentioned the shares.

'Hey, I was pretty impressed by that tip of yours. Should've followed your advice.' He gave a phoney laugh. 'Got any more where that came from?'

Franco shrugged, playing hard to get. Finally, he said, 'Between you and me, I heard DigiCorp is in for a tumble, so dump the shares, if you have any. But keep it to yourself, okay?'

Miraculously, DigiCorp's share price dropped the next day, exactly as Franco had forecast. As it turned out, Jed didn't own any of the stock, but all the same he was impressed by Franco's market savvy.

All in all, Franco gave the guy four sure-fire tips, and the accuracy of his predictions was uncanny. But not once did he approach Jed for money. Instead, Jed came to him.

'Look, I don't know what kind of crystal ball you're gazing into, but what do you say I get a bigger piece of the action? Hell, four hot tips just from casual acquaintance, makes me wonder what other opportunities I'm missing, know what I mean?'

So they'd agreed that Franco would make some short-term investments on Jed's behalf. They started small with five grand, which Franco pocketed and later returned, along with a twenty per cent profit. 'Predicted market movements' was how he explained it, but in reality the profit came from Franco's personal stash. They repeated the transaction a few more times, Jed's stake and confidence growing bolder with every move. It had killed Marty to see the money flowing out through their fingers. He'd thought for sure when they'd taken Jed's fifteen grand that this time they were playing for keeps.

Franco snapped his fingers and ducked away from the window. 'Places. He's here.'

Marty's gut hitched. He scurried after Franco into the other room, closing the door to wait for Riva's signal. Franco sat at the desk, tugging his cuffs, the only outward sign of his tension. Two minutes later, the desk phone buzzed, and Riva escorted Jed Sanders into the office.

The guy was shaped like a small Buddha, with a round head as smooth as a cue ball. He smiled at Marty, who showed him to a seat. People always smiled at Marty. They said he had a likeable face.

Marty made a pretence of sorting through some files, while Jed and Franco exchanged a few pleasantries. Finally, Franco got to the point.

'I'm assuming you want to do this in cash, as usual?'

Jed stole a glance at the briefcase by his feet. His gaze

always seemed to be on the move, never settling long enough to look a person in the eye. He shrugged.

'Keeps it simple for everyone, doesn't it?'

Franco opened a drawer and extracted the wads of notes he'd counted out earlier, adding another envelope on top. 'Your fifteen thousand, plus a healthy return of three thousand dollars.'

Marty riffled through a file of bogus paperwork, trying not to flinch at the sight of all that money going the wrong way over the table. Jed smiled, reaching out for the bundles.

'I don't know how you do it, I really don't. If I didn't know better, I'd think you had inside information.' His eyes flicked to Franco's, then slid away again as he laughed to show what a joker he was. 'Hey, what do I care how you get your information, as long as I'm making money out of it, right?'

Franco smiled, allowing a silence to lengthen between them, goading Jed as always into making the first move. The guy licked his lips.

'You mentioned on the phone you had something else? Something bigger?'

Franco shrugged. 'It may be too rich for you, but I thought I'd give you first refusal.'

'Maybe I can handle it. What's the deal?'

'I've an offer to bulk-buy MediLabs at rock-bottom price. Thing is, I know for a fact those shares are about to soar. The returns could be fifty, sixty per cent.'

'So what's the price?'

Franco hesitated. Marty looked up from his paper-work, waiting for him to sting the guy for thirty-five thousand dollars. Franco's gaze drifted to the door, where Riva was probably listening on the other side. He tugged at his cuffs and Marty frowned, making bullshit scribbles on his file. What the hell was he waiting for?

'Seventy-five thousand dollars.'

Marty's eyes flared wide. What the fuck was he doing? Jed looked dazed, as if he'd been hit with a mallet.

'Jeez. I'd need to think about that one.'

Franco shook his head. 'No time, that's the rub. We've got to close the deal today or we lose it. If those shares move up tomorrow, the offer will be withdrawn for sure.'

Marty recognized the classic deadlining tactic, but he wondered was it enough. Jed shifted his bulk in the chair.

'Can't we share the cost with another investor?'

Franco threw him a rueful smile. 'Dow Chemical were lined up, but they pulled out at the last minute. That's why this is so tight. Look, it's a sweet deal. You might just double your money.'

Jed swallowed, and slid a hand over his gleaming scalp. Franco tugged at his cuffs some more.

'I haven't steered you wrong yet, Jed, have I?'

'I know, I know.' The guy leaned back, shaking his head. Doubt oozed like sweat from his pores. 'I might've been good for half the stake, but jeez, seventy-five grand. That's a lot of money.'

Marty winced. Shit. Franco's original pitch of

thirty-five grand would have been right on target. And from the look on Franco's face, it didn't help to have it confirmed.

Marty fumbled with the papers in his file. The way things were going, that mob deal wouldn't be happening for a while. He should have felt relieved. Instead, all he could think about was Riva. He hesitated, then cleared his throat.

'Uh, Mr Morehampton . . .?'

Franco scowled at the interruption. Marty handed him a sheet of paper from the top of his make-believe file.

'This fax came in a little while ago, sir. I, uh, I should've mentioned it earlier.'

Franco's face was thunderous. 'What are you talking about?'

'It's Dow Chemical, sir. They want to come back in on the deal.'

Franco's brow cleared, softening his what-the-fuck glare. He nodded slowly, then turned back to Jed. 'This is good. We can split the purchase with them, lower your stake.'

Jed's interest quickened. Marty pictured Riva pressed up against the door, her slender frame clenched, ready for battle. She'd never give up; he knew that better than anyone. But maybe there was a way that Marty could still be a hero.

He stepped forward and pointed at the paper in Franco's hand. 'Sorry, sir. As you'll see from the fax, Dow Chemical won't share the deal. They're quite definite about that. They want to take the full amount. I'm afraid Mr Sanders here can't be involved.'

Franco shot him a direct look, and Marty read the understanding in his eyes. It was shaded with something else. Respect, maybe? Marty felt a warm glow at his own cleverness. In the trade, it was known as red-inking, and worked well on reluctant marks. Threaten a guy with exclusion from a deal and often it jacked up his motivation. Hell, no one liked to be left out of a party.

Jed stabbed the air with his finger. 'Hey, who are they to try and cut me out of this? They had their chance. What if I change my mind? What if I want in on the whole lot?'

Franco hesitated, as though considering the ethics of the situation. But Marty knew the deal was done. Five minutes later, Jed had shoved the wads of cash back across the table and was writing out a cheque for the rest.

Marty turned away to hide his smile. He felt like a jack-in-the-box, ready to explode. Finally, Franco escorted Jed out of the office, then he held up his hand and strode across to the window. Nobody spoke. Marty's blood sizzled through his veins, and Riva's grey eyes shone like wet granite. Then Franco turned from the window and grinned.

'He's gone.'

Marty whooped and punched the air with his fist, while Franco slapped him on the shoulder.

'A masterstroke, kiddo. I always said you were a great actor.'

Marty felt himself flush. Riva hugged him tight, whispered 'Thanks' in his ear. Her breath was warm, and adrenalin flared through him like a torch. He could almost picture his insides outlined with heat. He basked in the rush, in the heady camaraderie. They were untouchable. Unbeatable. A loyal trio on fire.

Franco was right. Think big.

It was all about the long con.

It took a few hours for the elation to simmer down. Even by nightfall, Marty's veins still pulsed with electricity. But the dizzying high had worn off, and he found himself picking over the details of the Forecaster scam. There was something about it he just didn't understand.

He glanced over at Franco. They were sitting on the veranda of one of the best hotels on the Strip. The oven-baked air was dry and dusty, but neither of them wanted to go inside. The bar was too noisy. At least out here, they could shut the clamour out. Luxuriate in the afterglow of the scam.

Marty sipped his beer. It was the first one Franco had ever bought him. Riva was upstairs with Andy, so for now they were alone; just two guys sharing a Bud.

'About the scam,' Marty said eventually. 'There's something I still don't get.'

Franco threw him a questioning look, and Marty went on.

'When you first gave Jed those hot tips? You know, to reel him in? How did you know which way those shares would go?'

Franco laughed. 'Haven't you worked it out yet, kiddo? I *didn't* know. How could I? Hell, if I knew, I'd have played the market myself.'

'That crossed my mind.'

'You think Jed was the only mark I had in play? I started with sixty potential guys, Marty. *Sixty.*'

'What the hell for?'

'They were the gene pool, kiddo. Only the fittest were going to survive.'

Marty frowned. 'I don't get it.'

'Look, I didn't just give that first tip to Jed. I gave it to every one of those sixty guys. Only I told half of them the stock would go up and told the other half it would go down. It had to do one or the other, right?'

Marty shrugged. 'I guess.'

'So the stock moves, and now I have thirty guys who think I got real lucky. So I play those thirty again. I pick another stock, tell half of them it'll fall, tell the other half it'll rise. The stock moves and now what have I got? Fifteen guys who think I'm a real smart sonofabitch.'

Marty felt his mouth form an 'O' as understanding filtered through. Franco continued.

'And on it goes, play by play. Natural selection, whittling the gene pool down. By the end, I'm left with three astonished guys who are seriously impressed with my market know-how. Chances are, at least one of 'em wants to invest their money with me.'

'And that guy was Jed.'

Franco grinned, raising his beer in salute. 'You got it, kiddo.'

Marty shook his head, marvelling at the simplicity of it all. They sat in easy silence for a while, the whir of night insects throbbing over the racket from the bar. Then Marty turned to Franco, his head swimming a little from the beer.

'It's a great con, best I ever heard. We gonna pull it again soon?'

Franco looked away and didn't answer. His jawline tensed and Marty wondered what he'd said to spoil the mood. Shit. He should've kept his mouth shut. Talking about the future always seemed to make the guy antsy.

Franco set down his beer and looked Marty in the eye. 'You did good today, kiddo. You stepped up.'

'Thanks.'

'So now I want you to promise me something.'

'Sure.' Marty blinked. The guy's expression was grim.

'If anything bad ever happens, I want you to take care of Riva and Andy.'

Marty stared. Franco's face looked tight, as though he was in pain. Marty shook his head.

'Nothing bad is gonna happen, what are you talking about?'

'Promise me, kiddo?'

'Oh, come on. Nothing's gonna happen.' He raised

his hands at Franco's expression. 'Okay, okay. Of course I'll take care of her. Though you know Riva, she prefers to take care of herself.'

Franco regarded him for a long moment, then nodded and settled back in his chair. Marty shifted in his seat. The guy's intensity always made him fidgety. And where did he get off, acting like he knew what was coming down the pike?

Marty reached for his beer, tried to recapture the mood. To hell with Franco. He was always uptight about something.

And besides, what could possibly happen to spoil it all now?

19

The Volvo roared through the pitch-black hills. Harry clung to her seat belt, like a dangling climber hanging onto her harness.

She flung a glance at Gideon in the driver's seat beside her. His hands were clenched on the wheel, arms fully extended. Up close, his skin looked cracked and sun-damaged, the joined-up freckles giving the impression of a light tan.

'So, Diego,' Franco said from behind, 'what part of Spain you got in that mongrel pedigree of yours?'

Harry twisted around to stare at him. His chattiness had an air of unreality about it, as though the loss of blood from his wound had made him light-headed. She tried to match his nonchalance.

'My ancestors were Basque whalers, or so I'm told.'

'Well, well, another member of the tribe.' He winced as Ginny checked on his wound.

He'd removed his jacket and sweater, and his bare torso was matted with dark hair. His physique had an old-fashioned burliness about it, from a time before men waxed or pumped up too much iron.

'You speak Basque?' he said, over Ginny's bent head.

'No.'

'Me neither. Oldest living European language, my old lady said. The Basques reckon they're the original Europeans. Probably gives 'em a kick to think they got here before anyone else.'

Harry shifted in her seat. The conversation seemed bizarre, given that she'd just stabbed this guy in the arm. She watched Ginny snip at the dressing they'd acquired from the barman. He'd handed it over without a word, leaving Harry wondering what other stuff went on there to make a stabbing seem routine.

Franco's eyes drifted to the window. 'The Basques may be as old as these quaint hills of theirs, but they're not as unique as they think. Matter of fact, they have a lot in common with the Irish, you know that, Diego?'

Harry shook her head, and flicked Gideon another look, trying to gauge from his face whether this kind of chit-chat was normal. His jaw looked cinder-block hard. She turned back to Franco, who was still talking:

'Some genetic study. The Basques are supposed to have

179

this special DNA? Turns out the Irish have it too. Maybe your pedigree isn't as mixed as you think, Diego.'

He broke off and hissed in through his teeth, swatting Ginny away. She shrugged and turned to the window, her manner careless. But to Harry, her slender frame looked braced, ready to duck at the next mood-swing.

Franco dragged his sweater over his head, and Harry took the opportunity to turn back and face the road. Franco kept on talking.

'They say the Basques ask themselves three questions every day: Where do we come from? Who are we? and Where are we going for dinner?' Franco snorted. 'All that nationalist identity bullshit. What the hell does any of it matter?'

Harry's mind flicked to her own rootlessness, her disconnect from home, then skittered neatly away from any underlying cause. She shrugged and ventured a comment: 'Maybe a sense of identity's only important when it's missing.'

Gideon shot her a wary look, and Franco missed a beat.

'That's very profound, Diego. Very fucking profound. Now shut the fuck up and let Gideon concentrate on the drive.'

Harry let out a quiet breath and made a mental note: conversation with Franco wasn't a team sport.

For the next half-hour she stared at the road, watching the headlights rinsing through the dark. She had no idea which direction they were headed, and it wasn't till she saw the crescent-shaped beach that she realized they were back in San Sebastián.

She peered out the window, trying to get her bearings, and noticed that her muddled inner compass had finally pieced some landmarks together: La Concha beach, curved like a necklace in the sea; two rounded hills forming the open clasps at either end; the Town Hall, with its turrets and elaborate colonnades, guarding the promenade. Behind that, the Old Quarter. Where Stephen McArdle had been killed.

Harry blinked and rolled the window down. Cold, briny air rushed in, hauling with it the crash of breaking waves. The onslaught to her senses flushed McArdle's image away.

Gideon yanked the wheel to the right and swerved the car inland. Harry clung to her seat. The guy's macho rally-driving made the smallest manoeuvres seem dramatic. He sped up a side road, and with a jolt Harry recognized Calle de la Infanta Cristina: the street where the Ertzaintza police station was located.

Harry's gut contracted. They cruised past the familiar triangular block. Was Zubiri inside, yelling on the phone, furious that his backup had lost her? She wanted to scream, let him know she was here. Sweat flashed down her back, and she clamped her mouth shut. Gideon drove on. Harry's muscles ached with the effort of keeping still. She fixed her eyes on the road, paralysed as they cut across the city. Fifteen minutes later, they pulled up outside an apartment block close to the mouth of the river.

At a signal from Gideon, Harry climbed out of the

car. She stared up at the modest four-storey building. Was this where McArdle had been headed when she'd followed him through the Old Quarter? She felt a sharp pang on his behalf. The old bullring wasn't far away. McArdle had almost made it.

Franco led the way up to a third-floor apartment and Harry followed him inside, Gideon close on her heels. The living area was poorly lit, and smelled of fried food. Brown paint deadened the walls, and the tweedy upholstery looked as though it might itch. Harry raised her eyebrows. It was clean and spacious, but still not the kind of place she'd expected for an outfit pulling in $900 million.

The door snapped closed behind her and she spun around. Gideon was blocking it, arms folded, his red-gold buzz cut glinting in the dim light. Harry's gaze flashed around, taking in the confines of the dark walls and the closed shutters that guarded the windows like bars. Gideon stepped closer and addressed her for the first time.

'From now on, you do as we say.' His voice was quiet, but his air of threat rang loud and clear. 'You don't go anywhere without us. No trips outside, no phone calls, no communication with anyone. One of us will be with you at all times.'

The roof of Harry's mouth turned dry. She wanted to nod and back away, but it occurred to her maybe Diego wouldn't take this shit lying down. She turned to Franco.

'Is this guy for real? Am I some kind of prisoner here?' The crabbiness came easily, a tension release-valve that she opened full throttle to cover her hair-raising fear. 'I don't need a stupid babysitter. I've got people to talk to, things to do that are none of your damn business.'

Gideon stepped forward, his speckled complexion dark. Franco lifted one eyebrow and gave her an assessing look.

'You want to work for me, you do as Gideon says. We get to trust each other, then maybe we'll see.' He turned to Ginny. 'Show her the room, get acquainted. We'll start in ten minutes.'

Ginny made a bored face. Then she drifted into the hall, not bothering to check if Harry was behind her. Harry trotted in her wake, glad to escape the tricky aggression in the room, and stepped into a small, drab bedroom with twin divans pushed against the wall. Ginny dropped onto one of them and rummaged in a drawer till she found a pack of cigarettes.

'You'll be sharing with me.' She angled her head to light up, her dark hair swinging over one shoulder. The man-sized shirt had slipped away from her neck, baring a fragile collarbone. She exhaled, blowing smoke up at the ceiling. 'Don't worry, half the time I don't sleep in here.'

Harry was about to ask where else she slept, when she got it. Ginny and Franco. She could picture it better than Ginny and McArdle, but still there was something about her subservience with Franco that made the image lopsided.

The haze of smoke prickled Harry's nostrils, and she crossed to the window to fling open the shutters. Street light flooded into the room, hosing away the shadows. In the distance, she could see the Zurriola Bridge, with its globed lamps like lighthouses lining either side. The city looked reassuring after the eerie isolation of the hills. She turned back to Ginny.

'Would he really have let me stab someone back in that bar?'

Ginny flexed her wrist and inspected the tip of her cigarette. Her make-up looked ghostly in the stark light.

'Maybe he would, maybe he wouldn't. He's a little unpredictable, in case you hadn't noticed.'

'Yeah, I'm getting that. Jesus. I don't know how you put up with that shit.'

Harry flounced across to the other bed, making up Diego's character as she went along. So far, her alias had turned out mutinous and cranky, and the effect was faintly liberating. She swung her legs onto the bed, leaning back against the pillows.

'What about Gideon? Franco just yanks his chain and he jumps?'

'Something like that.' Ginny's eyes flicked to the door. 'Just watch your back with him.'

'Thanks for the tip.' Harry hesitated. 'And for intervening back there in the bar. Things might've turned nasty.'

'I didn't do it for you.' Ginny stretched out on the bed, her petite shape lost in the billowing shirt. 'That whole thing was stupid, and frankly a bore. Franco needs you, he knows that. He needs you to replace Stevie.'

She blinked suddenly and looked away, sucking deep on her cigarette. Harry kept her tone offhand.

'Why did Franco hire Stevie? What does he want me to do?'

'Ask Franco.'

'I did.'

Ginny lifted one shoulder in a lazy shrug and didn't answer. Her nostrils had turned faintly pink around the edges, and Harry decided to change tack.

'So what was the deal between you and Stevie?'

'There was no *deal*. I felt sorry for him, that's all.'

'Why?'

Ginny flung her an impatient look. 'Why do you think?'

Harry's stomach hitched. She'd forgotten she was meant to know the guy. But Ginny went on, ignoring her blunder.

'He was a geek, wasn't he? Shy, spotty, overweight. Like some kind of goofy teenager. Franco gave him a hard time over it.' She flipped ash on the floor, as though flicking at a bug. 'But Stevie was good to me.'

She stalled a little more with her cigarette, then gave Harry a sardonic smile.

'I like to drink.' The look in her eyes was defiant, self-mocking. 'I like it a lot, if you want to know the truth. Being sober is tedious. I don't know how people can stand it. Living the same drab day, over and over. Jesus.'

She sucked in a lungful of smoke, head tilted back, savouring it the way other people relish the sea air. She exhaled reluctantly. 'But sometimes I overdo things, drink too much. Stevie always looked after me, made sure I was okay. He never minded. Said he used to do the same for his sister.' Ginny hunched her shoulders, as though she was cold, and hugged her arms around her chest. 'I wonder how she manages without him.'

Harry recalled the image Zubiri had conjured up: McArdle's sister lying dead, a needle still stuck in her arm.

'His sister died,' Harry said. 'A long time ago.'

Ginny blinked. Her make-up looked stale, separating from her skin like chalk dust. She shivered, and rubbed her arms. Somewhere down the hallway, Franco yelled.

'Diego, get out here!'

Harry stiffened, then swung her legs to the floor. 'Who murdered Stevie? What was he doing for Franco that got him killed?'

Ginny shook her head, stared into space. Had the girl checked out, the alcohol level finally kicking in? Harry got to her feet and planted herself directly in her line of vision.

'Hey, I'm supposed to take his place. Isn't it about time I knew what was going on around here?'

Franco roared again, but Harry didn't move. She waved her arms at Ginny, like a castaway making distress signals at a plane. Just Diego being belligerent. But Harry's heart was pounding hard. She needed answers, and the sooner she had them, the sooner she could bail out.

Ginny finally stirred, and jerked her chin at the door. 'Ask him. He's the only one who really knows.'

20

Harry wandered down the hall towards the sound of Franco's voice, and tried not to break into a run. Diego, she felt sure, wouldn't jump just because the guy said.

The door to the living room stood ajar, a slice of light illuminating the short hall. Harry wiped her palms along her thighs. Then a hand shot out and grabbed her by the wrist.

'Hey!'

Strong arms hauled her backwards into a darkened room. She stumbled, and opened her mouth to scream. A tall shape loomed and slammed her up against the wall, then Gideon thrust his face into hers.

'I don't like you, Diego.' His breath was hot, his scent a rush of fresh, male sweat. 'I don't like you at all. You may have fooled Franco with that stunt in the bar, but you haven't fooled me.'

Harry twisted her face away. His fingers were like iron cuffs around her wrists. A charge of panic shot through her as he shifted his body in close to hers.

'Franco needs me to look out for him.' His voice was low, almost a whisper. 'That's my job, always has been. I watch his back, I notice things he doesn't see. And there's something about you doesn't look right.'

Harry felt his breath caress her neck and she shivered. His fingers squeezed tighter. Then she summoned up Diego and made herself look him in the eye.

'You're hurting me, you lunkhead. Your loyalty to Franco's touching, but do you think he needs a hacker with broken wrists?'

He glared at her for a moment, then shoved himself away, releasing his grip on her arms. She massaged her wrists, trying to judge whether it was safe to move. His eyes were pockets of dark shadow. He was taller than Franco, with none of his burliness. The features she could see were neater, more finely drawn, but the set of them was harder to read.

He stepped towards her out of the gloom, his eyes hard and flat with suspicion.

'I'll be watching you. You and that lush down the hall.' He jerked his chin in the direction of Ginny's room. 'Don't bother getting too cosy with her, she won't be your ally. The women in Franco's life never last long enough for that.'

Harry snorted. 'Who needs allies? All I need is to do this job and get out of here. This may come as a

188

surprise, Gideon, but I don't like you either, and the sooner we part company the better, as far as I'm concerned.'

She turned and swept out of the room, her heartbeat drumming fast. Gideon's soft laugh pursued her down the hall, and she half-expected him to follow her. She scooted into the living room, tracking the sound of Franco's voice to another room off the dining area. She stopped up short on the threshold.

A full-sized roulette table filled her vision. It had to be almost eight feet long, and seemed to burst from the drab room in a riot of colour: the vivid green baize; the red-and-black markings; the stacks of gaily coloured chips. She stared at the wheel and thought of Stevie McArdle rubbing his eyes.

'Diego, where the fuck you been?' Franco tossed some chips onto the table with a clatter and gestured at the man behind him. 'Meet Clayton. Clay, this is Diego. You two will be working together.'

Gooseflesh prickled Harry's skin as she looked into the man's eyes: Clayton James, the American with the thatch of grey hair who'd cleaned up at Riva's wheels. Her gut swooped with a queasy, falling sensation. What were the chances he'd recognize her from the casino?

Clayton narrowed his eyes. He was squat and heavyset, with full cheeks, like a gerbil stocked up for the winter. He gave her a long, hard stare. Then he turned to help himself from a drinks trolley by the wall, flinging a comment over his shoulder.

189

'I hope to fuck she can play roulette better than fat-boy Stevie.'

Harry shot Franco a look. Tension snagged at the corners of his mouth, his mellowness on the wane. She hitched a thumb at Clayton.

'What's he talking about? I'm not here to gamble, I thought you needed a hacker.'

'Like I said, you want to work for me, you do what I say. You're taking McArdle's place at the roulette table.'

'Oh, come on. First you ask me to stab someone, now you want me to play roulette? What the hell is going on here?'

Franco's wide cheekbones turned dusky. 'What's the matter with you? Didn't I make myself clear in the bar? *I'll* decide when you're ready to know what's going on, you got that?'

Harry eyed him warily. His colour was high, his face an arrangement of jutting angles and planes. He was the only one who could tell her why he'd hired a hacker. Ginny and Gideon weren't in the mood to share, and by the looks of him, neither was Clayton. That is, if any of them knew. Stevie was probably the only one who knew for sure why he'd been hired, and he couldn't tell her anything.

Harry blinked. Or maybe he could.

She gave a small shrug. 'Okay, have it your way. Tell me when you're ready. But I'm just warning you, if I have to use Stevie's laptop, I'll need time to get acquainted with it.'

'What the hell for?'

She lifted an eyebrow, hoping she looked uppity. 'We're

not plumbers, you know. Hacking is an art, and craftsmen don't all use the same tools. I'll need to run through what he's got, put his box of tricks through its paces.' She shrugged again. 'I can either do it now or waste time later, it's up to you.'

Franco studied her for a moment. 'Let's see how you do at roulette.'

Harry sighed. 'What's the deal with that? Another kind of test?'

'We cheat the casinos. It's how we make our walking-around money.'

Harry folded her arms and looked sceptical. Clayton was ignoring them, busy nursing his drink by the window. Franco moved along the table and spun the wheel. Light bounced off its polished bowl, the slots a psychedelic whirl of black and red.

'How much do you know about roulette?' he said.

Harry shrugged. 'I know the rules.'

Franco flicked the roulette ball with a clack onto the wheel.

'What if I said that every time a number from twenty-five to thirty-six comes up, we're guaranteed to win seventeen-and-a-half grand?'

Seventeen-and-a-half grand. The amount Clayton had collected from Riva on each win, with a bet of five hundred euros. The ball swirled around the wheel. Harry shook her head.

'I'd say it's impossible. Not unless the wheel's rigged, or you're betting all twelve numbers every time.'

Over by the window, Clayton snorted. 'How dumb would that be? Each spin would cost us six fucking grand.'

Franco looked uptight at having his narrative interrupted. He focused on Harry, like an expectant teacher waiting for his star pupil to get it.

'No rigged wheels,' he said.

The roulette ball rattled around in the bowl, and Harry peered at it, tracking its course. Was Riva right? Were they using computers to predict the spin?

She threw him a doubtful look. 'You've got some kind of computerized device?'

Franco paused, and looked disappointed. Then he slid a phone out of his pocket and set it on the table. 'Works every time. In-built laser scanner measures the velocity of the ball and predicts just where it'll land. Sector targeting. Technique's been around a while.'

Harry squinted at his face. Something flickered in his eyes, piercing the dark intensity. Slowly, she shook her head.

'You're so full of shit.'

Franco stared, then threw back his head and laughed. 'Attagirl, Diego, you got it. No bullshit gadgets. We do things the old-fashioned way.'

He stowed the phone back in his pocket. Harry's chest lurched to see it disappear, a sharp reminder of how cut off she was from Zubiri. The ball clattered into a slot and Franco spun it around again.

'Ever heard of past-posting?'

192

Harry nodded. 'Sure. Betting when you already know the outcome. Like betting on a winning horse after it's gone past the post.'

'Exactly. Same in roulette. Soon as you know the winning number, you dump a big bet on it. Oldest trick in the book, which is why we use it. Bunch of eye-in-the-sky novices out there don't know jack-shit these days. Glorified camera jockeys, most of 'em.'

'So you don't get caught?'

'Never happened yet.'

Clayton turned away from the window, his face sweaty and pugnacious. 'There's always a first time.'

Franco ignored him, the twitch in his jaw the only sign he'd heard. 'Casinos don't like re-winding surveillance tapes. They gotta halt the betting, so right away they're losing money in table downtime. Plus it's bad publicity. Stop the game every time a punter hits a winner, and people will think you don't like to pay out.'

Harry frowned, still hung up on the mechanics of past-posting a winning bet. Her mind looped back over what she'd seen: Stevie's eye-rub; Clayton's noisy win; the floorman's grudging approval of the payout. She shook her head.

'I still don't get it. How can you pull off a move like that right under the dealer's nose?'

Franco smiled to himself. 'With timing. Finesse. A few artistic moves. Split-second precision, and creative sleight of hand.' He flicked her a sardonic look. 'Casino cheaters are craftsmen too.'

193

Harry inclined her head. 'Okay, point taken. But why use me? What about Ginny?'

'She's already in play, so are Gideon and Clayton.'

Harry blinked. 'How many people does it take?'

'Four.' Franco counted them off on his fingers. 'The two bettors, that's you and Ginny. The mechanic, that's Gideon, he does the move. Deft hands, softer than a magician's. Then there's the claimant, who scoops up the winning bet. That's Clayton here. Best role-player we got.'

Clayton drained his glass and looked unimpressed by the compliment. Harry raised her eyebrows at Franco.

'So what about you?'

He shook his head. 'I'm out of it. Can't afford to be seen just now.'

Clayton snorted again, and lumbered back to the drinks trolley. Seen by whom, Harry wondered. Casino security? Riva?

Franco went on: 'As well as betting, you'll be in charge of signals to the crew. Ginny's no good, it needs a sharp eye, and Gideon needs to focus on the move.'

Harry leaned against the roulette table, a worm of uneasiness wriggling in her gut. She rattled a pile of chips through her fingers.

'I don't know. I still don't get how it all works.'

'You will. We rehearse all night until you do. Then tomorrow we pull the move in the Gran Casino.'

Harry's hands froze against the baize. Riva's casino. Shit. What if she saw her? What if Riva approached her and blew her cover?

Clayton swung around, setting his glass on the trolley with a crack. 'Jesus, Franco, I keep telling you, we've milked that one dry. Pull it there again, and security will be all over us the minute I go in for the claim.'

Franco clenched his fists. 'Don't question me, Clayton.'

'Hey, you're not the one out there pulling the moves. I'm the one smiling for all the cameras. And fat-boy Stevie must've picked up heat from someone. He gave the emergency signal, remember?'

Harry was siding with Clayton on this one. 'Look, maybe Clayton's right. If you've done it there before, then shouldn't we try someplace else?'

Franco slammed his fist on the baize, setting the chips chinkling. 'We do it in the Gran Casino!'

Harry flinched, then covered the reflex with a scowl. 'Jesus. What's so special about the Gran Casino?'

Franco didn't answer. Clayton stepped closer, purple patches suffusing his cheeks like fruit-juice stains.

'He's got some kind of hard-on vendetta against the owner. Classy-looking woman, too, but I guess he has his reasons.'

Franco gave a bitter laugh. 'Yeah, real classy. Those casinos of hers got started with mob money, that's how classy she is.'

Harry flashed on Riva's elegance, on the frosty, businesslike air. Mob money didn't fit the image. She studied the venomous look on Franco's face with interest.

'Is that why you want to target her casino?'

His black eyes blazed into hers. 'Too many questions, Diego.'

Clayton flapped a dismissive hand. 'The whole thing is crazy. *You're* fucking crazy.'

Franco whipped around and lunged at Clayton's throat. 'You piece of shit!'

He thrust a forearm under Clayton's chin and jammed him up against the wall. Then he shoved against his throat until Clayton's eyes bulged.

'Don't you ever call me crazy.' Franco was panting, his voice hoarse. 'I should've left you where I found you, just some loser gambling his life down the crapper.'

He jerked his head back, then butted it against Clayton's nose. The crack was sickening. Clayton's head whacked against the wall, the blood already pumping from his nostrils. Harry stumbled backwards, trying to dodge Franco's orbit of rage. He yelled again.

'I'm running this show, you piece of filth!'

Franco punched Clayton in the gut, driving the air out of his lungs. Clayton gasped, his tongue lolling from his mouth. Franco pulled back his fist and punched him again, his arm a frenzied piston.

Harry clung to the wall. Jesus, he was going to kill him. She opened her mouth to yell, then Gideon stormed past her into the room.

'Franco?'

He put a hand on Franco's shoulder, his touch oddly gentle in the face of all that boiling fury. Franco jerked away, and looked as if he might round on Gideon.

196

'He's not worth it.' Gideon's expression was calm, the hand on Franco's shoulder firm. 'Look at him, for Chrissake.'

Clayton had slid to the floor, and lay there crumpled like a leaking beanbag, moaning softly to himself. Franco nodded, seemed to gather his self-control.

'Just get him out of my sight.'

Gideon hauled Clayton to his feet and dragged him out of the room. Franco stared at Harry as though he'd forgotten she was there. He was still breathing hard, and his close-set eyes looked concussed. A few wild grey hairs had escaped from his ponytail, giving him a deranged look.

'This crew is falling to shit.' His face was spangled with sweat. 'Gideon's the only one who's worth anything. We've known each other a long time, Gideon and me. Since we were kids. He understands loyalty. Lifelong friendship.'

He pressed a fist against his chest, punctuating every word. Then he stepped up close, lowering his voice to a whisper.

'But you know what? If Gideon ever put a foot wrong, I'd kill him. No hesitation.'

Something icy wedged in Harry's chest.

'Remember that, Diego. Anyone steps out of line with me, anyone at all, and they're dead.'

21

'Show me the signals.'

Harry paused, halfway out of the car, and twisted back to Gideon. 'Oh, come on. We've been over it a hundred times.'

'Do it.'

She sighed and lugged the passenger door closed. They'd been rehearsing all night and for most of the day, and by now her brain was punch-drunk with chip moves and orchestrated signals.

Gideon turned to face her, one arm draped over the wheel. His black tuxedo seemed to intensify the amber tones of his freckles.

'What happens when a number from twenty-five to thirty-six comes up?' he said.

'I rub my eyes.'

'Why?'

'So Clayton knows to come to the table and claim his winnings.'

'What are you looking for, every second we're in play?'

'Suspicion from the dealers. Floormen not buying the move. Any attention at all from security.'

'And if you see it?'

'I give the emergency signal.'

'Show me.'

Obediently, Harry smoothed a hand over her hair, the way Stevie McArdle had when he'd caught her watching him in the casino.

'Then what?' Gideon said.

'Then everyone gets the hell out of Dodge.'

His tight mouth told her he didn't appreciate the flip response, but Harry didn't care. A sassy exterior was the only thing choking back her fear. She rolled her eyes.

'Okay, okay. At the emergency signal, we drop everything, leave the premises and meet up back at the apartment. Come on, Gideon, I know all this.'

He nodded slowly, his air distracted in spite of the close-quarter grilling. He'd seemed anxious all day, and had hovered over Franco before they'd left the apartment, as though reluctant to leave him alone. Harry was starting to see why. True, Franco's episode of rage had burned out and today he'd been affable, if a touch erratic. But a pattern was emerging that made Harry uneasy: frenzied outbursts, followed by intervals of precarious calm. As though violence somehow soothed him.

She eyed Gideon's preoccupation, recalling Franco's

claim that he would kill his childhood buddy if he had to. She wondered what was behind Gideon's loyalty. Didn't he know how misplaced it was?

He roused himself finally, and turned to the door. 'Let's go.'

They climbed out of the car. The night air was cold, a boisterous wind gusting inland over the bay. They'd parked in a side street off Alameda del Boulevard, and Harry stared at the busy avenue up ahead. Her heart shifted in her chest. She'd been a prisoner in Franco's apartment for almost twenty-four hours. This could be her only chance to cut and run.

Gideon joined her on the pavement and placed a proprietary hand on her back, then guided her across the Boulevard. Something bulky nudged her from under his jacket lapel, a reminder that bailing out here wouldn't be a smart move. She'd seen him load the gun before they'd left.

They jostled through the crowded grids of the Old Quarter, the cobbles lumpy under Harry's thin soles. Ginny had lent her a pair of high heels, along with a black, halterneck dress cut too low front and back for Harry's taste. Gideon's touch was light against her flesh, but owed nothing to courtesy or the urge to feel her up. It was just his way of stalking her tail.

They reached the Gran Casino, and Gideon propelled her through the entrance and into the high-limit salon. The clack of casino chips filled the air, cutting through the genteel murmur of conversation. Harry threaded through the knots of well-heeled punters, her stomach tensing as she glanced up at the mezzanine floor.

There was no sign of Riva.

Gideon's hand pressed into the small of her back, goosing her further into the room. Ginny and Clayton were already there, but no acknowledgements passed between them, no hint of collusion.

Harry bagged a seat opposite Ginny at one of the roulette tables, while Gideon sat at the end furthest from the dealer, which was where he'd make his move.

She flicked another glance at the mezzanine floor, her insides churning at the notion that Riva might blow her cover in front of Gideon. According to Zubiri, Riva could even be involved. Harry wasn't sure exactly what that meant, but her instincts were all humming the same frenzied plea to lie low.

She bought in for a cheap stack of dark blue chips, surprised to find her hands steady. Ginny was already set up with low-value yellows, and Gideon had a mix of dark blues and blacks stowed away somewhere in his pocket. The chip colours were important. They'd steer the move, work the dealer like a marionette.

Clayton wandered over to the table and set a black chip down on number thirty-two. He beamed at the other punters, his friendly, American-tourist act hampered a little by the bandaged swelling around his nose.

The dealer spotted the bet, and gave Clayton a direct look. His name was Dario, according to the tag on his waistcoat. He was in his early twenties and looked new

201

at the job, which was one of the reasons they'd homed in on his shift.

Dario signalled to the floorman, who joined him at the table. Dealers were obliged to announce all high bets to the boss, who would then supervise the spin and authorize the payout if it won. The floorman studied Clayton as if memorizing him for a future police line-up. Then he nodded at Dario to carry on.

The ball whirled. Harry fiddled with her chips. The players pushed in two-deep around her, scattering their bets in a race against orbital motion. The ball skipped into a slot.

'*Quinze, negro, impar.*'

Dario set his plastic marker on the winning number fifteen.

Clayton shrugged, then drifted away. His bet had lost, but that didn't matter. What mattered was that Dario and the floorman had him pegged as a punter who bet black chips straight-up.

Harry's pulse kicked up a gear. The play was on. She snapped three blue chips onto each of the numbers from twenty-five through thirty-six. Opposite her, Ginny placed a stack of yellows in the third dozen box, a bet that encompassed all the same numbers as Harry's but at much reduced odds. But the odds didn't matter. It was the colour of Ginny's chips that would count.

Harry slid her a look across the table. Ginny's white dress was strapless, exposing thin shoulders and a collarbone that jutted out like a coat hanger. She'd pulled her hair into a ballerina bun, matching it with dramatic stage make-up. Harry couldn't see her eyes, and wondered if they were already slippery with alcohol.

The ball clattered to a halt. Red sixteen.

Harry and Ginny had lost.

Dario scooped up their stakes, and Harry immediately littered the baize with the same pattern of dark blue chips. She scoured the room, her fingers busy, ostensibly on the lookout for hostile security, but in reality wondering if Zubiri had installed a team in the casino.

The ball curled around the wheel. Arms stretched across the table, tossing chips onto the baize. Dario was supposed to keep track of every bet, but the reality was, on a layout this busy he couldn't.

Harry and Ginny kept on losing, kept on laying out chips. Harry flashed a look at Gideon, her whole body clenched with the overwhelming urge to run. What if she just walked up to security? What if she screamed for help? Gideon caught her eye, his gaze chilly. Her stomach swirled as she pictured the gun under his jacket.

She laid out another matrix of bets. Her brain looped in circles, scrabbling for a way out. All these cameras and security men, and still she was Franco's prisoner.

Something gnawed at her gut as she thought about Franco. How much longer before he'd tell her why he'd hired a hacker? If she cut loose now, she'd never find out. She'd return to Zubiri empty-handed. Harry shifted in her chair, not liking the notion. She was so damn close. She flashed on Stevie's laptop, and felt sure it had secrets to tell. Her stubborn streak argued she should stay and check it out. But her instincts screamed at her to run if she got the chance.

The ball trickled into a slot on the wheel.

'*Veintiséis, negro, par.*'

Dario placed his marker on number twenty-six, right on top of Harry's dark blue chips.

Her skin felt clammy. She and Ginny had won. Harry rubbed her eyelids, wondering if Clayton could see the signal through the crowds. But he had plenty of time. The dealer had to sweep away the losing bets before he got around to paying out.

Dario's hands brushed across the layout, rattling chips into the sorting machine. When the baize was clean, he began paying out to a few players in the middle of the table.

Soon, he'd get to Ginny's pile of yellow chips. To pay her, he'd have to grab two stacks of yellows from the chip well by his side. The yellows were at the extreme rear of the well. Which meant for one split-second, Dario's back would be half-turned.

Dealers were taught never to completely turn their backs, but almost all of them did. No two dealers turned in the same way, but according to Franco, a mechanic like Gideon could pull a move off against most of them.

Harry held her breath. They knew Dario's turn was tight. Gideon wouldn't have much time, and she still couldn't believe he'd get away with it. She'd seen his move a dozen times in the apartment. It was slick, no question. But in a roomful of punters and cameras?

Dario's eyes fell on Ginny's stack of yellow chips. He turned to the well. In the same instant, Gideon's hands surged towards the plastic marker. His right hand nudged Harry's three blue chips to the left, the marker still on top, and in their place he dropped the four chips he'd already cupped in his palm. Then he slid the marker on top of them while his left hand snatched Harry's chips off the table. The move was fluid, dextrous; a single smooth action. The whole thing took less than a second. By the time Dario turned back to Ginny, Gideon had melted into the crowd.

Harry surveyed the switched-in stack: three dark blues, just like hers, but with a single black chip on the bottom. To Dario, it would look like Harry had placed her three blues on top of someone else's bet.

'Well, hell, would you look at that!' Clayton had appeared on the opposite side of the table. 'Five hundred euros straight-up on twenty-six. I just hit me a jackpot!'

Dario jerked up his head, snapped his gaze to the marker. He paled when he saw the black chip. From his look of dismay, the blues were dark enough to persuade him he'd simply missed the black. He muttered something under his breath, then called the floorman over.

By now, Clayton had generated a buzz in the crowd. He whooped like a cowboy rounding up cattle, while people tried to clap him on the shoulder. He'd deliberately positioned himself on the other side of the layout, as far as possible from the move. No one could suspect him of past-posting his chip from there. Besides, he'd already bet a black chip straight-up at the table, which established his betting habits and made the win easier to swallow.

The floorman gave Clayton a long, hard look, then nodded and authorized the payout. Dario shoved two stacks of chips across the baize: €17,500.

Harry's fingers tingled. She lined up another row of bets. Ginny did likewise. Departing the scene now would only draw attention to their collusion. Clayton exchanged his winnings for regular casino chips from Dario, while Harry let her gaze drift up towards the mezzanine floor. Her hands froze on the baize.

Riva was staring right at her.

Harry's heart jolted. The woman looked furious. They locked eyes for a moment. Then Riva whirled away and marched out of Harry's sight.

Shit. Was the woman coming down to confront her? Was she calling security? Harry's eyes raked the room. Gideon had dropped back out of Dario's sight, and was cruising the outskirts of the table.

Her stomach went into freefall. She couldn't let Riva challenge her, not in front of the others. She had to get out of here, but Franco's damn crew still hemmed her in.

Something clicked in her brain. Slowly, she released her chips onto the baize, uncomfortably aware that the last person who'd done what she was about to do had ended up dead. But right now she had no choice.

She straightened her shoulders, then ran a hand across her hair in an unmistakable emergency signal.

22

The response was immediate; a synchronized drill.

Ginny moved first. She slipped from her seat and drifted towards the door. Then Clayton peeled away and headed for the cage to cash out. Harry checked over her shoulder. Gideon had dropped back and was already making for the exit. But any second now, he'd turn to check Harry was following.

Harry shot to her feet as though her legs were spring-loaded. She shouldered through the crowds, away from the exit, putting distance between herself and Gideon. She scoured the perimeters of the room, her breath hitching. There had to be another way out of here.

An unmarked door blended into the wall panels on her right. She flung herself against it, tugging at the handle, then lurched through to a deserted hallway. She snapped the door closed, whipped her gaze left and right.

An anonymous corridor. Bare walls. The muffled chinkle of chips sounded through them. Harry's legs quivered. Where to now?

She veered left and flew down the passageway, stopping up short at a door marked *V. Toledo*. Something stirred in her brain. Victor Toledo. The security guy who'd been tipped off about Franco. Harry rattled the handle, banged on the door. It was locked, and no one was home.

A moan escaped Harry's throat. She raced to the end of the passageway and blundered through to the stairwell. The air was cold, the white-tiled walls adding to the refrigerated effect. She stared at the zig-zagging flights of steps. The only way was up.

She took the stairs two at a time, her heels scattering *rat-tat-tat* echoes off the tiles. She launched herself at the door on the next landing, and burst out onto the mezzanine floor.

Harry jerked backwards, held her breath. She scanned the catwalk overlooking the casino. The lighting was soft, the walls lined with paintings, like some kind of stately home. Riva was nowhere in sight.

Harry tiptoed to the balcony and peered down, raking the heads below for Gideon's beige crew cut. She spotted him near the exit, craning his neck over the crowds, a phone pressed to his ear. His face looked taut. Then he wheeled through the exit, disappearing from view. Harry let out a long breath and edged backwards, her knees ready to buckle.

'Consider yourself fired, Ms Martinez.'

She spun around. Riva was watching her from the doorway to her office. The woman's lips were compressed, as though sealing back her temper, and it made her pointed features look pinched.

'My office. Now.'

Harry felt her cheeks burn. Riva stalked back inside and Harry followed, her legs still unsteady. The woman stood behind the desk. Her business suit was severe, a gunmetal grey. A match for her stony mood. She eyed Harry's low-cut attire. Harry felt like a child caught dressing in grown-up's clothes.

She lifted her chin. 'Perhaps I should explain.'

'I doubt if you can. I haven't heard from you in over a week, you haven't acknowledged my calls.' Riva hit a key on her laptop, and a printer juddered to life in the corner. 'I hired you to find out who was cheating my casinos, not to play roulette at my wheels.'

Harry chewed her lip. Her first impulse was to defend herself, to make good her professional reputation. But she bit it back. If Zubiri was right and Riva was involved, just how much could Harry afford to say?

Clammy sweat doused her back. Her brain felt splintered, caught in the dizzy space between truth and lies; between reality and sleight of hand. Between Harry and Diego.

Only she wasn't Harry now. She wasn't even Diego. She was Harry disguised as Diego, who in turn had to masquerade back as Harry. A nested doll of diminishing identities. The layers were making her head spin.

Riva snatched a sheet of paper out of the printer and scribbled her signature on the bottom. Her mouth looked tight. The baby-blonde hair was glossy under the lights, but the jaw-length bob was too blunt for her heart-shaped face. She shoved the paper across the desk to Harry, who read the bold-font heading from where she stood: *Notice of Contract Termination*.

Riva rapped the letter with her pen. 'I hired you to do a job, and I expected you to keep me posted. At the very least, I expected you to take my calls.'

Harry's mind raced. For now, she had to run with this charade. Maybe she could even dig for information about Franco. She jerked her head towards the picture window overlooking the casino floor.

'I needed to blend in down there. Act like a player. How far do you think I'd get stalking cheaters if I prowled around in a suit?' She borrowed some attitude from Diego. 'And not to sound rude, but when I'm working in the field like that, I never take calls.'

Riva's eyes were liquid steel, and Harry tried not to blink. She wondered how many messages Riva had left on her phone. It was back in her hotel, along with her other personal effects; the layer of identity she'd shed to become Diego. A twinge pierced her chest as she wondered who else had been calling her. Hunter? Her mother? Her eyes strayed to the phone on Riva's desk. She badly needed to contact Zubiri.

Riva stared at her for a moment, then flung down her pen. 'Don't bullshit me. You've accomplished nothing. Why don't you just admit it?'

'I've found your cheaters for you. Doesn't that count?'

Riva frowned. Her look was sceptical, though a flicker of doubt hovered around her eyes. She glanced at the window.

'Are you saying they're here now?'

Harry whirled through her options. If she said Franco's crew had been in the casino, then Riva would check the tapes to identify them. Which meant she'd see Harry's collusion in the move. She'd see Diego. And that could be tough to explain. Who knew which side Riva was really on?

Harry shook her head. 'I've been waiting for them to show.'

'So how are they beating my wheels?'

Riva's cold, grey eyes were challenging, and Harry's mind stalled. Should she tell her about the past-posting? She'd probably check the cameras for that, too. Harry's head felt jammed. She had to keep Riva away from those tapes.

Something cut through the gridlock; something Franco had said. Harry cleared her throat.

'Sector targeting.'

Riva missed a beat, then shook her head. 'That's not reliable. What equipment are they using?'

'Phones, wristwatches. Anything that'll take an in-built laser scanner and isn't banned on the casino floor.'

'But sector targeting's been around for years. It's just not accurate.'

'Looks like technology has caught up. They can capture the speed of the ball, calculate its decaying orbit and predict the sector where it'll land.' Harry was ad-libbing freely by now, and hoped it sounded plausible. 'It improves the odds of winning by eighty per cent. That's got to eat into your margins.'

Riva crossed her arms, and drummed the fingers of one hand against her sleeve. She studied Harry's face.

'How did you find this out?'

'I got lucky. I picked up on some signalling between people who weren't meant to know each other. Collusion between strangers.'

'In a crowd like this? That's hard to do, even for a seasoned surveillance agent.'

Harry shrugged. 'My father taught me to watch out for it from the time I was six years old. You spot it in a poker game, and you get the hell out.'

Riva looked at her with renewed interest, as though re-evaluating her talents. Then she glanced at the termination notice on the desk. Harry could almost see her wrestling with the notion that she'd been wrong, but in the end, thorny obstinacy won out.

'Your father has good instincts. But my Chief of Security can take things from here.' Riva took a seat behind the desk, and motioned for Harry to sit. 'If you can identify these people on tape, then we'll pursue them through normal channels.'

Harry's heartbeat seemed to skid. Those bloody tapes. She lowered herself into a chair, and threw Riva a doubtful look.

'Well, I can try. But I don't think they've hit your tables here recently. I found most of this out in the bar, in ways I'd rather not go into just now.'

She pressed her lips together and let that one hang, hoping to imply that her methods were less than ethical. She had the feeling someone like Riva wouldn't hold that kind of transgression against her.

Riva acknowledged the venial sin with a small nod, then lifted the handset on the phone. 'We have cameras in the bar. We still might have picked them up. How many people are we talking about here?'

'Four. Three guys, one woman.' Harry's brain scrambled. 'But the key player, Chavez, he won't be on any of your tapes. They hook up with him outside, and as far as I can tell, he never comes into the casinos.'

Riva punched in a number, her attention already shifting to the phone conversation ahead. Harry edged forward on her seat. Either she got some leads on Franco, or it was time she got the hell out.

Franco's face filled her vision: the close-set eyes; the wide cheekbones; the look of rage when Riva's name came up. A vendetta, Clayton had called it. Harry leaned her elbows on the desk.

'Maybe you know him. Big guy, burly chest. Long, black ponytail. Looks like some hostile Indian brave.'

Riva's body grew still. She fixed her gaze on the phone,

her eyes losing focus, as if she'd suddenly zoned out. Harry could hear a man's voice pick up on the other end. Riva didn't respond.

Harry pushed the description home. 'From what I heard, he's some mix of Spanish and Iroquois.'

Riva jerked her head up and stared at Harry. The grey eyes looked leaden, and her jawline had slackened a little. She spoke softly into the phone.

'Sorry, Victor. My mistake.'

She eased the handset back into its cradle, then clasped her hands in front of her on the desk. Her movements were small and precise, her posture rigid. She pinned her eyes on Harry.

'This Chavez. What else do you know about him?'

Her voice sounded hoarse, as though she hadn't used it in a while. Harry watched her closely.

'He's volatile,' she said. 'Dangerous, even. Doesn't seem to like you much.'

She squinted at Riva, trying to interpret her reaction. Clearly, Riva and Franco were well acquainted. And since Franco claimed to know how she'd financed her empire, the acquaintance probably went back a long time. But what was behind all the high-octane emotion?

She decided to pursue the point. 'Do you know him?'

Riva's gaze was distant, locked into hindsight. Finally, she said,

'I thought he'd be dead by now.'

She inhaled a deep breath, then got to her feet and wandered over to the window. She moved slowly, like a convalescent. Then she slipped a finger through the slatted blinds, separating the blades to get a clearer view of the floor. Eventually, she said,

'I used to love the old catwalks.' She widened the slats. 'They were always so dark, with that black, one-way glass. I used to prowl them for hours, watching the games with my binoculars. Watching my empire.' A smile fluttered around her lips. 'I still prowl this place late at night, sometimes.'

Her gaze lingered on the casino floor. She seemed cut adrift, as if one old memory had stirred up others, the eddying history pulling her away like a tide. Harry kept still, not wanting to disturb the mood.

'Chavez.' Riva shook her head. 'That's not his real name. Or at least, it's not the name I knew him by. But I suppose it doesn't matter.'

She released the blinds with a sudden snap. Her fingers curled into fists, and she seemed to fight for control. Then she turned and marched back to her seat, some of her earlier briskness returning. She glared at Harry.

'How do you know so much about Franco? About his operation?'

'I've got pally with the girl. She tells me things, lets things slip.'

'What's she like?' Riva looked at her hands. 'Is she close to Franco?'

'She's thin and attractive, dark hair. Ginny something. And they're probably sleeping together, if that's what you're asking.'

215

Maybe Franco and Riva had once been lovers, but Harry wasn't about to spare her feelings. Old jealousies were the least of her concerns right now.

Riva thrust up her chin. 'And he's never set foot in my casino?'

'He just pulls the strings from outside, as far as I can see.' Harry hesitated. 'If you ask me, this casino cheating's just a sideline.'

'What do you mean?'

'Something feels off. Their technique is pretty foolproof, but they're not going for big returns. They could hit you harder. More wins, higher stakes. It's like they're toying with you. Waiting for something.'

'Waiting for what?'

'I don't know. I was hoping you could tell me.'

Harry watched Riva's face, but her expression gave nothing away. The woman leaned forward across the desk, her eyes locked on Harry's.

'How do I find them?'

Her tone had undergone a shift. Harry shook her head.

'I don't know. But I can probably find out. I can use Ginny to get close to them, maybe make contact with Franco. But I'd need to know what all this was about.'

Riva gave her a long, penetrating look. She drummed her fingers against the desk, then snatched up the notice of termination and ripped the page in half.

'Do it. Get closer to these people. I want to know who's involved, what they're up to. But most of all, I want to know how to find them.'

216

Harry's brain seemed to tilt. If she was reading this right, Riva had just hired her to work undercover in Franco's crew. Those nested identities were starting to stack up to infinity. Like reflections in opposing mirrors. And still she had no idea what was going on.

She shook her head. 'These people look dangerous. Don't get me wrong, I don't mind a little danger now and then. But I need to understand what I'm getting into first.'

Riva shrugged. 'They're cheating my casinos. What else do you need to know?'

'Come on, we both know there's more to it than that. What's Franco got against you? Why is he gunning for you?'

Riva spread out her hands. 'I honestly don't know.'

'But what's your connection to him? Why are you so anxious to find him?'

Riva was silent for a while, then she gave her a level look. 'I can probably tell you that. You see, Franco killed my brother.'

23

Harry clipped down the stairwell, spattering echoes off the hard, white tiles. Hairs rose on the back of her neck. She had to call Zubiri.

She eased open the door to the ground-floor hallway. She'd hoped to get a chance to use Riva's phone, but the woman had broken off to take an incoming call and had immediately signalled to Harry they were done. Harry had seized the chance to slip away while she could.

She hesitated in the doorway. The ground-floor corridor was dimly lit, the swirl of roulette wheels deadened by the partition wall. Her pulse drummed at the notion of braving the open territory of the casino. Ditching Franco's crew meant she'd probably ditched Zubiri's backup team as well. Assuming they'd ever been there.

Harry edged into the corridor, rewinding her

conversation with Riva. She'd tried to quiz her more about her brother's death, but the woman had refused to be drawn.

'Franco killed him,' she'd said. 'That's all you need to know.'

The stairwell door clunked shut and Harry picked her way down the corridor. Something was different. A pie-shaped wedge of light was angled across the floor up ahead. Victor Toledo's office was open.

She inched forward and peeped around the door. The room looked empty. Fluorescent lights blazed down on pristine-white furnishings: white desk, white walls, white floor.

White phone.

Harry's pulse surged. The instrument gleamed like a beacon. She glanced up the corridor, then slipped into the office, lifted the handset and dialled. On the third digit, her fingers froze. Her brain faltered. She'd blanked on Zubiri's number.

Shit! What the hell was it? She clenched her fist.

Think!

She'd hard-wired it into her memory. For days, she'd been able to recite it at will, one number prompting the next like a catchy jingle. She groped for the rhythm, but couldn't latch onto it. Her head felt scrambled. Her memory had shut down.

Dammit!

Harry took a deep breath. Maybe oxygen would goose her brain into gear. Then something shifted in her head;

another number leaped into focus. She dialled it without thinking, her fingers trembling. Then she waited for the call to pick up.

'Hunter.'

His voice sounded taut, strung out on a short fuse. A lump sprang up in Harry's throat, a reaction she put down to relief at hearing a familiar voice.

'It's me,' she said.

'Harry. Jesus. Where the hell are you? I've been calling you for the last two days.'

She swallowed against the fullness in her throat, not trusting herself to speak straight away. Hunter didn't seem to notice. His tone said he had a lot to unload.

'I looked up those names, like you asked. Against my better judgement, I might add.'

She heard the tap of a keyboard and pictured him squinting at the screen, his expression mutinous at the confines of being tied to his desk. She wished she could see his face.

'Ginny Vaughan,' he said. 'Comes from one of the wealthiest families in Dublin. Yachting, horse breeding, opera buffs, art collectors . . .'

'No criminal record?' Harry noticed how much she wanted Hunter to keep on talking. For now, just hearing his voice was a help.

'Nope. But Clayton James does. Most recently for embezzlement and attempted blackmail.'

He started reading out a list of arrests that went back

twenty years. Harry soaked in the reassuring normality of his voice. Then she made herself interrupt.

'Hunter—'

'When are you coming back?'

She closed her eyes briefly, cradling the receiver in both hands, as if that could somehow bring him closer. 'Soon.'

'I . . .' Hunter hesitated, then tried again. 'It's the Tech Bureau guys, they need you. They don't want to deal with anyone else. Seems like you're quite a hit in there.'

'Am I?' Harry managed. Then, because she wanted him to stay on the line, she said, 'How'd you get all this information on Clayton?'

'Believe me, you're better off not knowing. Let's just say, I wouldn't do it for anyone else but you.'

He let that one hang between them for a moment, then cleared his throat, as though wrong-footed by what he'd just said. Maybe the guy was no closer to understanding this relationship than she was.

Harry's eyes flicked to the door. 'Did your sources have anything on Gideon Ray? He's Franco's sidekick, acts like he's his guardian angel.'

I will not be your guardian angel.

The random leap to Zubiri's words sent a voltage kick straight to her head. Somewhere, a memory cell stirred and said *Ah!*, then flashed up Zubiri's number. Whole and intact. Harry closed her eyes and sent up a silent prayer of thanks. Then she edged around the desk,

221

listening to the clack of Hunter's keys and knowing she had to end the call.

'Sorry, Hunter, something's come up. I've got to go.'

'Wait, there's more. You'll want to hear this. I've nothing on Gideon Ray, but I dug deeper on Riva Mills.'

Harry went still. 'Oh?'

'Did you know she has links to organized crime?'

'I heard she got a leg-up from the Mafia when she started her casinos.'

'That was back in the eighties. This is more recent. Nothing's been proven, but according to the FBI, she's suspected of involvement in ongoing racketeering and state crimes.'

'Jesus.'

'Then again, maybe her activities aren't relevant. It's Chavez you're going after, right? Maybe there's no real connection between him and Riva Mills.'

'There's a connection all right. She told me he killed her brother.'

Hunter paused. 'Hold on a second.'

Harry flicked another uneasy glance at the door, shifting from foot to foot. Hunter came back on the line.

'Brother, Andy Mills. Died in Las Vegas in 1989. Bullet wound to the head. Aged eighteen.'

There was a pause while Hunter seemed to read ahead. Harry's stomach went cold as she tried to picture Franco pulling the trigger on an eighteen-year-old boy. Was he really that crazy?

Hunter cut back in. 'That's all I've got on how he died. Seems he was brain damaged from birth. They're guessing Foetal Alcohol Syndrome. In other words, the mother was a drunk. From what I've got here, Riva more or less raised him on her own.'

Jesus. Mothers. Who knew the damage they could cause? Harry allowed her thoughts to hover experimentally around Miriam, as though prodding a fresh wound to see how much it still hurt. She dug her nails into her palm. Distracting pain with pain.

'Nothing more about her brother,' Hunter concluded. 'I'll see what else I can dig up, since that's the connection with Chavez.'

'Actually, there's another connection. Organized crime. It's probably not just Riva who's involved.'

She finally brought him up to date on what she'd learned from Zubiri's slides: the transnational criminal organizations; the global terrorists; the criminal proceeds of $900 million a year.

When she'd finished, Hunter was silent for a long moment.

'Colombian cartels?' he said eventually. 'Triads and Jihad movements? For fuck's sake, Harry. What the hell are these Basque cops playing at? This is huge. These are global syndicates, fucking dangerous. They've no business trying to recruit an amateur like you. Just stay away from Vasco, for God's sake, and make sure you don't change your mind. You can't go in.'

Harry looked at the floor and didn't answer. The

silence intensified, buzzing like a current between them. When Hunter spoke again, his voice was quiet.

'You're already in, aren't you?'

She closed her eyes. 'Yes.'

'Ah Jesus, Harry.'

Her palms grew damp. She waited for him to yell, but he sounded too scared to be angry. She pressed a hand to her mouth, realizing that somehow she'd got sidelined; distracted into thinking this was all about casino cheaters. She knew it wasn't; the slides had been clear enough. But she'd blanked it out, trying to hide in the layers.

And what layer was she in now? Sometimes it felt as if she was always acting a part. If she wasn't careful, the real Harry might soon disappear. Maybe one day she'd look at herself in a mirror and see infinity.

She shook her head. Fear was making the voices in her head start to babble.

She clutched the phone, as though clinging to Hunter. Hunter who never role-played, never used sleight of hand. Hunter was real.

'Where are you now?' His throat sounded constricted.

'Riva's casino.'

'Are you okay?'

'I'm fine.'

'You've met Chavez? He buys your cover?'

'I think so. But he's testing me.' She thought of the uneasy truce between herself and Franco. How fragile it was. 'He likes to frighten people, I think.'

Hunter groaned. 'Harry, you need to get out. Please.'

'I know. I will.' She rehearsed Zubiri's number, rattling it off in her head without a hitch. 'I'll do it now.'

Hunter exhaled a long breath. Then his voice grew more urgent. 'Just put the phone down and go. Call me when you're out. If you don't, I swear to Jesus I'll come over there and find you. I mean it.'

Harry swallowed. The lump in her throat was back. She whispered a promise to call, then slowly disconnected, reluctant to cut off his voice. She rubbed her palms along her dress, and reached out once more to punch in Zubiri's number.

Then her hands went still. A shadow had shifted in her peripheral vision. She raised her eyes.

Gideon was standing in the doorway.

24

'What the fuck do you think you're doing?'

Gideon's eyes locked on Harry's, and a small shiver rippled down her spine. How long had he been standing there?

She thrust out her chin and slammed the phone back into its cradle. 'Well, where the hell did *you* get to? I get collared by security and you guys make a run for it. What's that all about?'

She stomped towards the door, but Gideon didn't move. He reached out and grabbed her by the wrist.

'Who were you trying to call?'

His fingers dug hard into her skin. She tried to jerk her arm away, but his hold was lockjaw-tight. She ground her teeth.

'I could have called you or Franco if you'd trusted me with a number and a phone.'

Gideon shoved his face close to hers, and she squinted at his mottled complexion. The skin between the freckles was alabaster-white. He squeezed her wrist and she winced.

'If it's any of your damn business,' she said, 'I was about to call my own phone. I figured one of you had it somewhere, maybe you might have answered. How the hell else was I supposed to reach you?'

Gideon's eyes narrowed, suspicion etched in his face. 'What happened out there? Why did you give the emergency signal?'

'You didn't see her?'

'Who?'

'The woman on the balcony. She was staring right at me, just after you made the move.'

Something flickered across his face. 'Blonde woman? Grey suit?'

So he'd seen Riva too. Harry nodded.

'I'm telling you, her eyes drilled right into me. She knew. Suspicion from the floor, that's what you said to look out for, right?'

'But then you disappeared. That wasn't part of the plan.'

'Your plan sucked. Security collared me right after I left the table, dragged me up to her office. Turns out she's the owner, Riva Mills.'

Harry watched his face. It didn't change. He was eyeing her closely, like a lion with a gazelle, waiting for her to make a mistake.

'What did you tell her?' he said.

'Oh, come on. I just played dumb. She let me off with a warning not to come back.' Harry craned her neck to peer down the hall. 'Look, can we please get out of here? All she has to do is look at her stupid tapes and she can nail us.'

Gideon crushed her wrist till she thought her bones might shatter. A small sound escaped her lips. He glared at her for a moment, then shoved her hand away and stood aside to let her pass.

Harry started off down the hall, massaging her wrist. Gideon's glare scorched her back. She could tell he hadn't entirely swallowed her story, but at least he wasn't acting as though he'd heard her conversation with Hunter.

She found the door to the casino and slipped through, Gideon close behind. Harry picked her way through the crowds. A quick glance at the mezzanine confirmed it was empty, and she wondered if Riva was up in her office, watching through slatted blinds.

Harry scurried through the exit, back out onto the dark street. She hunched against the cold, peering through the cramped alleyway. Unfamiliar music thumped out from one of the bars. A gabble of Spanish eddied around her, but even that seemed alien, the Basque intonation sounding sing-song to her ears. She glanced at the street signs: Basque name on one wall, Spanish on the other. Her chest constricted with an aching disorientation. She felt off-course. Cut adrift from her allies.

How the hell was she going to contact Zubiri now?

Gideon placed a firm hand on her back, and she

228

allowed herself to be piloted out of the Old Quarter and onto the bustling Boulevard. Five minutes later they were back in the car, heading towards the river.

Harry slid a glance at Gideon. The bristles of his buzz cut were standing to attention, like copper filaments magnetized onto his head. The drive seemed to be smoothing his hackles a little, and she decided to let up on Diego's quarrelsome tone for a while. She sighed, and leaned back against the headrest.

'So where's everyone else?'

'Gone back in Clayton's car.'

'How come we didn't travel together? Too risky?'

Gideon shook his head. 'Can't stand the stink of ash that woman leaves in my Volvo.'

Harry raised her eyebrows. It never occurred to her a killer could be fastidious.

'You don't like Ginny much, do you?'

'What's to like? All she does is smoke and drink.'

Harry made a face, as though giving it some thought. 'I have to admit, it's hard to see the connection between her and Franco.'

Gideon snorted. 'Franco's like me. Tough, from the streets. But her.' He curled his lip. 'Top hats and tiaras, that's what she's used to.'

'So how'd they hook up?'

Gideon shrugged. 'She was running some antiques scam back in Nevada. Sculptures, fine art, that sort of thing. Franco got wind of it, checked her out. Decided he could use her.'

'Use her for what?'

'You saw.'

'Oh, come on, Gideon, I'm not stupid. There's more to all this than past-posting at roulette. What's he really up to?'

Gideon scowled and didn't answer. He wrenched the wheel hard, taking a corner too fast. Harry clutched at her seat and took note of his set jaw. He looked sore about something, as though the subject matter stung, and it suddenly occurred to her that maybe Gideon didn't know. Maybe Franco hadn't confided everything in his old friend. And it rankled.

She tried poking at the wound. 'What about you? Is that why you're out here, so Franco can use you too?'

'Franco and me are partners, always have been.'

'But aside from switching chips, why else does he need you? To kill people?'

Gideon threw her a scornful look. 'So what if he does? I never killed anyone yet who didn't deserve it.'

Harry felt a sharp clutch in her stomach, and decided to let the matter drop. They drove in silence for a while, cruising along the deserted riverbank. The water steam-rollered against the walls, churning up waves high enough to surf. She glimpsed a landmark: the Zurriola Bridge, backlit by the dazzling glass auditorium. The apartment wasn't far away.

They pulled up outside it a few minutes later. Harry eyed the tiers of dark shutters, picturing the brown

230

apartment where she'd been a prisoner for a day. Her mind flipped to Hunter, to her promise to come out. Her throat ached.

She followed Gideon upstairs to the third-floor apartment. Ginny was lounging on the sofa inside, and acknowledged their arrival with a lazy eyebrow-lift. She'd swapped her dress for leggings and a baggy T-shirt, the neckline so stretched it bared both her shoulders. Even dressed down, she still looked elegant, and it wasn't hard to see how she'd fit into the world of fine art.

Ginny's gaze flicked past them towards the door, and Harry turned to see Franco stepping inside the room. His aquiline features looked dark and fierce, and he turned the full force of them on Gideon.

'What the fuck happened back there?'

Gideon raised his palms in a placating gesture and started to fill him in. Given his distrust of Harry, his account was surprisingly objective. She had to guess any suggestion that she'd given him the slip would call his own performance into question.

Gideon finished up and Harry held her breath. Franco turned towards her with a dark, unfocused look, and she sensed Ginny shrinking into the sofa like a retracting snail. Harry's mind flashed on Riva's brother. *Bullet wound to the head. Aged eighteen.* She dug her nails into her palms. Which side of his mood-flips would Franco come down on now?

'So how did she look?'

Harry blinked. It took her a second to realize he was talking about Riva. He'd sounded hesitant, as though bracing himself for the answer. It was the way a person asked about an old lover or an arch-enemy. Though in Harry's experience, there was often little difference between the two.

'What kind of question is that?' she said. 'The woman looked pissed off, what do you think? She suspected me of cheating in her casino. Makes me wonder how the hell you guys haven't been caught before.'

Franco gave her an enigmatic smile. 'Maybe I want to get caught. Eventually.'

Harry frowned, and noticed a puzzled look creasing Gideon's face. Franco stepped closer, a forcefield of aggression simmering around him.

'You could have made a run for it,' he said.

'What the hell for? I've still got a job to do, right?'

He regarded her for a long, tense moment, then nodded towards the kitchen area. Harry followed his gaze. A laptop case sat in plain view on the counter.

'It was Stevie's.' Franco smiled, spreading out his palms in a magnanimous gesture. 'Now it's yours.'

Ginny jerked her head up. Harry's skin tingled, aware that she'd just been promoted. Officially inducted into the ranks. Her eyes were transfixed by the black case on the counter, her mind racing at the possibilities of what she might find inside it.

Gideon grew restless. 'Hey, Franco. You sure? She could still be lying.'

But Franco wasn't listening. He nodded at Harry.

'You can examine it later, pick up where he left off. But for now, get changed. You're coming with me.' He clicked his fingers. 'No more tests. It's time I showed you something.'

25

Marty hunched tighter into the doorway, his eyes fixed on the apartment block entrance across the street.

He shivered in the dark. He'd only been watching for five minutes, but already his bones were chilled. He checked his watch. Franco usually made a move around about now. All Marty wanted was a sign the guy was still in the same apartment.

He leaned against the wall, its dampness seeping through his jacket. The streets were quiet, apart from the angry rush of the river water close by. Marty shuddered. For a moment he was back on the bridge: icy waves punching through his airways; pooling in his throat. He wiped a slick of sweat from his forehead. Fucking river had given him the chills.

Light spilled from the entrance across the street. Marty straightened up and pressed back against the doorway.

Franco and the dark, Spanish-looking girl came out of the apartment block and climbed into a nearby car. Marty watched it pull away, his gaze following the glow of rear lights for a while. He watched them cruise along by the river, then veer towards the promenade that skirted the cliff-face of the bay.

Was Franco taking the girl to the warehouse?

Marty frowned, then dragged himself out of the doorway and trudged away from the river towards the well-lit city streets. He guessed Franco trusted her, but Marty wasn't so sure. He'd planned to pass on his suspicions to Franco, but then he'd seen Fat-Boy's face on TV. The poor guy's throat had been slit. Marty swallowed against a burning in his own larynx. His landlady had translated the story for him. The newsflash hadn't mentioned any link to Riva's casino, but the whole thing had spooked him and his instincts had been to lie low for a while.

He glanced back at the road the car had taken, and thought of what the girl would find when she got there. Marty had seen the warehouse before. Franco made the same trip every two or three days, and sometimes Marty would lie in wait by the pier to watch.

He'd always known there was more at stake here than roulette past-posting. Franco was just goading Riva with that, the same way Marty had goaded the English guy at the start of his poker scam. It was part of the set-up, a taunt to provoke the mark into a particular frame of mind.

235

Marty tugged his jacket tighter across his chest. He pictured the warehouse, and the men Franco mixed with down there: violent types with personal bodyguards; hard men who demanded respect and killed when they didn't get it.

Something rustled in the shadows behind him, and he snapped his gaze over his shoulder. The street was empty. He quickened his pace. Ever since Toledo had threatened him on the bridge, he'd had a sense he was being followed.

Marty worked his way back to the streets of the Old Quarter, searching for the warm glow of any bar that was still open. He didn't plan on returning to his rented room. Toledo could find him too easily there.

Sweat flash-flooded down his back. Toledo had given him two days to deliver up Franco. Maybe he should just tell him where the guy was holed up. As betrayals went, what could be easier? Marty winced, his head throbbing. Or maybe he should say nothing. Protect Franco. Let him run with his game plan, and sell Riva down the river instead.

Jesus. Which one was he supposed to rat out?

He groaned softly. Why the hell should he care about either of them after everything they'd done? Memories bubbled up, but he smothered them down, burying old loyalties. Instead he focused on a more familiar aspect of the problem: the fast buck versus thinking big. The short or the long con.

Echoing voices snagged his attention, and he followed the sound to a nearby bar in the Plaza de la Constitución.

Patrons were chatting beneath the shadowy archways, their voices hollow in the natural echo chamber of the plaza. Marty slipped under the portico, glanced left and right, then ducked into the cosy bar.

Warmth and glowing lights coddled him like a blanket. He eased his way towards the counter, another flash of sweat drenching him like a tide. His brain seemed to shimmy, and he clutched the bar for support. Jesus. That fucking river. He needed a drink. He had enough money to get through the night, but after that he'd be cleaned out. He closed his eyes. Maybe tomorrow he'd have the energy to drum up some more cash.

Marty's skin tingled, and he dragged his eyes open. Someone was watching him. He knew it as surely as if they'd tapped him on the shoulder. He slid his gaze to the right. An attractive redhead was sitting at the bar, stealing looks at him over the rim of her glass. It took him a second, but he knew who she was. The same redhead he'd flirted with last week in Riva's casino.

She gave him a shy smile and raised her wine glass in salute. 'Remember me?'

'Hey, sure I do.' Marty scanned the vicinity for the man she'd been with, the toady-looking guy whose black chip Marty had stolen. There was no sign of him. Marty moved up beside her and smiled.

'So how's the wheel been spinning for you lately?'

'Oh, you know.' She looked at her drink. 'You win some, you lose some. But I'm doing okay.'

She flashed him another smile, though this one looked

kind of brittle. She was older than he'd first thought, maybe late thirties, same as him. It was beginning to show around her eyes. But her hair was ageless: a corkscrew mane the colour of warm copper. Okay, so the shade probably came out of a bottle, but Marty didn't care. He admired her for going to the trouble.

She drained her glass, then nodded towards the door. 'You snuck in here like a felon. Are you hiding from someone?'

Her accent held a trace of southern belle that sent a warm buzz down Marty's spine. He shook his head and moved a little closer.

'Just some people I don't want to talk to right now.' He paused, glancing around the bar. 'Where's your, uh, husband?'

The redhead laughed. 'He's not my "uh-husband".' She looked at her hands. 'But I guess he does pay the bills.'

Marty's eyes lingered on what he could see of her curves, and for the first time he noticed the greenish bruising along her arms. She shot him a mischievous glance from under her lashes.

'Actually, he's away for a few days.'

Something warm pumped through Marty's veins, a sudden anaesthetic for the chill in his aching bones. Before he could respond, the barman arrived with the redhead's bill and Marty took the opportunity to peek at himself in the mirror behind the bar. He looked like shit. His colour was bad, and his eyes were ringed with circles darker than eggplants. But at least his hair was thick, still mostly blond. And people always told him he had a likeable face.

The barman was rattling something in Spanish, and Marty turned to find him holding up the bill and scowling at them both. The redhead was clutching her purse, her cheeks stained a hot pink. Marty glanced at her tab. It wasn't much, just a few drinks, but the notes in her hand didn't cover it.

The redhead threw him a mortified glance. 'I'm so sorry to ask, but is there any way—'

'Hey, my pleasure.' Marty fumbled for his wallet and managed to cover her shortfall and buy another drink for them both.

'Thanks.' The redhead's voice was small. 'I appreciate that. You caught me all tapped-out.'

'I guess the wheel wasn't spinning your way after all.'

She flashed him a grateful look, and Marty stowed his near-empty wallet away. He wasn't naive. He knew better than anyone there was a possibility he was being scammed. Maybe she'd waited all night for a mug like him to show. He took in the fiery cheeks, the flaming hair. So what if he traded a few drinks for her company? Right now, it seemed like a fair exchange.

The barman set their drinks on the counter, and the redhead clinked her glass against Marty's with a smile.

'To a gentleman.' She sipped her wine, then flicked him a curious glance. 'So, these people you're avoiding. You going to hide from them forever?'

'Maybe. I just need to make a decision first.' Marty looked down at his whisky. 'Guess I'm not ready to make it yet.'

'So decide not to decide. Works for me all the time.'

Marty smiled and sipped his drink, the whisky blazing a trail along his insides. Sweat washed over the back of his neck, and his vision blurred slightly. The redhead placed a cool hand on his arm.

'You okay? You don't look so good.'

Marty blinked, tried to laugh the moment off. 'Didn't sleep much last night. Couple of whiskies will knock me into shape.'

He swigged at his drink. Maybe the alcohol would burn away the toxins from that damn river. He'd spent the whole night lathered in sweat, his sleep fractured with feverish dreams about Andy. An image burst into his head: panicky crowds, people screaming; Andy's skinny body crumpled on the ground, a dark hole in his head. Marty slugged down the rest of his drink.

The redhead squeezed his arm, cutting back into his thoughts.

'I've got a better idea.' Her voice was soft and seductive. 'Why don't you come back with me? I may be broke, but I've still got a hotel room that's paid up for a few days.'

Heat flashed through Marty's body. He looked into her face, read the generosity and hunger in her eyes. She was snatching comfort. Some temporary relief, same as him. And what the hell was wrong with that?

She slid off her chair. He eyed her curves, then followed her out of the bar. He thought about Toledo, and the sanctuary her hotel room would offer. He'd lie low a while longer.

Decide not to decide.

His life had been one long list of bad decisions. Maybe this way, he wouldn't add to it for a while.

26

'Where are we going?'

Franco didn't answer. He eased the car away from the river, and Harry flicked him a glance. Street lights had sculpted wide planes on his face, accentuating his Indian chief look. Harry bit her lip. Right now, he was calm, almost benign. The last thing she wanted was to stir him up with too many questions.

They veered left towards the avenue that by now Harry recognized as Alameda del Boulevard. She hugged her chest, cradling her own throbbing heart-beat. Her instincts told her she was about to see some-thing important, but her mind flicked back to McArdle. *He knew too much*. Harry's spine hummed. Once Franco confided his plans, could he ever really afford to let her go?

They cruised to a halt at a set of lights, and Franco

gestured out the window. 'You haven't seen much of the city since you got here, have you?'

Harry stared at him. His tone was sympathetic, as though she'd just been too darned busy for sightseeing. She shook her head, marvelling at how easily he could doctor reality with the ludicrous.

'No, I haven't.'

'You got family around here?'

Harry pictured the grave in Cementerio de Polloe. 'No.'

'You don't look Basque, you know that?'

'I'm told there's a fisherman from Cadiz in the blood-line. You can blame him.'

Franco nodded, as if that settled the matter. The lights changed, and he eased the engine into gear. 'My old lady looked like a throwback from the Middle Ages. Long chin, big face.' He shook his head. 'Fierce woman. Only argument my old man ever won with her was when he called me Franco, after his own father.'

Harry shifted in her seat, not sure what to make of his cosy tone. Getting close to him felt dangerous, like playing a game of 'What's the Time, Mr Wolf'. You stepped nearer and nearer, until eventually the wolf just whirled around and grabbed you.

Franco made a sudden left, criss-crossing through the streets till he'd jumbled up Harry's internal map of the city. He slid her a sideways glance.

'You worked with McArdle often?'

'Not really.' She peered out the window. All these

café-lined roads were starting to look the same. 'We blitzed a couple of corporate databases, held them to ransom, but that was about it. Mostly, I prefer to work alone. So did McArdle.'

'Yeah, me too.' Franco nodded to himself, as though mulling it over. 'But sometimes you need help, whether you like it or not.'

'Maybe.' Harry turned and studied his dark, rough-hewn profile. 'But if it was me, I still wouldn't tell my associates everything.'

The look he gave her was shrewd. 'Clever girl. Tell nobody nothing they don't need to know. Especially the guy below you in the foodchain, right? Just in case he gets ideas.'

'Like Gideon, you mean?'

'Hey, I love the guy like a brother, don't get me wrong. But some things I just don't tell him.' He fixed his hard, black eyes on hers. 'And you won't tell him anything you see here tonight, either.'

She held her palms up, as though fending the notion off. 'Believe me, the less I talk to Gideon the better. He and I don't exactly hit it off.'

'Don't knock him, he's a good guy. The kind you want beside you in a pinch.' Franco slammed the car up a gear. 'But he doesn't need to know the whole picture. Nobody does.'

Harry was saved from answering by the sound of Franco's phone. He dug it out of his shirt and glared at the caller ID before answering in terse tones. His face tensed as he listened to the voice on the other end. Then he said,

'I'm busy, Gabino. I pay you to deal with this shit yourself.'

He listened some more, turning his face away. His responses were curt and monosyllabic, probably edited heavily for Harry's benefit.

Finally, he cursed and ended the call, then glowered across at Harry.

'I'm taking you back to Gideon. Something's come up.'

He speed-dialled a number and waited for the call to pick up. When it didn't, he whacked his fist against the wheel.

'*Shit!* Where the fuck is he?'

He spun the car in a one-eighty turn, heading back the way they'd just come. Harry made an impatient gesture.

'Look, I don't need Gideon to babysit. Just drop me back at the apartment, I can wait on my own.'

'Maybe you can, maybe you can't. But it's like Gideon said . . .' He gave her a direct look. 'You could still be lying.'

'But—'

'You're coming with me.'

They drove in silence for the next few minutes, Franco making frequent checks in his rear-view mirror. Eventually, they fetched up back at the river, the glass auditorium sparkling across the water. He drove along the embankment away from the city lights, winding his way towards the deserted headland where the river collided with the sea.

The cliff road was slick with ocean water. Waves exploded against the rocks, surging over the promenade barriers. Franco geared down, preparing to round the peninsula. Then an avalanche of water slammed into the car, slewing it sideways, and Harry's muscles went rigid. Franco corrected their course, slashing the car through the deluge.

Harry eyed the churning sea. Hulking waves prowled off the coast, waiting for their turn at the rocks. She shuddered. She'd never had much of an affinity for the ocean, despite all her seafaring ancestors.

Franco came to what looked like the end of the road. He pulled over, killing the engine.

'Let's go.'

Harry's heart started banging. She climbed out of the car. Needles of spray pricked her cheeks, and the boom of the sea was deafening. She followed Franco away from the cliffs, the wind cutting through her borrowed sweater and jeans. They picked their way over drenched paths, angling across the headland, until gradually the sound of the ocean fell away and Harry could detect the snap of tarpaulins in the wind. They'd emerged at a small fishing harbour.

Franco turned to face her, stopping her up short. His fists were clenched and his eyes held a menacing glint.

'You're going to see stuff here. Stuff that's dangerous

for you to know. That makes you dangerous to me.' He took a step closer. 'You don't tell anyone, not Gideon, not Ginny, no one. You got that, Diego?'

Harry lifted her chin. 'Is this another one of your tests?'

'You could say that. Fail this one, and you're dead.'

Harry felt her stomach tighten. He turned away and they continued along the dark wharf. Masts and rigging *tink-tinked* in the wind. The air was rank with the smell of old fish, and absurdly, she pictured her ancestors hauling in whales. She clung to the notion that they might be watching over her now.

Something growled in the dark. The sound vibrated along the quays. Then a vast blocky shape loomed out of the shadows, and Harry's eyes widened. It was a heavy-duty, armoured truck. Its headlights were doused, the driver's cab dark. It looked almost ghostly as it rolled, seemingly unaided, along the pier.

The truck wheeled towards a bank of unlit warehouses, its tyres making *slick-slick* sounds in the wet. Brakes hissed as it lumbered to a halt. Then the driver clambered down and Franco went to meet him, signalling for Harry to wait. She hunched against the wind, trying to guess at their cargo.

The two men conferred in low tones. Then Franco moved away towards the nearest warehouse, beckoning at Harry over his shoulder. She dog-trotted after him across the wharf, her step faltering as a man with a machine gun slid out of the shadows up ahead. He blocked the warehouse door, his stance combative. At a signal from Franco, he lowered his gun and turned to hit a lever behind him.

The warehouse door rumbled to one side, hosing the wharf with light from the interior. Harry moved closer. A rhythmic, rustling sound filled the air, like thousands of fluttering wings. She frowned, straining to identify it. Then she followed Franco inside.

The first thing she saw were the machines. Hundreds of them, like neat faxes, lined up on benches. They whirred like mechanical grasshoppers, spitting out mounds of paper at top speed while teams of men fed more stacks in from the other side.

Only it wasn't paper. Harry peered closer. It was currency. Thousands of banknotes, swishing out of the machines in a blur. *Flick-flick-flick*. Like the riffle of a roomful of cards.

She whipped her gaze around the warehouse. Bundles of cash covered every available surface. Pallets of the stuff were piled high on the floor and stacked on industrial shelves. Forklift trucks beeped around the storehouse, shifting blocks of shrink-wrapped notes like bales of hay.

Harry turned to Franco, who was watching his men unloading the truck. She stared at the containers they'd already dragged in: strongboxes, suitcases, duffel bags, bin liners. Another crew of men hauled the containers away, upending them onto benches. Harry gaped at the contents: stockpiled wads of grubby, dog-eared cash.

'What's going on?' She glanced at the machines still

whisking out banknotes. 'Is this some kind of counterfeit operation?'

Franco snorted. 'No funny money here, Diego. This is the real deal. At least, it better be.' He nodded at a group of men shining pen-shaped devices over the notes. 'Random ultra-violet checks. Last thing we need is to get caught because some cheapskate's passing duds.'

Harry squinted at the thin, crinkled bundles they'd unloaded from the truck. The wads were made up of small denominations, mostly ten-euro notes, and secured by a final banknote wrapped around the middle.

'Dealers' wraps,' Franco said, following her gaze. Now that he'd taken the step of allowing her in, he seemed almost chatty again. 'Street money, straight from the junkies. Probably got high levels of dope smeared all over it.'

Harry frowned. 'You said you weren't a drug dealer.'

'Hey, I'm not. Why the fuck would I get my hands dirty with that shit?' He looked offended. Then he held his palms up and gave an exaggerated shrug. 'Sure, some of my clients are drug dealers. But I've got contracts with a lot of organizations: smugglers, embezzlers, corrupt governments. One thing they got in common? Boatloads of cash they want to hide.'

Harry flashed on Zubiri's slides. Suddenly, that nine hundred million was finding a context. Franco turned and threaded his way between the benches, heading for a door on the other side of the warehouse. Harry glanced at the banks of cash-counting machines, at the floor-to-ceiling shelves where parcels of banknotes were packed into every corner. She scurried after Franco.

'This isn't your money?'

'Hell, no. I'm a broker. A facilitator.' Franco repeated the word to himself, as though he liked how it sounded. He reached the door, and Harry caught up with him.

'So you hide other people's money?'

He turned to face her, his hand on the doorknob. 'My clients have gone to a lot of trouble trying to make this cash. Just hiding it isn't enough. These people want to spend it.' A slow smile spread across his face. 'But you can't spend dirty money till it's been washed, now can you?'

Harry's ears buzzed. All around her, whispering banknotes fluttered through the counting machines. She felt her brain flicker in response.

'So you're a money launderer. Is that it?'

Franco's smile grew wider. Then he spread out his arms and gave her a playful bow.

'Welcome to my counting house, Diego.'

27

'Wait in here, I've some business to see to.'

Franco opened the door and flicked on a switch, ushering Harry inside. Strip lights stuttered overhead. Franco moved off, closing the door behind him, and Harry turned to do a quick survey.

The room was kitted out as an office, though with little concession to decor, making do with the same stone walls and concrete floor as the loading bays outside. The overall effect was stark and chilly.

And there was no sign of a phone.

She flicked a look at the closed door, then scooted behind the desk, sliding out drawers, sifting through paperwork. The documents didn't tell her much: invoices, receipts, bills of lading; the paper trail for cargo haulage.

She glanced back at the door. Outside, she could hear Franco's raised voice. She edged across the room to a bank of filing cabinets and jiggled the drawers, one by one. They were locked.

Her eyes strayed to the wall behind the desk. It was covered with an oversized map of the world, a rash of red pins studded across its surface. She moved closer for a better look.

'My business empire.'

She spun around to find Franco watching her from the door. He crossed the room and dropped into a chair behind the desk.

'I'm running out of push-pins,' he said. 'Have a seat.'

Harry did as she was told, her eyes straying towards the map on the wall. Franco leaned back and propped his feet up on the desk.

'Know how much dirty money gets washed around the globe every year? Three trillion dollars, maybe even four. That's one big sea of money, Diego.'

He looked at her expectantly, as though waiting for her jaw to drop. She played along.

'Wow, three trillion. I'm not even sure how many zeros that has.' She pictured the world's oceans awash with greenbacks, and in truth it wasn't that hard to look impressed.

Outside, the warehouse door clattered shut. They must have finished unloading the truck. Harry hitched a thumb over her shoulder.

'All those duffel bags and binliners. Where did they come from?'

'They belong to a client of mine. He delivers them to

the drop centres I've set up along the coast. Dummy retailers, restaurant fronts, places like that. My trucks round the money up and bring it here.'

Harry blinked. Franco looked as if he was enjoying the effect all this was having on her. Forklifts beeped and clanged outside, and she turned her head, following the sound. Then something on the far wall hijacked her attention.

A dark brown stain had muddied the brick. It had spattered from head-height down to the floor, exploding across the wall as though something had burst against it. At the epicentre of the mess was a cluster of small holes.

Harry stared at it for a moment, then dragged her gaze back to Franco. He gave her a blank look. Apparently, the bloodstain didn't warrant explanation and, under the circumstances, Harry wasn't about to ask. She scrambled back to a safer topic:

'So where does your client's cash go from here?'

'Ah.' Franco smiled as though he'd been waiting for the question all day. 'It slips back into the system. Goes legit. Worst thing a guy can have is large sums of unexplained cash.'

'But there must be close to a million stacked up out there. How can you hide all that?'

'With a little artistry and hocus-pocus. Peekaboo finance. It's all about sleight of hand, Diego.'

Harry frowned. She'd heard him use those words before. 'Like chip-switching, you mean?'

He gave her a sharp look. 'Yeah. Like chip-switching. Best place to hide money is with a load of other money, right? Just like past-posting a chip. Sneak it into place quietly enough, and no one can prove it doesn't belong.'

'I still don't get it. How can you make that amount of money look legit?'

Franco swung his legs to the ground, straightening up in his chair. 'Look, first we get the cash into the banks. That way it stops being street money, and becomes a number on a screen.'

'But wouldn't the banks question such a large deposit?'

'Good point, Diego.' He made a gun with his thumb and forefinger, and cocked it in her direction. 'Anything over ten grand triggers paperwork from the bank. So we break it up.'

'A million euros into ten-grand bundles?'

'Think about it. Twenty-five guys – smurfs, we call 'em – each depositing nine thousand nine hundred euros into ten banks a day. Shit, that way I can place a million into the banks in a single morning.'

Harry nodded, acknowledging his math. 'Okay. Then what?'

'Then we mix the money up, move it around. Switch it to other banks, other countries, other currencies. Flip it in and out of shell companies and different investments. Bonds, stocks, real estate, whatever. We scramble it up and create so much paperwork that the trail's impossible to follow.'

Franco tilted his chair back and contemplated his map

with a smile. 'That money outside, for instance. Tonight it gets couriered to smurfs across the province, and tomorrow it goes into the banks. After that, I transfer it to an account in Gibraltar, then switch it to London via a Federal Reserve bank in New York. In London, I'll convert it to certificates of deposit, which I'll use as collateral for a bank loan generated in the Bahamas . . .'

Harry felt her eyes start to cross. Franco kept on talking.

'. . . then I'll wire the loan proceeds back to a shell company in Gibraltar, and from there to a company in Chile, then from Chile to my client in Colombia.'

Harry shook her head. 'Sorry, I don't follow.'

'That's the point, Diego. You're not meant to.' Franco gave her a lazy smile. 'For one particular client, I formed thirty different companies and opened eighty bank accounts in fifty countries around the world. Shells within shells. Bewilder and confuse. Sounds complex, but the whole thing can be managed in a few days.'

Harry was still hung up a few sentences back, trying to figure out some of the details. 'But I thought the banks were tightening up on stuff like this. Getting tougher on money-laundering regulations.'

'Most of them are. Cayman Islands isn't the haven it used to be, that's for sure. But who needs banks? There's plenty of other ways to move cash and clean it up at the same time.' He nodded towards the door. 'That street money belongs to a Colombian. It's earmarked to pay his crop-growers and other personal expenses back home.

255

So he needs to get it back to Colombia in clean, legit pesos. I can broker that without any bank trail.'

Harry noted the smirk on his face. The guy was showing off, but what did she care? She'd stroke his ego all night if it kept his mood sweet.

'Okay,' she said. 'I'll bite. How?'

'Easy. I buy a few thousand fridges with those euros of his, then export them to a white-goods importer in Colombia. The importer pays for them in legitimate pesos which he deposits into my client's Colombian account. My client gets his clean pesos, the importer saves on exchange duties.' Franco beamed and spread out his arms. 'Suddenly, I'm a currency dealer. And I've plenty more moves where that one came from.'

Harry took in the smug, hey-presto gesture and didn't doubt it for a minute. She glanced around the makeshift office.

'You do all this from here?'

His smile faded, and a small pulse jumped in his jaw. Harry felt the mood-change like a flash of sudden heat, and rushed to make amends.

'Hey, not that I'm criticizing, but it just sounds like a sophisticated enterprise.'

Franco glared at her, and she held her breath. Dealing with him was like trying to stroke a rattlesnake. Finally he blinked, dissipating some of the heat.

'I operate from all over,' he said. 'No single point of failure, that's the key. Spread the risk. Different warehouses, different trucks, different drop centres. I rotate the drivers, the couriers, the smurfs, the lawyers.' He leaned forward and fixed her with his black-eyed stare. 'Point is, Diego, this is a big operation. Took me five years to set it up. I only know of one other outfit that could match it.'

His cheeks took on an ugly flush, a reminder that somewhere his rapid cycle of moods was still looping.

Harry heard a soft click, and his gaze cut past her to the door. She checked over her shoulder. A tall, stooped man had shuffled into the room. Franco frowned, addressing him in tetchy Spanish.

'What do you want, Gabino?'

The man called Gabino looked at the floor. 'We're short a courier.'

'How the fuck did that happen?'

Gabino shifted his feet, and flicked a glance at the grisly discolouration on the wall. 'Chico . . .'

He let the name hang. Franco stared at the bloodstain, as though noticing it for the first time. Then he clicked his fingers and pointed.

'You do it, Gabino. Double shift, back to Bilbao. We'll draft in another replacement for Chico tomorrow.' He jerked a thumb at the wall. 'And get that cleaned up.'

Something flickered across Gabino's face, then he nodded and slipped from the room. Harry turned back to Franco. This time, she had to ask the question.

'What happened to Chico?'

'He nosed around, knew too much. Then got caught with his hands in the till.' Franco shrugged. 'If I hadn't killed him, sooner or later one of my clients would have done it.'

Harry suppressed a shudder. Knowledge was dangerous around this guy. Already she knew too much, but there was still another question she had to ask.

'What about McArdle? What happened to him? Do you know who killed him?'

'Oh, I know all right.' The set of Franco's mouth hardened. 'That was down to Riva Mills.'

Harry squinted at him, her face forming the question long before she could find the words. 'What? But that doesn't make any sense. Why would she kill him? Did she even know who he was?'

Franco didn't answer. His eyes turned matte as he seemed to look inward. Eventually, he said,

'We'll get to that later. It was McArdle's own fault, he probably got careless.' Franco's dull black eyes were challenging. 'I'm hoping you're better than that.'

'Well, God, so am I. But we'll never know till you tell me what the hell it is you want me to hack.'

He looked at his watch. 'I'd hoped to do that tonight, but it's getting late. We'll be here for a while.' He got to his feet. 'But tomorrow, I'll show you.'

28

By the time Harry got back to the apartment it was close to four in the morning, and the place was as dark as a cave.

She paused in the hallway, letting her eyes adjust, while Franco locked the apartment door behind her. The room smelled of pizza. The takeout boxes were stacked on the kitchen counter, and Harry had a sudden vision of the banknotes stacked in the warehouse. It was hard to reconcile that hoard of cash with Franco's modest lifestyle.

Harry squinted at the boxes, then raked her gaze back over the counter. McArdle's laptop wasn't there.

She turned to Franco. 'The laptop—'

'In the morning.' He stuffed his keys into his pocket and headed down the hall to his room.

Harry stared after him. He'd been tight-lipped for most of the drive home, his chattiness snuffed out as though someone had flipped a switch. She turned her attention to the living room, groping for a light as she scanned the shapes and shadows. Right now, the laptop was her life-line; a precious connection to the outside world. To Zubiri.

Her eyes picked out a shadowy bulk on the sofa, and her hand froze against the wall. Gideon was lying there, covered to the waist with a blanket. Her nerve endings tingled. She could tell by his stillness that he was watching her in the dark.

Reluctantly, she let her arm drop and made her way down the hall. Hunting for the laptop at four in the morning might be hard to explain, even for Diego.

She let herself into the room that she shared with Ginny and found her perched on the edge of her bed, clutching a pack of cigarettes. Beside her, a laptop was plugged in and humming. Harry stared.

'Is that McArdle's?'

Ginny shrugged. 'Thought you might like to take a look at it when you got in.'

Ginny fumbled for a cigarette, lighting up with jerky movements. She still wore the oversized T-shirt from earlier, but had slung a roomy leather jacket over her shoulders for warmth. The ballerina bun was gone and her dark hair hung loose, slightly kinked from its recent stranglehold.

Harry sat on the bed opposite and took the laptop on her knees, waving off choking drifts of smoke. She adjusted the screen. It was waiting for McArdle's logon credentials.

'I don't suppose you know his password?'

Ginny laughed. 'You must be joking. Stevie was paranoid about stuff like that.'

Her smile slipped, and she lifted the collar of her jacket to her lips, holding it there like a comforter. She'd wiped away her pancake make-up, and without it her skin looked frail and washed out. Harry took in the dark circles and large, tired eyes. Had she waited up all night just to watch Harry work on the laptop?

'What made him so paranoid?' Harry said.

'Everything was a secret with Stevie. He loved all that cloak-and-dagger stuff. Secret codes, invisible ink. It was like a game.' Ginny wrapped an arm around her waist beneath the jacket and rocked gently on the bed. 'It got worse when he caught Clayton sniffing around his laptop. After that, Stevie didn't trust his own shadow.'

'Clayton? Why would he be interested?'

Ginny shrugged. 'That's what Clayton does. Tries to nose out information he can use against you later. Tried it once with me, but I don't have any secrets from Franco.'

She slid backwards against the wall, tucking her legs up under her, the leather collar still pressed to her lips. Peeling off the make-up had stripped away the years, and the jaded showgirl was gone. Now, she looked like a freshly scrubbed college student with good bones.

'The password,' Ginny said. 'Is it a problem?'

'Depends.'

Harry studied her face, wondering what made her so interested. Then she reached for the laptop case lying on the floor and started rummaging through it. Her own satchel was stuffed with paraphernalia: CDs, screwdrivers, antennae, storage devices, cables. But apart from blank paper, envelopes and pens, all McArdle had were five unmarked memory sticks.

She spread them out on the bed. 'Is this all the gear he had?'

'As far as I know.'

Harry frowned, then plugged one of the memory sticks into the laptop and rebooted the machine. McArdle may have travelled light, but any self-respecting hacker carried a lock pick for jimmying passwords.

She tracked the reboot, then interrupted it, redirecting the laptop to take orders from the memory stick, just as she had with Zubiri's. But the memory stick played dumb. Harry whipped it out and tried the next one. Nothing.

Shit.

She jammed in the remaining memory sticks and on the last one got a bite. The stick issued orders. The machine pricked its ears. Then it rolled over like a dog and let Harry massage its insides.

She let out a long breath. Ginny knelt forward on the bed, craning her neck to look, the oily incense of leather permeating her nicotine fug.

'What are you doing?'

'Blanking his password.'

Harry tinkered with McArdle's credentials, as she had with Zubiri's, and rebooted the machine. She sailed through the login who-goes-there and swooped into McArdle's files.

Ginny made a small sound. 'Wow. As easy as that.'

Harry worked the keys, hunting for outbound connections. There weren't any. No wireless links; no open channels. The laptop was as cut off as she was.

Harry closed her eyes briefly, aware that Ginny was watching. Then she plugged the memory sticks back in and scrutinized their contents. Two were blank, but the others were packed with an arsenal of familiar weapons: scanners, sniffers, crackers, tracers, botnets, Trojans, zero-day exploits. A line-up of hacker missiles, primed and ready for attack.

But none of them could wire her up with Zubiri.

Harry bit back a curse. Her legs twitched with the need for action. She dumped the laptop on the bed and strode the perimeters of the room, scouring the walls and peering behind the beds. No phone jacks for a dial-up, no dangling cables.

'If you're looking for an internet connection,' Ginny said, 'Stevie used a modem stick thingy.'

Harry wheeled around to face her. 'Where is it?'

'Franco took it.' Ginny slipped her legs under the covers and sat up against the wall, her shoulders still hunched under the jacket. 'Said you wouldn't be needing it for a while.'

'Shit!'

Panic corkscrewed up through Harry's chest. She caught Ginny's frown, and tried to backtrack with a show of pique.

'How does Franco expect me to work if I can't download any decent tools?'

263

'Stevie would've managed it.'

'Yeah, well Stevie probably had a phone. Look, why don't you lend me yours? I can piggyback on its modem, get to the internet that way.' Or better still, just put in a call to Zubiri.

Ginny reached for an ashtray and stubbed out her cigarette as though she was crushing a bug. 'Sorry. Don't have one. And even if I did, Franco's given strict instructions. You're to be kept incommunicado until he says otherwise.'

Harry groaned and flopped back down on the bed. Fatigue dragged at her limbs like pondweed, but her brain was too strung out for sleep. She lifted the laptop back to her knees. McArdle's files could still tell her something.

She plunged into the hard drive, scouting out its terrain: data files, system files, activity logs, installed programs. She thought of her own laptop with its powerful forensic tools for dissecting and analysing hard drives. Without her kit, this could take a while.

She glanced at Ginny, who was watching her closely. 'Gideon said you used to run an antiques scam. Fine art, or something.'

Ginny lifted an eyebrow. 'Said with a sneer, I bet.'

'He's not exactly a fan of yours, is he?'

'We come from different sides of the tracks, in case you hadn't noticed, and it really pisses him off. Nothing like a silver spoon for stirring up resentment in other people.' Ginny gave a lazy smile. 'I wave it in front of him whenever I get the chance.'

'You were born into money?'

'The country club set.'

'And you know about art?'

'Grew up with it. My mother considered herself a connoisseur.' Ginny leaned forward and hugged her blanketed shins, resting her cheek on her knees. 'I know how to act around the big auction houses. Cheating them was easy.'

'How did you do it?'

'I posed as a wealthy client, got them to trust me. Then I persuaded them to hand over paintings and heirlooms before my cheques went through. They bounced, of course.'

'But why turn to fraud? Why not settle for family money, if there was so much of it?'

Ginny lifted her head and frowned. 'Where's the bloody fun in that?'

Harry made a rueful face, acknowledging the sentiment. Then she turned her attention back to the screen and skimmed through a few more files: travel documents; music files; dozens of photographs, including some of Ginny. The girl shifted on the bed.

'What exactly are you doing?'

'Just checking out Stevie's tools in case I need to use them for Franco.' Harry flicked her a glance. 'What made you hook up with a man like him, anyway? The guy's a loon.'

'What's it to you?'

'Just making conversation. You know. Girl talk.'

Ginny looked sulky and slid further down in the bed. 'He wasn't so bad at first. Passionate, dangerous. Sexy as hell. But the mood swings are getting worse.'

'Sounds to me like he should be on medication.'

Ginny's shrug was listless. 'Even Gideon says he wasn't always like this. I'll say one thing for Gideon, he's pretty even-keeled. Keeps Franco on track.'

Harry flashed on the blood-soaked wall in the warehouse. Even Gideon couldn't control Franco's rages all of the time. She blocked the image out and turned back to the screen, nibbling at her lip. Something wasn't right with these files.

Ginny's voice cut into her thoughts. 'Franco bullied Stevie. So did Clayton. At least Gideon left him alone. But I'm the only one around here who misses him.' She touched the leather collar of her jacket back to her lips. 'I wear his clothes sometimes. Makes me feel like he's still close. Stupid, isn't it?'

Harry gave her a level look. That explained the man-sized shirts. She shook her head and said, 'Not really.'

Ginny's gaze was distant, snagged on some internal landscape. Then her eyes refocused on Harry.

'Be careful of Franco,' she said. 'He's still testing you.'

Harry threw her a wry look. 'Maybe he's the one who should be careful. Last time he tested me, he got stabbed in the arm, remember?'

Ginny contemplated her for a moment. 'You know, I didn't like you at first. Thought you were cocky. Still do, as a matter of fact.' She shrugged off her jacket, letting it drop to the floor, then rolled over to face the wall. 'But you're not so bad.'

'Well, thanks, that's good to know.'

Harry's eyes strayed to the discarded jacket. The leather was cracked and wrinkled, like an old woman's face, and on the back, the familiar DefCon logo was visible. A coveted prize for any young hacker. Despite its age, the jacket looked soft, and Harry pictured McArdle caring for it over the years with saddle soap and sprays.

She watched Ginny settle herself in the bed, and recalled Riva's interest in her. Harry couldn't help comparing them: Ginny, frail and indolent, dependent on McArdle; Riva, full of steely determination. Harry dropped her gaze to the list of files on the screen. Had Riva really killed McArdle? Was that what Zubiri meant when he'd said that she might be involved?

Harry stepped through another audit trail of activities, and wondered what McArdle had done to end up dead. She sighed, and flipped the file closed. Whatever it was, there was no evidence of it here. In fact, there was very little evidence that he'd used the laptop at all. The thing had been sanitized. No web history, sparse audit logs, no temporary files. Nothing to hint it belonged to a professional hacker. No attack strategies, no reconnaissance records, no trial intrusion results.

To all intents and purposes, the hard drive was clean. And that in itself suggested it was hiding something.

The question was, where?

29

Cloak and dagger. Secret codes.

So McArdle liked James Bond games.

Harry drummed her fingers on the laptop base, her eyes gritty from trawling through his benign-looking files. She leaned back against the wall. The laptop was warm against her legs, and the urge to sleep was suddenly overwhelming.

Her gaze drifted over Ginny. She was motionless under the quilt, her soft breathing the only sound in the room apart from the occasional swish of cars outside.

Harry turned back to the screen. McArdle had been working on something for Franco, so where the hell were all his files? A hacker didn't operate in a vacuum. He broke into a system the way a jewel thief planned a heist. The thief acquired floor plans, blueprints and schematics. He scrutinized security, probed it for weaknesses: guards, locks, alarms, sensors, radar, CCTV. Then he sharpened his tools and devised a stealthy break-in strategy.

A hacker did the same. True, McArdle was no Indiana Jones, but any expert staked out his target. And good reconnaissance generated a lot of data. Data that had to be stored here someplace.

Harry massaged the corners of her eyes and tried to picture McArdle. Pasty complexion, Tweedledum-shape. What did she know about him, really? He was secretive; easily bullied. Socially awkward, maybe. Only four years older than her. A smart hacker gone bad. Then she remembered his sister and bit her lip. He hadn't really had much choice.

Ginny murmured in her sleep, and Harry glanced over. McArdle had probably been half in love with her, and it sounded as if she'd clung to him with a neediness of her own. Harry turned back to the laptop and tapped a few keys, locating the photos of Ginny she'd found earlier. They were casual shots, mostly taken in the apartment: Ginny lounging on the sofa; Ginny eating spaghetti; Ginny laughing easily at the camera. The poses had a childlike spontaneity about them that suggested Franco probably hadn't been around.

Harry flicked through the shots, skimming past dozens of snaps of the river until she found one of McArdle himself. He was standing in the kitchen, smiling shyly at the camera, dressed in a blue-and-white apron. The stripes curved over his bulk like staves on a barrel. He looked large and dishevelled, like an untidy, agreeable sheepdog.

Harry snapped the photo shut. McArdle was dead. It wouldn't help to start liking him now.

She reached for a pen and paper and scribbled out a list of what she knew: McArdle, dead; casinos and past-posting; a warehouse full of money by the pier. She doodled a large dollar sign, shading it in, and waited for her brain to engage.

Nothing.

Harry scrunched the paper up and climbed off the bed, wandering over to the window. She pressed her nose to the glass. The world looked black. To her left, the globular lights of the Zurriola Bridge burned like fireballs in the dark.

Somewhere close by, the counting machines were probably still rattling. Harry wiped a peephole in the misted-up window. Odd how easy it was to accept Franco as a heavyweight money launderer. He struck her as a man who played many parts. Casino cheater; money dealer. What other layers did he have?

She was guessing Zubiri knew about Franco's money laundering, given the information on his slides. Harry pictured the Basque copper's blunt, unsmiling face, and felt her jaw tighten. Okay, so he'd tried to talk her out of it, but the fact was, he and Vasco had knowingly used her as bait. And in an underworld where one rookie mistake could get her killed.

She scowled at the laptop over on the bed. She'd been desperate to find it and contact Zubiri, but in all honesty she wasn't sure what she'd say. She'd promised Hunter she'd come out, but was she really ready to leave? She still didn't have the answer to the one thing Vasco wanted to know: why did Franco Chavez need a hacker?

Harry huffed out a breath, then turned back to the window. Some mule-headed part of her wasn't prepared to fail. She stared out at the river. Then her eyes narrowed, and she cocked her head to one side. Her gaze shot to the laptop. Back to the window. Her pulse quickened.

She reached the bed in two strides and snatched up the laptop, unplugging it from the wall and carrying it back to the window. Balancing it in the crook of her arm, she stepped through McArdle's photos till she found his snaps of the river. She studied them in turn, comparing them with the view out the window. There was no doubt about it. They'd all been taken from here. Right from where she was standing.

But why would anyone do that? The angle was bad, the window pane smeary. The quaint lights of the Zurriola Bridge were only partially visible. If McArdle had wanted a keepsake shot, he'd get a better view down in the street.

She peered at the photos again. Most of them were grainy, all taken in daylight, except the last one, which was shot in the dark. McArdle had probably snapped them with his mobile phone. But why so many? What was his interest in the Zurriola Bridge?

Harry frowned at the night shot, the closest in composition to her own vista. The sky and river were bands of black, the golden globes on the bridge the only contrast. She squinted at the lamps. The nearest one

271

looked smudged, as though someone had taken an eraser to its edge. She checked the view out the window, then flicked through the other photos. In every other case, the lamp was intact. Harry noted the date on the night shot. It had been taken the day McArdle died.

Harry stared at the smudge.

Cloak and daggers. Invisible ink.

She raced back to the bed, her heartbeat thudding. It was a long shot, but right now it was all she had. She grabbed one of the memory sticks, jammed it into the laptop and scoured its catalogue of tools.

Nothing.

She whipped out the memory stick and plugged the next one in. It had to be here somewhere.

Invisible ink. She should have thought of it before. Steganography: Greek for 'concealed writing'. Invisible data, masquerading as something else.

As a photograph, for instance.

She found what she was looking for on the third memory stick: HideGoSeek. A common steganography tool. She launched the program and fed all McArdle's photographs into it. Then she hunched over the keyboard and waited.

If she was right, McArdle had embedded his files inside the photos. He'd used HideGoSeek to doctor the images, pixel by pixel, replacing a morsel of digital colour with a scrap of sneaky data. The result: a microscopic change in pixel shade, invisible to the naked eye.

Hiding data with other data. More sleight of hand.

But you had to use the right images, and some were better than others. You needed busy detail, lots of different colours. That way, it was harder to spot the shade anomalies hiding the secret data. A waterfall in a forest would do the job. A cloudless blue sky over a blanket of snow would not. And nor would a jet-black night shot.

Harry opened the photo and stared at the smudged lamp. Its subtle aberration against the uniform darkness was the only clue the shot had been tampered with. McArdle must have been in a hurry to settle for that one.

Her gaze darted back to HideGoSeek. It had finished sifting through the images, and was spitting out a folder of successfully reconstructed files. The folder was called RECON.

Harry's stomach gave a leap, and she knew she'd got it right. She jumped into the folder and burrowed through its contents. It was a lengthy reconnaissance dossier. She hunted for McArdle's starting point: the name and address of his target. It didn't take long to find. He'd stamped it on most of the documents:

Aztec International, Avenida del la Libertad, San Sebastián.

Harry frowned. What the hell was Aztec International?

She shook her head and pored over the rest of McArdle's recon. First came the corporate data: employee names, departments, email addresses. Then the floor plans: IP addresses, domain names, network blocks, routers. Then came the schematics of perimeter security: firewalls, alarms, intrusion-detection systems. And finally, a record of his attacks on Aztec's barricades.

Harry's eyes widened. McArdle had bombarded his target ruthlessly. He'd fired off exploits and complex code injections; he'd unleashed multi-headed worms and viruses with malicious payloads. Among them, packaged and primed, was a small slug called Dormouse that for the moment Harry didn't recognize. All in all, McArdle's attacks seemed exhaustive and advanced, but none of them had managed to drill through Aztec's defences.

Harry turned back to the odd little program called Dormouse, and wondered what it did. She scanned it for meaningful symbols and text, but the program had been stripped and only a handful of fragments were readable: 'detonate'; 'gotcha'; 'network's been nuked'. But they told her all she needed to know.

Dormouse was a logic bomb; a deadly piece of code that would snooze inside a system until a special trigger was pulled. A certain date, perhaps; or a particular user login. The trigger would detonate the dormant bomb, exploding it across the system.

So Dormouse was going to annihilate Aztec. By now, Harry was willing to bet that Aztec belonged to Riva.

30

'I checked McArdle's files.'

Harry glanced over at Franco and waited for him to respond, but he kept his eyes fixed on the road ahead, squinting against the sun. He'd seemed distracted since they'd left the apartment, and she wasn't even sure he was listening. She flicked a look over her shoulder at McArdle's laptop in the back seat, then went on:

'From what I saw, he was trying to infiltrate a company called Aztec International. Is that my target?'

Franco slammed the horn with his fist, blasting the driver in front. Then he cursed, and dragged a hand over his face. His usual ruddy complexion looked grey and waxy, the hand a little unsteady. What the hell was the matter with him?

Harry's instincts told her to stay quiet. Then again, Diego was more thick-skinned. She cleared her throat.

'I'm just guessing here, but does Aztec belong to Riva Mills?'

Franco's mouth tightened at the name. 'You ask a lot of questions, Diego. Relax. I said I'll show you and I will. We'll see the place on the way back.'

'On the way back from where?' Harry checked out the window and felt a flicker of recognition at the steep, winding hill. 'Can't you show me now?'

'No.' Franco flexed his fingers on the wheel, as though unsure of his grip. 'Got to meet a guy first.'

'Who?'

'A prospective client.'

'Is he the reason you're so uptight?'

Franco snapped his black eyes to hers. 'Just watch your mouth, okay?'

He rammed the engine down a gear, and Harry felt a tug as the car bit into the climb. Eventually, Franco said,

'He's not my usual type of client, that's all.'

'Meaning what? He's not a drug dealer?'

'Hey, drug dealers, smugglers, these are people I can understand. It's all greed with them, pure and simple. I can relate to that, you know? But these other guys.' He shook his head. 'Different rules. A whole new set of extremes.'

Harry felt a flicker of unease. 'Are you saying he's a terrorist?'

'Financial manager for some Egyptian group. Fucking terrorists, worst kind of client.' Franco ground the gears hard. 'A lot of brokers like me won't take them on any more.'

'Because they're too dangerous?'

'Because the agencies investigating them are too dangerous. They don't play by the same rules as traditional cops, know what I mean? They don't care about evidence, they just want to stop the fuckers.' He threw her a meaningful look. 'So their interrogation style can turn a little fatal, if you get my drift.'

Harry nodded, and when Franco spoke again, his voice was low.

'But that aside, I still wouldn't want to deal with this guy.'

A flash of alarm moved up Harry's frame. 'So how come I need to tag along? Can't you leave me at the apartment?'

'After what you saw last night?' Franco cut her a look. Suspicion had triggered a disconnect in his close-set eyes. 'You know stuff now. I told you that was dangerous. So from now on, you stick with me. Period.'

Before Harry could ask any more, he pulled into the kerb and motioned for her to get out. She paused to gape at the old sandstone church across the road. The sun had warmed its brickwork to a buttery yellow, and Harry read the familiar sign over the old archway: *Cementerio de Polloe.*

She climbed out of the car. 'You're meeting him in a cemetery?'

Franco strode into the courtyard and didn't answer.

He was dressed in a long black leather trench coat that made him look like a wartime commanding officer. But the jittery expression didn't match his military bearing.

Harry followed him through the archway, her pace slowing as they reached the avenue of large, ornate crypts. The place was busier than last time. People lined the walkways, chatting in small huddles. Fresh wreaths and posies carpeted the graves like vibrant tapestries. Harry caught up with Franco. They'd obviously arrived at the end of some kind of ceremony, and her pulse rate climbed at the thought of bumping into Olive.

'Why are we here?' she said.

'To make a bid for this guy's cash.'

'You're buying his money?'

Franco made an impatient gesture. 'It's a straightforward business transaction. He's got a load of dirty cash he wants washed, so he auctions it off in blocks to money brokers like me. We bid against each other, offering to buy it from him at a discount and clean it up.'

'So he just puts his cash out to tender? Like he's procuring office supplies or something?'

Franco waved the question away. 'Hey, it's a business like any other. Everyone likes to keep costs down and get the best deal.'

He picked up the pace, criss-crossing through the orthogonal layout of the cemetery as though he knew where he was going. Harry trotted to keep up.

'And if you win the bid?'

'Then I take on the risk of laundering his cash, and in return, I pocket my cut.'

'So he ends up with less money.'

'Yeah, but what he gets looks like regular income. A bogus loan from an independent shell company. Phoney consultancy fees paid out to him by some offshore entity. Or maybe I do an exchange deal with a fridge importer in the Middle East who lodges payment with the guy's arms supplier over there. I can do anything. I can turn dirty cash legit, or I can make it disappear.' Franco flourished his fingers in a sleight-of-hand gesture. 'Like a magician.'

Harry threw him a doubtful look, then did a quick survey of the nearby headstones. By now, they'd left the lavish crypts behind and had reached the more modest-looking graves. The air was fragrant with incense and flowers, and Harry noticed she was getting closer to where her own family grave was located.

Jesus. Were Diego and Harry about to collide?

She opened her mouth to quiz him some more, but Franco cut across her. 'Zip it, Diego. You're too mouthy for your own good. When we meet him, I want you to keep it shut. Understand?'

Harry shrugged, and tried not to look offended. 'Am I allowed to know his name?'

'*I'm* not even allowed to know his fucking name.' Franco lengthened his stride. 'All I know is people call him Pontius Pilate.'

'What kind of name is that?'

Franco scratched his chin. The shadowy stubble made his complexion look ashen. Eventually, he said,

'He likes to crucify people. You don't pay him what you owe, he comes around to your house and drives spike-nails through your hands and feet, and pins you to your own floor timbers. Hammers a skewer through your brain, too, in case you feel like moving your head.'

Harry winced at the image. 'Jesus.'

'Yeah.'

She squinted at Franco's tense profile, and finally understood what was making him so edgy. It was fear. Who would have believed this raging bull of a man could be afraid?

Franco turned away from the main avenue, and motioned at her to keep up. Knots of people still gathered along the verges, and Harry kept her voice low.

'I don't get it. If you don't want this creep as a client, then why the hell are we even here?'

He jerked around to face her. 'What's the matter with you? You don't just not turn up when a guy like this invites you to bid. There's a protocol here, you got to show some respect.' He glared at her for a moment, then continued along the path. 'All I got to do now is bid high.'

He strode ahead of her, still talking.

'He may not want you there. He doesn't like strangers, so if I tell you to, just move away.' He shot her a sharp look over his shoulder. 'But stay where I can see you. Don't try anything stupid.'

Harry murmured her assent. Then she glimpsed a familiar photograph on one of the graves, a silver-haired lady with a shy smile, and she felt her chest squeeze. She glanced down a narrow pathway to her right. The Martinez plot was less than a hundred yards away. But it was deserted, with no sign of Olive.

She hurried after Franco, the grave of her ancestors exerting a pull like a magnet. Franco had stopped in the middle of the path and Harry joined him, following his gaze. A heavyset man was walking towards them, his long, pleated overcoat swirling like a cassock around his ankles. Two other men supervised his progress from a nearby grave.

Harry felt her muscles tense. Beside her, Franco breathed in deeply through his nose. Then he tugged at his cuffs, cleared his throat. As the stranger drew closer, Franco nodded in salute.

The newcomer stared at Harry, and she tried not to flinch. His face was large and middle-aged, with plumped-up hog jowls and full, pouty lips. The eyes were round and doleful. He turned them on Franco and said,

'So many dead people.'

He gestured at the graves. A small crucifix dangled from his fingers, and Harry realized he was holding a set of rosary beads. His gaze settled back on hers. Beneath the mournful expression was a look of ill will that had her edging away.

He turned back to Franco. 'You have a proposal for me?'

His voice was soft, the accent hard to place. Franco held up his palms and dipped his head; the kind of gesture people make when they're getting ready to beat about the bush.

'Truth is, my overheads are high right now,' he said. 'I've had some unforeseen setbacks. A few unexpected losses. I'm sure you can appreciate, the risks in this business are increasing all the time.'

'It's the same in any business, my friend. Spoilage, spillage, theft. Law-enforcement intervention.' The hog jowls quivered slightly. 'You factor it in and calculate your receivables accordingly.'

'Sure, sure, that goes without saying.' Franco scratched his chin. 'Look, I'll call in a few favours. I can do you a two-week wash-cycle for fourteen per cent.'

The man called Pontius Pilate laced his fingers together as though in prayer, the rosary beads still draped across them. Harry detected a faint scent of incense in the air around him.

'This is very disappointing,' he said. 'My sources told me you owned the market here. That you could offer me less than one per cent for a two-day turnaround.'

Harry sensed Franco shifting beside her.

'Well, under normal circumstances, that'd be true,' he said. 'And as you know, most other outfits can't do it for less than ten per cent. But right now, I just don't have the resources.'

'Perhaps your reputation has been exaggerated.' The man fingered his rosary beads. 'Or perhaps you've lied.'

'Hey, don't misunderstand me, I appreciate the opportunity to bid, I really do. Maybe this time we just can't do business, but I can still do you a favour. From one businessman to another?'

Franco flicked his wrist, and conjured up a slip of paper between his fingers. Harry blinked. Had he been palming it all this time? The man with the rosary beads eyed it with suspicion.

'What kind of favour?'

'I can give you insider information that'll help you get the best price. Information us money dealers usually keep to ourselves.' He waved the slip of paper. 'Then maybe when my operation recovers, we can do business again.'

The man with the rosary beads closed his eyes briefly, nodding as though giving a blessing. Franco gestured with the paper.

'This is a contact number for my main competitor, they've been trying to undercut me for years. Normally I wouldn't give them the business, though sometimes we help each other out—'

'I'm not interested in your turf wars.'

'What I'm trying to say is, I can tell you how to knock down their fees.'

'Go on.'

'I know for a fact they can do it at cost for five per cent. Normally, I can beat that, but if they think I can't and that five per cent will steal the business from me, they'll do it. Just tell them I offered you six and they'll go one better.' Franco held out the piece of paper. 'It's

283

the best handling fee you'll get in the market without me in the picture, and I think you know that.'

The man with the rosary beads stared at the slip of paper, but didn't take it. Franco persisted.

'You've probably dealt with them before. They have the wherewithal to meet your requirements. Three hundred million, like you said. One third to your business acquaintance in Port Said, the rest in clean US dollars.'

The other man's face darkened, and he snapped his eyes to Harry. 'I dislike discussing such personal details in front of strangers.'

Harry took an involuntary step backwards. She'd been hoping he'd forgotten about her. Franco shot her a look, clicked his fingers. She nodded, hitching a thumb over her shoulder.

'I'll be right over here.'

She edged away with relief, following the path to her right, putting a little distance between them. She could feel the man's malevolent gaze on her back like a branding iron. She strolled on for a few more yards, then glanced over her shoulder. Franco was still watching her. She sauntered on, fetching up beside a large, worn headstone, engraved with the familiar words, *Familia Martinez*.

Harry paused to look, as though casually browsing, unprepared for the burning ache that seared through her core. Her ancestors were laid out in front of her, the grave close enough to touch, yet it made her feel more isolated than ever.

She tried not to think about what Olive had told her the last time she'd been standing here. Maybe later she'd dig that up and re-examine it, but for now she had other distractions.

She ran her eyes over the gravestone, over all the names she knew: the tough old Basque ladies, Irune and Aginaga; her own grandmother, Clara; then Cristos and Tobias, her uncle and cousin. The old ladies' spirits seemed to reproach her. She'd tracked them down to reinforce her identity; to draw strength from the lives that had delivered her and made her what she was.

So why the hell was she here pretending to be somebody else?

31

'Let's get out of here.'

Harry's pulse tripped. Franco was standing behind her, a few feet from the grave. His skin looked drawn, greasy with sweat, and his gaze slid uneasily over his shoulder.

'Fucking place gives me the creeps.'

He turned away, gesturing for her to follow. She trotted after him, burying the urge to slip one last look at the grave. Instead, she took refuge in Diego for another while.

She followed Franco out of the cemetery and back to the car. The interior was stuffy from sun-baked upholstery and she cranked open a window, letting the air seep in. Franco fired up the engine and shot the car into reverse, hooking his arm over Harry's seat to check his rear-view. The move released a wave of acrid sweat; the raw kind that comes from fear.

Franco ground the gears. 'Let's get the hell out before that psychopath changes his mind.'

'What happened back there?'

'Bastard didn't trust me, can you believe that?' Franco snatched at the wheel, whipping the car into a two-point turn. 'He's gonna make a bundle on the information I gave him, but he still had to squeeze me. Made me commit to a rate of less than half a per cent next time we do business.'

'Will there be a next time?'

'Not if I can help it.'

Harry gripped the seat as they sped downhill. 'That guy's really spooked you, hasn't he?'

'Damn right. He's fucking deranged. Started talking about crucifixion. Said it's where we get the word "excruciating". Slow and agonizing. Jesus. What kind of person does that shit?'

Harry slid him a look. She recalled the bloodstain on the warehouse wall, and Franco's orders to stab someone in the bar. On a slide rule of violence, he probably saw himself at the acceptable end of the scale.

'Maybe you should have brought Gideon along,' she said. 'Just to watch your back.'

Franco shook his head. 'I told you, Gideon's not in on this. And you keep your mouth shut, just like I said.'

Harry shrugged and let her gaze wander out the window. As far as she could see, they were heading back the same way they'd come.

'You said we'd go to Aztec International.'

'We'll be there in fifteen minutes. No more diversions.'

'You didn't answer me before. When I asked if it belonged to Riva Mills.'

'It belongs to Riva all right. Aztec's the headquarters for her whole damn empire.' Franco rammed the car up a gear. 'Her seat of high command.'

His tone was sour. Harry wondered what Riva had done to make him hate her so much. By rights, the vendetta should have been the other way round, if her claims that he'd killed her brother were true. Maybe Harry was misreading the situation.

'So, just to be clear. Aztec is your target?'

Franco nodded, his jaw tightening. 'I want you to bring the bitch down.'

Harry's eyes widened. No crossed signals there. She thought of Dormouse, McArdle's pet bomb, snoozing in harmless hibernation. She'd unpicked the code the previous night and taken a closer look. Her instincts had been right. It was a kill-switch for the network. Nerve-centre meltdown. Harry nibbled her lower lip.

'You realize I can't permanently destroy her opera-tions? They'll have backups and recovery procedures. I can put her out of commission for a few days, maybe a week, but that's all.'

'A few days is all I need.'

Harry squinted at his fierce profile. His expression was wooden and gave nothing away. She risked probing further.

'Why do you want to disrupt her casino business?'

'Who said anything about her frigging casinos? Gambling's not the only game she's in.' Franco gave her a hard look. 'She's a money launderer, just like me.'

Harry's brows shot up high. She pictured Riva: tough businesswoman with dainty, fox-like features; gutsy runaway with a record by the age of fourteen. But a money launderer? She cut Franco a disbelieving look. Despite the harsh exterior, she'd admired Riva. An underdog who'd done good. But if Franco was telling the truth, the woman was as much a criminal as he was.

Franco tossed her a look. 'What? You find that hard to believe? Riva Mills, philanthropist and businesswoman of the year? Don't be taken in by all the window-dressing, Diego.'

Harry shrugged. 'Makes no difference to me, I hardly know the woman. Just didn't think there'd be room for someone else in this business with you around.'

'You think I'm the only one in the money-laundering game around here? I told you, Diego, this is big business. Everyone needs to wash their cash. Crooks, corporations, governments, political heads of state. Believe me, there's plenty to go around for everyone.'

'And you know for sure Riva's involved?'

'Oh yeah.' Franco nodded slowly, and when he spoke again his voice was low. 'I was the one who got her started.'

He eased the car to a halt at a set of lights, turning

to stare out the window. Harry followed his gaze. By now, they'd reached the river, and the lunchtime traffic was clotting along the bridges. Water churned against the embankment walls, thick and oily-looking. Harry ventured a question.

'Does that mean you and Riva used to be partners?'

'I taught her all she knew.' Franco kept his face turned away. 'She always was a quick learner. It started with cards, before we got into the big stuff. Cons, casino cheating. She was something else. She could stack a deck, fake a shuffle, deal from the bottom, peek at the top. Best damn card mechanic I ever knew. Better than Gideon.'

'You know her pretty well, then.'

'We were on the road together for a couple of years. But that was over twenty years ago.'

'Was Gideon with you?'

Franco shook his head. 'Just me, Riva and her two kid brothers. Well, one was her brother. The other was some stray she sorta took under her wing. Felt sorry for him, I guess.' He blew out a breath and massaged his stubble. 'Guy was a fucking liability half the time.'

'What about her brother?' Harry kept her voice light. 'Is he in the business with her now?'

Franco clenched the wheel, and his profile turned ugly. 'He's dead.'

The lights changed, and he revved up the engine, tyres chirping as he accelerated across the bridge. Harry changed tack, retreating to safer ground.

'So you haven't seen Riva Mills for twenty years, but now you want to bring her down?'

'Hate can last a long time.'

'I guess it can. But don't they say it's like drinking poison and waiting for the other person to die?'

'Not in my world.' Franco locked his gaze on hers. His eyes looked as cold and leaden as the river water. 'In my world, I hate someone, they die.'

A cold shiver washed over Harry's frame. She judged the time had come to shut her mouth and shrank back against the seat, as though by getting smaller she might defuse his mood.

They drove in silence for a while, cutting left over the bridge towards the newer part of town. They sailed along the broad, tree-lined streets and Parisian-looking avenues until finally Franco coasted to a halt in a No Parking zone. He switched off the engine, leaving the hazard lights ticking, and pointed at an elegant, sandstone building across the street.

It was five storeys high, its blush-pink façade ringed with tiers of wrought-iron balconies. The entrance was discreet, recessed well back from the wide, chequered pavement. As far as Harry could tell, there were no signs or branded logos to advertise what went on inside. She turned to Franco.

'That's Aztec International?'

'Full of accountants, bankers and crooked lawyers.'

'Doing what, exactly?'

'On the face of it, managing her casino empire.'

'And behind the scenes?'

'You name it. Cooking up shell companies and dummy bank accounts. Arranging wire transfers, false invoices, loan-backs, front companies. Injecting cash through the casino books. And all in one building.' He gave Harry a meaningful look. 'Single point of failure. Big mistake.'

Harry stared across at the pretty stone building. 'So that's her nerve centre.'

'Exactly. And I want you to sabotage it. Bring her infrastructure down. Cripple her access to the bank accounts, the cashflows, the transactions, the money trail.' Franco held up a finger. 'But only on my command. Not before, not after. We need to reel her in, a little at a time. Then when I tell you, we move in for the kill.'

Harry frowned, still not getting it. Sure, she could torpedo the Aztec network, but like she said, they'd recover in a few days. What the hell had Franco planned for the downtime?

His eyes narrowed. 'What's the matter? Can't you do it? McArdle said he had it all worked out.'

'He did, up to a point. I've seen his files. He planned to nuke Aztec with a logic bomb called Dormouse. He was trying to tunnel through their network to sneak Dormouse in. After that, he planned to detonate it remotely. There's a website Dormouse checks every few minutes. If it sees the message, "Mousetrap", then it explodes. Network Armageddon.'

'So? You can take up where he left off.'

She shook her head. 'It's a good basic strategy, but it

wasn't working. I've seen his attack files. Aztec's defences are locked down tight. He was getting burned by the firewalls, couldn't get Dormouse inside.'

Franco was breathing hard through his nose. 'What about you? I thought you were this hotshot hacker? Are you saying you can't do it either?'

Something clutched at Harry's stomach. This guy wouldn't tolerate failure. 'Oh, I can do it all right. But not the way he was going about it.'

'So what exactly do you suggest, Diego?' His voice was low and dangerous.

Harry stared at the recessed entrance across the street. Sunlight flashed off the glass doors as a young man emerged and ducked into a neighbouring coffee shop. The hairs tingled on the nape of Harry's neck. Maybe there was a way she could break free from Franco for a while. She gave a casual shrug.

'Hacking's not all about the technology. Sometimes it's not enough to just sit at a laptop and fire off malicious code.' She nodded at the Aztec building. 'Sometimes you've got to walk inside.'

Franco's gaze shot across the street, then back to Harry's face. 'You're going in there? What for?'

'To hack the human firewall. Smuggle Dormouse in.' She was playing for time. 'The best hackers are social manipulators, didn't you know that? Forget the geeky misfit, that's just a myth. The real expert is a skilled social engineer. Part-opportunist, part-actor, part-con artist.'

'Now you're talking my game.' Franco's black eyes burned into hers. His look was almost admiring. 'How come you know so much about this shit?'

Harry gave another shrug. 'I had a lot of time on my hands as a kid. What about you? How come you know so much about money laundering?'

'That's easy.' His eyes were still fixed on hers. 'I used to be an undercover cop.'

32

Firearms cracked, ripped the air. Marty moaned. Buried his face. Someone was screaming Andy's name, over and over.

Marty's eyes flared open. A juddery breath racked his chest, and the sheet that clung to him was sodden with sweat. He squinted at the unfamiliar wallpaper. Faded yellow flowers. They seemed to recede, then rush back in. Like someone fiddling with a zoom lens in his head.

'You're awake.'

Marty turned, his neck creaking. A woman stood framed against the window. Soft-looking curves. Copper-coloured hair. He swallowed, then wished he hadn't. His throat felt lined with jagged, white-hot coals.

'Hey,' he managed. 'I been asleep long?'

The redhead shrugged. 'About ten hours. It's past noon.'

She moved closer to the bed, arms folded across her cushiony chest. Her perfume was sweet, and Marty hoped it masked his own stale aroma. He took in the rest of the room: small and drab, a low-budget hotel. But better than his own place near the river.

The redhead shifted her weight, her eyes on the floor. 'You were talking in your sleep most of the night.'

'I was? Hey, sorry about that.'

Marty's gut cringed. Had he blacked out on her? Was she pissed because nothing had happened, after her generous invitation to come back to her room?

Then a memory lit up: a snapshot of heat; of slow, clinging movements; of agonizing release. He glanced at her face, at the blazing mane of hair, and remembered that her name was Josie.

She flicked him a look from under her lashes, and gave him a slow smile. 'I'll get you some water.'

She moved away and Marty's stomach relaxed. Maybe last night had been okay. He tugged at the damp sheet.

'I'll get dressed. Get out of your way.'

He lifted his head, leaned on his elbows. The room tilted and spun, and pitched him back against the bed. He lay there sweating.

'Stay where you are, doesn't bother me.' Josie's voice echoed in the bathroom acoustics. 'You're running quite a fever.'

Marty's eyelids dragged, and he worked hard to keep them open. No more sleep. Sleep brought dreams.

Only they weren't dreams, were they? They were memories. Solid, 3-D fucking recall that left him buckled in pain.

'Here –' Josie was somehow back by his side, holding out a glass of water. Funny how her voice still sounded echoey. 'I told you, he won't be back for two or three days.'

Marty tried not to visualize the toady-looking guy whose bed he'd taken for the night. He sipped some water. Ice on fire. He winced, and handed back the glass. Josie's eyes didn't quite meet his.

He hunched under the sheet, stiffening against a wave of shivers. 'Just give me a minute. Soon as my head stops spinning, I'll get up.'

'No need. You did me a favour, now I'm doing you one.'

'You were short some ready cash. I just helped you out, that's all.'

Josie set the glass on the bed stand and leaned back against the wall, her palms wedged flat behind her hips. The pose thrust out her curves in a way that reminded Marty of last night. She made a face.

'I'd been stupid. Put a bundle on the wheel when I should've known better. Looking for that big win. The one that'll change your life.' Her hair looked vibrant against the dingy yellow flowers. 'Get you out from under, you know?'

'Yeah, I know.'

Josie tugged at the cuffs of her sweater, the long sleeves

hiding the faint bruises he'd noticed the night before. She lifted her chin.

'You haven't asked me why I stay with him. Most people do.'

Marty managed a shrug. 'Survival calls the shots for people like you and me. I know how that works.'

She stared at him for a moment, then looked away. 'I waited over an hour for someone like you to turn up. Someone who'd pay my bar bill.'

'Yeah, I figured.'

She flicked him a sheepish smile. Then she tilted her head, studying him. 'How'd you get sick, anyway?'

'Took a dunk in the river. Musta caught a chill.'

She was silent for a moment. Her body looked seductive. Soft and warm. If he got cleaned up, would she slide back under the sheets for a while?

Josie sighed and pushed herself away from the wall, then started to pace the room. Marty stared at the drab yellow flowers where she'd been.

Zoom in. Zoom out.

'Got any cash left?' Josie was hunkered down by the bed, her face inches from his. Up close, the lines around her eyes were etched deep.

'Haven't you already checked?' Marty said.

She gave him a wry smile. 'I only found twelve euros.'

'That's all I got.'

Her smile grew fixed. She nodded, straightened up, then pulled on a jacket.

'I'm going out for a while. I'll find a drugstore and get you some pills.'

'Sure.' Marty watched her all the way to the door. She looked small and far away, as if he were viewing her through the wrong end of a telescope. 'Put five on for me, okay?'

She hesitated, then left the room. Marty's eyelids were heavy. The yellow flowers receded, grew smaller than pinheads. He couldn't help himself. He closed his eyes and drifted.

'What do you think, Marty? Think this'll look good when we get to Spain?'

Marty turned to find Riva standing by the door, clutching a gypsy-red dress. The colour looked rich against her smoky-grey eyes. He shrugged and turned back to the suitcase on the bed.

'All you need are the castanets.'

Her silence was testy, but he ignored it. Beside him, Andy was struggling to fold a stack of shirts.

'God, lighten up,' Riva said. 'This is supposed to be fun.'

Marty didn't answer, and waited till she'd left the room. Then he fired a sweater into the suitcase. This dumb-ass vacation had been planned for weeks. They were flying from Vegas to Madrid in the morning, and from there Franco planned on driving north through Spain to a town called San Sebastián. Marty would've been happy to cut loose in the capital and avoid the five-hour drive. But

299

Franco kept talking about fishing ports and hills and soft, sandy beaches. Jesus. The way he went on, you'd think he was planning on staying there for ever.

Marty rammed a pair of trainers down the side of his case. He'd been surprised when Franco had suggested the trip. It had been a while since they'd included him in any of their plans. According to Riva, that was just for his own protection, but he was almost eighteen, he could take care of himself. He slapped the suitcase lid shut. Truth was, they just didn't trust him.

He yanked at the zip. Beside him, Andy grunted, still grappling with his shirts. Riva was right, this trip was supposed to be fun. So why did his damn gut feel so sour? If they could just go someplace else. Chicago, maybe. What was wrong with staying Stateside? But this Spanish backwater seemed to mean so much to Franco, and it had Riva all fired up. That excluded Marty even more, somehow.

Andy let out a sudden howl and hurled his shirts to the floor. Marty shot him a glance. Angry splotches pooled on the boy's cheeks, and his heavy-lidded eyes had turned dark. Marty shook his head. Small things frustrated the kid more and more these days, and he looked just about how Marty felt.

Riva drifted back into the room, picked up the shirts, and laid a hand on Andy's arm.

'Come on, I'll show you again. You spread them out, then fold them over, like this.'

Her voice was calm; a cool trickle on white-hot rage.

300

Marty wished she would use it with him sometimes. Andy turned his face to hers, absorbing every word.

The phone rang in the other room and Riva moved off to answer it, fixing Marty with a look.

'Help him, okay?'

He waited till she'd left, then glanced at Andy. The boy's fair head was bent low over the bed as he folded a shirt with care. Riva's voice murmured from the other room, and Marty slipped closer to the door. Eavesdropping was the only way he found out anything around here.

'That's not what we agreed,' Riva was saying.

Marty guessed she was talking to the casino. That was where she spent most of her time these days, though not as a blackjack dealer. She and Franco had stepped things up a grade.

Money brokers, they called themselves. Independent contractors who worked for the mob. For now, they operated out of their client's casino premises, but soon they planned to establish counting houses of their own. Riva managed the casino back rooms, taking receipt of money shipped in from nameless sources. She counted the cash, parcelled it out. Some got blended with the casino takings; the rest she morphed through a series of black magic tricks: smurfed bank deposits; cross-border exchanges; real estate flips. Marty didn't really understand any of it, but Riva had it all down pat. Franco only ever had to explain a thing to her once and she got it.

'But why tonight?' Riva was saying. 'We're set up to take delivery next week, like we agreed.'

Marty guessed it was another cargo of cash. They'd used him as a smurf once or twice, sending him scurrying from bank to bank to make dozens of small deposits. But he knew they didn't really trust him. He pictured the tempting wads of notes he'd handled, and squirmed. Shit, they were probably right. But hey, that wasn't his fault. He'd been living hand-to-mouth for most of his life, and the habit was hard to break.

Marty slumped against the door jamb. They hadn't pulled a con together in almost a year. Riva said they didn't need to, now that they'd funded the start of their laundering operation. But Marty missed the cons. He missed the adrenalin, the daredevil impulses. The power-surge of fear. Half the time, they'd made a play just to see if they could get away with it.

Riva slammed down the phone and Marty jumped. He giant-stepped back to Andy's side just as she poked her head around the door.

'I'm going out.' Her thin face looked taut. 'Tell Franco the trucks are coming in early.'

Marty nodded, though she'd already gone. Andy straightened up and stared after her, clutching a shirt in both hands. He turned to Marty.

'We're still going to Spain, aren't we?'

Marty glanced at the sharp, pointed features that looked so much like Riva's. The kid hadn't grown much in the last twelve months, and Marty was already a head taller.

'Yeah, we're still going,' he said.

Andy looked doubtful, and began wadding the shirt into a ball.

'Hey, not like that.' Marty took it from him. 'Lay it out flat, like Riva said. Then fold it over, see?'

Andy's brows puckered. 'Can you write that down for me?'

'Write what down?'

'Write down how to fold it so I don't forget?'

'Hey, it's only a stupid shirt. So what if you forget? Riva'll keep reminding you.'

'But Riva might die someday. Who'll remind me when she's gone?' Andy fixed him with solemn, wide-set eyes. 'You won't stick around, will you?'

Marty stared. Something nasty crawled around in his gut, and he let his gaze drop. Then he snatched at the pile of shirts on the bed.

'Gimme those. Jesus. Talk about morbid. Why wouldn't I be around? You're three months older than me, you're probably going to die first anyway.'

They packed in huffy silence for a while. Then the door burst open and Franco stormed into the room.

'Where's Riva?'

Marty spun around. The guy was pale, his black eyes wide and staring. Something in his face turned Marty's skin cold.

'She's gone to the casino, said to tell you the trucks are coming in early. Why, what's wrong?'

'Shit!'

Franco wheeled away and dragged a hand over his

face. Then he whipped back around and stared at the suitcases on the bed.

'Get in the car!'

'But—'

'Grab your stuff and get in the fucking car!'

Franco strode across the room and slammed the lid shut on Andy's suitcase. The boy blinked, shook his head.

'That's not right, I've got to fold—'

'GET IN THE FUCKING CAR!'

Andy flinched. A shiver whisked between Marty's shoulders. Franco never yelled at Andy.

Franco was already out of the room, Andy's suitcase in tow. Marty snatched up his own, then grabbed Andy by the arm and dragged him out of the apartment.

Franco had ignored the elevator and was barrelling down the stairwell. Marty tore after him, Andy close behind. Following. Trusting. Together they clattered down the steps, and Marty yelled out over the din.

'What's going on? Has something happened to Riva?'

Franco didn't answer.

They got to the car, clambered inside. Franco gunned the engine and took off before they'd slammed the doors shut.

Marty's chest was pounding. In the back seat beside him, Andy was panting. Between breaths, the boy said,

'I thought the plane was tomorrow.'

Franco locked eyes with Marty in the rear-view mirror. 'Looks like we're taking off a little earlier than planned.'

Marty's insides flipped. What the hell was going on?

He eyed the back of Franco's head. Took in his hard, wide shoulders; his death-grip on the wheel. Trust Franco not to tell him anything. Marty wanted to quiz him, but something dangerous radiated from the guy; something fierce that warned Marty off.

The traffic moved freely this time of night, and they reached the Meridian Casino in less than five minutes. The place was located away from the main strip, a dazzling clone of its rivals. Just another neon explosion. Franco parked the car and climbed out.

'Stay here.'

He slammed the door before Marty could object, and sprinted towards the rear of the building. Marty stared after him.

If anything bad ever happens, I want you to take care of Riva and Andy.

Marty's scalp prickled. He watched Franco disappear, and clenched his jaw at the powerlessness of being left behind. Who the fuck put Franco in charge, anyway? Since when did he get to make all the rules? Marty eased the door open. Edged out of the car. To hell with following orders. With being shut out.

He slipped across the tarmac and headed after Franco. The night air was cool, and pulsed with a ripple of lights and chirping insects. Somewhere, a diesel engine throbbed, and Marty followed the sound. He dog-trotted around a corner and stopped up short. Nosed into a delivery bay up ahead was an eighteen-wheeler truck.

Marty eased back against the wall and into the

305

shadows. Half a dozen men were unloading the cargo, grunting as they passed each other duffle bags and boxes, bucket-brigade style.

Marty allowed himself a moment to picture all the cash you could carry in an eighteen-wheeler. He eyed the men up ahead, and was thinking about turning back when Franco strode out of the delivery bay towards him. He was hauling Riva by the arm, his face dark and urgent. But Riva hung back, trying to wrench free.

Marty tensed. Something wasn't right. Neons stuttered across Franco's face. Then new lights strobed from behind the truck, fracturing the darkness. Tyres shrieked, car doors *whunked*. Franco broke into a run, dragging Riva with him. Marty edged away. Gunfire tore the air, and he scrambled backwards.

'Get down!' Franco yelled.

The whizz-by of a bullet hummed in Marty's ear, and he moaned. Franco cannoned into him, tackled him to the ground, holding him and Riva close.

Marty pressed his face into the tarmac. Gunshots blasted behind him, around him. He squeezed his eyes shut, didn't move. Couldn't. Then Riva screamed, fought to get away. He felt Franco struggle to hold her, but she broke free. Marty twisted his face, saw her running towards the car park. Then she flung herself on the ground beside the body of a fair-haired boy.

Marty's brain jangled. Seized up. The picture was wrong. That wasn't Andy. Andy was in the car.

Something wrenched inside his chest.

The kid was in the car!

Marty's vision blurred. He closed his eyes, and his head swam.

The rage of bullets slashed the air. But all he could hear was the sound of Riva screaming.

33

Harry gaped at Franco. 'You used to be a *cop*?'

He nodded, then twisted in the driver seat to face her, his eyes locked on hers.

'I worked undercover for twenty-five years. Went deeper than most. It messes with your mind, after a while.' The black eyes glittered. 'Fucks you up.'

Harry stared at his hard, ugly features. Tried to picture him on the side of the angels. Couldn't do it.

She groped for a response. One wrong word, and the guy's mood would flip. Then she remembered Diego, and she scowled.

'I don't do business with cops.'

'Me neither. I'm not a cop any more.'

'No one stops being a cop. Not after twenty-five years.'

'You think?' His mouth formed a hard line. 'What if

your own organization turns against you? Forces you out on some dumb-ass charge?'

'That what happened to you?'

He glared at her for a moment. 'Let's just say I don't have any lingering allegiances, and leave it at that.'

'Hey, you brought it up. Now I want to hear more. If I'd known I was hooking up with an ex-cop, I wouldn't have taken the job.'

'You saying you don't trust your contacts in Belfast? They vouched for me, didn't they?'

'Sure. Same way they vouched for me. But you didn't take that on trust, so why should I?'

Franco's stare hardened. Harry returned it with a mulish look of her own, trying to ignore her drumming pulse. Trying not to imagine how an undercover pro might have seen through her own rookie efforts from day one.

The Volvo's hazard lights ticked into the silence. When Franco spoke again, his voice sounded low and dangerous.

'They stitched me up. Wanted me out. So they cooked up some bullshit about a missing packet of cannabis on a raid.'

Harry eyed him with suspicion. 'Why'd they want you out?'

'Said I was making bad calls. Becoming unpredictable.'

'And were you?'

Franco shrugged. 'According to the department psycho-fucking-analyst, I'd been living too long under too many different identities.'

'Goes with the territory, I'd have thought.'

'Exactly.' He looked pleased she'd got it, as though somehow that vindicated him and put them on the same side. 'I had dozens of aliases. Different briefcase for each one.'

'Briefcase? For what?'

'For swapping personas. You empty your pockets into one briefcase, then kit yourself out from another. Wallet, credit card, watch, driving licence. Everything compart-mentalized. Total context switch.'

Harry took in the animation in his rough-hewn face. The guy had more layers than she did.

'I can see how that might mess with your head.'

'Hey, the life takes a toll, no question. I'd go under for two, three years at a time. Nothing but hotel rooms and secrecy. Who could have a normal life with that?'

'Sounds unsociable. No wife and picket fence with that package.'

'Tried that once, didn't last three months.' A shadow passed over his face, a sliver of pain that undercut the macho swagger. 'I lost family, friends. That's the one thing they don't train you for.' He seemed to battle with something for a moment, then the animation kicked back into his face. 'But that was the game. A good operation could take years. You had to build things up slowly, reel people in. Like a con artist. Same skills: acting, manipulation, getting through people's defences.' He frowned and clicked his fingers at her. 'What did you call it? Hacking the human firewall?'

Harry nodded, not liking the buzz he seemed to get from discovering common ground.

'So you got burned out?' she said.

'Bullshit. Other guys got burned out, but not me. You got to be strong to work undercover. Disciplined, confident.' He thumped the wheel to emphasize the point. 'You're alone most of the time, so you need an ego that'll feed you. But the most important thing . . .?'

He held up a finger, as though snagging her attention on it, then went on:

'You don't ever forget who you really are. You're an agent making a case, bottom line. Problem with most guys is they fall in love with the role. With the money, the flash cars. They forget who they really are.' Franco's eyes turned solemn. 'Never forget who you are, Diego.'

Harry blinked; shifted in her seat. 'Okay, so you didn't get burned out. Why'd they get rid of you, then?'

Franco shrugged. 'Maybe I crossed the line now and then. But with me in charge, the perps got nailed. I just didn't pay much attention to the technicalities involved, that's all.'

Technicalities. Harry's pulse drummed harder. Like whether the perps lived or died?

Franco was still talking.

'My partner warned me to cool it. Said I was starting to look as dangerous as the scum we went after. But he saw things my way, protected me as long as he could.'

Something clicked in Harry's brain. 'Your partner. I'm guessing here, but was that Gideon?'

Franco tilted his head in acknowledgement. 'Very good,

311

Diego. Now cut out the bullshit questions. I hired you to do a job.'

Harry folded her arms across her chest. 'So now suddenly I'm working with *two* cops.'

'Ex-cops. Gideon left as soon as I did.'

'Cop, ex-cop, what's the difference? No one in Belfast said anything about this to me. I don't like it.'

'Who cares what you like? And don't give me that once-a-cop-always-a-cop bullshit. Nothing's for ever in this life.' Franco's face grew dark. 'Nothing.'

Harry eyed his ruddy features, then let her gaze drift to the Aztec building across the street. The place tugged at her like a magnet. In a few minutes, she'd walk inside. She'd ditch Franco on the pretext of deploying Dormouse behind enemy lines, then she'd call Zubiri and get the hell out. She watched a trio of men emerge from the building and stream into the coffee shop next door. Then she turned back to Franco. A few last questions, and she was done.

'What about Riva Mills? Were you a cop when you met her twenty years ago?'

For a minute, she thought he wouldn't answer. His face looked shuttered; closed for business. Eventually, he said,

'I was setting up an undercover op in Vegas. A money-laundering sting to hit the mob where it hurt. Seize their truckloads of cash.'

'Riva was in the mafia?'

He shook his head. 'She was just a pawn. Worked as a dealer in their casinos, did some smurfing for them now and then. But she had links to some of the kingpins, so I used her as a way in. Fooled her into thinking I was on her side.'

'Did it work?'

Franco nodded slowly. 'Took more than two years to set it all up. Then the sting came down, and we raided their delivery trucks, their houses, their business premises. Seized assets worth more than eighty million dollars and made over a hundred and fifty arrests.'

'Riva among them?'

Franco shook his head. 'I kept her name out of it. Like I said, she was just a pawn. I'd planned to get her out of town before the raid even happened, but something went wrong.' He jerked away to face the front. 'Things came down earlier than I expected.'

Something about the way he said it made her think of Hunter's words: *Brother, Andy Mills. Died in Las Vegas. Bullet wound to the head.*

'You said her brother died. Was he involved?'

Franco gripped the steering wheel. 'He was just a kid. Caught a stray bullet. Like I said, things went wrong.'

Franco killed my brother.

Harry kept her voice soft, cradling the mood. 'And Riva blamed you?'

'What do you think?' His lip curled. 'She hated me, threatened me. Swore she'd kill me one day. Hated me for lying to her all that time. No surprise. Betrayal's the name of the game in undercover work.'

His brusque tone had a dangerous, bitter edge. Harry moved the topic along.

313

'So after that, she started a money-laundering outfit of her own?'

Franco nodded. 'Built it from scratch. My department only started tracking her six or seven years ago. Never made anything stick.'

'Were you still a cop by then?'

'Just about. I worked background intelligence. I knew how she operated, so I could help them dig deep, tell them what to look for. We were getting close. Real close.' He flexed his fingers on the wheel, and his jawline looked rigid. 'That's when she decided to make good on her threats.'

Harry felt her eyes grow round. 'She came after you?'

'Threatened to kill me. Left anonymous warnings through the department, trying to scare me off the investigation. I knew too much about her, you see. I could help make the case against her stick. When I didn't back off, she tried to get to me through someone else. Went after someone close to me.' Franco was breathing heavily now. 'She should've known better. Someone strikes out at what's mine, I retaliate. I never back down, she should know that.' He snapped his gaze to Harry, his eyes hot and dark. 'Remember that, Diego, I've told you before. Someone becomes a threat, I take them out.'

Harry's heartbeat stalled. She recalled the bloodstain on the warehouse wall, left there by a guy who knew too much. Like her. She averted her gaze from Franco's cross-eyed stare. Had Riva killed someone close to him to try and warn him off? Was that why he wanted to take her down?

She thought about the years he'd spent undercover: the long-term stings, the meticulous planning. Then she thought about the money-laundering outfit he'd built up over the last five years. Her brain shifted, re-ordering her perspective. Then she stared at him and said,

'It's just another elaborate sting, isn't it? All your warehouses, your trucks, your money-laundering stunts. It's all a front. Just like before. Part of some kind of set-up to take her down.'

Franco looked impressed. Then he shrugged and said, 'Damn right, it's a front. Who the fuck could run a business on the crazy margins I charge? I've got to keep my rates low to stay a player in the market, but it barely covers costs. All those people you saw in the warehouse, they all got to get paid. Along with the smurfs, the couriers, the cross-border merchants. Plus all the officials who need bribing along the way.'

'Sounds like an expensive business.'

'You got that right. I use the casino scams to bankroll it when funds are getting low.' Franco's smile turned slightly manic. 'What could be sweeter than taking her down with her own money?'

Harry's brain did another shuffle, flipped her perceptions a little more. 'That slip of paper. The one you gave the guy in the cemetery. It had Riva's name on it, didn't it?'

'No one goes by their real name in this business. Take Pontius Pilate. I don't know his name, he doesn't know mine. Same with Riva. Besides, her financial manager does all the deals. Now his name, I know. It's Victor Toledo.'

Something twitched in Harry's brain. Riva's Chief of Security? Franco was still talking.

'Me, they call Mojave.' His smile was nasty. 'But yeah, I gave him Toledo's name.'

'So you opted out of the bid because you want Riva's outfit to take his money.' Harry frowned, working her way through it out loud. 'Then you pull the plug on her operations so she can't launder his cash. She's trapped into a commitment she can't fulfil.'

Franco nodded, watching her figure it out. Harry flashed on the man with the rosary beads, the man who drove spike-nails through people's hands when they couldn't pay what they owed. Her mouth felt dry.

'But she can just give him his money back, can't she? Maybe sweeten it with a little extra on top? I don't get it. What's the pay-off?'

'Sure, she could try that. He might even let her off, just this once.' Franco's mouth twisted. 'But what if it's too late? What if she doesn't have his money any more?'

Harry felt her brows pucker. What the hell was he talking about? What was he planning to do when Riva's networks went down? She was missing something here.

She found herself staring at the Aztec building, and realized it didn't matter what she was missing. She didn't need to know his plans. She knew who his target was, and most of the reasons why, and as far as she was concerned that was enough. It was time to bail. Time to shake Franco off and keep her promise to Hunter to come out.

Her mind raced. This could be her only chance. A

flash-flood of sweat clung to her shirt, and she buzzed the window down, cracking open the claustrophobia of the car. The swish of traffic sounded loud, as though she'd emerged from a long spell underwater. She flicked another glance at the Aztec building and gave a testy sigh.

'Look, I don't know what you're planning, and quite frankly, I don't care. If I'm going to sabotage that nerve centre, then it's time I went inside.'

Franco inhaled the clean air, nodding his approval. 'I like that, Diego. Businesslike. No bullshit. Just concentrate on your part of the deal and we'll get along fine. How long will this take?'

Harry shrugged. 'Not long. Thirty or forty minutes in there should do it.'

Long enough to find a phone, call for help. Not so long that it raised his suspicions. Franco nodded again.

'Good, because we don't have time for anything more. There've been enough delays. With McArdle, everything took weeks.' He held a finger up. 'There's just one more thing.'

Harry's heartbeat juddered. 'What's that?'

Franco smiled, and his eyes turned shrewd. 'I'm coming in there with you.'

34

Harry blinked. Felt as if she'd crashed into a wall.

She shook her head. 'I don't take tag-alongs.'

'This time you do.'

'I work alone, I told you that before.'

'Where you go, I go.'

Harry's breathing felt shallow. Franco's gaze seemed to strobe into her brain like a searchlight. He still didn't trust her. Natural caution? Or had he figured out Diego was a fake?

She played for time. 'I'll need some equipment. Cloned employee badges, wireless access points—'

Franco was already shaking his head. 'No time for bullshit paraphernalia. You're either good enough to do this right now or you're not. I want this logic-bomb sucker in place, ready to detonate.'

'But that's crazy. If you want this done right—'

'I want it done fast. Things are in motion. I can't afford delays.' His eyes narrowed. 'Sometimes I don't know about you, Diego. You ask all these questions, then you don't do as I say.'

Harry went still, made her face bland. Did he know? Maybe he'd known for a while. Maybe he'd kept her around because he needed a hacker, and nothing else mattered right now.

But if that was true, what would he do when her usefulness was over?

She blanked the thought out, and studied the Aztec building. She'd started this. Now she had to finish it.

'Okay, but I'm warning you, this comes with no guarantees. If I had time to prepare, I could deploy McArdle's Dormouse, no problem. But on the hoof, here and now?' Harry shook her head. 'Our best chance is fifty-fifty.'

'Just shut up and do it.'

Harry shrugged. Then she reached into the back seat for McArdle's laptop and hauled the case onto her knees. Her brain was scrabbling, scouring for a plan. Truth was, she hadn't formed any kind of strategy. All she'd cared about till now was cutting loose from Franco.

She extracted the laptop, along with McArdle's memory sticks, and booted up the machine. There were plenty of ways she could do this. Probably the simplest was to engage with an Aztec employee over the phone. Social engineering: the hacker's long con. Bamboozle a mark with enough persuasive lies, and you could get him to do almost anything: click on a malicious email

319

attachment; download hostile programs from a bogus website. With the right amount of flimflam, Harry could persuade someone to whistle Dormouse in and let it nest there in Aztec's back yard.

She chewed on a thumbnail. Scamming over the phone wouldn't help her lose Franco. Her eyes slid to the building across the street. She had to go inside. Find a way to ditch him in there.

The laptop whirred. Harry let her gaze drift beyond the Aztec building to the coffee shop next door. A scenario flashed up. Unfolded in her head. She plugged one of the memory sticks into the laptop and went to work on the keyboard.

'Can you lift someone's wallet?' she said. 'If I distract them?'

'Are you kidding? I've got light hands. Cons, card tricks, sleight-of-hand cheating. It's why I got recruited for undercover.'

'To play cards?'

Franco shrugged. 'They like you to have a specialist skill. Never know what they're going to need. Lorry drivers, chemistry graduates, plumbers, pilots . . .'

'What was Gideon's speciality?'

Franco gave her a long stare. 'He served in the Special Forces for a while. He's got plenty of useful skills.'

Harry's stomach dipped. *All we know about Gideon Ray is that he kills people.*

Her fingers jittered across the keyboard. Franco squinted at the screen, watching every key she hit.

'What are you doing?'

'We need to get Dormouse inside, right? Catapult it over the fence, launch it past their blockades?'

'So?'

'So, I'm priming up the slingshot.'

She flicked a glance at his face. It looked tight with suspicion. She switched the stick out, snapped another one in. Flitted her fingers across the keys.

'Now what?' he said.

'Two slingshots. Let's increase our odds.'

She sensed him leaning back a little. Relaxing, even. Maybe she was wrong. Maybe he hadn't seen through Diego. After all, he didn't trust anyone, not even Gideon.

She shot him a look, ventured a question. 'What does Gideon think is going on?'

'Thinks I'm here to take down Riva's casinos.'

'He has no idea what you've been doing for the last five years?'

Franco shrugged, his eyes tracking the hieroglyphics on the screen. 'If I'd told him, he would've tried to talk me out of it. Besides, we lost touch. Went our separate ways.'

'So why's he here now?'

Franco gave an unpleasant smile. 'Let's just say I've got a use for those specialist skills of his.'

Harry's insides squeezed. She blundered through a few more commands and snapped the memory stick out. Then she dipped back into McArdle's reconnaissance and took note of two senior executives' names: Rico Cardona,

Head of Human Resources, and Fabio Perez, Head of Operations. Then she closed the laptop and retrieved paper, pen and a handful of plain envelopes from the case.

Franco frowned. 'You writing a fucking letter now?'

Harry ignored him, and leaned on the laptop to scribble out a short note in Spanish. Franco's eyes followed her pen across the page, and she could tell by his expression that he understood. She copied the same note out a second time, then slipped each one into a separate envelope, which she marked 'PRIVATE & CONFIDENTIAL' along the back. She tipped a memory stick into each one before tucking in the flaps.

Harry glanced at Franco. He was studying her closely, suspicion and curiosity chasing each other across his face. She packed the laptop away, sliding the two envelopes into the case. Her palms were damp with sweat. She turned to Franco with a challenging look.

'Let me do the talking out there. And if anything looks off, we get the hell out. We'll use your emergency signal.'

She smoothed a hand over her hair to demonstrate. Franco's lip curled, his eyes looked mocking.

'Bullshit. I have my own way of dealing with problems. Here's *my* emergency signal.'

He reached into his jacket and whipped out a bulky-looking gun. Then he jammed it under her chin, snapped her head backwards. Harry gasped. Froze. He shoved the pistol hard into her trachea, and she gagged. Couldn't swallow. Franco's face loomed close.

'You better make sure nothing goes wrong.' He looked cross-eyed. Psychotic. 'I'll be right beside you, so don't do anything stupid.'

Harry stared, wide-eyed. Blood pounded in her throat, throbbed against the metal. She tried not to swallow, tried not to choke.

Then suddenly, he pulled away. Harry dragged in air, and touched her throat. Felt the indentation he'd left there. She watched him tuck the gun back in its holster. Then he clicked his fingers at her and said,

'Let's go.'

35

Harry pushed through the glass doors of the Aztec building. A tremor pulsed along her arms. Behind her, Franco was so close she could hear him breathe.

She eased into the spacious lobby, cataloguing her surroundings. Reception desk straight ahead, manned by a security guard. Sofas on one side, steel turnstiles on the other. Beyond the turnstiles, a short corridor with restrooms and a single glass door.

Harry strolled towards the reception desk, waiting her turn behind a stocky woman who was chatting to the guard. Harry stood to one side and studied her. Casual business shirt and trousers. Photo ID badge slung around her neck. Electronic key fob clipped to her belt loop.

The woman caught her eye, nodded to the guard and moved off towards the turnstiles. Harry watched her go.

Saw her hold up the key fob to a sensor on the turnstile before ratcheting through the barrier. Same thing by the door at the end of the corridor, only this time she punched in an access code as well. When the glass door opened, Harry glimpsed a second door beyond.

Her insides sank. Security lockdown. Dead space. There was nowhere for her to go.

She tightened her grip on the laptop case and stepped up closer to the desk. Franco moved with her, his hand sliding under his lapel. Harry smiled at the security guard, addressing him in Spanish.

'Excuse me, can you tell me if I'm in the right place? Is this Aztec International?'

'That's right.'

'Oh great.' Harry patted her chest. 'I was afraid I'd got it wrong. Only there are no signs on the door.'

The guard's stare was blank. He was middle-aged, with a beach-ball gut that seemed to wedge him into his chair. Corporate signage didn't seem to interest him, so Harry pushed on.

'We've an appointment with Señor Cardona in a little while. I just wanted to make sure we had the right building, that's all. Thanks for your help.'

She started to edge away, but the guard was already lifting the phone.

'I'll tell him you're here. Name?'

Harry raised a hand. 'Oh no, we're too early, I don't want to bother him yet. Our appointment isn't for another forty minutes. We'll come back.' She moved off towards the door, then turned as if in afterthought. 'Maybe there's a café where we can wait?'

The guard dumped the handset back in its cradle. 'Next door.'

Harry thanked him, and headed for the exit. His surly voice trailed after her.

'Stay away from the pastries. They're stale.'

'So how're we going to get past security?' Franco slurped his coffee. 'Tailgate in behind someone else?'

Harry shook her head, and kept her eyes on the café entrance. 'Won't work. The guard's watching the turnstile, and the other door's a man-trap.'

'It is?'

Harry nodded. 'Two sets of doors. First door has to close before the other one opens. An air-lock. Pressure sensor in the floor measures weight distribution and only allows one person in at a time. No tailgating in through that dead space.'

Franco jiggled his knee under the table, his gaze flitting around the café. 'So what's your idea, Diego? How the fuck do we get in there?'

Harry tried to ignore him, kept her eyes fixed on the door. The guy was like a time bomb, waiting to go off. Behind her, the baristas slammed out coffee dregs, and the espresso machines gushed and gurgled. The place was busy, and a favourite with Aztec employees. She could spot them by their ID badges and key fobs.

Harry profiled each newcomer that came through the

door. She needed a lone employee. Preferably young, preferably a guy. Preferably not an alpha male.

Five minutes later, she saw him.

Short, mid-twenties, narrow-chested. Glasses and centre-parted hair. Harry watched as the guy flattened himself against the door, letting someone else jump the queue. He sidled up to the counter, as though ready at any moment to step aside for someone more important.

Harry looked at Franco. 'That guy with the glasses. Can you lift his wallet without being seen? When I make my move?'

Franco glanced over and shrugged. 'Sure.'

Harry watched the guy queue up. She felt bad about the trouble she might get him into, but it couldn't be helped now. She took Franco's coffee cup and lifted her own. Then she got to her feet, a half-full latte in each hand, and strolled up behind the guy with the glasses. She waited till he'd paid, waited till he was turning. Then she barged right into him, jerking her hands upwards, spilling one cup over his shirt and the other one over herself.

The guy gasped and leaped backwards, bent at the midriff as though someone had yanked a cord behind his waist. His arms were outstretched, one hand clamped to the lid of his still-intact coffee. He gaped down at his latte-stained shirt.

Harry spread out her arms, surveying her own sodden blouse. Lukewarm coffee trickled down her abdomen. She looked at the guy and said in Spanish,

327

'Oh my God, I'm so sorry!'

He blinked, wordless. Franco materialized behind him, leaning over to pass a wad of napkins from the counter.

'I'm really so sorry.' Harry picked at her own shirt, separating the wet fabric from her skin. 'I was heading for the condiments, I didn't see you turning.'

The guy with the glasses managed a weak smile. 'It's okay, I'll dry off.'

'But your shirt, it's ruined.'

'So is your blouse.' His cheeks coloured slightly. 'Really, don't worry. I can clean up back in the office.'

Harry gave him a rueful smile. Apologized again. He smiled back, then tried to edge unnoticed towards the door. A nice guy. Didn't want her to feel bad. Someone pushier probably would have got riled.

Harry watched him go. Franco came to stand beside her, then without warning took her hand and kissed her upturned palm. A sickening charge shot through her, and she worked hard not to pull away. His smile was slow and provocative, his fingers tight around hers.

'Who knew we'd make such a good team?'

They waited five more minutes, then headed back into Aztec. Bored recognition flickered over the guard's face, and he raised his eyebrows at the state of Harry's blouse.

She made a rueful face, jerked her thumb over her shoulder. 'I had a collision with one of your guys back there.'

'So I see. He just came in. He was a mess.'

328

'God, I feel awful. And I hate to bother him again, but I think he left this behind.' She held up the wallet Franco had given her. 'His credit card says his name is Ramirez, is that right?'

The guard sighed. 'I'll get him down.'

He spoke into the phone, and two minutes later the guy with the glasses had emerged from the man-trap and was pushing his way through the turnstiles.

He looked startled to see her. Harry nodded.

'Yeah, me again. Sorry to be a pain, but I think you left this behind.'

She held out the wallet. The guy frowned. Patted his back pockets. Stared at the wallet and paled. Then he took it from her and riffled through it. Harry clasped her hands together.

'I hope everything's there?'

'Yes. Yes, it is. Thank you.'

He looked a little dazed. Harry noticed he'd tried to dry himself off, though his shirt was still badly stained. She plucked at her own blouse, giving the fabric a little shake.

'I'd better get cleaned up somewhere. I've an appointment with Señor Cardona upstairs in ten minutes.'

She edged backwards, gave him a shy smile. He blinked and seemed tongue-tied, his social awkwardness blinding him to his cue to return the favour. But he recovered in time, and gestured behind him.

'Why don't you use the restrooms here?'

Harry's smile widened. If he hadn't offered, she would

have asked. The guy with the glasses checked with the guard.

'That'd be okay, wouldn't it?'

The guard glared. 'No one's allowed through without a pass.'

He turned his glare on Harry, and she could see the internal debate in his face. A stranger off the street would have got a straight refusal. But he had a context for her now. A social pedigree of sorts. He'd met her twice. She had an appointment with Cardona, which constituted an endorsement by proxy. And she'd just returned this guy's wallet intact. What could be more trustworthy?

The guard clicked a release button for the turnstiles. 'Just don't take too long about it.'

'Thanks, I appreciate it.' Harry shot Franco a look, and noticed his clenched jaw. 'I'll be right back.'

She clanked through the turnstiles before he could object, and pushed open the door marked *Servicios*. Her heart rate climbed. She stepped inside and, for the first time in days, slipped out of Franco's reach.

The door swung to, and Harry found herself in an outer vestibule with a choice of Ladies or Gents.

Her limbs trembled. She ducked into the Ladies, scouted out the room. Three stalls, all vacant. Coffee-coloured tiles. Floral air-freshener.

No windows.

Shit.

Harry charged into the nearest stall. Scoured the walls, the ceiling.

No windows, no skylight.

She tried the next two stalls. Same solid enclosures.

Lockdown. No way out.

Harry's head reeled, and she felt herself sway. She dropped the laptop case, covered her face with her hands. Panic torpedoed through her, ricocheting to a frenzy inside her.

No way out. No place to go.

She wheeled around to the basins and leaned her palms on the cold tiles, her head bent low. Why the hell had she started all this? What had she thought she'd solve by shedding her identity and hiding?

A sob juddered through her. She clamped her hands over her mouth, staring at herself in the mirror. Her hair looked wild, a mass of dense curls, and beneath it her face looked white. She breathed deeply through her nose. She had to stay calm. Had to figure a way out.

Slowly, she removed her hands from her mouth. Maybe Dormouse could help her. Maybe she should deploy it, just like Franco wanted. Then if he wanted her to detonate it, he'd have to link her to the internet. Let her open a channel to the outside world.

A jab of adrenalin flared through her. She snatched up the laptop, fished out the two envelopes, and ducked into the middle stall. She left one envelope in full view on the toilet tank, then swung out of the Ladies and into the Gents next door. The place was empty, the décor much the same, though the air wasn't nearly so floral. No windows, either, but Harry hadn't expected any. She elbowed her way into the nearest cubicle and left the second envelope on the tank.

Someone would find them eventually, and probably open them. The note inside was addressed to Cardona in Human Resources, and purported to come from Fabio Perez, Head of Operations. According to Fabio, the enclosed USB stick contained the list of names for a first round of employee redundancies. For security reasons, Fabio said, the list was being hand-delivered rather than emailed over the corporate network.

Harry surveyed her handiwork. In these uncertain times, who wouldn't want to take a peek at that?

And when someone got curious enough to insert the stick in their computer, its covert payload would catapult Dormouse straight into the Aztec network. Dormouse would email Harry to announce its safe landing, then scamper into a corner and snooze until detonation day.

Harry left the Gents and stood in the vestibule, steeling herself to go back outside. She took a deep breath, then pushed through the door and marched back out to reception. Franco glared at her from the other side of the turnstiles. She ratcheted through to join him, then he grabbed her elbow and steered her out the door.

Outside, the pavement was clogged with shoppers. Franco guided her towards the kerb, heading for the car, when suddenly she felt him pull away. Then he released his grip on her arm.

She whipped her gaze around. He was backing down the street, his eyes wide with alarm. He fixed her with a warning look, then slipped a hand under his lapel and smoothed the other over his hair.

The emergency signal.

What the hell?

Harry snapped her eyes back, raked the busy crowds. Then she froze. Riva was crossing the street towards her, heading for the Aztec building. A tall, fair-haired man strode by her side.

Harry stared. Recognized him with a hard, body-slamming jolt, the kind that punches the air from your lungs.

Sandy hair, cut schoolboy-short.

Lean, athletic build.

Harry squinted, shook her head.

The man coming towards her was Hunter.

36

Harry felt paralysed. Her eyes were riveted on Hunter's face. On his achingly familiar features. What the hell was he doing in San Sebastián?

But she knew the answer to that. He'd come here to find her.

He stepped onto the kerb, and saw her the same time that Riva did. His eyes flared, his stride faltered. For a moment he looked too stunned to move.

Beside him, Riva's bony face tightened. 'What are you doing here?'

Harry checked over her shoulder. Franco had vanished into the crowds, but her instincts told her he was somewhere watching, looking for false moves. She hitched a thumb at the Aztec building, improvising wildly.

'I came here to see you.'

'I have nothing more to say to you. Just stay out of my way.'

'What? I don't—'

'Detective Hunter here can explain. Apparently, he's been looking for you.'

Hunter moved in close to Harry. Close enough to touch. She looked up, hungry for his face. His eyes held hers, full of unspoken messages. He made as if to reach out, then stuffed his hands into his pockets.

'I warned you I'd track you down, Ms Martinez.'

Harry felt a rush at the sound of his voice, and battled with a fullness in her throat. She drank in his hazel eyes, the light stubble, the wavy fatigue lines on his brow. She raked his face, trying to guess the story he might have spun for Riva. The woman stepped closer.

'I don't hire felons,' Riva said. 'So consider our arrangement terminated.'

Felons?

Harry opened her mouth to answer when something flashed across the street: sunlight slicing off metal. Harry squinted. Stopped breathing. Franco was staring out at her from the Volvo, the bore of his gun propped discreetly against his open window. His smile looked deranged.

Blood roared in Harry's ears. She threw Hunter a desperate look. Saw the answering fear leap into his eyes, urgent and questioning. Beside him, Riva's face was hard and pinched.

Harry hesitated. Whose side was Riva on? She'd killed McArdle. If she knew Harry had links to Franco, would she kill her too? Her brain whirled. She felt as if she were trapped in some deadly blind man's buff, groping in the dark for the other players.

Hunter gripped her arm. 'I'm taking you back. We're getting you out of here.'

Her skin tingled at his touch, and for a moment, she savoured it. Anchor-strong. Safehaven-warm. Then she flicked a glance over at Franco and stiffened. His gun was drifting slowly back and forth, as though tracking stray passers-by. He mimed a series of pistol kickbacks, as if picking people off, one by one. His eyes flicked to hers to make sure she was watching. Then he smiled and centred the barrel on a sight line to her chest.

Harry felt cold. Numb. Then the words tumbled out.

'I've found him.' She addressed herself to Riva, but the message was meant for Hunter. 'The man you were looking for. He's holed up by the river. Unit 310, Apartamentos Urumea.'

Hunter tightened his grip on her arm. Riva looked at her sharply, ignoring the phone that suddenly rang out from her bag. Then the woman briefly closed her eyes and shrugged.

'Maybe I don't care any more.' Riva moved away, digging out her phone. 'She's all yours, Detective.'

Riva turned aside to take the call, covering her ear to block out the din of traffic. Harry snapped her eyes to Hunter, lowering her voice.

'I can't come with you.'

'What—'

'Across the street, don't look, don't look. He's got a gun, I have to go.'

Hunter stared. 'Jesus, Harry.'

'Apartment 310, tell Zubiri.'

Hunter clenched his teeth, squeezed hard on her arm. 'You can't stay! Come with me. Just run.'

'He'll shoot. He's crazy, he won't care who he takes down. Me, you, Riva. All these people.'

'I don't care about all these people.' He looked fierce. Bewildered. 'I came to get *you*.'

Harry felt a crushing heat in her chest. Then her eyes darted across the street. Franco's smile was menacing. She took a deep breath, the words coming in a rush.

'He's set himself up as a money launderer. Riva, too. He's out to get her. Tell Zubiri.'

'Come with me and tell him yourself.'

Harry closed her eyes. 'He's an ex-cop, used to work undercover in Vegas. You could get a line on him there. He was part of the sting that got Andy Mills shot.'

Hunter shook her arm. 'I don't give a shit. You're coming out.'

Harry shook her head. Across the street, Franco was looking restless.

'I can't come with you,' she whispered.

'Jesus, Harry, don't do this.'

She edged away. 'I've got to go back.'

'Bullshit.'

Hunter was breathing hard through his nose, shaking

337

his head. She could almost see his brain scrambling, desperate for another way.

'Jack.' She said his name softly. It felt good. 'You can't help me.'

He looked as though she'd slapped him. Then his face darkened, and she sensed his body clench. Felt his urge to rail against her. His gaze tore through the crowds, hunting for a way out. She prayed he wouldn't do anything stupid. That he'd realize there were some things you couldn't just bulldoze through. Slowly, finally, he seemed to get it. His eyes turned bleak. Then he loosened his grip on her arm.

Harry felt a surge of panic. Like the sudden fright you get when you find yourself drifting out to sea. Hunter's eyes sought hers. She looked at him for a moment, feeling light-headed. Ordinary life clamoured around her. Horns blared. Shoppers bumped into her. A harmonica coaxed out a mellow jazz note in some bar.

She wrenched her gaze away and blundered back across the street to Franco.

37

'I can't believe you pulled a gun on me. In the middle of the *street*?'

Harry glared at Franco, waiting for him to answer. He revved the engine, cutting across the avenue, his roughcast profile set in hard lines. Harry yanked at her seat belt and rammed the buckle home, using righteous outrage as a cover for the tremor in her limbs.

'What if you'd been seen?' she said. 'Who's going to pay me if your ass gets slung in jail?'

She exhaled a huffy breath, ignoring the tug in her chest that urged her to look back at Hunter. She fixed her eyes straight ahead. He knew where to find her. Already, he was probably calling in the address to Zubiri, along with the Volvo's number plates. All she had to do now was play out the final charade.

'You were looking real cosy back there.' Franco's voice

was low, simmering with a fury that was ready to come to the boil.

Harry squinted. 'Cosy? Are you kidding? The woman's an ice cube. Last time we met, I was cheating her roulette wheel. Take it from me, she wasn't pleased to see me.'

'What did she say?'

'What do you think? She wanted to know what I was doing outside her corporate headquarters.'

'So?'

'So I tried to sell her the coincidence. Told her I didn't know it was her stupid headquarters, that I was in the café next door when I collided with some guy and was just returning his wallet.'

Franco paused, as if replaying the ruse frame by frame, checking it for holes. 'Did she buy it?'

'No.'

Franco whipped his gaze to hers. His teeth were clenched: a dam choking back an eruption of hot rage. Harry made an exasperated sound.

'Would you just relax? I gave her Ramirez's name, told her to call him up if she didn't believe me. She spoke to him right there, you saw her on the phone.'

'So your story held up?'

'Sure, why wouldn't it?'

Franco's knuckles bulged like mini-mountain ranges on the wheel. 'Who was the guy?'

Harry shrugged, suddenly seized by paranoia. Could one seasoned cop possibly scent out another? The notion had her shifting in her seat.

'We didn't get introduced. Some lackey of Riva's. Did you see the way he grabbed my arm? I thought he was going to haul me back inside.'

Franco paused. 'You have an explanation for everything, don't you, Diego?'

She shrugged again, kept her face neutral. Franco went on.

'I'll get Gideon to check him out.'

Harry experienced a sharp stab of unease, and leaned back against the headrest, her brain strung out from trying to keep track of all the lies. She thought of the story Hunter had given Riva to try and track Harry down. He knew the woman was involved, so had to be circumspect about what he told her. A felon on the run. Not a bad choice. The kind of ruse she might have ad-libbed herself.

An image of Hunter suddenly flooded her head: the short tawny hair; the eyes that always drank in the sight of her with such intensity. A dull ache squeezed her chest.

Franco wheeled left into a narrow side street. 'You done good in there, Diego. Set-up, convincer, pay-off. I like it.' He nodded to himself. 'Now tell me about the envelopes. I'm guessing you left them in the john, so what happens now?'

'You saw the note. Someone's going to get curious and plug the memory stick in. And when they do, Dormouse will burrow into the network. Mission accomplished, logic bomb deployed.'

'No one will know?'

341

Harry shook her head. 'The USB just throws up a blank document. No evidence of what's going on behind the scenes.'

'What if they don't plug it in? What if we get some conscientious prick who just hands the envelope in to security?'

'Then we're screwed.'

Franco shot her a black look, and Harry held up her palms.

'Hey, I told you there were no guarantees. You rush me, this is the best you get.'

'Not good enough, Diego.'

He hung a hard right, grinding the gears. Beside them, the river snaked into view, which meant they were getting close to the apartment. Harry eyed Franco's profile. All she had to do was keep him calm until Zubiri came to get her. She spread out her palms in a mollifying gesture.

'Look, chances are it's going to work, and if it does, it'll be soon. Maybe it's already happened. Maybe there's an email waiting for me now, saying Dormouse is in place. We can nuke Riva's network any time you want.'

Franco nodded, and gave a smile that goosed Harry's flesh. She thought of his scheme to bring Riva down: the long-term planning; the careful chess moves. The obsession.

'If you hate her so much,' she said eventually, 'why didn't you just shoot her back there when you had the chance?'

342

He gave a scornful laugh. 'What do you know about hate, Diego?'

Harry looked at him doubtfully, and he went on.

'You hate someone, you don't just want them to die. You want them to suffer. You want to see it in their face, watch it in their eyes.' The sneer on his lips was ugly. 'I want to watch her when everything she's built goes up in flames. *Then* I'll fucking kill her.'

Harry felt her eyes flare, and she kept her mouth shut for the rest of the journey. Five minutes later, they pulled up by the apartment and Harry climbed out of the car. She dawdled by the kerb, checking left and right. A feathery breeze brushed her skin as she took in the deserted road.

Too soon for Zubiri.

Franco gestured with his arm, hustling her inside. Slowly, she led the way up to the apartment, where he unlocked the front door and strode ahead of her into the living room. Then he jerked to a sudden halt.

Harry stopped up short behind him as he put out a hand.

'Don't move.'

Harry frowned, peering around him.

Ginny was lying on the floor beside the sofa, as though searching for something that had rolled away underneath it.

'Ginny?'

She was dressed in leggings and a long shirt. Probably another one of McArdle's. Her hair was jumbled into a matted bun that looked too heavy for her graceful neck. Then Harry saw the clumps and sticky darkness that weighed it down.

'Fuck it.' Franco snatched out his gun. '*Fuck it!*'

Harry gasped, clapped both hands over her mouth. She squeezed her eyes shut, swallowed up by a nausea in her gut.

Franco whirled away and raced down the hallway, kicking in doors, checking the other rooms. Harry breathed through her nose. Opened her eyes. Waves of sweat broke over her skin. She edged closer to Ginny, averting her gaze from the explosive mess that had once been the back of her head. Harry knelt beside her. Touched a smooth, white wrist, so slender it could have been a child's.

'Get away from her!' Franco charged back into the room, his gun trained on Harry. 'Don't touch anything!'

Harry scrambled backwards. His eyes were black holes. He gestured with the gun.

'Into the bedroom. Pack everything up. *Now!*'

Harry flinched, then hurried into the bedroom she'd shared with Ginny. The floor seemed unsteady, as if she was clambering over a boat deck. Franco watched as she flung open the wardrobe, hauled down a suitcase and grabbed an armful of clothes.

'Who did it, Franco?'

'Shut your mouth! Keep packing!'

Harry stuffed the clothes into the suitcase and stumbled back to the wardrobe for another armful. Hangers jangled, echoing the clamour in her brain. The clamour that drowned out images of Ginny's burst skull.

Harry flattened the clothes in the case, shoving McArdle's beloved DefCon jacket on top. Harry caught its dusty scent: old leather and cigarettes. She flashed on Ginny, huddled into it, inhaling memories of her dead friend. Harry's sinuses flooded with the threat of tears. Ginny was the closest thing to an ally she'd had around here.

'*Move!*'

Harry jumped, and zipped up the suitcase. Franco herded her across the hall and stood over her while she cleared out the wardrobe and shelves in his room. Then he grabbed one of the suitcases and flicked the gun towards the door.

'Let's go.'

'What about Ginny?'

'Gideon will take care of her.'

Harry's brain jarred, refusing to picture what that meant. Franco hauled her outside, shoving her towards a white van parked beside the kerb. She flicked a look at the Volvo across the street.

'We're switching cars?'

'Switching cars, switching apartments.'

A cold stone of dread dropped into Harry's stomach. Franco's eyes burned into hers.

'Somebody knows where we are.'

38

The new apartment turned out to be shabbier than the old one. Threadbare carpets. Musty, wet-dog smell. It was located on the other side of the river, huddled in a side street far from the embankments.

Far from the bullet-torn wreckage of Ginny's skull.

Harry shrank back against the sofa, watching Franco prowl the kitchen. They'd been cooped up in the apartment for almost twenty-four hours, Harry sitting hunched, rocking to and fro, waiting for the rhythm to calm her. Franco yelled whenever she asked about Ginny. Yelled even more when there was still no word from Dormouse.

He slammed a drawer shut, sending cutlery crashing. Then he turned and reached for the laptop that lay on the counter between them.

'Check it again.'

Harry dragged herself to her feet. Her body felt heavy,

as though shock had somehow thickened her bones. She waited while Franco snapped a modem stick into the laptop, then under his sharp gaze, she checked Diego's email.

Nothing.

Franco whacked the counter, making Harry jump. 'What the fuck, Diego? I ask you to do one simple thing and you screw it up.'

'Hey, it's not over yet. Maybe whoever has the envelope is lying low, just waiting for a quiet moment. It's not the kind of thing you want your boss to catch you with, is it?'

'We're running out of time, Diego. *You're* running out of time.'

He whipped out the modem, burying it in his fist. His rage had been bubbling all morning, a molten fury ready to spew out and scald someone.

Harry edged back to the sofa. Radio silence from Dormouse might be a hitch in Franco's plans, but it was probably the only thing keeping her alive. Once the Aztec network toppled, her usefulness to Franco was over.

She curled up on the stale-smelling couch, her eyelids drooping. Images of Ginny had stalked her sleep, along with anguish over the part she might have played in the girl's death. What if Riva had killed her? Harry had been the one to tell her about Ginny in the first place. It was Harry who'd given Riva the apartment address. She squeezed her eyes shut against a crush of regret.

'Where the fuck is Gideon?' Franco paced the kitchen.

He'd called Gideon from the van the previous day as they'd pulled away from the old apartment. He'd ordered him to find Clayton and clean the place out, get rid of anything they'd left behind.

Had that included Ginny's body?

Harry hugged her knees, trying to get warm. Maybe Zubiri's men had already stormed the apartment. Maybe they'd barged in on Gideon and caught him covering their tracks.

Or maybe they'd just found the place empty.

Franco shoved the modem back into the laptop. 'Again.'

Harry trudged over to the counter and re-checked her email. This time her pulse climbed. One new message. She pulled it open.

Dormouse was in.

Franco's gaze jumped back and forth from the screen to her face. 'That's the email we've been waiting for?'

Harry nodded. His broad features widened into a ferocious smile. Then he made a pistol with his fingers and cocked it at the screen.

'Detonate it.'

'What? Now?'

'We've already wasted too much time. Just do it.'

Harry hesitated, her scalp prickling. Then she summoned the special website McArdle had created, which right now consisted of a single blank page. Franco shifted closer, watching her every move. She slipped into the internals of the page and slowly, carefully, in the top left-hand corner, she inserted the word 'mousetrap'.

'Now what?' Franco licked his lips, hungry for more.

'We wait for Dormouse to check its new instructions. It won't take long.'

Harry flipped back to her email, knowing Dormouse had one last message to send. It arrived two minutes later:

doomsday initiated

Franco barked out a laugh. 'It's started?'

Harry nodded. She pictured Dormouse exploding across the network, blasting communications, torpedoing data; a Molotov cocktail hurling fireballs through Aztec's core.

Network inferno.

Franco's eyes glittered, as though he'd seen it too.

'Okay, Diego.' He looked restless. Febrile. 'You're done.'

But nothing changed.

For hours, Franco paced the apartment, fuelled by some internal fire. Harry stayed huddled on the sofa, trying to ward off a cold fog of fear. When Gideon and Clayton finally showed up, the fog turned icy. So much for Zubiri.

'Where the fuck have you been?'

Franco drew Gideon aside, and chewed him out for a while. Then he swept out of the apartment, leaving Gideon in charge.

Harry curled up smaller on the sofa. It was the first time Franco had left her side in two days. Was he finished with her? Finished with Riva? The notion made her stomach queasy.

A day later, Franco still hadn't come back.

'What's he doing, anyway?'

Harry swung her legs off the couch, waiting for Gideon to answer. She watched him deal poker hands on the coffee table for himself and Clayton. The two of them had been playing cards for five hours straight.

Gideon ignored her. The only sound in the room was the *slip-slap* of cards and the tinkle of ice in Clayton's drink. Harry stretched, her limbs crackling like twigs.

'God, this is so boring. Why can't we go out?'

'Franco says to stay here.'

'You always do what he says?'

Gideon's freckles turned dark. Clayton flung down his cards and got to his feet.

'I've had enough.'

He stomped into the kitchen, taking his drink with him. His bandage was gone, exposing the bulge of livid flesh that was his nose. He switched on the radio, cutting snatches of static into the room as he trawled for an English station.

Harry hunched her shoulders, massaging her arms. Why couldn't she get warm? She wandered into her bedroom in search of a jacket, her eyes lingering on the small, rear-facing window. They were six storeys up. No balconies, no ledges. Just sixty feet of sheer, concrete drop. She slipped on McArdle's leather jacket, hugging it close, inhaling the smoky leather aroma. She tried not to think of Ginny.

'Hey you, get the fuck out here where I can see you.'

Harry closed her eyes briefly, then drifted back out to the couch. Gideon glared at her, then started dealing himself blackjack hands. In the kitchen, the radio hissed and buzzed, spitting out shredded sound. Gideon smacked down his cards.

'Jesus, Clayton, would you cut that out?'

Clayton slid him a look. Then he snapped the radio off and carried his glass and a bottle of whisky into his room.

Gideon shook his head and turned back to his cards. His shirtsleeves were rolled up, revealing sturdy forearms more freckled than his face. Harry eyed the hard set of his jaw. Somehow it was easier to picture him as a cop than Franco.

He caught her stare. 'What are you looking at?'

Harry shrugged, opting for the truth. 'Franco told me you two used to be undercover cops. I was just wondering why you quit.'

His eyes narrowed. 'He said that?'

'Sounds like he got burned out.' Harry leaned back against the sofa. Something hard dug into her back and she shifted. 'Is that what happened to you?'

'Mind your own fucking business.'

'Maybe you just left when you saw what it did to Franco.' Harry groped under the jacket at the small of her back. Felt something solid in the lining. 'He ended up in psychoanalysis, didn't he?'

'Shut your mouth.'

'Didn't someone close to him die? Maybe that sent him over the edge.'

Gideon slammed the deck of cards onto the table. 'What the fuck do you know about it? Franco gave his life to that outfit, and for what? For a filing cabinet of backslaps, then one last stitch-up? Damn right I got out.'

Harry fingered the hard shape at her back. Had McArdle hidden something in his jacket? Her mind raced as she dragged her attention back to Gideon.

'So you left the force. What did you do then?'

For a moment, she thought he wouldn't answer. Then he said,

'Same thing I'd been doing for the last twenty years. Only now I wasn't fooling.'

Harry frowned, and he went on.

'My best undercover role. Contract killer.' His voice grew soft. 'Play a role long enough, and it starts to get real.'

Harry felt a hitch in her chest. She stared at Gideon, and her hearing seemed to buzz. Then she inched forwards on the sofa and got to her feet.

'Where the fuck are you going?'

Harry drew herself up. 'If it's any of your business, I need to go to the bathroom. That okay with you?'

'You got two minutes.'

Harry made her way to the toilet and locked the door.

Then she whipped off the jacket and knelt on the floor to examine it.

Her hands trembled. She groped at the lining, felt the hard shape. Small. Rectangular. She probed along the seams, hunting for a weakness. Her fingers hooked into a small opening near the sleeve, and she ripped into the stitches, pulling them apart. Then she worked the object out with both hands.

It was a drawstring pouch. Black, velvety. Secretive. Harry yanked at the puckered neck, then upended its contents onto the floor. Adrenalin flared through her as she stared at McArdle's cache.

A memory stick and a mobile phone.

39

Harry picked up the phone.

She turned it over, cradling it in both hands, afraid her jitters might send it clattering to the floor. Her thumb hovered over the power switch, and she hesitated.

Who knew what noise the thing might make? Probably some cheery start-up jingle. She glanced around the dingy bathroom, assessing its tiled acoustics. She might as well sound off a fire alarm.

She clasped the phone to her chest. Then she slipped it back into the velvet pouch, along with the memory stick, and slotted the pouch into the lining of McArdle's jacket. She got to her feet and shrugged the jacket on, her heart drumming so hard she could feel the pulse in her neck. Then she opened the door and made her way back out to Gideon.

He was still at the coffee table dealing cards. The back

of his neck looked hard and muscular, glinting with buzz cut regrowth. Harry trudged past him towards her bedroom.

'I'm taking a shower. This dump is making my skin crawl.'

She grabbed some fresh clothes from the suitcase on her bed, then headed back out, making a detour into the kitchen to nab the radio from the counter.

'Don't lock the door.' Gideon's voice was flat.

Harry jerked her head around. He'd twisted in his seat to face her, his eyes stony.

'Are you out of your mind?' she said. 'Of course I'm going to lock the stupid door. You think I want you and Clayton walking in on me?'

'I said, don't lock it.'

Harry held his glare for as long as she could, then turned and fled to the bathroom. She slammed the door shut and switched on the shower, a basic model installed in the grimy bathtub. No screen, no curtain. But the power was good and the motor was pumping loud. She set the radio on the sink and scratched through the stations till she found a music channel. Then she cranked up the volume till the speakers buzzed.

Harry pressed up against the door and held her breath to listen. The gushing water and drubbing bass buried all other sounds. Gently, she snicked the door lock closed. Then she slipped off the jacket and massaged the phone back out of the lining, like toothpaste through a tube.

She switched the phone on. It flickered to life, emitting

a tinkle that she smothered between her palms. Fear strummed through her like a shuddery chord. If she got caught, there'd be no talking her way out of this one. She checked the screen. The signal was strong, but the battery was close to empty.

Steam billowed around her, wringing sweat from her pores. She punched in the number with shaking fingers, and got him on the second ring.

'Zubiri.'

Harry closed her eyes, relief leaking through her. 'It's me, Harry Martinez.'

There was a pause. '*Jainko maitea!* Where are you? We thought—'

'I don't have much time, this phone's going to die. I'm in a side street off José Maria Something, east of the river, a six-storey block, apartment 601.'

Muffled echoes blocked the phone as Zubiri covered it and yelled out something in Basque. Harry pictured his dark, woolly head, the scowling tangle of brows. He came back on the line.

'How many are with you?'

'Two. Gideon Ray and Clayton James.'

'Not Franco?'

'He's been gone since yesterday, I don't know where he is.'

'Are you okay? Are you hurt?' His accent sounded stronger; more Spanish, less transatlantic.

'I just need to get out of here.'

'We thought—' Zubiri stopped. Tried again. 'Your

friend Hunter got in touch. We found blood at the apartment.'

She hugged her waist. 'That was Ginny's.' So they hadn't found the body. Harry's back felt suddenly drenched, a clammy blend of sweat and steam. 'She's dead. Someone shot her, I don't know who.'

'Stay calm, we'll get you out.'

'I found out what you wanted to know. Why Franco needed a hacker. He's taking Riva down. He's a money launderer, they both are.' She remembered the slides. 'You probably knew that.'

She brought him up to date in quick snatches, recounting bits of what she knew: how Franco had manoeuvred Riva into a high-risk deal with the man called Pontius Pilate; how he'd crippled her network, preventing her from honouring the pact.

Harry frowned. Somehow, the set-up sounded incomplete. As if she was missing some final play.

She shook her head, dismissing the notion. 'I don't know what Franco's doing now, but I don't care. I've done my job, I just want out.'

'Is your cover still intact?'

Harry thought of Franco's tests, of his penetrating suspicions. *You have an explanation for everything, don't you, Diego?*

'I'm not sure,' she whispered.

'If Franco comes back, just stay out of his way. The guy's dangerous.'

'You think I don't know that?'

'We tracked him down in Vegas. His real name's Franco Santoyo. Twenty years ago, he was a hotshot agent. Got cosy with Riva and her brother. And some other kid, Marty LaRosa. Used them to engineer a sting on the Mafia almost single-handed. Now he's blacklisted, classified as burned.'

'He told me his organization set him up, wanted to get rid of him.'

Zubiri made a *pff*-sound through his lips. 'Who knows? He'd been unstable for a while, but he went into meltdown after an investigation six years ago.'

'What happened?'

'He'd been receiving death threats, warning him off the case. When it didn't work, the threats switched to someone else.'

'Who?'

'His ex-wife, Sara Kowalski. She got shot in the back of the head. They say it put him over the edge.'

Shot in the back of the head. Just like Ginny. Harry flicked a look at the door, lowered her voice.

'He and his ex, they were close?'

Another *pff*. 'Marriage was over before it started. But she was seven months pregnant. His kid.'

'Oh, Jesus.' Her scalp felt damp, and tendrils of hair clung to the back of her neck. 'Do they know who did it?'

'No.'

'It could have been Riva. She killed McArdle, too, maybe even Ginny. Tell Hunter to stay away from her, she's dangerous.'

358

Zubiri paused. 'I can't.'

'Can't what?'

'I can't tell him.' He hesitated. 'Hunter's missing.'

Air rushed out of Harry's lungs. 'What?'

'I don't know where he is. He got to the apartment before us, and when he found the blood, he just went crazy, almost tore the place up.'

Harry's head felt jumbled. 'Missing? How can he be missing?'

'He was supposed to meet me here yesterday, he didn't show up. We can't reach him on his phone, he didn't sleep in his hotel room last night. He's gone AWOL. A loose cannon.' For the first time, Zubiri sounded unsure of himself. 'I don't like it.'

Harry felt a choking dryness in her throat. What had Hunter done? Had he done something reckless, put himself in danger? She sank to the floor, hugged her chest. Tried not to picture Hunter with a bullet in his head.

Zubiri cut into her thoughts. 'We'll get you out. It'll happen in the next few hours, so be ready.'

Harry closed her eyes, allowing herself a brief image of Zubiri hustling her into an unmarked car, whisking her away, shepherding her into the familiar, grey block that housed the Ertzaintza station.

Sanctuary.

Relief slackened her muscles for a moment. Then she opened her eyes and slowly shook her head.

'No.'

'What?'

'I'm not coming out.'

Zubiri missed a beat. 'What are you talking about?'

'You heard me, I'm not coming out. I have to find Hunter.'

'Listen to me—'

'How can I find him if I come out?'

'That isn't your job. Leave it to us, we'll find him.'

'Like you found me?'

Zubiri was silent for a long moment. 'You can't do this.'

'I'm staying in, Zubiri. This world, these people, someone here knows what happened to him. It's the only way I can find him.'

The bathroom door rattled, and Harry jumped. Someone was testing the handle.

She shot to her feet, whispered, 'Someone's coming.'

Then she thrust the phone under her pile of fresh clothes on the floor. A fist pounded on the door. Adrenalin blasted through her, and she kicked off her shoes, ripped off her shirt. The door shook on its hinges, as a foot lashed out on the other side. Harry stripped herself naked and scrambled into the shower.

The hammering stopped. Hot water drilled into her skin, soaked through her hair. Then her eyes widened. The phone was poking out from under her shirt on the floor.

She made a move towards it. A loud crack split the air, and she leaped backwards. Wood splintered, the lock shattered. The door burst open and Franco stormed into the room.

He held a gun in one hand, the barrel overly long. A silencer? He let it hang by his side as he stared at Harry. His gaze brushed down over her body. Lingering.

Harry's insides shrivelled. A cold draught bled into the room, chilling her bare flesh. She wanted to cover herself; to cower and turn away. Instead, she thrust her shoulders back, arms by her side, spine straight. Then she flung him an I-dare-you look, Diego-style. Anything to keep his gaze from straying down to the floor.

Franco switched off the radio. The silence rushed up like a wind between them. He swallowed hard, his eyes still roaming her body.

'Gideon told you. No fucking locks.'

Then he backed out of the room, closing the door behind him.

Harry hunched her shoulders, covered her chest. A weakness shook her knees, juddered up through her legs and arms. She slid to the bathtub floor, letting the tremors take over.

Beside her, the phone fluted a soft, dying note to tell her the battery was dead.

40

Marty studied himself in the bathroom mirror.

His skin looked slack, and his eye-sockets were sunken pits. But he was showered and dressed, and whatever he'd caught from that stinking river had finally slithered away. Taking the dreams with it, thank Christ. No more nightmares. No gut-wrenching memories butchering his sleep.

He turned away and headed back to the bedroom. He'd been holed up in this third-rate hotel long enough. It was time to go. Time to decide.

'You're dressed.'

Josie stood by the door, looking startled to see him up. She cut a vibrant splash against the drab room: copper-coloured hair, vivid yellow dress. Maybe a little flashy, but the curves made it work and he wasn't going to fault her for that.

He smiled, enjoying the view. 'Hey, I've been under your feet long enough.'

He'd lost track of time, but he must have been here a couple of days. Josie had drifted in and out, checking on him occasionally and dosing him up with Tylenol. But he could tell she was already bored with playing nurse.

He reached for his jacket. She took a quick step towards him and put a hand on his arm.

'You're leaving right now?'

Marty's brows shot up. He'd thought she'd be relieved.

'Time I got going. But thanks for the bed.' He smiled into her eyes. 'I mean that.'

Josie frowned, slid her gaze away. Then she squeezed his arm, shifting her body closer till he felt her breasts brush against his chest. The invitation was unmistakable. But mechanical. Brittle. Not like the easy, sensuous heat she'd burned with a few nights before.

Marty let her push him into a sitting position on the bed. He looked up past those soft handfuls of flesh into eyes that still wouldn't meet his. For a moment, he thought she was going to straddle him. Then she seemed to change her mind, and instead climbed up behind him and started massaging the back of his neck.

She had to know the fake mood wasn't working. This way, she didn't have to look him in the eye. She kneaded his muscles.

'God, you're tense.'

Marty bent his head, letting her fingers roam, and wondered why she was so anxious for him to stay. Maybe she didn't want to be alone when the toady-faced guy came back.

Her fingers worked small circles into his neck. 'So, have you decided yet?'

'About what?'

'Those people you were avoiding. You know, when I met you in the bar?' The circles spread out to his shoulders. 'You said you needed to make a decision.'

'So I did.'

Marty closed his eyes. Decide not to decide. Josie's fingers squeezed, coaxing heat into his muscles. Who to sell out? Riva or Franco. Heads or tails. He let out a long, slow breath.

'Guess decisions aren't my strong point.'

'What's the problem?'

'It's a question of loyalties.'

'You're kidding. Loyalties? Not money?'

'Well, yeah, that too.' The taste in Marty's mouth was suddenly sour.

Josie's touch hardened. 'Loyalty's overrated. People change.'

'You got that right.'

They'd all changed. Riva, Franco, himself. Maybe Riva more than anyone. She'd always been driven. Single-minded. With Franco around, she'd been more alive, less in conflict with the whole damn world. Happy, Marty guessed. But after Andy got killed, she'd just turned ruthless. Obsessed with building up her casinos, chopping down every rival in her way.

It had wrenched Marty's guts out to watch her grieve for Andy. But it was hard to feel the same about her now, after what she'd done to Franco. At least Andy's death had been an accident.

Josie dug hard spirals into his shoulders. 'You just got to be loyal to yourself, that's what I say. Screw everyone else.'

'The Judas approach. Yeah, I got that down pat. Story of my life.'

Betrayal, snitching, breaking faith. It was a small slide from there to police informant, which was what he'd become in the years since Andy's death.

Franco had been the first to get back in touch. Marty hadn't seen him for three years, not since the ambush at the casino. The guy had aged. His nerves seemed raw, more savage than usual, and he looked in the grip of something manic. A fast, bad mood that never let up. Marty recalled the man he'd hero-worshipped; the man who'd let him down.

How could you love a person and hate them at the same time?

Franco had wanted to put Marty on the department payroll. Not to snitch on Riva, just to target other people on the fringes. There was plenty of scum in Vegas. Marty needed the cash, and told himself it was just another way of surviving.

Bad decision number three million and fifty-five.

Riva found out about his association with Franco, and had predictably disowned him for good.

Josie rubbed his flesh in rhythmic circles, melting the tension in his muscles. 'You can only betray someone if they trust you first, right?'

'I guess.'

'These people you think you owe some kind of loyalty to. Do they trust you?'

'Probably not.'

'Well, there you go.'

Her soft breasts nudged his back, and a deep-tissue heat spilled through his body. She brought her lips close to his ear and whispered,

'Do you trust me?'

Her warm breath sent a charge into his groin. He turned around, laced his fingers through her hair and drew her face closer to his. Her eyes looked heavy-lidded, her cheeks flushed.

'Probably not,' he said.

Her lips parted slightly, and her mouth looked hungry. 'See? We know where we stand.'

Marty twisted on the bed, his turn now to massage soft, warm flesh. She closed her eyes, leaned her head back and moaned.

Then a hard fist hammered on the door.

Marty froze. Josie gasped, then scrambled off the bed. He threw her a questioning look, but she was no longer meeting his eyes. She edged towards the door and opened it a crack. Then she let it swing wide as she turned and moved away.

Two men stood in the corridor, shoulder-to-shoulder.

Hefty. Expressionless. They stepped apart to reveal a third guy behind them: elderly, slightly built, with a walking stick clasped in his gnarly old hands.

Victor Toledo, Riva's Chief of Security.

Marty's pulse drubbed hard. He shot Josie a look. She was leaning against the wall on the other side of the bed. She flicked him a glance, gave a small shrug, her expression a mix of apology and defiance.

She'd sold him out. She'd known he was on the run. Had seen him get back-roomed, heard him talk in his sleep. She knew the casinos. An easy leap from there to guessing they might pay a price to find him.

He turned back to the door. What the hell. Survival called the shots, right? Who was he to hold it against her? He probably would have done the same thing.

Besides, it was time.

41

By the time Harry got out of the shower, Franco had gone. Gideon was alone in the living room and when he saw her, he grabbed his jacket.

'Get your coat, we've an errand to run.'

Harry clutched the bundle of clothes she'd carried from the bathroom and didn't move. She felt concussed, her senses dazed to a slow-motion hum that made moving around a chore.

Was Hunter really missing? Or worse?

'I said, get your coat!'

Harry jumped, and moved past him into her room. She dumped the clothes on the bed and retrieved McArdle's jacket from the pile. Then she hiked back to the living room, trying to galvanize some adrenalin into her veins.

'What kind of errand?'

'You'll see. Won't take long.'

Gideon headed out the door and Harry followed, flicking a backward glance at the apartment. Was Zubiri already on his way? Maybe she should find some excuse to hang back; seize the chance to escape Diego for good.

She closed her eyes briefly, then followed Gideon down the stairwell. She couldn't break cover, not now. She had to stay deep; try to find Hunter. Her brain lurched away from the notion that she might be too late.

Outside, the darkness rolled through the street like a mist. She inhaled the chilly air, felt it slice into her lungs. It was the first time she'd left the apartment in two days.

Gideon bundled her into the passenger seat of a black sedan, then slipped behind the wheel and took off. Harry shot him a look. He was dressed all in black, the glint of his hair the only break in the slick silhouette.

He zig-zagged with assurance through a web of side streets, his expression tight-lipped. Harry leaned back against the headrest. The guy might be surly, but right now she'd take it over Franco's explosive moods.

Traffic was light at this late hour and they sped through streets that Harry hadn't seen before. Her thoughts spiralled inwards, hurtling straight to Hunter. Panic whipped through her.

Had he made some kind of reckless move? Pushed Riva too far, maybe? Showed his hand? If he'd thought the blood in the apartment was hers, who knew what kind of knee-jerk response he might have had?

The chaotic what-ifs stampeded through her head. She

recalled how Franco has asked about Hunter; how he'd planned to get Gideon to check him out. Harry stole a glance at Gideon's profile. Maybe he already had.

'What's Franco been doing all this time?' she said. 'What's he got *you* doing?'

Gideon didn't answer. She tried again.

'Don't you get tired of just babysitting me?'

He turned his head. His eyes were dull and empty. 'I don't like you, Diego.'

'Yeah, I got that, you told me before.'

'So let's just keep this businesslike. Professional.' He turned back to the road. 'You don't talk, I don't need to listen. The sooner we do this job, the sooner we can part company.'

'What job?'

'Jesus. You don't stop, do you?'

He clamped his mouth shut and kept his attention on the road. Harry glanced out the window, recognition stirring as they turned left onto a main thoroughfare. They were approaching the Zurriola Bridge.

The globed lamps shone like a series of moons, picking out movement in the black, churning water below. Gideon accelerated over the bridge and turned right along the embankment, heading seaward towards the angry mouth of the river.

Harry squinted at the deserted road up ahead. This was the route to Franco's warehouse. Was that where they were going? But Gideon wasn't supposed to know about that, was he?

They followed the embankment road, curving away from the city towards the stark, windswept headland. Waves stormed against the cliffs, punching fists of foam high over the sea wall. Further out, the water looked thick and leaden, swollen with giant prowler waves.

They rounded the peninsula. Seawater slapped onto the road ahead and pounded on the roof of the car. Harry clutched her seat belt. Gideon held the wheel steady, and two minutes later he jerked the car to a halt by the promenade.

'Get out.'

'What, here?'

Gideon ignored her and climbed out of the car. Harry felt a trickle of unease as she opened the door and stepped out onto the pavement. A furious wave exploded against the sea wall, and she hunched against a batter of spray and salt-laden wind. She squinted at Gideon.

'What are we doing here?' She had to yell to be heard over the thunderous water.

'Wild, isn't it?' Gideon looked out to sea. 'When I cleaned out the apartment, this is where I dumped Ginny's body.'

Harry caught her breath. Went still. Behind her, the water crashed and hissed. She fought the gruesome image but it thrust itself up: Gideon heaving Ginny over the wall, abandoning her to the marauding waves.

Harry licked her lips. They tasted salty. She stared at Gideon and suddenly knew he'd brought her here to kill her.

She edged away. Then a jolt of electricity fired up her limbs and she ran. She raced along the drenched promenade, but Gideon cut across her and lunged. He grabbed her sleeve. She screamed, wrenched away, scrabbling to extract her arms from the oversized jacket. He yanked it free, whipping her off balance, and she sprawled down hard to the pavement. In one stride, Gideon was standing over her. He'd flung the jacket aside and was two-handing a gun that he aimed directly at her face.

Harry's insides gave a sickening lurch. Gideon's face was impassive. Detached. A professional doing a job. She raised her hands and slowly scrambled to her feet.

'What's going on?' Her voice sounded cracked over the driving wind. 'Is this Franco's idea?'

'Franco doesn't need you any more.'

'So he kills me? What kind of crappy business deal is that?' She backed up against the waist-high wall. Cold seawater bludgeoned against her, drenching her shirt. 'He hired me to do a job and I did it.'

'No one trusts you, Diego.' Gideon was yelling too. His face and jacket were slick with spray. 'Except maybe Ginny, but she can't help you now.'

A moan rose up in Harry's throat. She risked a backward glance. Below her, the tide swirled high, seething over giant boulders at the base of the cliff. The drop had to be over sixty feet, and the sea looked colder than death.

She turned back to Gideon. 'I'm no threat to Franco. He can trust me. Hey, he doesn't even have to pay me.'

'You know too much.' The wind ripped through Gideon's short, pale hair and whipped at his jacket. 'And you lied about that phone call in the casino. You called someone else, didn't you?'

Alarm screamed through her like a siren. She shook her head, picturing Hunter's face; his tired, hazel eyes pleading with her to come out. Behind her, the ocean roared and crashed. Then a deluge rose up and slammed into her back, knocking her forwards. She gasped. Seawater slopped into Gideon's face and he shook it out of his eyes, blinking. Then he snapped his gaze back to Harry.

She retreated against the wall, soaked and shivering, and stared at the gun; at the empty road. There was nowhere to go. She flicked a look at the heaving sea. Another monster wave skulked off the coast, slowly gathering steam.

'It's over,' Gideon yelled. 'You're done. Franco doesn't trust you.'

'You think he trusts you?'

Gideon's eyes seemed to flicker. Could she stall him? She yelled over the booming waves.

'Don't you get tired of being left out of his plans?'

'Shut it, Diego.'

Out to sea, the wave swelled. Rolling, arching.

'Come on, Gideon, what made *you* so loyal?' Echoes of Olive asking her the same question. Harry blundered on:

'Franco's not loyal to you, don't you get that?'

'I said, shut it.'

Harry checked over her shoulder. The wave curled, stampeded towards the cliff. She yelled at Gideon.

'Why do as Franco says all the time? The guy's on the edge of crazy!'

'All the more reason for me to stick around and keep an eye on him.'

Gideon squared his stance, adjusted his sight line. Harry felt numb. She'd have maybe a second, probably less. She saw his knuckles tense, getting ready to squeeze the trigger. Then an avalanche of water smashed over the wall.

For a split-second, Gideon was blind. Harry twisted, shouldering into the charging water. She vaulted onto the wall, eyes wide, transfixed by the drop and the thrashing foam below.

Then she jumped.

42

The ocean swallowed Harry up.

It snapped her head back, pumped into her nostrils. Then it gulped her down into a deep, spinning vortex.

Her brain screamed. She squeezed her mouth shut, choking back air. The ocean thrashed against her. Packed into her ears, compressed her lungs. Sucked her down.

Don't breathe! Don't breathe!

The maelstrom spun her, then hurled her against rock, jarring her bones. Her lungs felt congested. Bursting.

Then suddenly, she surfaced. She hauled in air, gagged on salt water. Waves erupted around her. And above her, Gideon's dark silhouette was leaning over the wall.

The ocean surged back over her head and buried her, plunging her into another black spin. Water rumbled inside her head. She opened her eyes. Couldn't see through the murky swirl. Then a white spear of backwash sliced past her.

A bullet?

Harry's chest heaved, fighting for air. She thrashed her legs, panic screaming through her. Then the current snatched her and whacked her up against the boulders. She grappled for a finger-hold, but the underwater surface was slimy.

Dizziness sideswiped her. The suffocation was crushing. Unbearable. What if she opened her mouth? What if she inhaled?

Don't breathe!

An image of Hunter's face floated in front of her. Was he already dead?

Her brain swirled.

Maybe she'd see Ginny's body. Maybe she was down here with her.

The undertow ripped at Harry's limbs and flung her back against the rocks. Pain fractured through her, and she felt herself grow limp. Felt her eyes roll.

Her mother's face. Always so relieved by Harry's absences. What would she think when Harry was dead?

Her brain drifted. Floated. She felt light. Euphoric, almost. The temptation to breathe was seductive.

Harry couldn't help it. She opened her mouth. Inhaled. Cold water sluiced down into her lungs, and she choked. Swallowed.

She tried to have you aborted.

Something raged suddenly in Harry's brain. Like a sleeping monster jolted awake.

Damn Miriam to hell! Had Harry survived her mother's need to be rid of her, just to die like this?

The water swelled and pitched her back into the rocks. She flung out her arms, scrabbled for a hold, and this time her hands found a crevice. She clung there by her fingertips, her lungs exploding. Her feet scrambled, found a toe-hold. Then she hauled herself upwards through the water. Her arms ached, her feet slipped. She heaved and pulled until finally her head broke the surface.

She dragged in a breath, her lungs rattling. She cleaved to the rock. Coughed and retched. Then she lay her face against the cold stone. Could Gideon see her? She hadn't the strength to look. Eventually, she lifted her head. The boulder was blocking her view of the wall, hiding her from Gideon.

She closed her eyes and pressed her cheek against the wet stone. The ocean thrashed around her, over her. She clung to her bedrock, breathing in its brackishness, her arms trembling. Salt crusted on her cheeks, tightening her skin, and the wind sliced through her drenched clothes.

A roar sounded in the distance. The ocean? Or an engine pulling away? She couldn't be sure. So she stayed where she was. She stayed till the tide receded. Till the waves sank back and barely covered her knees. She stayed till her body was stiff and racked with pain.

Then she lifted her head. Peered up at the sea wall. Gideon's silhouette was gone.

Slowly, Harry groped her way over the rocks, scrabbling from one slippery foothold to another until she reached the sea wall.

Shivers convulsed her battered body. She fumbled in the dark along the slimy wall, scouring for purchase while the water fizzed and foamed around her legs.

Her fingers knocked against something hard. Rough metal. She closed her hand over it, peering upwards at a line of geometric shapes: rusty ladder rungs, hammered into the wall like croquet hoops.

She hauled herself up, battling against the spinning sensation in her head and only half-trusting the corroded bolts to take her weight. The wind pummelled her all the way to the top. With a final heave, she flung herself over and slid to the ground on the other side.

Harry hunched against the wall, the glacial wind slicing through her sodden clothes. Something shifted in the dark, scuffing against the kerb. Moonlight picked out a silvery-black skull, and Harry caught her breath. McArdle's DefCon jacket.

She pounced on the jacket and huddled into it, her body temperature rising by a blissful few degrees. Then she got to her feet and eyed the empty road.

Where to now?

The road to her left led back to the city. To bright lights and warmth. To Zubiri. She pictured him storming

Franco's apartment. Thought of her own hotel room that she'd left only a few days ago. She could go back. Reclaim her life. Get a plane ticket out of here.

Her gaze strayed back to the road on her right, which skirted around the headland and led to the pier.

To Franco's warehouse.

Harry hugged her chest, trying to crush away the tremors. Franco: casino cheater, money launderer, cop, avenger.

Killer.

How could one person be so many things?

Play a role long enough, and it starts to get real.

She shook her head at the memory of Gideon's words. Diego's hard shell had long since deserted her. All she had left now was Harry.

Cold spray pricked her cheeks. She glanced at the headland; at the sea that rippled into peaks and ridges like the surface of a dark moon. There was a chance that Franco was in his warehouse. And there was a chance he might know where Hunter was.

Harry hunched into the wind, and set off towards the pier.

43

'You've run out of time, Roselli.'

Rope gnawed at Marty's flesh. Toledo's men had strapped him to a chair in Josie's room, after tossing the redhead an envelope and telling her to take a hike.

Toledo stood in front of Marty, his crooked old hands resting on the top of his cane.

'I gave you two days. That was almost a week ago.'

Marty tried to shrug, but the ropes were a hindrance and he figured the effect was lost. He aimed for a rueful smile instead. The key here was to stop this before it got started. He'd already taken more than enough beatings for Franco.

'Hey, I admit, I didn't come looking for you.' Marty flicked a glance at the pumped-up men by his side. The guy with the shades was the one who'd back-roomed him in the casino. 'But these goons of yours make me nervous. I've had run-ins with them before. You should tell them I'm working for you.'

Toledo's thin lips curled. 'Being a scum informant does not make you an employee.'

Marty averted his eyes. The look of contempt was nothing new. He'd seen it in Franco's face every time he'd paid Marty for information.

Toledo's knuckles tightened on his cane. Then he raised the stick up, two-handing it over his head, and whacked it down on Marty's skull.

Marty yelled. Pain crunched through him, jarring his spine. Jesus, who'd have thought the old man had the strength? He squeezed his eyes shut against the throbbing pangs, then opened them to see the cane looming.

'Wait! I'm ready to talk! I'm ready, I'm ready!'

Slowly, Toledo lowered his arms. 'I know you're ready.'

Then he leaned forward on his cane to stare into Marty's face. The old man's eyes were hooded slits.

'You see Luis here beside you? Seven years he's worked for me. Take a good look at his face, Roselli. Because if he ever hears that I can be pushed around by some lowlife like you, I'll have to kill him and everyone else that might start wondering who's boss around here.'

Without warning, Toledo whipped the cane across Marty's face. Marty's head snapped sideways, wrenching his neck. He cried out, but the cane cracked down onto his skull, over and over.

Pain shattered behind Marty's eyes. It reached into his gut and whirled up something queasy. For a moment, his brain seemed to drift, floating through the agony. Welcoming it, almost. Anything to block out the self-loathing.

The whacking stopped.

Marty's head lolled on his chest, his thoughts cutting in and out like a radio tuner scrabbling for signals.

Franco or Riva. Heads or tails.

I can't treat you like a grown-up till you start acting like one, kiddo.

Marty heard himself moan. Air whistled and the cane thwacked his ear, bursting his brain into a hodgepodge of images.

The warmth of Riva's hands as she glued a twinkle to his finger.

The way Franco entered a room, like a proud Indian brave.

The invincible trinity.

You can't keep letting us down like this, kiddo.

A hard knot of pain lodged in Marty's skull. He felt groggy. Punch-drunk. The collage of images flickered.

Riva screaming Andy's name, over and over.

Franco's face stark with grief, explaining how his unborn child had died.

Marty himself at nine years old, peering at his father's body in a rancid dumpster.

Marty's gut heaved. It'd be so easy just to tell Toledo everything. Let him in on all of Franco's plans. He dragged his eyes open. Saw the old man's withered face looming over his.

It's a simple choice, Marty. Sucker or scammer. Top dog or victim.

Marty groaned. Toledo lowered his cane and cracked its metal tip on the floor.

'So talk. Tell me about Chavez. About this roulette team.'

Marty licked his lips. His tongue felt thick and dry. The time had come to hand over something valuable. He couldn't meet Toledo's eyes.

'I can go one better than his crew of casino cheaters.'

The old man's gaze sharpened. Marty went on, aware that his speech sounded slurred.

'Supposing I said I could give you his money-laundering operation?'

Toledo went still. The hooded eyes looked uncertain. Marty wanted to swallow, but his spit had all dried up. He took a breath and went on:

'Franco's more than a casino cheater. He's a laundryman. Big league. Goes by the name of Mojave. He's been using your casino to bankroll his outfit. Been laughing at you, probably.'

Toledo paled, and Marty noticed a tremor in the claw-like hands. He squinted through the pain that still pulsed in his skull.

'Look, if he has any money belonging to you, I'd try to get it back.' He watched the old man closely. 'Franco's not in this for the long haul.'

'What does that mean?'

'This money laundering, it's just a front. A set-up for something else. It's what he does.'

'What the hell are you talking about?' Toledo's voice was a gravelly whisper.

'Hey, he really does have money belonging to you, doesn't he?' Marty's brain felt light-headed, in spite of the throbbing. 'Well, however he got it, he probably conned you. Think about it. I bet you were manoeuvred into giving him your money. Am I right?'

He watched Toledo's eyes lose focus as the old man seemed to rewind some mental tape. Some slow-motion replay of a deft conjuring trick. Marty could almost see him pinpoint the sleight of hand. With Franco, there was always sleight of hand.

Marty made a rueful face. 'I hate to tell you this, but you're probably not going to see your money again.'

Toledo's slack jawline quivered. Then he swished the cane and whacked Marty on the side of the head. For an instant, the room went black. Marty tilted, felt the chair topple. Strong arms caught him and hauled him upright. He prised open his eyes. Toledo was staring at him, his mouth clenched with rage. But the eyes held something else, too. Terror?

'You piece of garbage!' The old man raised his cane. 'Is that all you've got to tell me? How do I find him? Tell me how to find him!'

Marty shook his head. Kept on shaking it. 'He's moved apartments, I don't know where he's gone.'

The cane whistled down and sliced Marty's face. His cheek burned, and something warm spilled down his neck. Toledo swung the cane again and Marty yelled.

'Wait! The money! I know where he keeps the money!'

Toledo's arms froze. 'Go on.'

'There's a warehouse on the pier. Third from the end. A counting house.'

Toledo lowered his arms. Marty nodded, swallowed, licked his lips. Hated the eagerness he knew was in his face.

'And it's not just your money.' Marty was talking fast now. 'All his clients' cash is there. You could double your money, triple it even. You could take him down.'

Toledo blinked, the crêpey lids drooping to half-mast. Marty went on.

'The cash is moved every night, you probably don't have much time.'

The hooded eyes stared. 'How do you know so much about him?'

Marty let his gaze fall to the floor. The little saliva he had left tasted sour. 'I used to work with him once. Long time ago.'

Toledo seemed to think about that for a moment. Then he snatched a phone from his pocket and headed out of the room. His sidekicks stayed put, one hand each on Marty's chair. Outside the door, the old man's voice was low and urgent.

The sourness in Marty's mouth burned down into his gut. His head pounded, and he wished it would just black out.

Eventually, Toledo returned. He looked shaken, and his colour was bad. He signalled to Luis, who flicked out a blade and started to cut through the rope. Marty's arms burned. Toledo stepped closer and tossed an envelope into his lap. Marty didn't look up. Didn't care to see the contempt in that dried-up, reptilian face.

Toledo snapped his fingers and left the room, Luis and his buddy in tow.

Marty sat where he was, the envelope untouched on his lap. He let his chin sink to his chest. Longed for unconsciousness to hijack his thoughts. He recalled all the other envelopes; how Franco had handed them over saying, 'Keep in touch,' and how Marty had hated himself because he'd known he would.

If anything bad ever happens, I want you to take care of Riva and Andy.

The invincible trinity.

Somewhere outside, a church bell chimed. Marty closed his eyes. Wanted more than anything to leave this city with its chapels and statues of pious-looking saints. He longed for Vegas. That counterfeit town where no one asked too much of him because everyone was working a racket.

The searing pain in his head dulled. After a while he staggered to his feet, ignoring the envelope as it slipped to the floor, and crossed to the window to get some air. He leaned his forehead against the cool glass, his gaze floating to the pavement below. Toledo was still outside the hotel.

Marty frowned. Tilted his head. Then his eyes flared wide, and alarm rocketed through his body.

He shook his head. That couldn't be right. He stared down at the pavement, then jerked backwards, scrambling out of sight. His gut turned over.

What the hell had he done?

44

It was a while before Harry figured out she was bleeding.

The icy water must have numbed the pain, but the walk around the headland was thawing her out and she could feel the lacerations burning. She probed her shoulders under McArdle's jacket, and winced. Her skin was shredded, and so was her shirt.

Gingerly, she zipped the jacket back up and continued her hike along the headland. The wind shouldered into her, knocking her off-balance, and salt water seeped like acid into her wounds.

She rounded the cliff-face, and her step faltered. The road terminated about a hundred yards ahead, which meant the pier wasn't far away. Harry pictured the warehouse: the flickering notes, whisking through money-counters; the strongboxes, the pallets, the trucks.

The guns.

Her stomach lurched, the same way it had when she'd jumped off the sea wall.

She cut left, preparing to angle across the headland, when she noticed the white van that was parked at the end of the road. Nondescript, no identifying logos. It was the only vehicle in sight.

Franco's?

She eyeballed the windscreen for telltale silhouettes, but the van looked empty. She hesitated, then made a quick detour to check it out, cupping her gaze against the passenger window. Something slim and rectangular was propped up against the foot well. A laptop? It was hard to tell, but it could have been McArdle's.

Harry blinked, suddenly remembering the memory stick in the lining of McArdle's jacket. She groped at her back till she felt the small oblong, still tucked in beside the phone.

Her fingertips tingled. What was so important that McArdle had needed to hide it in his jacket?

She stared out to sea. The waves pounded against the breakwater, unfolding like a line of powerful, butterfly swimmers. She turned her collar up against the wind, touching the leather to her lips. Recalled how Ginny used to do the same.

Ginny.

Harry frowned. Ginny had worn the jacket, same as she had. Wouldn't she have found the memory stick too? Harry remembered the girl's uncharacteristic interest in the laptop; how she'd watched as Harry sidestepped McArdle's logon password.

Had Ginny wanted to see how to bypass his credentials so she could check the memory stick out?

Harry stared at the ocean. Where Ginny's body was.

Ginny and McArdle. Both dead.

Small hairs rose along Harry's arms. Suddenly, it seemed vital to know what was on that memory stick.

She jiggled the door to the van, but unsurprisingly it was locked. She scoured the ground for a weapon, pouncing on a heavy stone by the kerb. Taking aim, she smashed it into the window, shattering the glass, then reached inside to open the door. Splinters tinkled to the ground. She whipped off McArdle's jacket, used it to sweep the seat clean, then hopped into the van and hauled the door closed.

The shelter from the wind was a blessed relief. Harry lifted the laptop onto her knees, powering it on, then fumbled with the jacket till she'd prised out the phone and the memory stick. She tossed the phone onto the driver's seat, then stared at the memory stick in the ghostly, laptop light. Knowledge was dangerous in Franco's world. But she already knew too much, and right now she was desperate for anything that might help to find Hunter.

She wriggled back into the jacket, wincing as it chafed against the gashes on her shoulders. The laptop powered up. It was McArdle's all right. She plugged in the memory stick and leaped into its files.

Her heart sank. More photographs. Another set of doctored images? If so, she was out of luck. The tools

389

to decipher hidden data were on McArdle's other memory sticks. Harry skimmed through the first few photos: shots of Aztec International, probably taken as part of McArdle's routine reconnaissance. She felt her shoulders droop, and flicked through a few more shots. Then she frowned, and peered at the screen.

Zoomed in on the image.

The face was unmistakable.

What the hell was Gideon doing coming out of Riva's headquarters?

Harry sat upright, ignoring the blistering pain in her shoulders. She stepped through another batch of photos, all of Gideon. Gideon on the street; Gideon in his car; Gideon in the company of men Harry didn't recognize. She felt her brow furrow. Had McArdle been following him? Keeping him under surveillance after unexpectedly spotting him at Aztec?

Harry flipped to the next shot. A close-up of Gideon in conversation with an elderly man: withered skin, guarded eyes, arthritic-looking hands resting on a cane. McArdle had posted a label on this one: 'Victor Toledo'.

Harry squinted. Riva's Chief of Security. And according to Franco, the guy who handled her money-laundering deals.

Why was Gideon hobnobbing with Riva's right-hand man?

The wiring in Harry's brain felt faulty. She shook her head and brought up the last photo: Gideon in the company of a heavyset, middle-aged man.

Harry froze. Wind whistled through the broken window, saturating the car with its briny cologne. She stared at Gideon's companion: round, doleful eyes; full, pouty lips; a long, pleated overcoat that looked like a priest's cassock. She zoomed in on the man's hands. Laced through his fingers was a delicate string of rosary beads.

Harry's gut turned icy. Pontius Pilate. What was Gideon doing with a man who scared even Franco?

She flopped back in the seat and massaged her eyes, trying to loosen the gridlock in her head. According to Franco, Gideon didn't know about any of his money-laundering schemes. He didn't know about Pontius Pilate, or Victor Toledo. Yet McArdle's photos suggested he was heavily involved.

Was it possible Franco was wrong about his lifelong pal? Maybe Gideon wasn't all that he seemed.

Jesus, was anyone?

Harry shook her head and scrolled back through the photos. There was no getting away from it, McArdle had amassed compelling evidence that Gideon was a player of some kind. Were he and Riva a team? Harry shifted in her seat. She didn't see it. Gideon was an ex-cop who'd been involved in the sting that had led to her brother's death. Surely Riva would never have hooked up with him?

Harry flipped a mental somersault, turned everything on its head. If Franco was wrong about Gideon, then maybe he was wrong about Riva. Supposing she was never involved?

Harry blinked. Viewed from that angle, things started to look a whole lot different.

Maybe Riva hadn't killed McArdle. Maybe Gideon had killed him, once he'd realized the hacker was on to him. Maybe he'd killed Ginny, too, because he knew she'd seen the photos.

You know too much.

Harry's eyes widened. The logjam was clearing. Gideon had said that Ginny trusted her. Was he worried the girl had confided in Harry about the photos? Or that Harry had found them herself? She pressed unsteady fingers to her lips. Out there on the headland, she'd thought Franco had wanted her dead. But maybe killing her was Gideon's idea.

She whipped her gaze around, raking the shadows, seized by the notion that she'd see Gideon's black-panther silhouette. She hunched down in her seat, shuddering.

She thought of Franco and his meticulous planning; his enduring hatred and schemes for revenge. Revenge for what? If Riva hadn't killed Ginny or McArdle, there was a good chance she hadn't killed Franco's ex-wife either. Had Gideon been responsible for that, too? Had Franco's bid for retribution all been for nothing?

Harry closed her eyes. Fatigue suddenly swamped her, bogging her down. Even if she was right, how the hell would any of this help her to find Hunter?

45

Marty snuck another glimpse out the window, squinting at Toledo's companion on the pavement below. Franco's buddy, the guy with the freckles. What was his name? Gideon.

Gideon and Toledo.

It didn't make sense.

Pain lurched across Marty's skull. He leaned back against the wall, closing his eyes. Toledo was Riva's guy. Why the hell was he talking to Gideon?

Marty's head felt squeezed. Was Franco at risk from something out of left field?

He took another peek at the dark street below. Gideon was looming over Toledo, invading his space. The body-guards kept their distance, as though all loyalties had been neutralized by the presence of a higher command.

Toledo looked like a frightened old man.

Marty flattened himself against the wall and eyed the envelope on the floor. He should take it and run. Go back to Vegas, pick up where he left off. Scamming, hustling, cheating at cards. He thought of the plays Riva had taught him. She'd been good, but Franco was better. Together, they'd pulled off some slick cons. Marty closed his eyes briefly. Without them, he wasn't so smart.

Riva and Franco.

Gideon and Toledo.

Something wasn't right.

His gut had always told him that Riva wasn't a killer. Maybe he should've listened.

He balled his hands into fists. Then he crossed the room and snatched up the envelope, stuffing it into his pocket.

Maybe it wasn't too late. Maybe for once, he could make the right decision. Make up for the shit he'd been pulling all his life.

46

Harry crept along the wharf, hunching into the shadows by the wall. Halyards clanked around her in the dark, and somewhere the hull of a boat knocked against the pier.

The place looked deserted. No trucks, no guards. No signs of life.

What if Franco wasn't here?

Harry squinted along the pier. The harbour was a pincushion of masts and cranes. On dry land beside her, she could make out the dinghies piled high on the jetty, in between racks of skiffs and upturned canoes. She crouched down low, taking cover behind a boat rack, and stared at Franco's warehouse.

It looked abandoned.

Harry closed her eyes briefly. Franco wasn't here. And suddenly the notion of quizzing him about Hunter seemed stupid. Why the hell would he know where he was? Supposing it was Gideon who'd somehow got to Hunter?

You lied about that phone call in the casino.

A twist of panic wrenched through Harry's gut. Had Gideon traced her call to Hunter? If he was tight with Toledo, he could have accessed his phone records. Maybe Gideon had even crossed paths with Hunter as he'd fled the apartment.

Harry leaned her forehead against the boat rack, breathing in the tang of seaweed and muddy shellfish. Her wet clothes sucked at her skin like tentacles, chilling her bones and ripping at the gashes on her shoulders. Slowly, she straightened up, easing out of the shadows. There was nothing more to do. It was time to go back to Zubiri.

'What the fuck are you doing?'

Harry whipped around. Her gaze raked the boat-shaped silhouettes, and picked out a crouching, burly outline on the jetty.

'Get down!' Franco's eyes glittered in the dark. 'What's the matter with you, you want to get yourself killed?'

Harry ducked low, huddling back behind the boat rack, and Franco stole up beside her. His hair hung loose, freed from its ponytail, giving him a wild, hunter-gatherer look. His gaze flitted around the pier.

'Where the fuck is Gideon? I told him to keep an eye on you.'

Harry studied him. He had a phone in one hand, a gun in the other. 'Is that all you told Gideon to do?'

Franco frowned, then seemed to register her bedraggled appearance. 'What the hell happened to you? You're a mess.'

Harry wanted to shrug, but knew it would chafe the raw flesh on her shoulders. His ferocity was faintly reassuring. It was run-of-the-mill Franco. Not the reaction of a man who'd expected to see her dead.

He tilted his head, the wide planes on his face casting geometric shadows. 'What's up, Diego? Run out of comebacks?'

Harry gave him a level look. 'Gideon tried to kill me.'

Franco went still. Below them, the water lapped at the pier, and the moored boats creaked and rocked. His eyes became slits.

'What are you talking about?'

'He brought me to the headland, pulled a gun on me.' Harry's teeth were chattering, the tremors brewed from a mixture of cold and fear. 'He's not what you think, you can't trust him.'

Franco turned away and stared at the warehouse. 'I don't need your bullshit right now, Diego.'

'He killed McArdle. Ginny, too.' She bit her lip, trying to skirt around things that Diego couldn't possibly know. 'He probably killed anyone else you've blamed Riva for, too.'

Franco's expression underwent a shift. He turned dull eyes towards her, his face unreadable.

'You don't know shit.'

'I know he's been meeting with that Pontius Pilate

guy.' Something flickered across Franco's eyes. 'And with Victor Toledo, too.'

'Bullshit.'

'I have photographs, I can prove it.' Harry heard the urgent pitch in her own voice. 'McArdle had them, it's why he died.'

Franco shook his head, waving the gun at her as if he were backhanding at ping-pong. 'I don't have time for this crap.'

'You think Gideon's loyal, but what if you're wrong? What if you're wrong about a lot of things, Franco?'

Suddenly, he rounded on her and jammed the gun into her throat. Harry made a choking sound, and the barrel dug hard into her jugular.

'What's your angle, Diego?' His eyes looked crossed. Dazed. 'What are you trying to pull?'

'I'm telling you the truth!' Her voice was a croak, and she tried not to gag. 'He's lying to you, Franco.'

But his gaze looked fixated. Blinded by obsession. He thrust the gun under her chin, tilting her head back so that all she could see were masks spiking the sky.

'You don't say another word, you got that, Diego?' His breath was hot against her face. 'You just sit there and wait.'

Harry swallowed. Tried to nod against the pressure that was closing off her throat. Finally, he eased the gun away and turned his attention back to the warehouse. Harry huddled against the boat rack, a weariness crushing through her bones. He'd never believe her. He'd invested so much in his hatred of Riva, he didn't know how to give it up.

Her larynx felt bruised, and she kept silent for a while. Around them, tarpaulins whipped in the wind and boat rigging tinkled like someone playing the triangle. She waited for his episode of rage to pass, then eventually, she said,

'What are we waiting for?'

He didn't answer. She listened to the water slapping against the pier, then tried again.

'How come there's no one guarding the place?'

This time, he flicked her a look. 'I sent them away.'

'The warehouse is empty?'

He shook his head. 'There's over three hundred million euros in there.'

Harry gaped. Franco went on.

'Most of it belongs to our friend Pontius Pilate.' He gave a slow, satisfied smile. 'I managed to persuade Riva to part with it.'

Harry's head felt woolly. 'She *gave* it to you?'

'Sure. Or at least, her front-man, Toledo, did. That was the whole point. I thought you got that, Diego.'

She shook her head. Franco clicked his tongue.

'Look, I manoeuvred things so that Pontius Pilate offered his business to Toledo, right? And sure enough, Toledo made a deal with him. He took that lunatic's cash and promised to launder it in double-quick time.'

'But then his network gets sabotaged.'

'Exactly. There he is, sitting on all of this psychopath's

money, with no way to fulfil his contract. Suddenly, he's desperate. Old Pontius isn't the kind of guy to take excuses, he'll expect Riva's outfit to honour the deal, no matter what. Toledo's only option is to lay off the money with someone else.'

Harry threw him a doubtful look. 'And he laid it off with you?'

'Hey, it's just like any other business. You do each other professional favours, as long as there's something in it for you. I've done business with Riva's guys before. Claimed I couldn't fulfil a transaction, paid them to do it instead. Paid high, too. They know how to screw the opposition.'

'Wouldn't they rather see you go under?'

'Sure, except I had something they wanted at the time. A slick, cross-border exchange they wanted a piece of, so I agreed to route some of their assets through it. Everyone's a winner. They've swallowed the convincer and I've reeled them in. So now, when they're in the shit, who do they come to? Me.'

'And they'd trust you with that amount of money?'

'What choice do they have? No one else around here can handle that kind of cash, not at such short notice. Plus, I've handled their money before, so they trust me, up to a point. They weren't crazy about the commission I charged, but that's business. Besides, anything's better than screwing with Pontius Pilate.'

'They didn't think you'd double-cross them?'

'And make off with the cash? That's the last thing

they'd expect. I'm a serious player here, an established money broker. My reputation is my business. If I get sticky fingers, no one deals with me again, and a lot of scumbags are on my tail, Pontius Pilate included. I'd end up on the run, abandoning a thriving operation.' He flashed her a wide, manic-looking smile. 'Only a crazy man would do something like that, right?'

Harry took in the feverish light in his eyes; the dancing animation in his face. A small chill shivered over her as she thought about all his years of set-up; all the camouflage and the sleight of hand that were only a means to an end.

'So what are you going to do?' she said. 'Take the money and leave Riva to the mercy of Pontius Pilate?'

The light in his eyes was suddenly doused. He turned away.

'Yeah, sure, I could leave her to him.' His voice was quiet. 'But I want to see her face when she knows everything she's built has been destroyed. Her operation, her empire, her money. Her life. I want to be the one to finish her.'

Harry's gaze swept the harbour. 'You're expecting her to show up here?'

'She's already figured out I'm not going to honour the deal. She's screwed, and she knows it. Her only option now is to get the hell out.' He gave a nasty smile. 'Only not without the money. She'd never leave without that. Plain old greed, the downfall of every mark.'

'And if she comes? What then?'

'Then it's all over.' He held up the phone in his hand. 'Just one call, that's all it'll take.'

'What call? To who?'

Franco laughed softly. 'To you, Diego. How'd you like that? To you.'

Harry squinted at him. What the hell was he talking about?

She eyed his gun, and strained for sounds of movement on the pier. Ropes creaked somewhere behind her, and flags snapped overhead in the wind. Harry ran her tongue over her lips.

'What if she doesn't come? What if I'm right, and it's Gideon you should be worrying about, not Riva?'

A spasm of fury twitched across Franco's face. 'Look, if she's not coming, then why did she send one of her lackeys to scout the warehouse out?'

'She did?'

'I found him creeping around here yesterday.' He looked mildly puzzled. 'Still haven't figured out how he knew about it then, but I guess things don't always go according to plan.'

'What did he say?'

'Not much. I whacked him over the head and the prick never woke up.' He nodded at the warehouse. 'I dumped him in there.'

'Then how do you know he was working for Riva? He could have been working for Gideon, couldn't he?'

Franco shook his head. 'I saw him and Riva together.

So did you. Couple of days ago, outside Aztec. You spoke to him, remember?'

Harry stared. Blood beat loud in her ears. Clogged up her brain.

Outside Aztec.

Riva and Hunter.

Fear screamed along Harry's spine as she choked back an image of Hunter lying dead in the warehouse.

47

The harbour stretched and groaned in the dark.

Harry crouched against the boat rack, paralysed by the images of Hunter that crushed into her head. She squeezed her eyes shut. She had to get into that warehouse.

'Get down!'

Harry jerked backwards into the shadows. Franco had ducked low, and was peering through the stacks of canoes. She followed his gaze and saw a dark silhouette skulking by the warehouse door.

Light flooded the shuttered entrance. The stranger's movement must have tripped a motion sensor, and he spun around like a startled animal, flattening himself against the door.

Franco straightened up. 'What the fuck?'

He edged around the boats, shoved the phone in his

pocket and sketched a furious wave with his gun. 'Marty!'

The guy by the door shot a look in their direction, then scurried across the wharf towards them. He was panting when he reached them, and Franco hauled him by the lapels behind the boat rack.

'What the fuck, Marty?'

The name dislodged something in Harry's brain, but she fumbled it.

The man called Marty was eyeing her with suspicion. She took in the rumpled blond hair, the tired good looks. A memory stirred. She'd seen him before. At the casino? The image snapped into place. He'd been flirting with a redhead at McArdle's table.

Marty jerked a thumb in her direction. 'What's she doing here?'

Harry's pulse leaped. Had he seen her watching McArdle?

Franco shoved his face into Marty's. 'Never mind her, what the hell are *you* doing here?'

The guy hesitated. 'It's your buddy, Gideon. You need to watch out for him.'

Franco drew back, and Harry squinted at Marty in the dark. His eyes were bruised, and a fresh-looking gash glistened across his cheek. He ran a tongue over cracked lips.

'I saw him with Toledo. You said he doesn't know anything. So what the fuck was he doing with Toledo?'

'You saw him?'

'He was right there! It didn't look good, Franco, I'm telling you. He was giving the guy orders. You got to be careful, you can't trust him.'

Harry's skin tingled at the echo of her own guesswork. She glanced at Franco. Maybe now he'd believe her. But he shook his head, rasping a hand over his chin.

'Come on, kiddo, this is bullshit.'

Harry blinked. Kiddo. Marty. Another brain cell jostled: Zubiri, talking about Franco.

He got cosy with Riva and her brother. And some other kid, Marty LaRosa.

Marty leaned forward, moonlight leaching the colour from his bruises. 'I'm telling you, it didn't look right.'

But Franco's face had shut down. Harry could almost see the deadbolt turning, blocking the information out.

Marty thrust out his chin. 'Hey, I know what I saw, you can't treat me like some dumb-ass kid here. I did everything you said. I told Toledo you were cheating his casino. You were right, it was the perfect convincer. After that, he was ready to believe everything I said.' Marty looked at the ground and shrugged. 'Once a snitch, always a snitch, right?'

Franco's jaw tightened, and his eyes looked glazed. Marty edged further into the shadows of the boat rack and went on.

'I kept out of his way till you gave the word. Wasn't easy, prick kept running me down. But I kept my mouth shut till it was time. Then I told him about the warehouse and he swallowed it whole. Every damn word.' Marty smiled, an easy grin that crinkled the corners of his eyes. 'Toledo's shitting himself, Franco. He knows you're making off with his money.'

Then the smile disappeared, and he leaned forward, looking Franco full in the face.

'But who did he run to? Not Riva. I'm telling you, he went straight to Gideon. And from what I saw, your buddy was ready to kill him. Something's off here, I can feel it.'

Franco's face looked wooden, and he didn't answer. Water sloshed against the pier, and the docked boats plopped and bumped. Harry's brain raced, playing catch-up. So Marty had been Toledo's source. He'd tipped him off about the cheaters, and now he'd told him Franco was bailing out with Pontius Pilate's money. A lure to entice Riva to the warehouse? Harry flicked a glance at Franco's closed expression. It looked as if his plan wasn't playing out the way he'd intended.

Marty shifted against the boat rack, firing anxious looks over his shoulder. 'It's gone wrong, hasn't it? We've got the wrong mark this time.'

His gaze slid back and forth, and suddenly he froze. His eyes widened. Then he turned and leaped at Franco, tackling him flat to the ground. A gunshot cracked. Two shots, three. Harry gasped, hurled herself face down on the pier. Another burst of gunfire shredded the air. Marty jerked. Yelled. Arched his back. Harry hunched her shoulders, screwed her eyes shut.

Scuffling sounds made her open them again. Franco

had grabbed Marty under the arms and was hauling him backwards, retreating behind a stack of skiffs away from the warehouse. He up-jutted his chin, gesturing for her to follow. She hesitated, then scrambled after him.

Franco propped Marty up against a nest of coiled ropes, and Harry hunkered down beside him. Marty's eyes were closed, and even in the dark she could see his face was ashen. Her eyes raked the wharf, and she jammed her knuckles against her mouth, cutting off a scream.

Franco craned his neck, gun at the ready, and peered through the shield of skiffs and tarps. Marty's eyelids fluttered.

'Behind the warehouse.'

His voice sounded hoarse. He stirred, tried to sit up. A bubbling cough erupted in his chest and his face twisted as he tried to catch his breath. The spasm passed. He sank back against the ropes, then turned to Franco.

'Hey, Franco?'

'Shut up, kiddo.'

'I almost sold you out, you know that, Franco?'

'I said, shut it.'

'Thought about it every day. How easy it'd be. Just tell Toledo everything. How the whole thing was a trap.' His lungs gurgled, and he hacked out another cough, then went on. 'Cash in now, I thought. Take his snitch money and go. Why wait for the bigger play? Stupid, right?'

'Shut the fuck up, I'm trying to think.'

'Came close a coupla times. But in the end, I stuck to

the plan. Sold Riva out instead.' Marty closed his eyes. 'Only that wasn't right either, was it?'

He slumped down further against the ropes, his eyes still closed. His chest rattled like a percolator, and Franco shot him a quick look.

'Hang in there, kiddo.'

Harry stared at the blood that was seeping out onto the ropes. Marty opened his eyes.

'Hey, Franco?'

No answer. Marty kept going.

'You ever think about Andy?'

For a moment, the only sound was the rhythmic creak of the harbour. Then Franco said,

'What do you think?'

Marty shook his head. 'I never shoulda gotten out of the car.'

'Don't be a jerk. I should've got you all out. We should've left Vegas together for good, like I'd planned.'

Marty coughed again, and Harry flinched at the wet, gargling sounds. Franco scooted closer and gripped Marty's hand in a man-to-man, arm-wrestling clench. There was a strength behind it, a kind of binding grip that said, *I've got you covered.*

'Come on, kiddo, think of the money. You want to stick around for that, don't you?'

Marty smiled his easy grin. 'Played my part well, didn't I, Franco? You always said I was a good actor.'

'Sure. The best.'

The smile faded, and Marty's look turned bewildered.

'How'd we get it so wrong, Franco? It wasn't Riva. It was never Riva, was it?'

Franco didn't answer. Then Marty's head rolled a fraction sideways. He seemed to grow limp, and the bubbling in his chest went quiet. Harry's eyes sought Franco's, but he was no longer looking at his friend. He was staring past Harry, over her shoulder. His expression looked frozen.

Her flesh prickled and, slowly, she turned her head. Gideon was standing by the boat rack.

48

'He's right,' Gideon said. 'It was never Riva.'

He stood with his legs apart, his arms locked straight and stiff. Harry stared at his gun. The barrel obscured his right eye as he nailed them in his sights.

Icy crystals formed along her spine. Gideon stepped closer.

'Get up!'

She did as she was told. Beside her, Franco moved more slowly, as though his limbs had geared down while his brain took up the slack to work things out.

'Gideon?'

'Toss it.'

Franco glanced, trance-like, at his gun, as though he'd forgotten it was there. Then with an easy action, he pitched it across the jetty where it clattered into the shadows.

Gideon jerked his head. 'Now move away.'

Franco edged left in the direction of the warehouse, his gaze fixed on Gideon. Harry followed. She raised her arms, sickened by her crushing urge to look submissive.

'That's far enough.' Gideon's face was stony.

He shifted his stance, adjusting his sight line on the gun. Harry stared at his knuckles, her gut churning, as she watched for the telltale squeeze of his fingers.

Slowly, Gideon shook his head. 'All this time, you were Mojave. My biggest fucking rival.'

Franco looked dazed. 'You're working with Riva?'

'Haven't you been listening? Riva's got nothing to do with this. Never did.' Gideon flexed his fingers on the gun. 'I should've known Mojave wasn't for real. No one could operate on those crazy commissions. But you weren't in it for the money, were you?'

'All the trails, they led to Riva.'

'Sure they did. How else do you think I've gotten away with it all these years?'

A low rumble sounded in the distance, and Harry's gaze slid along the wharf. A truck was rolling out of the shadows. It hissed to a halt beside the warehouse, growling into reverse against the entrance. A dark figure clambered down from the cab and Gideon hollered, his eyes still trained on Franco.

'Luis, get over here!'

The driver of the truck jogged across the pier. He was tall and blocky, and moved like a rhino: lumbering but surprisingly fast.

'Search them, Luis.'

The guy loomed over Harry and with a backhanded flip, he smacked her arms out wide. His palms roamed under her jacket, exploring along the length of her sodden clothes. Then he flicked down over her shoulders and groped inside her jacket pockets. He straightened up and held out McArdle's memory stick.

Harry wet her lips. Gideon signalled for the stick and Luis obliged. At the same time, she sensed Franco inching closer, and a delicate touch brushed her jacket. Something solid dropped into her pocket.

She held her breath. Fixed her gaze straight ahead. What the hell was he doing?

Luis turned back to Franco, patting him down, while Gideon glared at Harry.

'Thought I'd left you to fucking drown.' He held up the memory stick. 'McArdle's?'

She found her voice. 'You killed him, didn't you? And Ginny, too. Because they found you out.'

Gideon ignored her, and slipped the memory stick into his pocket. Luis finished frisking Franco, then stepped away, producing a gun of his own. Franco was breathing heavily, and when he spoke, his teeth sounded clenched.

'Tell me about Riva.'

'What's to tell? She got out of the business way back when her brother was killed. I saw my opportunity and took up where she left off.'

Franco shook his head. 'Her casinos, her whole empire—'

413

'Built the old-fashioned way, with sweat and hard work. Very admirable. But she left a gap in the market I knew I could fill. The department still had their eye on her, so I figured I'd use her as a smokescreen.'

'What the fuck are you talking about?'

'I dogged her footsteps, grew my business under the shadow of hers. Recruited all my key people from within her own ranks: accountants, lawyers, financial managers. Almost everyone's open to corruption, if the rewards are high enough.' Gideon's sneer was eloquent. 'On the face of it, they continued to manage her casinos, but in the background they were working for me.'

'They washed cash for you through her casinos?'

'Sometimes. Just enough to keep the finger pointed at Riva. Mostly, they ran sophisticated shell networks and wire transfers.'

'So you hid behind Riva.' Franco's voice was flat.

'Every step of the way. Vegas, Atlantic City, Reno. I branched out when she did, infiltrating her operations, putting her people on my payroll.'

Franco's face clouded. 'So when she moved to Spain, you came too.'

'What could be better? Place is a stepping stone for the cartels into Europe. I recruited Toledo as my point man, along with some handpicked lawyers and accountants in her corporate HQ.'

Harry slid a glance at Franco. He'd been right about most of it. Riva's empire *was* a front for a money-laundering operation, but it was Gideon, not Riva, who'd been pulling the backstage strings.

'You set her up to take the fall.' Franco spoke slowly, as though his brain had disengaged. As though he was busy deconstructing what he'd believed for so long and painfully trying to rebuild it.

For Riva, read Gideon.

Gideon shrugged. 'Just protecting my ass in case things went wrong. Cops would have no trouble believing she was behind it, you saw that for yourself.'

'But *you* were a cop.'

Gideon didn't answer.

Harry flashed on Riva: the runaway waif; the hard-working businesswoman. The only one of them who was exactly as she'd seemed all along.

Harry's arms were starting to ache. She thought about lowering them, maybe checking out whatever Franco had dropped in her pocket. She eyed the two guns and kept her arms in the air.

'So Diego's right.' Franco's voice was quiet, but Harry saw his fists clench. 'You killed Stevie and Ginny. Who else did you kill, Gideon?'

A muscle jumped near Gideon's eye. When he didn't answer, Franco drew himself up.

'WHO ELSE DID YOU FUCKING KILL?'

Snip-snap.

Luis's weapon was cocked. A spurt of electricity zipped through Harry's frame. Gideon shifted his feet, the pulse still twitching near his eye.

415

'I tried to warn you off, Franco. You were getting too close, I couldn't allow it. I had to do something.'

Franco's burly frame looked pumped up, and he was breathing hard through his nose. 'Sara called me that night. Said she was being followed, the house was being watched. She didn't want to go home. I tried to get to her. But you got to her first, didn't you? *Didn't you?*'

Franco's profile looked savage. Blood vessels flooded his cheeks, ready to erupt. He took a step forward. Luis's fingers squeezed.

A shot cracked the air, and Harry flinched. Luis jerked, slumped to the ground. Gideon swung his arms left and blasted at the boat rack, then recovered his aim on Franco before anyone else could move.

Harry's breath froze in her throat. Marty lay sprawled on the ground by the boat rack, and she stared at the gun resting in his hand. Couldn't look at the shattered, bloody remains of his head. Her stomach swivelled, and she turned back to Gideon.

Sweat sparkled on his upper lip. He glanced down at Luis, who lay groaning on the ground.

'Get up!'

Luis clambered to his feet, clutching his left arm, which hung uselessly by his side. He swayed. Steadied himself. Then with his good hand, he trained his gun on Harry.

Gideon glared at Franco. 'The warehouse. Now!'

Franco hesitated, then unexpectedly did as he was told. Harry followed close behind, Gideon and Luis tracking alongside them. Masts clanged by the edge of the pier, and the mineral tang of seaweed grew dense. Harry eyed Franco's back, half-expecting him to make a sudden move.

Franco kept on walking. Harry inched her arms lower, as if her biceps were weighing her down. By the time they reached the warehouse, her elbows were almost by her side.

'I don't trust you, Franco.' Gideon's eyes flicked over the door. 'I don't like that there are no guards.'

'You think I've set some kind of trap?'

'Let's just say, I'm not taking any chances. I figure you must have had something planned for Riva when she got here.'

'Sure.' Franco shrugged. 'I planned to shoot her.'

Harry frowned, drawing her elbows in to her side. She recalled Franco's venom when he'd talked about Riva; about how shooting her would never be enough. She nudged her pocket. Detected something small and solid.

A phone?

Just one call, that's all it'll take. To you, Diego.

What the hell was he planning?

Gideon stood back, signalling at Luis to wait. 'Open up, Franco. You go first.'

Franco hauled the door aside and stepped into the warehouse. Motion-sensor lights stuttered to life and Harry followed him inside, her eyes widening.

Bales of banknotes filled the shelves. The floor space was a stockpile of shrink-wrapped currency, some of it stacked in cartons and crates, the rest in free-standing cubes. The money-counting machines still lined the benches but no one was using them now.

Gideon leaned against the door jamb, Luis by his side, and surveyed the parcels of cash. He nodded and gave a satisfied smile.

'The king is in his counting house.'

Harry edged in further, past a waist-high wall of cartons, then her step suddenly faltered. Nausea hit her with a sickening punch. She stared at the floor near the back of the warehouse; at the image she'd been trying to block out for the last few hours: the image of Hunter lying face down on the ground.

49

'Against the wall. Now!'

Harry jumped, her heart banging. Gideon hadn't seen Hunter's body. For now, he was invisible, hidden from view by a wall of shrink-wrapped cash. She closed her eyes, overwhelmed by the urge to rush across and touch him.

'Move!'

Harry opened her eyes and backed away, stumbling against the towers of cartons. Franco moved with her as they edged towards the wall.

'What happened, Gideon?' he said. 'You were a good cop.'

'You think I wanted to end up like you?' Gideon's nostrils flared. 'All burned out, with nothing at the end of it?'

Franco didn't answer. Harry had almost reached the

wall. She fetched up beside another pile of boxes, and something in the top one caught her eye. A bright orange block, like a mammoth cheddar cheese. She let her gaze stray for another peek, then froze.

A phone lay on top of the plasticine loaf, hooked up to a set of AA batteries. Which in turn were attached to a thin wire fuse.

Fear plucked at Harry's spine.

Gideon levelled his gun at Franco. 'You should've stayed in Vegas. I thought you'd gone to ground, then I got word you were sniffing around out here.'

'So you got in touch.' Franco was beside Harry now. 'Just like old times.'

Her nerve endings crackled, prickling her flesh. All phones looked alike, but something told her this one was hers, confiscated by Ginny at the bar.

Just one call, that's all it'll take.

Gideon's gun never wavered. 'I knew you were targeting Riva somehow. And targeting her meant targeting me, so I had to stick close. Let the play roll out.'

Harry was barely listening. She was picturing Franco dialling her number; picturing the signal rippling through the airwaves, triggering her phone's vibrator. Sending its metal head spinning into the wires.

Completing the circuit.

Igniting the fuse.

I want to watch her when everything she's built goes up in flames.

Another remote detonator? Another bomb, expertise

420

courtesy of McArdle? Only this was no Dormouse. This time the payload was deadly. Harry's eyes strayed back to the putty-like, orange slab. She was willing to bet it was some kind of plastic explosive.

She slid a glance at Franco, and he held her gaze with lit-up, manic eyes. He knew she'd seen the phone. He drifted closer, and she backed up against the wall. Was he trying to slip a hand into her pocket? Did he plan to blow them all to kingdom come, just to make sure he killed Gideon? She stared at Franco's glittering eyes. The guy was just crazy enough to do it.

'I should have killed you six years ago when I had the chance,' Gideon was saying. 'It's hard to kill a pal, but now I guess I have no choice.'

He tilted his head. Lined up his sights. By his side, Luis did the same. Harry's spine turned to ice.

Gideon slid a glance at Luis, as though checking he was ready, and his eyes lingered for a moment on the guy's useless left arm. He hesitated. Then he darted a look around the warehouse, at the mountain of boxes and pallets he needed to move.

Harry held her breath.

Gideon narrowed his eyes. Drilled them into hers. Then he jerked his chin at Franco.

'Open the truck, start loading these boxes. You, Diego. Start lifting. *Move!*'

Harry jumped. She flicked another glance at the orange slab and suddenly felt her eyes flare. Was there still a chance? And would she have the nerve to do it?

She turned to a nearby carton and bent low, trading looks with Franco as he passed. A droplet of sweat meandered down her back. Would he get it? She hauled up the carton, her arms trembling, and stacked it over the detonator, hiding the orange cake from view. Franco looked away, his expression unreadable. Then she lifted both boxes and followed him out to the truck.

Hot sweat flooded over her like a shower. What if she dropped it? Would the stuff explode in her face?

She heaved the cartons into the truck without incident and returned for another haul. By now, Franco had chipped in, hefting three more boxes from the same spot. Harry watched him pack them close around the detonator.

More explosives?

Her mouth felt dry. She reached for another carton, her skin prickling with awareness of Gideon and Luis by the door. And of the guns that tracked every move.

Her heart thumped against the boxes in her arms. Running wasn't an option. The bullets would cut her down before she'd crossed the wharf. Her only weapon was Franco's explosive.

She pictured the bright orange slab. Timing was crucial. Detonate now, while she cleared the cargo near the door, and she'd be caught up in the explosion. Leave it too late, and Gideon might kill her before she ever got the chance. Ideally, she'd wait till he drove off down the pier, but something told her he wasn't going to let her live that long.

She heaved at the parcels of shrink-wrapped cash, labouring with Franco until box by box, they'd worked their way to the rear of the warehouse.

Harry bent to retrieve another carton from the floor, her back turned to Gideon. In a few more trips, the wall of money would come down and Hunter's body would be out on view. She dragged at the carton, fumbling with its weight, and under cover of her clumsiness slipped the phone out of her pocket and dropped it into the box.

The jolt lit up the display. Her own number flashed into view, ready to go. All she had to do was press 'send'.

She glanced over at Franco, who was stacking boxes a few feet away. For a moment, they locked eyes, and Harry's brain gave a dizzying lurch.

Were they far enough from the truck to escape the blast? Maybe he'd used enough explosive to blow up the whole pier. Maybe no one would come out of this alive.

She closed her eyes briefly. Pictured the two guns by the door. Then slowly, she smoothed one hand over her hair, and with the other, she made the call.

50

A white flash filled Harry's vision. Seared her brain.

The blast that followed tore through her ears, then a rush of air yanked her from the floor and hurled her in a high arc against the wall.

She plummeted to the floor. Fragments of metal whipsawed through the air, though they seemed to make no sound. Harry's ears felt plugged; numbed against all noise. For a split-second, everything was black. Then an orange fireball bowled through the warehouse, cremating everything in its path.

Flames spilled along the floor. Harry clawed her way backwards, the heat scorching her flesh. Black smoke mushroomed towards her, and her nostrils filled with a harsh, sooty smell.

Franco was nowhere to be seen.

The avalanche of fire billowed upwards. The explosion

had ripped a crater in the ceiling, and the flames quivered towards it, scenting oxygen. Debris swirled through the air, and a shower of sparks rained down on Harry's head. Beside her, one wall had collapsed into a pile of pick-up sticks on the ground.

Somewhere underneath it was Hunter.

Harry squeezed her eyes shut. Her vision shimmered with white-light images still burned onto her retina. She put a hand to her face. It was wet. Blood? But she felt no pain. Just a floating numbness. The world was exploding in a silent movie around her, but her body was drifting. As though she were back underwater.

When she opened her eyes again, she was staring at the night sky. The air seemed cooler, filled with the scent of wet, charred wood.

How much time had passed?

White ash floated down like snowflakes. Solemn faces appeared, hovering over hers. Worried men in protective clothing.

Their mouths were moving but no one was making any sound.

51

Gentle fingers lifted her eyelids. White lights came and went. The silence persisted.

But gradually, Harry's hearing returned. Muffled voices gathered in the distance, and she opened her eyes to see a young man adjusting an IV drip by her side. He flashed her a smile, and she tried to smile back but her face felt sore and tight. Her eyelids grew heavy. They drooped, and she drifted.

The next time she woke, Zubiri was sitting by the bed. He was leafing through a magazine, his head bent low as though his mass of shaggy curls weighed him down. The sight of his familiar, shabby figure squeezed at Harry's chest in a curious mixture of rage and relief.

He looked up from his magazine. 'You're awake.'

Slowly, she took stock of her vital signs. Her head felt thick, as though packed with insulation, and her limbs ached to the bone. Dressings tugged at her arms and legs when she moved. She recalled the blinding flash, the deafening blast, and suddenly thought of her family.

Had anyone contacted them? It was what people did in times of crisis, after all. Humans were hard-wired to need a mother's love whenever things went wrong. The thought filled Harry with a low-level dread.

Zubiri studied her face. 'You think you could answer some questions?'

'I can try.'

He quizzed her gently and she brought him up to date, halting now and then to block out the memories of smoke and rolling flames. She ached to ask if anyone else had survived.

Couldn't.

But Zubiri must have sensed the question in her face.

'Detective Hunter is in a critical condition down the hall.'

Harry's head reeled. 'He's alive?'

'Just about. Internal injuries, burns, severe concussion . . .'

She closed her eyes, grogginess smothering out the rest of his words. Hunter wasn't dead. Her brain floated on a sea of relief.

Zubiri's voice cut back in.

'. . . haven't identified all the body pieces yet. But if you're right, then at least we know the body on the pier is Marty LaRosa. Clayton James is dead, too.'

'Clayton?'

'We found him in the apartment. Shot in the head with a bullet that matched one of the bullets in Marty LaRosa.'

Harry's eyes widened. Gideon had been cleaning house. Another thought struck her.

'You've got ballistics already? How long have I been in here?'

'Two days.'

Harry's eyebrows rose, creasing against the tightness in her skin. Her first impulse was to mourn the missing chunk of time, but on reflection, it was probably a haze of pain that was best left forgotten.

'What about Ginny? Have you found her body?'

Zubiri's mouth pulled down, and he shook his head. Then she remembered she hadn't told him that Gideon had dumped Ginny in the sea. Harry studied the weary folds on Zubiri's face, and felt her own jaw tighten. An icy fist lodged in her chest.

'You bastard.'

His tangled brows jumped a fraction. Harry felt her whole body clench.

'You and Vasco. You knew the whole time what you were sending me into. Don't think I didn't know. You set me up. Disposable bait. Now Vasco's got his man, he's got the whole crew, except they're all dead. I nearly ended up dead, too, so did Hunter. Would that have mattered?'

He looked at his hands. She heaved herself into a half-sitting position, pain scorching the flesh on her arms and legs.

'Where was the backup team, Zubiri? What the hell happened? Did they ever really exist?'

Slowly, his eyes met hers. He gave her a long, level look, but seemed to have nothing to say.

When Zubiri had gone, Harry flung back the covers on the bed. Later, she'd rail at that bastard Vasco, but right now she wanted to see Hunter.

She eased into a sitting position on the edge of the bed, her feet dangling to the floor. Gauzy white dressings encased her legs, though here and there angry red flesh was visible. She inched forward on the bed. The room listed like a boat on high seas and her peripheral vision shimmered.

Maybe this was a bad idea.

She flopped back down against the pillows, and lay there sweating till her brain fogged over and she drifted off to sleep.

Some time later, a plump nurse arrived with a phone.

'You have a caller,' she said in Spanish, holding out the receiver.

Harry flicked it a wary look, hoping it wasn't her mother.

It wasn't.

Riva's businesslike tones came over the line, making perfunctory enquiries about Harry's health and explaining that Zubiri had filled her in on events. Harry winced. Had the woman called to tackle her about all the lies she'd told? But Riva paused, as though uncertain how to proceed. When she spoke again, her voice was hesitant.

'Zubiri tells me you were there when Marty LaRosa died.'

Harry blinked. 'That's right.'

Another silence. 'Can you tell me how it happened?'

Harry hesitated, not crazy about reliving those moments on the pier. Riva jumped in, misinterpreting her silence.

'It's not just idle curiosity. I knew him a long time ago, when we were kids. I was fourteen when we met, he was only eleven.'

Harry flashed on the mugshot of Riva at fourteen: the undernourished waif with the bony shoulders and the pinched, heart-shaped face. She inhaled a quiet breath and told her all she knew about Marty: how he'd tried to warn Franco, and the bullets he'd taken trying to save him. When she was finished, Riva was silent for a long time. Eventually, she said,

'He was a good kid. Weak, maybe, but he'd do anything for Franco. The man was his hero.' She sounded bitter. 'For a while, he was my hero, too.'

Harry chewed her lip. For reasons she couldn't name, she felt an urge to defend Franco.

'For what it's worth,' she said, 'I think he planned to skip town with you for good before the raid that killed your brother.'

Riva exhaled a long breath. 'I think that's probably

true.' Her voice was flat. 'But I'm not sure it's worth anything.'

Harry persuaded the plump nurse to find her a wheelchair and roll her down the hall to see Hunter.

He was laid up in a private room that smelled of spirits and adhesive tape. The nurse angled Harry in beside his bed, then left with a warning that she'd be back in five minutes.

Harry stared at Hunter's face, shocked by how defenceless he looked. His eyes were closed, and his hair was rumpled and matted against the pillow. Purple contusions mottled his skin, and tubes snaked from his nostrils and arms to a bank of blipping monitors by the bed. According to the nurse, he'd been in intensive care until the previous day.

Slowly, his eyes opened and he turned an unfocused gaze to hers. Harry's throat constricted at the sight of the hazelnut eyes.

'Hey.' His voice was cracked and slightly delayed, as though out of synch with his lips. His eyes took in the wheelchair. 'Zubiri said you were here. You okay?'

Harry nodded, working hard to get her throat under control. 'The chair is just in case I keel over and faint.'

'You're not the fainting kind.' His voice was a thick blend of concussion and heavy medication. 'You look like shit.'

'Thanks. So do you.'

431

But Hunter was right. She'd checked the mirror before she'd left her room, giving in to a self-conscious moment of vanity. Her face looked sunburned, and the ends of her hair were scorched and frazzled. The one-size-fits-all hospital gown made her look like an escaped prisoner.

Hunter offered her his hand, palm upwards on the sheets, and she grasped it. He squeezed so hard she felt her fingers crack.

'I thought you were dead.' He seemed unable to go on.

Harry wrapped her free hand around their clasped fingers. 'I thought the same about you when I saw you lying in the warehouse.' Then she gave in to a sudden rush of perplexed frustration. 'What the hell were you doing there, anyway?'

'I was looking for you.' He sounded indignant. 'I thought there was a chance you were still alive, that you'd left some kind of message about where they'd taken you. So I ransacked the apartment, found a balled-up sheet of paper in one of the rooms. It had your hand-writing on it.'

Harry frowned. Then her brow cleared as she recalled the list she'd made while examining McArdle's laptop. *McArdle. Casino. Warehouse by the pier.*

'So I went to the pier,' Hunter was saying, 'but someone jumped me in the dark.'

'That was Franco.'

Hunter nodded. His eyelids looked heavy. 'Is he dead?'

'Probably.'

For a while, neither of them spoke. Hunter's eyes creased slightly. His smile was always slow to form, but when it came, its affect on her was magnetic. She found herself smiling back, then Hunter said,

'What are you going to do now?' His voice was drowsy. 'Go back home?'

Harry shrugged, and watched his eyelids close. Her gaze traced the faint lines in his forehead and the unshaven set of his jaw. Would she go home? The notion didn't appeal. Maybe it was all down to her itinerant childhood. Maybe she was inherently nomadic.

She contemplated Hunter's face. Was her mother right? Was she the same with men? She closed her eyes briefly, suspecting her injuries were scrambling her brain.

The plump nurse came back. Harry slipped her hand reluctantly out of Hunter's and allowed herself to be propelled down the corridor and back to her own room.

When she got there, Miriam was standing by the window.

52

Harry couldn't meet her mother's eyes.

The nurse wheeled her over to the bed, then Harry waved her away and clambered unaided under the sheets. Her skin was fiery under her dressings, but a show of weakness in front of Miriam was out of the question.

Her mother watched impassively from the window. Her fawn-coloured suit looked soft and expensive, a perfect match for the pale, gold hair that was twisted into a knot so high it had to hurt. At sixty, she was still a beautiful woman. Harry recalled Olive's story of how Miriam's own mother had been jealous of her.

'The Spanish police told us what happened.'

Miriam's smoke-cured voice had an accusatory tone, though Harry was unsure of the charges. Was her mother put out because Harry had got herself blown up? Because she hadn't called home?

She looked at the woman who was so different from herself. Different in appearance, different in soul. Her presence had never brought Harry any comfort. Impossible that this woman could be her mother.

Miriam flung her a challenging look. 'The nurses say you're doing well.'

Harry blinked. Hadn't she seen the burns? But her mother's eyes dared her to contradict her, and Harry let it pass. She didn't need the woman's sympathy.

'I'll survive.' Harry indicated the visitor's chair beside the bed. 'Have a seat.'

Miriam moved closer, but didn't sit. Instead, she stood with her hands clenched on the back of the chair. Harry regarded the woman who'd tried to get rid of her and wondered just what she should feel. Should she apologize for her existence? Try to prove her worth?

Look, Mom, I'm still here. Whether you want me or not.

'Your father couldn't come.' Miriam's lip curled delicately. 'No one knows where he is. Another gambling trip, so God knows when he'll turn up.'

Harry nodded and looked at her hands. Her father had spent his life gambling in some form or another: investment banking; high-stakes casinos; illicit insider trading. Not all of his bets had paid off, and for a long time his family had suffered the collateral damage.

Harry glanced at her mother. To her credit, Miriam was tough. She'd moved them from a mansion in the leafy suburbs to a world of bedsits and dingy thrift stores with her head held high and her spine ramrod straight. She'd brought her small daughters through the upheavals intact, on a practical level if nothing else.

Harry plucked at the sheet. At least Miriam was here. Her father was absent and her mother was here: the pattern from her childhood. She cleared her throat.

'Look, thanks for flying out. I appreciate you making the trip.'

Miriam shrugged and examined a nail. 'It was Amaranta who made me come.'

A spasm jolted in Harry's solar plexus, and she felt as though she'd been winded. So much for giving the woman credit. Jesus. Would she never learn?

'So.' Miriam was still examining her nails. 'Did you meet with Olive?'

Harry paused, her diaphragm still pounding. Was this the real reason her mother had come? To bury anything Olive might have said? Harry's head felt giddy at the prospect of saying the truth out loud.

Don't say it, don't say it.

Maybe once the words were out, she'd want to snatch them right back. Maybe some things were better left unsaid.

Harry wet her lips. 'Yes, I met her.'

Miriam paused, giving up the pretence of inspecting her manicure. She lowered her hand back to the chair.

'How does she look?'

Harry pictured Olive's face: the pallid skin, the too-large mouth. 'Old.'

Miriam's mouth twitched. Harry's heart drummed hard

against her breastbone, and she fixed her eyes on her hands, which had a tremor all of their own.

'She told me you tried to have me aborted.'

Miriam went still. Somewhere out in the corridor, a trolley crashed and dishes clattered to the floor. Miriam's knuckles tensed on the back of the chair. Then she swept away to the window and stood with her back to Harry.

'She always was a vindictive woman.'

'Are you saying it's not true?'

'Don't be ridiculous.' Miriam snapped open her handbag and dug out a pack of cigarettes. Belatedly, she realized where she was and stuffed them back in her bag. Her hands were trembling.

Harry hugged her chest, suddenly chilled. Wouldn't it be easier to keep on pretending? The way they always had? She stared at Miriam's back.

'Why would Olive lie?'

'She hates me, always did.'

'She said when I was born, you didn't want to touch me.' Harry flinched, as though in pain. 'That you got the nurse to take me away.'

'That doesn't mean anything.'

Harry shut her eyes. Squeezed the words out. 'You never loved me.'

'Don't be ridiculous.' Miriam's voice was husky.

'Olive said you can pretend better with Amaranta, because you're so alike.'

'Stop this, Harry, you're being dramatic.'

'Is it because I'm so like Dad?' Now that Harry had

started, she couldn't stop. 'Are you punishing me for being my father's daughter? Is that why you don't love me?'

Miriam's fists were clenched by her side. 'Every mother loves her child.'

'Is that really true? What if it's just a myth? All this unconditional love, the maternal instinct bullshit.' The words erupted in a rush, all her emotions coming to the boil. 'Maybe sometimes it doesn't work. Maybe sometimes it's just broken. Look at your own mother. Are you telling me she loved you?'

Miriam twisted around, startled. All the colour had bled from her face. Her skin looked slack and the glare from the window had etched deep lines. But it was the look in her eyes that shocked Harry the most. They were wide and staring, and filled with fear.

Fear of what? Of speaking the truth out loud?

Miriam pinned her gaze to Harry's. Seemed to plead with her not to say any more. Not to push for any kind of admission.

Harry looked away. Then she sank back against the pillows and closed her eyes, all her churning emotion suddenly flat-lined, leaving her cold and drained.

Presently, she heard her mother leave the room. Miriam, always so relieved by Harry's absences, and now Harry understood why. She was a mirror for her mother's greatest failure: her unnatural, unthinkable inability to love her own daughter.

And keeping that secret was more important to her than her daughter was.

438

53

Harry knelt on the grass beside the Martinez grave.

A spiced-honey fragrance oozed from the posy of carnations and lilies in her hand. She placed the flowers on the centre of the plot, then looked up at the headstone with its roll-call of ancestors, like the credits after a movie, listing everyone who'd had a part in the person she'd become.

She glanced through the generations of tough old Basque ladies and wondered how far back the ripples of influence went. She thought of her lineage on her mother's side, with its flawed maternal bonds. That was a legacy she didn't plan on handing down.

Slowly, Harry got to her feet. She'd been released from hospital three weeks earlier, and the skin on her legs and arms was healing well. But sudden moves still triggered stinging reminders of her ordeal.

She fingered the folded sheet of paper in her jacket pocket. Zubiri had given it to her earlier that morning, and she'd already read it three times. She closed her fingers over it, her thoughts rolling back to Miriam.

She hadn't talked to her since the day she'd come to the hospital, and wasn't sure when they'd ever talk again. By now, she'd figured out that the woman's inability to love her own daughter had nothing to do with Harry. Miriam had problems of her own, and was probably too damaged to be able to love anyone.

Harry sucked in air quickly through her nose, trying to vacuum up the tears that stung at her sinuses. It was tempting to rush after her mother with forgiveness, and hope that all would be healed. But nothing would change. Harry would be trapped in the same futile game, wanting her mother to love her. The only way to win was not to play.

The wind rustled through the conifers that lined the cemetery paths. Harry watched a group of women laughing and chattering as they filled up their watering cans from a nearby tap supply. Their camaraderie and casual irreverence made Harry smile.

She inhaled a shuddery breath. She and her mother needed a break. No contact, no visits. She'd heard of children divorcing their parents, disconnecting from the power of the past. The notion seemed wildly liberating.

She took a last look at the Martinez headstone, then firmly turned away from her procession of ancestors and headed out of the cemetery towards the car where Hunter was waiting. She was tired of digging up roots planted by others. Maybe it was time to bed down a few of her own.

The sheet of paper crackled in her pocket. She slipped it out, unfolding it for another look. The handwriting sloped in old-fashioned strokes. Zubiri had kept the original, along with the envelope that had been addressed to Diego, care of the Ertzaintza in San Sebastián, and posted two weeks ago from Aruba. It had taken a while to find its way to Zubiri's desk.

The hairs on the back of Harry's neck tingled as she read the note again:

I salute you, Diego. Blowing us up took guts. I hope you got out alive.

You know what the thing about you is, Diego? You're someone who could've gone bad. You're prepared to cross the line, break the rules. That's what made you so convincing.

But me, I'm hard to fool. I knew you were working undercover. I knew it from the minute you stabbed me in the bar. You know why? Because it's what I would have done myself.

Two mongrel Basques. Who knew we'd make such a good team?

Never forget who you are, Diego. And look me up if you ever come to Aruba.

There was no signature, but Harry didn't need one.

A fluttery sensation started up inside her chest. Franco had known all along she was working undercover. He'd kept her around just to get the job done, and now she'd never know for sure what he'd planned for her afterwards.

She pictured him sitting with his feet up on his desk, plotting an escape route on his map of the world, planning a life on the run. A life of aliases, personas, briefcases and layers.

She found herself hoping he'd make it.